This is a book seven years in the making, and is therefore dedicated to everyone who was a part of my life in those seven years, and to everyone who will have this book in their lives from now on. It's especially dedicated to those who have struggled from discrimination, whether they made it through or not. It's for those who don't feel worthy of a dedication. You are. Never forget that.

# THE DEFINED ROLE

ANNIE O'QUINN

ISBN: 978-1-7330604-0-0 (Paperback)
ISBN: 978-1-7330604-1-7 (Hardcover)
ISBN:  978-1-7330604-2-4 (Ebook)

Library of Congress Control Number: 2019905577



Front cover image by Annie O'Quinn
Editing managed by Morgan Greenfield
Editing by Morgan Greenfield and Carrie Miller
Formatted by Carrie Miller
Proofreading by A. E. Hayes

Printed by Ingram Spark
First printing, 2019

Annieoquinn.com

# FOREWORD

T he very first time I read *The Defined Role* was just the second day I knew Annie, a few years ago, at an anime convention where we both happened to share an artist table. After discovering she was writing a book, it didn't take long to grab the opportunity to read it. I had no idea those twelve hours would lead to several more rereads and becoming her head editor.

These last few years of working on *The Defined Role* have reminded me of exactly why I love editing: assisting the evolution of an early draft into a final product which can then be shared with others. I watched a draft from 2017 become what is now published here, and I couldn't be prouder to have been a part of it.

When talking about this foreword, there was one thing Annie specifically made sure would be included: sensitivity warnings. While written with extreme care, we understand that some topics may cause discomfort, and we want everyone to know what to expect for their own safety and well-being. There are very heavy suicidal situations and discussions along with mentions of self-harm. There are no detailed scenes of a character harming themself. There are moments where a sexual assault is implied, but there are also no details of the events. There are moments of implied domestic abuse and the resulting evidence of it. There is violence, including violence against children. There is also a moment of homophobic language. We understand completely if this warning means you can't continue reading. That being said, you can be reassured that none of these situations are glorified, and that this story has gone through many sensitivity readings by a large variety of people. Any errors in this are completely unintentional and are no fault of the sensitivity readers. Education on the matter is welcomed.

While the topics are heavy, they are very real, and that was something that stood out to me while reading. This book is a commentary on people, how dangerous assumptions can be, and the different paths that are created based on a small nudge. It's about how anyone can fight through, even when your life doesn't pan out the way you planned. It is a story of hope and of asking for help. Annie has taken the common concept of demons and angels and given them humanity. It gives every human an opportunity to become *more*, both in life and after death. I believe that, after reading this book, people will be reminded this opportunity is real. I also hope everyone will love Jenkins, who everyone will learn is my favorite character.

# THE DEFINED ROLE

This was a journey Annie started, I joined, and now, you get to take. We both hope it's nothing but enjoyable, even though there is angst. And, as they say in the theatre, let the story begin!

–Morgan Greenfield

# PROLOGUE

If Robbie Hodge could write a letter in his last moments, it would happen twice.

The first letter would have been an apology. It would have been filled with agony as he begged and begged for forgiveness. He had been afraid of death, of what he was about to face. It wasn't a fear of the unknown, but of what he did know. When you died, one of three things could happen: you could receive an offer to become an Angel, an offer to become a demon, or you could receive no offer at all.

Robbie had been possessed by a demon. In those last moments, he knew everything that was happening, everything his body was doing. He knew the bitterness that had led to his vulnerability, and he knew he didn't deserve forgiveness.

He would have written a love letter, something to express that yes, he understood now. He was dying, but he had figured out why a demon had targeted him, and he had conquered it. When he died, he knew he was fading without a chance for last words. There were so many regrets, so many events that led to his possession and death. However, he did not regret the end, and he would have done it over again.

When it came time for the offer, he prepared himself to refuse the demon. He didn't die for nothing. He lived with too many demons for him to spend death as one.

No demon came. Instead, there was a light, a figure that was terrifying enough to make him cower. He didn't know who was behind the mask, but he knew the Angel had once been human. He wished there were words to describe it, to send home. He wished he could send out invitations for the celebration: Robbie Hodge's Acceptance of the Angel Offer.

At first, being an Angel seemed like what he thought Heaven was: freedom. There were far fewer Angels than demons, but demons required a human Host to be on Earth, while Angels just had to make sure nobody knew who or what they were, but were otherwise allowed to roam. Robbie learned so many things, including how it took more to receive an Angel offer than a demon's—it was a lot easier to live your life easily than properly.

There wasn't a way for him to send a letter. He wasn't allowed to contact his loved ones. He had a job to do.

The second letter wouldn't have been too different from the first, minus three points.

The first would be a warning.

In Robbie's last moments as an Angel, he had been building a house when he witnessed a blood-ied, rotten, dying Host take the side of the demon who had possessed them. He was doing his duty, trying to help save the Host while unable to harm it, as human hands clamped down on his wrist. There was panic and desperation, emotions he thought had disappeared with his humanity.

He was dying, despite being an Angel, and he had to sound the alarm.

The second difference came after a wash of calm. It was the same thought but a different tone: He was dying, despite being an Angel. It was a fact and there wasn't a way to add that warning. There wasn't anything he could do, and that took the urgency away. He wouldn't talk about the demons that had swarmed around the Host and himself that evening, where the bones of the house had become sharp shadows of cages. He wouldn't describe his soul being ripped apart. He would have written how there was much less regret when you have done everything you could, even after death. He felt that his debt had been paid.

The third difference was his signature. While before he would have simply signed his name, now it would end with "Love, Robbie." It was significant, if only to him, because it was the sign of one thing: He was still human. Yes, he had become an Angel, but he could still feel as he did before. He was done being an Angel and he was relieved. Now, someone else could take over, and he could finally, *finally*, rest.

# CHAPTER ONE

When Samuel Stewart was told to decide his future, he knew there were three paths in front of him. If he were to visualize them, he would describe each of them as something vastly different.

One was a dirt road. This was the path he would have to take if he were to live up to his mother's expectations. Which was to say, the lowest expectations. He would fail to finish high school, fail to get into college, fail to get a job, and fail to be anything more than a burden to her and to anyone who had the misfortune of breathing the same air as him. The dirt road would not be something he traveled along. It would be something he became.

The second was a paved road. Hot against bare feet, long and winding, cracked and faded, but steady. Survivable. That was the path of college, of getting a degree in something he was good enough at, of hopefully working his way into a job where he could feel useful and important rather than simply replaceable. It was the path of *potential*.

The third path was always at the center, laid in marble, carved into stairs that led up to heaven. This was the path where he could do more than survive. This was the path where he could *live*. It was the path he wanted most of all. It would allow him to escape, to run, to feel free and fulfilled spiritually, which he wished for even more than he wished for guaranteed meals.

There were many letters and brochures that came in the mail, telling him to apply to this college or that program or this job. It was the time in a teenager's life when the applications were sent off and prayers were said with more heart, and it was the time he received the only letter that mattered. It was a simple letter, thin enough to hold just one piece of paper. There was a seal in the corner, and the words Cleanser Academy printed underneath.

That single letter made his marble staircase crumble.

"Is it really so surprising?" his mother asked as she caught his expression. She sat at their small kitchen table in their quaint, pastel kitchen, watching him as he stood in the low doorway. He didn't know what he must have looked like to her. Was there an expression for crushed dreams?

Samuel held the letter in his hands, staring at it, wishing the letters would rearrange themselves, yearning for a different answer, struggling to see if he could rebuild that marble staircase.

He couldn't.

"No," he answered his mother, his heart heavy.

The ink was dried. He wasn't qualified to be an Exorcist. "I suppose not."

He chose the paved, but broken, path.

Samuel was obsessive about checking e-mails. There were rejection letters right next to suggestions on how to heighten his performance in bed. Most could be glossed over, but there was always a high enough chance one was life changing. That made it seem so dramatic, but he was borderline paranoid at this point. Samuel read every word of every e-mail carefully, even if it was just to find the real unsubscribe button.

Just before Samuel's second year at college, he received an e-mail that didn't necessarily affect him, but he could *feel* the effects it would have on others—and the potential it brought to him. It warned of Davis Turner, who would be a student the upcoming semester. With this single e-mail, every student and faculty member at the College of Charleston would know he had been possessed as a child. He could no longer have secrets. His future was limited. Being possessed was not like getting a cold. You didn't build an immunity to it; you became a beacon. The chances of being possessed again doubled. Tripled even.

Samuel had heard many stories through his church but had rarely seen a case of someone being possessed so young and turning out so...normal. The fact Davis was being let into college was a huge risk for the school and for the students.

Samuel was inexplicably curious.

Of course, Samuel was woefully incompetent at being social in nearly any form, so actually seeking Davis out to…talk? Ask questions? Observe like some creepy stalker? That was never going to happen. There was nothing to do but ignore his burning curiosity, his want to maybe help this boy, and so because of this he kept himself busy.

Theatre was a major that definitely helped with that. First it was just classes. There were small whispers ("He killed his dad;" "He killed an *Exorcist;*" "He's going to get *us* killed—or worse;" "He doesn't even care about anyone but himself if he's here and not in jail"), but Samuel stubbornly ignored them. He couldn't give himself hope for something he had already been denied. He couldn't get involved. He *could* put his best into his schoolwork.

A year passed without him even seeing Davis, despite them sharing a campus that was hardly anything more than three square blocks. That is, minus the occasional graffiti of his face on brick walls that were not so nice.

He decided becoming Assistant Stage Manager at the start of his third year would keep him focused, and he wasn't wrong. He had nearly forgotten by then that Davis was a student there at all. He had only given in to his curiosity when it came to his church. Whether it was criticisms of the nontraditional Exorcists who were a part of the government or rumors of warnings from Angels, the information had satisfied him enough in the Exorcist-and-demons department while he continued with his degree.

It was a week into the semester and he found himself organizing scenes and actor applications, wordlessly handing them out to actors. It was positions like this where he excelled, where there was a clear process and he wasn't obligated to be friendly, just efficient. He sat at a table pulled from the props room, positioned outside of the audition room, when one of the actors decided to try speaking to him.

"Can I audition?"

Samuel looked up to see a boy standing there, eyes focused but hesitant, eyebrows furrowed, his weight shifting from one foot to the other. His accent was not from Charleston, but of somewhere else Samuel couldn't quite place. He asked the question not as if he already knew the answer, like so many actors did, but more as if he was requesting to participate in something strictly off limits. The boy had the looks for an actor, with perfectly clear, brown skin, and it certainly wasn't fat surrounding his bones. His tight black t-shirt didn't hide that fact.

Samuel tapped his fingers on the stacks. "Which part?"

There was silence for a moment before Samuel looked up, annoyed with the lack of response, only to see wide, hazel eyes staring at him. Samuel squinted and looked away, then back at him. "What?" Samuel asked.

"I can audition? Really?" the boy asked, his face bright and hopeful.

"You're a student here?"

"Yes."

"Then yes. Which part?" Samuel asked.

"Uh. Harry. Yes."

Samuel handed him the appropriate scene and application. "Just fill this out and good luck."

With a whispered word of thanks, the boy leaned over and filled out the application right there instead of going elsewhere. Then, handed it back. Samuel took the paper and was about to place it with the others when he paused at the name.

Davis Turner.

Many things went through his head. He questioned the idea of fate, the inevitability of this meeting, and his own ability to not look invested. His eyes flickered up and Davis was still there, looking sheepish as he scratched his fingers through his messy brown hair. He prayed to Mary for self-control and berated himself for imagining Davis looking much different. White, scrawny, short. That was not this Davis at all.

"You're not going to give it back, are you?" Davis asked, his jaw clenching. He looked like he was preparing himself for rejection.

"No—no, you're fine," Samuel said, fumbling to keep himself looking unbothered, fiddling with the edge of the table, which he absently noticed was chipping. "Good luck, still."

"Thank you," Davis said, and Samuel could tell he put meaning into both words with how he controlled his voice. It brought Samuel's eyes back to him. He was truly and genuinely grateful to Samuel for the privilege, he noticed, even though it should have been a simple right.

Samuel gave a curt nod and made himself look busy while Davis walked away. For the first time,

Samuel felt genuine in wishing someone luck. Maybe he would see Davis again. Maybe there was no way to escape this curiosity.

Samuel was disappointed to find out Davis did not get the role.

# CHAPTER TWO

"Is there a word for being biased against people who have previously been possessed?"

"Logical?" Davis supplied, his words muffled in a pillow. "Self-preservation? Both of which do not describe you, by the way."

"No, like 'racist' or 'homophobic'—prejudiced!" Tommy said with elation, waving off Davis's comment. "We'll just go with prejudiced. They're all prejudiced assholes."

There were many ways to describe Tommy. Blond was one of them. Another could be That Guy Who Always Wears Pajamas. Davis preferred The Guy Stupid Enough to Be His Roommate, but none of them were wrong. Out of all the other Honors students, Tommy was the only one willing to share a suite with Davis. While Davis had a single room, it shared a kitchenette and living room with Tommy's— which was a bedroom meant for two, but their third roommate backed out at the last minute, leaving just the two of them. Davis solemnly understood. Tommy was thrilled. This somehow happened both years he had been attending.

Davis sighed and rolled onto his back, his long legs stretching out over the dorm couch. It was uncomfortable, but he couldn't be bothered to get up. He was too disappointed. "There are lots of factors that go into casting a role. I might have just not fit their vision."

Tommy glared from where he stood in their kitchenette. His pajamas had shirtless cowboys on them, which made it very difficult to take him seriously. "Davis, I'm trying to help you feel better. Let me. What, do you want alcohol instead?"

"Underage," Davis grumbled. "Not to mention, demons don't take a day off. The minute I get wasted is the minute I'd have another attempted possession, and boom." He gestured an explosion. "At least two more deaths, another protest against me, maybe even a lawsuit, and I would lose everything I've worked for. Probably because I'd be dead."

"Okay," Tommy said, frowning as he pulled out his own beer despite being underage himself. Davis had no clue where he got it, but he was sure it had to do with his perfectly tanned skin, haughty eyes, and overall beach boy charm. Tommy was well aware of the consequences Davis could face. He'd had a front row seat to Freshman Year and had since burned every death threat left at their door without a word to Davis, but a report to the dean.

"Not even one beer?"

"Not even one," Davis said, throwing an arm over his eyes. It was much too bright for how dark of a mood he was in. He peeked at Tommy. "But thanks for trying."

"I just do it for the discount on my housing. A happy Davis makes it tolerable living with you." Tommy paused. "Well, except when you're trying to imitate Brendon Urie. You can't sing, buddy."

Davis laughed and threw his pillow. "You are such a jerk."

"And you love me for it," Tommy said, sticking his tongue out and popping the beer open. It's not that Davis had never had a drink before. It was that when he did, it resulted in such a crippling panic attack (among all of the previously-mentioned fears) that he chose to stay away from the stuff. Better safe than sorry. That was a motto forced upon him, and one Tommy willfully chose to ignore.

"There will be other auditions," Davis whispered. He wasn't even sure Tommy could hear him. This was just the start. Actors got rejected all the time. He would have to get used to that and used to trying again and again until he landed something—and he *would* try again. Later, when he was done pouting.

Tommy walked over and forced Davis to sit up to take an offered can of soda. "Cheers," he said, tapping their drinks. "To not dealing with prejudiced people, and to other opportunities."

"Cheers," Davis said halfheartedly as he took a sip. Then he gave a small laugh. He had come a long way from the child who feared living, but he still looked at Tommy and wished he could be just as carefree.

# CHAPTER THREE

That was it. That one moment during auditions was the only time Samuel talked to Davis Turner. It was like a blink in his junior year. A month had gone by, then another: the show had opened and closed and with it, Samuel's excuse of being too busy to even have a chance at seeing Davis ended. How could he pretend to be an Exorcist when a show was overtaking his life? Now Samuel was well into the school year, just starting to fret about what the hell he was going to do once he graduated next year and how he was going to survive until then.

Assistant managing transformed into costume technology. He preferred concentrating on a single project rather than being the communication hub of the cast and crew. His major went from undecided to mostly decided, depending only on if he could rationalize the income he might eventually receive.

Mostly, he stayed on campus late into the night, working on student-run shows that sucked every bit of soul that was available. It kept him busy. It gave him back the excuse he wanted.

It kept him away from his mother.

His mother, who not so long ago decided that Samuel was going to have to pay his own way now that he was twenty-one. He wondered where, exactly, all his student loans and scholarships were going if they exceeded his tuition. But he couldn't argue that. Like always, he lost all words when he tried to oppose her.

He liked being inside the theater much better than being home, even if the building was empty with only a few scenic flats for company. It wasn't a fearful place. He sat down in the audience seating, placed his bowler hat beside him, unbuttoned his vest, and perfected what he could of the costumes for the upcoming show.

He flinched when the door clacked open.

"Oh, sorry," Davis said, standing in the doorway, looking just as surprised as Samuel. He was wearing yet another fitted shirt, this time a V-neck, but once again dark in color. There was a graphic design that burst blues and purples from his hip to his opposite shoulder in swirls and dots. "It's...really late," he stated. "Why are you here?"

Samuel squinted at him in defiance. "Why are you?"

"Audition practice," Davis said. "And my room-mate is trying to get laid. I think. There were noises."

Samuel had absolutely nothing to say to that. He simply gestured to the stage and went back to work.

The opportunity to approach Davis as Someone Who Was Possessed had passed. Samuel worked and tried to think of Davis as some victim he could help so he could somehow bring back up those hero-like feelings he used to have. Now that was gone. There were new categories Davis now fit, such as Someone Interested in Theatre and Someone Hot Enough to Sleep With, but because those two separate categories weren't allowed to intersect, Samuel settled with the first and he promptly treated him like anyone else in the department: he ignored him completely.

"Won't I distract you?" Davis asked, stepping into the small theater and walking into the row directly in front of Samuel. Samuel did not dare look up or, yes, he could be distracted, and he would be reminded of that second category.

"I'm used to distractions. I can tune you out," he said instead as he changed out his thread, focusing on each small step. Threading. Doubling. Tying. Clipping.

Davis hadn't moved. Samuel paused and huffed, glaring up at him. "What? I thought you didn't want to distract me."

"I never said that. I bet I will," Davis said. "But you look like you haven't slept in three days and, if I'm remembering right, last time you were much nicer to me." He looked up at the grid above them, a series of pipes connected to hold ancient lighting instruments, donated to the students when the theatre was renovated. He seemed disinterested until his eyes flickered down and caught Samuel's, his attention solely on him. "Isn't theatre supposed to be fun?"

Samuel thinned his lips, his heart heavy. "Sorry," he muttered. He knew he held some bitterness now. Even if he pretended, he couldn't be an Exorcist. It wasn't fair to take that out on Davis. "I didn't mean to come off as rude."

"It's still an upgrade from some people," Davis said, plopping down in one of the seats and throwing his legs over an armrest. "So, what's bothering you?"

"Hm?"

"What's bothering you?" Davis repeated. "You look exhausted, you're here at a ridiculous hour with no shows opening this weekend, and you've been focusing on that one stitch since I came over."

Samuel looked down at his lack of progress and placed the garment in the chair next to him with a sigh. "Shouldn't someone be asking you that? If you're okay, I mean. You don't look bothered, but...I think I have it a bit easier," he said, his words catching. He hoped not to offend.

"Oh, well, no?" Davis said, looking at his boots as he rolled his ankles. "Life's normal, for the most part." He glanced at Samuel. "I can't spend all of my time just moping about bullies and demon possessions, now can I?"

Samuel flushed. "I didn't mean—you're just— people can be worse than demons sometimes."

"I've found some good ones," Davis said, the corner of his mouth tugging. "Have you?"

"What?"

Davis's eyes were filled with laughter as he repeated himself again. "Have *you*? You know, found good people to surround yourself with?"

Samuel stared at him in bewilderment, unsure of how he should answer, or even what the answer actually was. After a moment, he simply shrugged.

"Well," Davis said, tilting his head back enough to stare at the grid again. "I found you." Then his eyes darted back to Samuel. "Do I have to prove anything to you?" Samuel raised an eyebrow in response. "You know, to make you believe I'm good?"

"I'm not going to tell you why I'm upset, or whether you're good or bad," Samuel said. "And for me to decide which you are, or if you're somewhere in the middle, I'd have to know you, Davis Turner."

"Then get to know me, Samuel Stewart." Davis grinned, showing his perfect teeth. (How did he have such perfect teeth, Samuel wondered. Did he have braces before? Was healthcare different if you were prone to possessions? But maybe this wasn't the time to fixate on that.) Samuel scrunched his eyebrows in confusion, trying to juggle his own thoughts and Davis's extremely confusing interactions. Then Davis said, quietly, gently, "I'd remember the name of a guy who gave me a chance."

"It wasn't—you were just any other student," Samuel said. He wanted to call out how corny Davis sounded, but decided it was more important that no one thought he gave special treatment.

"But you paused when you saw my name," Davis said. He sat up and leaned towards Samuel over his seat, forcing Samuel to lean back. "You knew who I was and you still let me audition."

"I'm a decent human being," Samuel said. "Why

wouldn't I?"

"I don't know. Maybe ask the others who wouldn't," Davis said. His gaze was sharp and serious.

Samuel broke eye contact. "Weren't you going to practice?"

Davis hummed. He stood up in that way actors do: with pure confidence in their body. He didn't seem like someone who needed help in any way. If someone like him, who had the world assuming who he was before they met him, was able to hold himself so well, what was Samuel doing wrong?

Samuel quickly gathered his things. "I have to go," he said, having no idea where to go, but knowing he had to.

"Good luck, then," Davis said, "with whatever made you come here tonight."

He could have been referring to the technician work, but Samuel doubted he was. He said, "Thank you," sincerely, before he left.

# CHAPTER
# FOUR

He got it.

There were many things Davis wasn't sure of. He wasn't sure if he would be threatened with a knife when he walked into the dining hall. He wasn't sure if he would pass Chemistry, and he definitely wasn't sure he would get the part in the play.

He got it. He got it. *He got it.*

It felt like one of those moments when you had to keep repeating the fact over and over to convince yourself of its truth, and this time it really *was* true. He got the role. He would be a part of a production. He would be acting in front of hundreds of people. He had a chance to convince them he was more than they assumed. He was Davis Turner, possibly future famous actor—and famous for more than being possessed by a demon.

He would never admit to squealing when he

reached his dorm room, no matter what Tommy said.

But as with every good thing that happened to him, there were waves of consequences. Two people dropped out of the production when they heard of his casting. Three others actually cared enough about the opportunity to stay, but their venom was clear. Davis resisted tiptoeing into the read-through. It took place in one of the dance-studios-turned-meeting-rooms. There, he stayed silent during the design presentations and was more than a little disappointed Samuel was not working on the show. At least with Samuel he knew he had an ally. Well, at least a good chance of an ally.

Yet there was Ashley, whose presence was equally quiet and loud with her bright blue hair, her clothes in shades of pastels, and her skin a smooth ivory. She was the costume designer and she was clearly not afraid. When it was time to present Davis's character design, she turned to him directly.

"As you might agree, your character has a strong presence. You're already tall, so we're going to emphasize that even more with vertical lines..." Davis didn't know a single thing about clothes, so he nodded in all the right places, trusting her, and taking notes on how she interpreted the character. Then, after a moment, she said, "Do you agree? Do you have any suggestions?"

There was a moment of silence where Davis realized he had been given permission to speak. He gaped like a fish before saying, "I think it's perfect. I trust you with this completely."

Ashley beamed at him. "Good. You should. I mostly know what I'm doing."

Davis laughed and a few others joined in. Apart from the Glaring Triplets, as he deemed them, he was surrounded by people who wanted him there. His director, Eric Goodwin, had specifically chosen him and was aware of what could go wrong, and still, here he was. He had never felt so at peace.

There were some, those who opted out of the play, who still made Davis hunch his shoulders whenever he walked by. He wasn't sure what they would do, if anything. He had more knives pulled on him than he wished to remember. Still, it seemed there was more avoidance than aggression. Tense shoulders relaxed, and soon, Davis only noticed the ones who paid him attention. He didn't have to second guess if laughing was okay when someone ripped their costume. He didn't have to look over his shoulder or think about how to carefully construct every sentence he said. He could breathe, and he hoped this would never end.

# CHAPTER FIVE

Samuel was well aware of Davis getting cast. He knew because of the posting, because of the gossip, because of Ashley, but mostly because he wanted to know and so he paid attention to the previously mentioned things. He let out a sigh, surprised it was a relieved one, and then he promptly stopped paying attention.

That is, he stopped paying attention until he was forced to. This happened at two very separate times. The first time, he had been working inside of the costume shop, having somehow managed to snag the job for a few hours a week. The room was probably too small for the number of tables inside and Samuel had to quickly get over his dislike of accidenttal physical contact, but the people were nice enough and they enjoyed the gossip of those outside the shop more than anyone *in* the shop, which was even better. It was a normal, hectic day.

Samuel had already fixed one of the sewing machines, converted a dress to a skirt, resized a pair of pants, and was currently taking apart a large patterned shirt they'd grabbed from Goodwill.

Davis stumbled in.

"Steven ripped his pants again," Davis said casually, as if he had not just tripped on his own feet. He was in a toga, which didn't make any sense for the play he was in, but no one was going to question it when he was nearly shirtless. His hair was even more unruly than normal, waves ruffled in a way that somehow always stayed aesthetically pleasing, which was just unfair when Samuel had to constantly hide his mess of stringy hair under a hat. Davis was looking around and caught Samuel's location. His face brightened. "Hi, Samuel."

Ashley looked at Samuel. Samuel saw her look, squinted as if to ask what she was looking at, and went back to work. Ashley sighed.

"Don't worry, I'll get it," she said to Davis. "Just tell him to leave it. I'll fix it for rehearsal tomorrow." Which most likely meant Samuel was going to be the one fixing them. On the bright side, at least he would get paid to do it.

There was more casual chatter that Samuel tried very hard to ignore, but the fact was he was still extremely curious, now more than ever. Davis seemed happy. He seemed perfectly in control, and that made Samuel's stomach feel tight. What use would he be? He remembered Davis saying he surrounded himself by good people, that he wanted Samuel to be one of those people, but what else could Samuel offer him? Nothing, yet again. He had nothing to offer anyone.

He was the one who fixed Steven's pants.

The second time Samuel was forced to pay attention was the day before opening night. Samuel made his normal, mentally necessary rounds, which included walking around the building, checking that all fire hydrants were still accessible, the stray cat was fed, the name of the building hadn't changed, and there was no paint splatter on the ground from set construction. It was tedious, like a list of chores, but he wouldn't be able to focus on anything else, let alone sleep, if he didn't do them.

He did not expect to find Davis there, in the dark, sitting crouched against the side of the building, clutching his head.

Samuel stepped closer and was about to call out when he noticed Davis was actually crying. Shaking. Muttering under his breath, "Stop, *stop*, please..."

It was clear Davis was having some sort of crisis or panic attack and Samuel was the least equipped person to be able to handle these sorts of things. He turned to leave, to avoid what he couldn't handle, but then he remembered the gossip. He remembered the two people who dropped out, the wary glances and hushed whispers of concern. He remembered that Davis was vulnerable and wanted Samuel around. He would have felt unbearably guilty if he left Davis, just as so many others probably had. He took a deep breath and turned back around, approaching Davis cautiously.

"Hey..." Samuel started, feeling awkward and completely unprepared. "Are you okay?"

Davis's head shot up and he stared at Samuel as

if him being there was the worst possible thing that could have happened in that moment.

Samuel held up his hands, eyes wide, and said, "I won't hurt you. I can leave, if you want me to. I just..."

"I'm not worried about you hurting me," Davis said, his voice strained. His eyes tried to focus as he blinked rapidly. "I don't want to hurt *you*."

Samuel froze at the words, realizing Davis's vulnerability went past social issues. He had been possessed and he could be possessed again at any time—and it was looking very likely at that exact moment. Samuel considered running. He even took a step back to consider letting someone *else* deal with this so he could be safe. But looking at Davis, even through the spike of fear, Samuel knew there was no demon in control. Davis was fighting it off, struggling to keep more than just himself safe.

Samuel wanted to help. He wanted to be useful. He wanted to be given his own chance.

"What can I do?" Samuel asked earnestly, kneeling in front of Davis, placing a hand on his knee delicately.

Davis looked at Samuel, his eyes dark, his hair matted to his forehead. "Don't let me hurt you," he said, his voice labored. "If I—if I can't stop." He winced and ducked his head, hiding it with his arms and knees. "Don't let me hurt anyone. Not again."

# CHAPTER
# SIX

A possession was not something that happened quickly. It was slow. It was silent. It was unpredictable.

Davis knew the feeling of it. At the beginning, it was just influence. Through his psychology class, he had learned the term 'intrusive thoughts,' and while it usually applied to suicidal or obsessive thoughts, it still seemed to fit. They were thoughts that weren't his own, building up his emotions, attempting to convince him of easy solutions. Those solutions were typically very illegal. If he noticed them, that was his first sign.

Sometimes, they were too subtle. Sometimes, it was as innocent as imagining an applause or receiving an award. It was when those thoughts turned into plots of sabotage or bribery that he caught it—and sometimes, even catching it at that stage was too late.

And it *hurt*. It was as if the entity sprang into attack mode once Davis was aware of it. Sharp spikes of pain in concentrated areas that soon after spread like fire, leaving his nerves exposed and his body sounding the alarm. It took everything he had to not give in. He knew if he gave in, the pain would be gone. The demon would grant him that. But there would be pain afterwards, if he survived it. He knew it too well and he could not, *would not*, live through it again.

A possession was slow, from beginning to end, and it hurt the whole time.

# CHAPTER SEVEN

She watched silently and warily from just around the corner of the Albert Simons Center. If only the other boy hadn't come along...it would have all been a lot easier. Now there was his life to consider, too, on top of Davis's. It was always more difficult when civilians were involved. Sure, *she* had given up on saving people, but government rules were government rules.

She kept low, kept quiet, kept aware. She had to be ready, whether that meant capture or kill.

Someone stepped up beside her. She lowered her gun.

"He'll be okay," her boss said, his voice as demanding as it was reassuring. "He's not dangerous."

"You call that 'not dangerous?'" she spat in a harsh whisper. She pushed herself off the side of the building and thrusted her gun in its holster. "It's been hours. You think he'll beat it?"

"I believe so. *Inshallah*," he said. "Watch, if you don't believe me."

"I believe you," she hissed. "It just isn't normal."

"He's our responsibility now," he said. "It is not our responsibility to kill a civilian."

"It *is* to protect them," she said, crossing her arms and leaning against the side of the building. She could hear him even from here, the noise of pain and torture. If she couldn't kill him to protect others, what about ending his misery? She looked at her boss and rolled her eyes with a sigh. "Fine, let's go."

Sometimes being an Exorcist was more frustrating than fun.

# CHAPTER EIGHT

Samuel was not too sure he could stop Davis from doing anything. Davis wasn't a body-builder, but he was in much better shape compared to Samuel, whose only exercise was the walk to and from his car. He nodded nonetheless, still kneeling, at the back of a building at night, hoping a demon wouldn't kill him.

He did not expect it to take hours. He expected minutes, maybe as much as fifteen, before Davis calmed down. But when it became eleven o'clock, then midnight, then one in the morning, Samuel started to worry. He had repeated The Lord's Prayer a dozen times, created new ones, quoted most of Genesis, and there was no change at all. His mental schedule had already been broken, which made him extremely uncomfortable. He was so sure some disaster would happen if he wasn't home in time. That was bothering him enough, let alone the fact he was also *tired*. If there was any chance of him defending himself before, it was near nonexistent now.

What was worse, Davis seemed like he was in *so much pain*. Samuel couldn't very well *leave* when there was a potential disaster right in front of him. But he could only watch as Davis trembled and let out pathetic moans and cries, biting his lip until it bled, digging his nails into his palms, rocking in place, arching his back with hisses. It was painful to *watch*, let alone experience. Davis had to experience it for *hours*. If he could do that, then Samuel could sit there for just as long.

It was nearing two in the morning when Davis let out a shuddering breath and his entire body sagged.

"I'm me," he whispered, as if testing what he said was true. His dark skin seemed pale, and not from the streetlight. He was still shaking, but it seemed more from the cold now rather than pain. He slowly uncurled himself and raised his head. His eyes caught Samuel's, as they always seemed to, and he seemed truly shocked.

"You're still here," he said.

"I couldn't have left you like that," Samuel said factually. "You were..." *Vulnerable*. "You seemed like you were in pain. Are you okay?"

Davis nodded, but his breath still seemed to come in short pants. His hand clutched his t-shirt, over his heart. "Now I am. Just...tired."

"Well, it *is* almost two."

"Shit. *Really?*"

"Really," Samuel said. "Is it not normal for it to last that long?"

"I…Yes?" Davis said, seeming unsure. Despite the fact he appeared tired, he didn't look like he had just been fighting a demon possession at all. "I never timed it."

He looked only at Samuel, nowhere else, and Samuel understood, if just for a moment, why some people liked undivided attention so much.

"Thank you," Davis said sincerely, "for staying with me. You didn't have to."

"I wouldn't have slept well if I hadn't," Samuel said. Even having said that, he wanted to sleep now, even if there were so many questions in his head pushing to come out. Not tonight. Not now. "You're really okay now, though? Can you stand?"

"Yeah," Davis said, proving so by standing up, if a bit wobbly. Samuel got up with him and helped steady him. "I'm good."

"Can you get back on your own?" Samuel asked-ed.

"It's not far," Davis said, gesturing in some vague direction. He smiled tiredly at Samuel. "Thank you again. I can't thank you enough."

"You have to do that—go through that—to protect others," Samuel said. "Thank you for fighting for us."

Davis's lips parted and he blinked. "I've never been told something like that before."

"Well, now you have," Samuel said. He took a step back. "Good luck tomorrow."

"Not luck," Davis said, his smile back. "I need to break a leg."

"Right," Samuel said, feeling himself give the smallest of smiles, even if this seemed like a very bizarre end to the type of night they had. "Right, well, see you tomorrow. At the performance." He gave a nod, not knowing why a nod was necessary at all, but giving it no mind as he turned and walked away.

"Goodbye until tomorrow," Davis said, a soft but hoarse melody behind it, a reference to a musical, and Samuel did smile then, because no one could see.

# CHAPTER
# NINE

The days of the performances flew by in a whirlwind. It all seemed like a dream, close enough to feel, but far enough to question it. There hadn't exactly been a standing ovation, but there was applause and not one person questioned why Davis was cast during the talk back. It might have been because the performance was such a small one that people didn't honestly know who he was. He wasn't some great actor yet, but he also wasn't just A Brown Possession Survivor, and he was perfectly fine with that.

Even though it wasn't a dream, it felt like one enough that, after the show ended, the reality of how much school work he had sunk in. And yet, he had difficulty thinking about anything school related at all, even while hunched over a textbook in his dorm.

"Samuel Stewart?" Tommy hummed as he scanned over his literature reading, looking much more invested in his reading than normal.

"That is his name, yes," Davis said. This was the first time Davis had mentioned him, feeling like maybe Samuel was a friend he could smuggle just for himself. He was sure he had enough room in the dorm for Samuel and what appeared to be a quite large collection of hats. The only problem was he wanted to share his joy too much. Still, Tommy was acting odd. "What, do you know him?"

"Depends on your definition of 'know,'" Tommy said, flipping a page. Davis was beginning to think Tommy was purposefully avoiding eye contact, but Tommy rarely gave anyone his full attention. Davis was not an exception in most cases, which he appreciated greatly. So, he tried to focus back on his school work.

He knew the extra work piled onto him wasn't strictly necessary. He was in the Honors program, expected to do more, *be* more, and that was exactly what he wanted. He wanted to Be More than someone feared. He wanted to Be More than a terrifying headline. He wanted to Be More than even just a simple man making a living.

He did not, however, want to be an Exorcist.

This thought came to him in a strange sort of way. It could have to do with the fact he was so completely bored of his literature reading, or that could just be a side effect of having too much energy that he couldn't let loose sitting while staring at a book, or all of it could be mixed in with the sudden and strong hit of *missing*. Missing something from his life, missing someone from his life, or in a less general sense, missing his ex-girlfriend, who had very adamantly wanted Davis to become an Exorcist.

"You know what I miss most about being in a relationship?" Davis said aloud. He suspected it was just to himself because Tommy was invested in his reading. "Being able to have sex without the worry of a demon trying to be a third."

Tommy made a strange sound that caught in his throat before bursting out as a laugh that sounded suspiciously guilty.

Davis smiled, even though it felt like it stretched his cheeks a bit too much. If he had just given in to her want, if he had said he would still try to become an Exorcist, maybe Rachael would still be around. Maybe he could act like a typical college student, where he could join in on the parties, drink alcohol, be stupid, make mistakes, let loose and forget about his own fear and the fears of everyone else.

Maybe he didn't really want all of that, but he wanted the option.

Instead, he had literature homework and a hope for a headline without 'demon' anywhere near it. He felt another spike of loneliness, brought on by his *missing* before he realized there were ways to fill the void Rachael left. Maybe there was not another like Rachael, who saw the worst that he was and still decided he was worth it, but Tommy was there, lazily studying, and he had been able to perform with people who supported that career choice.

He tilted his head back, again thinking of Samuel Stewart. Samuel, who stayed with him for hours in the midst of a potentially dangerous situation and still met his eyes the next day with no trace of fear.

Samuel was not someone Davis was going to let go so easily.

"Turner, are you fucking *smiling*? We're reading about child labor laws and you're *smiling*?" Tommy gave an exaggerated sneer of disgust. "Man, I *knew* there was a reason no one else would be your roommate. And I thought it was because you did yoga."

This time Davis laughed, and he continued laughing as Tommy bickered and continued to scorn him for his lack of heart for children, and he smiled because he certainly didn't *need* that void filled. He had a wonderful friend. He had opportunities. He had hope. However, he, like always, wanted more.

He thought he was so sure what that more was.

# CHAPTER
# TEN

Becoming Davis's friend was not something Samuel really expected. It didn't feel like Davis was doing it just because he felt indebted. It felt *genuine*, a word that kept coming up in his mind.

There were couches in the hallways of the department where the theatre students would gather between and after classes. Davis would be there. He would call out to Samuel as he walked by, asking if he wanted to join in a card game or silly debate. The gestures were done so naturally Samuel felt like it was something he had been doing for years, not just days. When Davis stole Samuel's phone to text himself, Samuel didn't even mind. It even became common that Davis would ask Samuel to lunch or coffee.

"I don't drink coffee," Samuel said one afternoon when he received a call from Davis. He was smiling because he couldn't remember the last time someone wanted his attention so much. It felt nice. Plus, Davis couldn't see it, so he couldn't be teased.

"*How?*" Davis asked. "I mean, you must stay awake somehow. Don't tell me you have insomnia and can naturally function on lack of sleep. I'll be very jealous."

Samuel laughed, which drew the attention of a student walking by and he quickly covered his mouth, his face warming. Maybe it wasn't such a good idea to call Davis back on his way between classes. "Nothing as absurd as that. I drink hot tea instead."

"Oh, well, *that* I can accept," Davis said cheerfully. "So, tomorrow? I know you have class at nine. I do, too. You can't get out of it. If you don't want to commute earlier, you can just stay at my dorm."

Samuel had not been to Davis's dorm and didn't plan to ever sleeping anywhere that wasn't his own bed. "I think I can manage," he said.

"I know I said I accepted you drinking tea," Davis said the next morning, "but I don't understand how you can stand seeing the leaves at the bottom."

They had picked a small local café, which was nice mostly because it wasn't overrun with people who were in a hurry. It was a place you could take your time. Samuel was sold when he realized there wouldn't be a crowd.

"At least I can *see* what's in my drink, which is rarely anything but clear," Samuel said, sipping his tea as he nodded towards Davis's. "Who knows what's in that. Beans? Powder? Spiders?"

Davis blanched and set his cup down. "Well, thanks for that," he said, smacking his lips in disgust.

Samuel hid his grin. "You're very welcome." He watched Davis contemplate risking the cup of coffee anyway. Apparently, it was worth it, because Davis took another sip.

"I don't care. This is fucking delicious," Davis said, and Samuel watched him savor it.

"Don't say I didn't warn you when you reach the bottom," Samuel said, too amused at Davis's skeptical look at the cup of pure caffeine.

Samuel wasn't sure this was how all friendships worked. He was called a friend by those who worked in the shop with him, but nothing else felt like this, feeling wanted for more than just his skill set. There were no obligations, just an equally shared fondness of the other's presence.

One shared visit to the café turned into a welcomed habit before class. It was not uncommon that lunches would be shared, as well as the occasional dinner during late hours. Soon enough, Davis's absence was more noticeable than his presence. Samuel noticed it during finals, when their schedules conflicted and yet still, when Samuel could sleep in, he was up at his usual time to meet Davis. When he finished an exam, he felt lost as to what to do next, without Davis being available for lunch or dinner.

He hoped the summer, when Davis went back to Atlanta, Georgia and when Samuel stayed in Charleston, would bring a reminder of what he used to do before he met Davis Turner.

# CHAPTER ELEVEN

Davis felt nauseous.

The music pounded in his ears, which was usually *such* a good thing. When he first got a job, experiencing the *joys* of being a cashier, the very first thing he saved for was a pair of cordless, noise cancelling headphones. Sure, it cost him any extra money he made from his first few months of paychecks, but they were worth it. Davis loved music and he loved the freedom to *move*.

The music was loud and blaring, but he didn't have any room to move at all. People surrounded him, solo cups filled with beer or soda or ping pong balls, and there were very distinct smells that Davis did *not* want to name. This was supposed to be fun, a chance to be at a party before everyone left, a moment to not worry about studying or deciding his honors' thesis or finding another job. It was supposed to be carefree, yet the world was rocking back and forth, a boat on dry land.

Maybe nausea was just the symptom of the very real truth that he was *scared*. Whether it was the crowd, the temptations, or the very real possibility of him becoming possessed and killing everyone here, he wasn't completely sure. He was just *mostly* sure.

There was medication advertised for those who were vulnerable to demons. SSRIs that helped with the depression, but that also stunted any other emotion. Each one affected people differently, and Davis had gone through many in high school. It wasn't that he was anti-medication. Some worked well for others, balancing their emotions rather than stunting them. It was just his was meant to make him numb, and how was he supposed to act, or dance, or perform in any way if he couldn't *feel*? He had some of the medication still, waiting, seeing if there was a time he would need it to get by.

He wondered if maybe this was one of those moments he should have taken it.

The air was pounded out of his lungs from the back and Tommy laughed as he moved his hand to grip Davis's shoulder, grounding him.

"Relax!" he said. This was one of the only times Davis had ever seen Tommy out of his pajamas, and he picked a palm tree printed button-down and polka dot boxers. Maybe they *were* pajamas. It was so like Tommy he felt comforted by it.

"You know very well that's not exactly something I can do," Davis muttered, flinching as a few people pushed past him, loud and reckless, with Greek letters stitched on jackets.

"*You know very well*," Tommy mocked, "that you

will stop a demon from possessing you. Come on. One drink." He pushed a solo cup into Davis's hands and Davis scowled at it. Tommy hadn't seen what it was like to fight a possession. He was playing with matches and Davis did not want combust.

He felt twitchy and the urge to hide in the bathroom was starting to beat out what pride he allowed himself, when he caught sight of a hat. Sandy blond hair curled from under it, covering a worried expression. Samuel approached him.

"You look like you're about to have an aneurism," Samuel said. 'Said' might have not been accurate considering the volume level of the room, but he didn't yell, either. It was something in between: loud enough to be able to be heard over the music, quiet enough to still be coming from Samuel. "Are you okay?"

"Define 'okay,'" Davis said.

Samuel shook his head. "Not you at the moment." He swapped Davis's solo cup for another before Davis could deny it, and he added, "It's just water. Come on." He waved his hand, gesturing for Davis to follow. He did.

The porch was much less claustrophobic and much quieter. There were others sharing in conversation and Davis remembered elementary school, being told to use his "inside voice" to quiet down. But now that they were outside, everything seemed backwards. He could smell what could only be described as *Charleston*. Alcohol. Horse manure. Sulfur. Beach. Ocean. Night. There was something else he couldn't quite place, that extra bit that make it unique and not so disgusting. It made it *real*. It let

Davis know he was himself standing there and not just a shell.

Samuel's knuckles tapped against the wooden rail a few times. There were lanterns strung above them which casted a shadow from Samuel's hat, hiding his eyes. Then he tilted his head, looking up at Davis, and the light played over his pale eyelashes and cheeks. "Better?"

It took a moment before Davis nodded, nearly overwhelmed by exactly how much better he was. "I'm worried it'll happen again," he confessed. "It just takes one moment, one slip up, and I could be giving up control to something that has no care about any of the lives here." He closed his eyes, rubbing his thumbs over his clasped hands.

"I don't worry," Samuel said, pulling Davis's attention back to him. He looked serene, at complete peace, even if he knew exactly what it took for Davis to stay in control. Samuel leaned forward, stretching his hand over the railing, reach-ing out to something Davis couldn't see. "Maybe it's because I know I can go to a party, I can drink alcohol, I can go home with a guy and sleep with him, and I have never been possessed." He took a breath, then there was the softest huff of a laugh. "Maybe going to church actually balances that out, but I don't think so. I think..." He trailed off, his eyebrows scrunching, the shadow from his hat growing. "I think intention matters and you care too much about the results."

Davis had just gained too much information to trust himself to react correctly. He paused and then looked at Samuel. "You go to church?"

Samuel laughed, soft and startled. "Catholic

baby," he said, as if he was almost embarrassed or sorry for it. His words always seemed to have an accent, but never one Davis could pin down. It was as if there were many accents all stringed together to form one melody. Then, perhaps because of Davis's expression, whatever it was, Samuel again asked, "Are you okay?"

"Yeah," Davis said unsurely. Then, "Yeah," again, more surely.

"Good," Samuel said, pushing away from the railing. "Then I'm going to…" He tilted his head back towards the house.

"Oh, yeah. Yeah, I think I'm going to go back," Davis said. "To my dorm, I mean. Could you tell my roommate, Tommy? Tommy Rider. Do you know him?"

Samuel cleared his throat. "Mhm. I'll tell him." Then he gave the smallest of smiles, his eyes downcast, and he left, leaving Davis feeling strangely like he was on the outside, watching some-one else's story. If he was to be a side role in anyone's tale, he would be glad for it to be Samuel's.

# CHAPTER
# TWELVE

"*Do you know me?*" Tommy whispered into Samuel's ear from behind, his hand reaching around, gliding over Samuel's chest.

This was always the part that took Samuel's breath away: the seduction of it, even more than when clothes were gone and bodies were connected. He needed that, but he wanted this.

Tommy had come out to the porch as soon as Davis left. Samuel hadn't been surprised and he certainly wasn't upset by it, but now his eyes were closed and the beauty of the night was gone, replaced by the fact they were at a party and it seemed not all of his chances for getting laid were gone. In fact, they seemed pretty high at the moment.

"I don't," Samuel finally managed to say, "know you. Not in the way Tommy meant."

"We're well acquainted," Tommy said, his lips against Samuel's neck. "At least in the way it matters."

Samuel pushed out a breath before turning around, putting his hand up between them so he could look at Tommy. "I know your name, I know you're Davis's roommate, and I know what you like in bed." He frowned. "I will *not* lie to Davis if he asks."

"Then he can ask," Tommy said. "What would be the answer?"

Samuel had never felt any sort of guilt about sex in years. Not who it was with, not how it was done, and not even *when* it was done. It was a part of his life, simple as that. Yet now, looking at Tommy and thinking about Davis, he felt guilt.

"We've hooked up," Samuel said, his voice low, his eyes now on the crooked floorboards under their feet. He was certain the floorboards of his porch at home needed a new coat of paint. Logically, he couldn't do it while it was dark out, so it would have to be done tomorrow. That didn't stop him from wanting to leave and do it now. Tomorrow could be one day too late for his mother's expectations. Then again, any day would probably be a day too late. He squeezed his eyes shut and looked back up to Tommy's expectant gaze.

"More than once?" Tommy asked. It was an offer, or at the very least, an inquiry.

Samuel hummed to himself, leaning back against the railing. "Twice would make it much more significant than it is," he said.

Tommy moved forward, boxing Samuel against the railing. "Only if we made it significant."

There was definitely alcohol on Tommy's breath, but he didn't seem too gone. Samuel observed him, the question in his gold eyes, and the expectation of an answer. Samuel could say no if he wanted to. He didn't.

"Okay," Samuel said, then pointed at Tommy when he grinned. "You have to make it as insignificant as possible."

"What could be less significant than hooking up at a frat party?" Tommy said, rolling his eyes.

Samuel still thought the 'who' factor mattered, but he dismissed that thought. He needed to be distracted and he needed to *stop thinking*.

"Then come on, I need a few more drinks," Samuel said. He slipped past Tommy, and entered the house without looking back.

# CHAPTER THIRTEEN

It was slow walking back to the dorm. Davis felt calmer now, thankfully, but walks always helped him get any excess energy out—and he had a *lot* of excess energy. He gave a passing hello to a few of the homeless men he knew, carefully avoided drunk students, and stayed clear of the roads.

He was approached just a few feet from campus.

"Davis Turner!" a woman called, latching onto his shoulders. At first, Davis thought she was just another drunk partier, but there was not a scent of alcohol. "You *must* let us talk to you!"

"What?" Davis asked, leaning away from her. Her hair was pinned up in a tight bun, and she was close enough to his face that, even in the dark, he could see four different shades of brown in her eyes. He glanced away, only to see three other people behind her. They were all dressed differently, but there was a symbol on their jackets. A pin, maybe, red and black in the shape of a reptile's eye.

Davis chilled.

He wasn't sure who they were, but all he could think about was why he had the major he did—to get away from demons. To get away from his past and from people who only saw that.

"Please speak with us. Let us know of your experience. We know what really happened," the woman said. "We know you're a demon walking among men. And we want—we *beg* for your acceptance of us." Now Davis thought maybe something besides alcohol had been involved, but the pins made that look unlikely.

"I'm *not* a demon!" Davis said. "I'm a *performer*."

"Yes! The devil's choice. It's good to know how to disguise yourself," the woman went on.

Davis pulled away from her. "What are you, Satanists?" Although he said it, he knew they weren't. He had met Satanists before and they had actually been really understanding.

The woman looked offended. "Of course not! We are followers of the truth, of demons alone. We call ourselves The Demon's Offerings. That is exactly what we are to you: an offering."

"Look, I'm just Davis," he said as innocently as he could. "A boring *person* who just really wants to sleep—"

"I think you misunderstand us," one of the men said. He had thin hair on his head and facial hair that was trying its best. "We do not think it's a *bad* thing you are a demon. We want to know how you did it— how do you receive the demon offer? Is sinning all it takes?"

"*What?* Why would you *want* the demon offer?" Davis asked, taking a step back towards the campus.

"To have a guaranteed life after death," another man with a round face and curved nose said. His eyes were narrow and dark, with lines running all around them.

Davis started to put together these strange pieces. These people weren't there to hurt him. That had become obvious enough. They were lunatics who had given up on the idea of becoming an Angel.

So have I, Davis thought. Could this be what I become?

No. This is what he was working so hard to prevent. He was *human*. That's all he wanted.

These four people seemed like they weren't giving up any time soon.

"I'm not a demon," he said. "That's what I'm trying to prove here. I want to act *roles*. As a *human*." He remembered in high school when he had first said his ambition. He remembered auditioning for a play and receiving the cast list. He had been cast all right. As a *demon*. There hadn't even been a demon in the play.

"You don't have to act with us," the woman said frantically. "Lord Turner—"

Davis blanched. "No, don't call me that. I didn't want to be hated as a demon, but this..." It was almost worse. He never wanted to be praised for what he had done. What about all the deaths? Demon possessions were common. He had many neighbors who had either been possessed and died themselves, or witnessed one or the other. Only very few survived. Did no one really understand the epidemic? Did no one get how far away they should try to be from it?

Davis's breath was becoming shorter. He was *terrified* of this, terrified of these people always connecting him to demons.

No one could get away from them. Especially him.

He took another step back, then another.

"We just want to help!" the woman said. "We want to give you strength! We want to learn what you need from us. Is it sacrifice?"

They weren't walking toward him anymore.

Davis looked down and realized he had officially crossed onto the campus.

They weren't allowed to walk on campus ground. Whether this was because they were banned by campus security or some other reason, Davis didn't know, but he would take the chance to get away.

"Just...leave me alone," he said, turning his back to them.

"Davis!" a man shouted. "We understand what you're saying! We'll be here, waiting, for any need you might have. We are your servants—your slaves!"

Davis wanted to throw up. He tucked his head down, and he tuned them out as he quickly made his way to his dorm.

He was definitely staying on campus for as long as he could before flying home. Tommy could get the groceries.

# CHAPTER FOURTEEN

There were many opportunities that Samuel had been presented with. Still, there were some nights all Samuel could do was mourn the one he lost. He remembered the rejection letter from the Cleanser Academy, a private school strictly for the Exorcist position. Out of the six positions within an Exorcist squad, two involved specific, uncontrolled conditions, two required an outrageous amount of degrees and experience, one required a specialized talent, and then there was the Cleanser. They were who performed any required ceremonies; they were who studied religions and knew demons the most intimately. Cleansers were also those with the most combat specific training.

Samuel had dreamed of finding a guaranteed way to help those who were possessed. He had been brought up believing that Priests were the only ones who could purify a spirit. As for himself, he believed that to be mostly true. A Priest was his connection to God. That's what he had been taught, even though he had learned differently since. For now, it was chance—a hope that the Host was religious enough, or even simply aware enough to recognize the ceremonies at all. Ceremonies, no matter what religion, didn't matter at all unless the Host truly believed in it.

The urge to become an Exorcist hit so strongly that it paralyzed Samuel's work on anything else. He had alerts on his phone, constantly updating him on local Exorcist news, church updates, or global breakthroughs. He had given up, completely switched paths, but he couldn't stay away.

He mostly received death announcements. Not many survived exorcisms. Davis was such an odd case because of how young he had been. There were other possessed children; it was just that none had survived. Or, cynically, none that could pay off the right people to keep it covered. Davis's case might have even been affected because of the color of his skin. Samuel didn't know. But it also wasn't just the fact he was a vulnerable survivor. It was that his survival was directly connected to the death of Exorcist Robbie Hodge. There was something there, an unknown connection to the case that made it to much more frightening...and interesting.

Samuel couldn't stop obsessing over it all. He thought of Davis, thought of his sister, thought of Robbie Hodge and demons and Angels.

He gave in to one specific notification. He knew Davis didn't want to be involved, and that there could even be a risk by including him, so he kept it to himself. When it was announced there would be an Exorcism open to the public, Samuel took no time in deciding whether to go or not.

It was held not at the Exorcists' Headquarters, but at the Hindu Temple and Cultural Center. Samuel was very careful when entering, taking slow steps so as to not disturb others or to accidentally offend those of the Hindu religion.

The building itself was simple, blending in with other buildings on the outside, while the inside felt as though stepping through a veil—not to a different world, but to a different *feeling*. Samuel knew the lights were usually much brighter from his search for directions, but even dimmed as they were, it reflected so smoothly over the floor he was afraid he would slip.

"Name?"

Samuel flinched and looked at a man. He was in a guard uniform and seemed taller than even Davis, and much wider. Samuel felt very small.

"Uh," he said. "Samuel Stewart?" He hadn't meant for it to come out as a question. He had expected this, but it was exactly like his fear. He debated just leaving.

The man sneered. Samuel glanced away nervously, but then tried to at least *look* for a name tag to be respectful. Yet, when he found what must have been the guy's name tag, it was as if he couldn't quite focus on it.

There was a sigh.

"Walk away, Jenkins. He can't see you," another man said. He had red hair and an amused expression.

He had a black and silver jacket in his hands. Samuel gaped.

"Don't mind him," the Exorcist said. He was Cillian O'Doherty, the Optic of the Charleston squad. Samuel couldn't connect any words in his head, let alone out of his lips as Cillian continued. "He's our Nondefined, Jenkins Perks. Are you here for the viewing?"

Samuel blinked. He registered the words. Nondefined, one of the uncontrolled conditions. It meant that whatever Samuel saw or heard from Jenkins was based only on his own assumption and prediction. It was possible that nothing he just experienced from Jenkins was real at all, including his physical appearance and words. He looked back at Jenkins, who didn't actually seem as tall as he thought, and maybe his facial features *did* look a little like the ID photo online. Samuel looked away. It was all giving him a headache.

"I'm, um. Well, I hoped to watch, if that's okay?" Samuel said carefully.

"Absolutely. Feel free to sit in the pews." He gestured towards the long, light wood pews. Then he gave an unsure smile. "You do have to sign a form, though. We can never predict what happens at an Exorcism."

"Yes, of course," Samuel said too quickly. He felt like a child, but he didn't care. He found the disclaimer form and signed.

When it was clear the exorcism was about to start, Samuel felt like a child for a completely different reason. Where before he was giddy, now he was cold. There were many people there, most of whom looked as if they were of Indian descent. There were a few men wearing white attire (lungi, Samuel guessed, but wasn't sure) and women in brightly colored sari and choli, who were cleaning their arms and hands in a basin. That was all normal enough, but then the screaming pierced through the doors.

Samuel was not the only one gripping the pew as musicians banged on their drums or clapped their manjeera. There were those who started to sing, or maybe chant, but Samuel couldn't understand the language. During the music, the doors burst open and a man was dragged into the room by two guards and thrown onto a bright pile of fabrics on the floor. The musicians—who were probably not so much musicians, as they were unofficial exorcists— sat around the man. A woman in a black and silver jacket held the man down, the words of the chant flowing perfectly from her lips.

It was Andy Rogers, the Cleanser of Charleston. She did *not* look pleased. Nor did the civilian exorcists. Andy pushed the man's head down and lodged her knee at the back of his head, holding his arms steady.

"*Fuck,*" she said, slipping up her chant and glaring to the side, where there were two other Exorcists. "I *told* you this shouldn't ever be public."

"It's going fine," one of them said.

Samuel couldn't avert his eyes. He just kept staring at the man, writhing in Andy's arms, spouting nonsense that was probably in at least four different languages, spitting, growling. It made Samuel agree with Andy. Maybe this shouldn't have been public at all.

The man went still.

"*Dancers*," Andy snapped. She hauled the man up onto his feet and practically dragged him off the fabrics as dancers made a path towards the door. Cillian was at the door, opening it—and then the man started thrashing violently.

The dancers didn't stop, but there were three Exorcists who came in to help Andy hold the man, and yet it was still unclear if four against the one possessed man was enough.

"This is the end!" Andy shouted. "The demon is rejected! It just needs a place to—"

The lights sparked out.

Everything and everyone stopped.

Samuel held his breath as he felt wind gust through the room.

Then, the lights were back on, fully bright. Samuel looked over the limp man and Andy's exhausted body...and he saw something in her hand, white dripping out of it.

A *coconut*, he observed. It was small enough to be palmed. It must have been a part of the ritual. His heart was in overdrive. He had so much to learn.

Andy pushed the man away from her and stood up, brushing herself off. The man was unconscious, but others immediately went to check on him without seeming fearful at all. Andy glared at the audience, then towards her teammates. "That was *not* a traditional exorcism. You have to understand it's *rare* someone believes strongly enough for the ritual to work—and the demon is still *alive*, since we weren't able to direct it properly." She waved at the entrance with both arms. "This was *stupid*." Then, she stormed out.

It was the Head of the Charleston Squad, Paul Duggar, who addressed the crowd. "I apologize for the behavior of my subordinate. I hope everyone was able to learn and see the true power of belief and exorcisms. Thank you and goodnight."

And just like that, all the Exorcists left.

Samuel felt like he was in a daze.

Even after witnessing all of that, he still wanted nothing more than to be a part of it.

# CHAPTER FIFTEEN

When someone looked at Jenkins Perks, they did not see Jenkins Perks. When they listened to him speak, they did not hear him. He was not, as far as the rest of the world was concerned, Jenkins Perks.

He was a Nondefined. A person who, as the name suggested, held no definition—or rather, they *had* one, but it was lost, leaving only an impression behind. This impression was created only by the perception of others. They were alive, but they left blanks for the rest of the world to fill in. He would try to order a pizza and receive a salad with an "I hope you enjoy it, ma'am." He would try to compliment someone he found attractive and instead receive a slap. He could not convince the city of Charleston that, yes, he was alive enough to still live in his house. No one saw him. No one heard him. He wasn't sure what he would say or do if they did. He felt dead and alive at the same time, as if he might as well be a ghost.

One day Jenkins received a letter in the mail. The envelope was crisp and clean with no signs of being handled through the post office. It simply had his name on the center and a seal on the top left corner. He received his black and silver jacket and an ID with the same seal the next day. Cillian O'Doherty had stood in front of him, shook his hand, and greeted him as Jenkins Perks. Jenkins asked questions, more on instinct than actually expecting an answer, but Cillian responded, his words heavy with an Irish accent. Then he asked Jenkins questions, and he heard Jenkins' answers, and there was a hope that built inside him. He was Lost to the world, but Cillian was his way to finding it again. It had been this way for seven years.

There were other Nondefineds around the world. They were called in, assigned what Jenkins learned was called an *Optic*. Someone who, like Cillian, was not affected by the condition. Optics were the translators, the ones who gave Nondefineds a purpose again, even if it didn't mean they Found themselves. They represented that connection to humanity otherwise lost.

Cillian was Jenkins' hope.

The weather should have been stormy. It should have been dark and unpleasant. That's what Jenkins would have assumed the weather was, if someone was retelling this moment. Instead, they were by the ocean near the Battery park, the sun was shining, the temperature was warm, and the tide was low and calm over the metal rail barrier.

Cillian was spouting obscenities, his fingers digging into his scalp, his breath labored, his legs stumbling. He was the only thing breaking the calm.

"Exorcists think they're doing good. You're doing nothing but helping us!" he spat.

No, not him. Not Cillian.

The exorcism had been a success: the demon was removed from the Hindu man. There had only been one small error: the demon needed to be contained and instead, got away. With the dancers guiding the direction, it had been led in a straight path—directly into Cillian O'Doherty.

"Cillian," Andy whispered. She was the one who actually exorcised hosts, who freed them from possession, yet there was nothing she could do now. She held the knowledge and the means to do so, but Cillian's eyes were on her, a finger pointed to keep her back.

"Don't you dare," Cillian gritted out, his accent thick as he struggled to do anything but collapse. It was so clear when Cillian was himself and when it was the demon using his body.

"I dare," the demon said through him, moving Cillian's eyebrows in a way he never would. "Come on, little girl. You can't kill your friend, can you?" It was Cillian's tongue that licked Cillian's lips, and Jenkins was holding himself back from punching the jaw that held them.

"I'm not needed," Andy said, lowering her fist and her gun, her brown eyes fixed on the ground. She looked resolved. "He knows his job. He can do it."

"Andy," Jenkins pleaded, even though she

couldn't understand him. "Andy, please, don't let this happen."

"It has to happen, Jenkins," Cillian said, who was stepping back, towards the railing, where the tide was a dozen feet down, too low to cover the glimpses of rocks and barnacles. Cillian knew what he was doing. Andy was right. Even as the back of Cillian's knees hit the railing, even as he tipped back and his arms flailed, even as he dropped those dozen feet head first, Jenkins could not look away. He didn't try to stop it. His fellow Exorcists didn't try to stop it. They watched.

"It's my fault," Andy whispered, the only sign of guilt Jenkins had seen from her. Her expression shook, her jaw tightened, her eyes teared…and then she took a breath and saluted.

From a distance, Jenkins heard Paul make a phone call, whispered words filled with orders, then grief. When he hung up, he did not move. He simply said, "*Innallahi wa inni ilahi rajioun.*"

None of them looked over the railing. None of them could. Their teammate, and Jenkins' hope, was dead.

# CHAPTER SIXTEEN

Classes were over. The campus was emptying, but the theatre department still buzzed with activity. The Spoleto festival, where talented groups from all over the world gathered to display their skills in the different theatres of Charleston, was in production and Samuel wasn't wasting the opportunity to be a part of it. The exorcism he witnessed still burned in his mind, but another feeling had crowded in, making it easy to search for any distraction.

There were only a couple of days left before the dorms closed, which meant Davis would be leaving for the summer, back to Atlanta soon. Because of this, there was a small group gathered at the couches with him, chatting away and milking the last bit of time together.

Samuel did what he normally did in groups of people, which was completely ignore them. He played a game on his phone, casually thrilled at the idea of beating his high score, when his hands vibrated.

Before he looked at the alert, he assumed it was either his mother, reminding him of all the chores he had yet to do or some other way to demean him, or Davis checking in to see if he was okay, and, if he was okay, teasing him for ignoring everyone. But it was neither of them. He stared at his phone, his heart pounding in his chest, his stomach churning. He had considered the possibility of commentary on the exorcism, perhaps a notice there would be no more public ones, but when he tapped the link to the article, he immediately felt sick.

He received the "Are you okay?" text from Davis. He looked up just as Davis's eyes shifted away from his other friends and to his own, catching his, not by chance, but by the fact Davis kept looking. Samuel jerked his head once to the side.

"Cillian O'Doherty died," Samuel said, his voice low enough to not interrupt any other conversation. Except the words still broke through and the gathered friends fell silent.

"Who is that?" Ashley asked, her now neon pink hair clipped back from her concerned gaze. "Should I know?"

Samuel thought she should know, but not everyone had the same interests as he did. He couldn't list all the actors from her favorite TV show, after all. He, however, had just met Cillian, had looked at him in awe. He had dreamed the night of the exorcism that maybe Cillian would remember his face—that Samuel could stop by again, maybe prove he could help in some way.

He had been dreaming selfishly.

"He was an Exorcist here," Samuel explained, dropping his gaze to his phone, reading the article's title again and again. "It says he committed suicide."

*Suicide*, of all things. Why? *Why?*

The silence grew heavy. That part of the world, the part that fought the war against demons, always seemed so far away when there were exams to pass and shows to put on. Distractions were necessary, but at that moment there was a break where reality could not be ignored.

Guiltily, each one of the friends gathered looked to Davis.

Davis was looking at Samuel. "Was there a demon involved?" he asked, too used to the word 'demon' to be afraid of it. Davis had already been a part of the war. He chose to stay out of it.

"Nothing's confirmed," Samuel said, scrolling through the article, more to keep his hands and mind busy than to actually read it again. "They suspect so." The Hindu exorcism was mentioned. The very same one he had witnessed. Had it really been so dangerous that someone *died* as a result? He hadn't understood each part of it, and he knew something hadn't gone quite right, but he didn't know what until he had a chance to research it.

Demons needed somewhere else to go. The dancers were used as a distraction, a way to keep the demon within the Host before it was guided somewhere else. It had been guided--toward the exit, where Cillian had been holding open the doors.

The coconut being smashed had signified the

end of the exorcism, but only of the Hindu man. The same ceremony wouldn't work on someone with a different belief.

The horrible feeling in his gut wouldn't go away, no matter how much Samuel willed it to.

But why *suicide*?

"Aren't Exorcists the ones who keep demons away?" Steven asked, his expression serious, his dark eyebrows low.

"Yes," Samuel said.

"Then who do you call when they fail?"

"No one," Davis said, his expression changing to something Samuel had never seen on him before, something ugly and filled with disgust. His hands were clenched in his jeans.

"What about the church? They were the original Exor—"

"No one," Davis repeated, his voice even and final. "No one who can really do anything." He closed his eyes, pulled in a breath through his nose, and stood. Samuel stood, as if pulled along with Davis's motion. He followed Davis down the stairs, through the building, and out the doors until they were in a parking lot.

Samuel watched the frustrated silence, heavy pacing, and nervous hand gestures. He waited until Davis gathered himself enough to face Samuel. "There's nowhere private to go. Not before work."

Davis, Samuel realized, wanted to tell him something. His hazel eyes were focused sadly on Samuel, the green in them shining more in the natural light.

"No one can hear," Samuel said, softening his

voice.

Davis raked a hand through his perfect hair, showing lighter streaks amongst the brown. "It's not something—I need to show you something."

"Show me?" Samuel said. It was becoming obvious that Davis left the others specifically to have a moment with Samuel. He had known, or expected, or wished, for Samuel to follow him. It wasn't like his mother, who tried to train Samuel how to read her mind, but more of a shared knowledge: they both cared if the other was okay. So, Samuel repeated himself, but changed his tone: "Show me."

Davis's eyes flickered around, a moment of hesitancy before he walked around the building, only slightly more private than the side. This was where he had fought off his last attack.

Then he pulled off his shirt.

"Whoa, wait, what—"

Davis turned around, showing his back, and the image stopped Samuel's words. He could see the pale color striking against Davis's brown skin, jagged and textured as it trailed down his spine and across his shoulders. A scar in the shape of a cross, stretched as Davis had grown despite it. Samuel could not look away until he was forced to as Davis turned back around.

"You're Catholic," Davis said, his voice quiet, vulnerable, guilty.

Samuel's lips parted in disbelief as he realized what Davis was trying to share with him. "I am. But that..." Samuel said, still seeing the scar in his mind. "If whoever did that to you claimed to be Christian, they were liars." The words came out much harsher than Samuel intended, but when he saw Davis's shock, he kept steady.

"They were trying to cleanse me," Davis whispered. "After I was possessed. It was a trial version of a new exorcism."

"Clearly, it didn't work," Samuel growled. "Clearly, they tried to take such a power into their own hands and the result was *scarring a child*. They are not true followers if they did not do it out of true guidance. That is the job of an Exorcist—I would know. I applied to the Cleanser Academy. You have to study for that and it's—no good Christian would try what they did to you. They need to respect *your* beliefs if they expect it to work. They were just pretenders."

Davis's eyes were steady on him, searching without moving. "How can you say that?" It wasn't asked as an accusation or out of disbelief. It was clear Davis was just looking for an answer.

An answer wasn't simple. How could Samuel say that, as someone who attended church most Sundays? How could he say that, believing in his faith when it was questioned? How could he say that, knowing Davis was a threat, knowing the Exorcists weren't a perfect defense, knowing he himself was not exactly the perfect example of a Christian?

He answered anyway, the only way he knew how to: with honestly. "I choose to believe people have emotions for a reason," he said carefully. "We have physical symptoms of them. When I look at your back with the knowledge I have, I feel sick." He did not hesitate to match Davis's gaze like he normally would. "I choose to believe that's God telling me something is wrong. And nothing else about you, not your past possession, not your near possession, and certainly not anything else you've done, has felt this type of *wrong*. I'll listen and believe in that."

Davis's gaze remained steady, digesting the information, then he took in a deep breath and let it out, slowly and evenly. He gave a single nod. "Thank you." Then he grinned. "I don't think I've ever heard you preach before."

"I don't, usually," Samuel said. "There hasn't been anyone to listen."

Davis dropped his gaze. "You applied to the Cleanser Academy?"

"Right next to college applications," Samuel said. He rubbed and twisted his fingers. "I didn't get in."

"I'm sorry," Davis said, although it was hard to tell how sincere he was.

"It's fine," he said, because it didn't matter now.

"Samuel?"

"Yes?"

"I'm not Christian."

"I know."

"I don't think I ever could be," Davis said.

Samuel bowed his head. "I know."

# CHAPTER SEVENTEEN

Summer came. People were separated by cities and states and, sometimes, countries. Samuel was still in Charleston. He worked at a small shop at the outdoor market, selling oddities and small recycled metal sculptures, meanwhile fighting his anxiety over *people* every day. It wasn't that the general public was horrible. He found most customers were tourists and being tourists meant they were on vacation with time to breathe and money to spend. It was more of the fact Samuel was forced to *smile* and make small talk, which he was never any good at. But the money was under the table, which meant his parents had no way to track it.

He took out most of his frustrations by scowling at one particular sculpture. It should not have reminded him of Davis, should not have made him miss Davis, but the frog had long limbs, a guitar, and its head was thrown back with a sort of joy Samuel didn't think frogs could actually feel, let alone express. It was nothing like Davis. So, Samuel passed the time by trying to convince each and every customer to buy that particular sculpture, all so he didn't.

No one else ever bought it.

# CHAPTER EIGHTEEN

Daniel Collins was a man whose story was already over. He wasn't dead. He wasn't Lost. It was simply that he felt the Epilogue had been written and the rest was left up to the imagination.

He was *not* content with this.

There might have been some resentment as part of the aftermath. He lived, but others didn't, and it was for them that he felt like such a wrongdoing had occurred.

Life went on and there was nothing he could do except keep working.

He adjusted his silver and black jacket, checking that his sleeves were crisp and straight. It was a new jacket, even if the position that came with it wasn't. The stiffness of it reminded him of that position, of why he was here, standing in front of the Exorcists' Headquarters after a fellow Exorcist had died. This was not his home and it was certainly not his team, but there weren't enough known Optics available to fill the position.

The front door opened after he knocked and a girl stood in the doorway, small but with an over-powering presence, her brown eyes glaring before they widened in surprise.

"Daniel?" she asked. She wasn't wearing her jacket, instead wearing nothing more than a tank top and short shorts with heavy boots and fingerless gloves, showing large patches of her brown skin. Practical, he thought, if someone relied on speed instead of brute force.

"Andy Rogers," he said, tipping his head politely. "It's been a long time. I'm sorry for your loss."

Andy shifted her weight back and crossed her arms. There was a moment of hesitation, but she said, "He did his job."

"Is that how you're handling it?"

"Yes."

It was clear Andy didn't want to talk more about it, so Daniel looked inside the house. "May I come in?"

Andy looked around the house that served as the Headquarters as if she were observing it—judging it, really—for the first time and was not pleased by it. "Sure," she said and stepped out of the way.

If it had been someone's house, Daniel would have been impressed. There were high ceilings and iron railings along the stairs and bypass, mimicking the gate work around the city. There were paintings that made the walls look less bare, and fake plants in corners. The furniture was scarce, but the pieces looked like antiques that were well maintained. It was a beautiful home.

It was not an Exorcist Headquarters.

Daniel tried not to show his judgement, but Andy sneered at him anyway. "We have less funding than your team. The house was donated."

"You don't have less funding," Daniel said, who was highly aware of all financial situations. "It's delegated differently."

A door opened across the foyer, spilling in light and a man covered in paint.

The man looked at Daniel. His eyes dark and hollow, his hair black and mussed so that it was directed towards the center, his skin pale under light blue paint.

"Jenkins?" Daniel asked, his eyes steady on the man.

"Yes," Jenkins said warily.

Daniel looked at the paint disdainfully. "Re-decorating?"

"Something like that," Jenkins said, recognition bringing some emotion to his face—not quite hope, but something close. The potential for it, at the very least.

"I know we haven't met," Daniel said. "I'm Daniel Collins, Head of the Atlanta squad. I'm here as your temporary Optic."

"Head?" Jenkins asked. "How were you able to leave your team?"

"I have a capable team," Daniel dismissed, ignoring the way Jenkins scowled at that. "Where is Paul?"

"In a meeting with Carol," Andy said, pointedly ignoring Jenkins, whom she couldn't understand. She pivoted on her heel and went to exit into a room to the left. "Welcome to Charleston. Make yourself at home."

Paul Duggar arrived a few hours later. Daniel filled those hours locating the gym (which was not a gym, but simply gym equipment stuffed into an extra room) and ignoring anyone else. This would be his team for a while, he realized. He needed to speak to them, but he knew he had to speak to Paul first. It wasn't that he had anything he needed to say, but that he knew Paul did. So, he waited.

Paul entered the gym looking tired and completely out of place. His skin was a light brown, covered precisely with his white thobe. His black hair and trimmed beard were peppered with white. The years were catching up to him, but Daniel knew how much experience those years held. He paused in his workout and straightened his back respectfully.

"Sir," he acknowledged.

Paul waved him off. "As far as I'm concerned, even here we're equals, Daniel. We are both leaders," he said.

"You have questions for me," Daniel said.

"Yes," Paul said, sighing. "Are you sure you can do your job here?"

"Yes," Daniel said without hesitancy.

"Despite Davis Turner living here?"

Daniel lowered his gaze but still, without hesitancy, said, "Yes."

"Why not Bailey?" Paul questioned.

Daniel shook his head. "That would bring up too

many questions. You needed an Optic. I'm here."

"And your own Nondefined?"

"Noelle is in good hands," Daniel said confidently. He waited for another question to which he could give a simple answer, but none came. "As far as Davis," he said carefully, "I was planning to pay him a visit."

"Daniel."

"He knows who I am," Daniel said at the warning. "I have nothing against him."

"You have everything against him," Paul said sadly. "You lost a teammate because of him."

"No," Daniel said, feeling quite tired himself. "I lost a teammate the same way you lost Cillian." Then he leveled his gaze on Paul. "I will not waste the life Robbie Hodge saved."

"Then wait," Paul said. "Find your place here first and then you may go."

Grudgingly, Daniel nodded. He couldn't help but feel this was where his sequel started.

# CHAPTER NINETEEN

After a summer filled with late night texting, the school year started all too soon, and so did the auditions for the year's shows. As promised to Samuel before the summer, Davis auditioned for all of them. Now he sat on the couches, trying to focus on math homework. He was so nervous that the words and numbers looked more like Elfish than English. The cast list was going to be posted in a few minutes, and he couldn't stop humming or tapping his foot or fiddling with his ear cuff. Anything to not be still.

The last show of the year was going to be a musical. He had no natural singing voice, but he had worked and paid for vocal lessons over the summer because he wanted to dance and act on stage, which is difficult to do if your voice sucked. So, he practiced, and he lost his voice numerous times before he figured out how to match a note.

He was not a singer. It was not his strong point at all, but he tried his best and he wanted that part more than anything.

He watched as the professor posted the cast listing and students rushed to see it. He didn't move an inch. He was frozen, trying to not let his fear build in case it turned into something worse.

"Have you looked?"

Davis looked up from his math book to see Samuel, who looked simple and calm and happy. He was wearing his normal proper attire, his favorite gray vest over a pastel striped shirt, topped with a pale blue homburg. Davis only knew the name of the hat because he once called it a fedora and then was educated at length about the differences.

It used to be that Davis would have to drag Samuel over to the couches to be social with the other students. He had never met someone who didn't like human interaction so much. Now he was here, standing at the center of social gatherings and hanging out with Davis by his own choice. He even hung out with Tommy occasionally. It was strange, but in a good way.

"I haven't looked," Davis admitted. "I am so terrified of not getting the part I want that I would almost rather just not know."

"Come on," Samuel said, nodding his head towards the list. He held out his hand. "Let's go look."

Davis took his hand and allowed himself to be pulled from the couch and to the board where the list was. He covered his eyes with his free hand. "I can't look. Samuel, just tell me?"

"No, you have to look yourself," Samuel said,

patiently stubborn.

Davis tried to push back the panic building in his stomach and just dropped his hand, focusing on the list.

There were so many names, but there it was. The character's name. The role he wanted. And then after a series of dots…his own.

"Oh my god," Davis said, or he might not have said. He wasn't quite sure if any words came out at all. "Oh my god, I got the part!"

And then he did possibly the stupidest but most instinctual thing. He grabbed Samuel's face and kissed him on the mouth. Adrenaline rushed through his veins, a small voice in his head going *Oh* before reality crashed back in the same moment Samuel pushed him away.

Samuel was scared. Davis could see it in his eyes and in the way his shoulders hunched, and he was holding one hand with the other. It was the way Samuel stepped back, away from him, and Davis's stomach twisted and his chest felt heavy with bricks.

He had been so afraid that Samuel would disappear after realizing just how vulnerable to demons Davis really was. He worried about possessions and his experience with the church. He never once worried about scaring Samuel away by his own actions.

"Samuel—"

"Congratulations," Samuel said, clearing his throat and clasping his hands together, his eyes not meeting Davis's. That was the worst of it, realizing that it didn't take a demon to have someone not want to look at him.

# CHAPTER
# TWENTY

Ten minutes after Davis kissed Samuel, Samuel was in the streets, phone to his ear and walking aimlessly.

"'Ello," Tommy said in a terrible British accent. "A phone call from Samuel Stewart? And what is the cause for such an honor?"

"Are you home?" Samuel asked, ignoring the warnings in his head telling him *this isn't what I want.*

Tommy hummed and Samuel wanted to snap at him to hurry it up. They only had so much time before Davis would come back to their dorm. Then he felt sick for wanting to hide this. Why did he need to hide it? Wouldn't he tell the truth, if Davis asked? Shouldn't he be making it obvious?

He couldn't. He wouldn't. He wasn't sure at all what he was doing.

But this was a need, not a want.

"I'm home," Tommy finally said. "Needy thing,

aren't you?"

"Yes," Samuel said, because he knew it would get him what he needed faster. He was sure the Saints would see him as shameful. At the moment, he didn't care. The guilt would be there anyway. "What dorm do you live in?"

"Rutledge."

Samuel paused. Rutledge was one of the Honors dorms. He never realized Tommy and Davis were Honors students. Before he let himself think too much about that, he said, "I'll be there in two minutes. Let me up."

"Aye aye."

It took a few minutes for Tommy to come down and get him signed into the dorm. Then it took an agonizing minute of walking up the stairs before Samuel just growled and pushed Tommy against the wall.

"Kiss me," he said.

Tommy looked stricken, noticing a side of Samuel he wasn't used to. "I'm not—"

"I know," Samuel said quickly. "Kiss me and then fuck me." *Make it mean nothing* was left unsaid.

It was clear something was wrong. Tommy noticed it, but, bless him, he ignored it, and he kissed Samuel with the hard disconnect that he needed.

It was nothing. It was biology. That was all.

# CHAPTER TWENTY-ONE

To be a Cleanser meant to be *willing*. Willing to work long hours, willing to lose sleep, willing to hurt, willing to kill; willing to do whatever it took to finish the job. A Cleanser position could never be drafted. The school was specifically designed to gauge exactly how much one was *willing*.

Typically, one began schooling at the Cleanser Academy at eighteen, but Andy started much earlier than that. She was shipped off by her parents because too many people thought her brazen attitude without discipline would lead her to become a serial killer. Which, honestly, she thought was *absurd*.

Except she was one now, wasn't she? She just did it in a way that was legal. Still, she didn't get *enjoyment* from killing. She was trained to not feel anything about it. There was a logic to it, a taught necessity to better the world.

She felt something about Cillian's death. She felt it was her doing. It was impossible not to remember him, even if she just wanted to replace him. It sounded so unkind, but it was a kindness for herself she couldn't give. Maybe remembering was her punishment.

She wasn't even sure what happened to Cillian after death. Knowing so many religions made it difficult for her to know exactly which one she believed in. They all fit together and, for the most part, none of them looked kindly on what she did. She believed in demons. She wasn't so sure about Angels.

She wondered if this was a repeat of the Salem Witch Trials. It was true that their logic was very skewed, and her knowledge of that time was probably not completely accurate, but there was also very little Andy factored before making the decision to take a life. She did what she could, but there were very few ways to kill a demon, and Cillian was a result of her sparing another's life.

Or was Cillian her only human kill? What if all the others were just the demons? Was she allowed to think that way?

She wasn't supposed to be thinking of any of that. She was supposed to simply do her job and be *willing*.

Her adult coloring book was halfway full by the time anyone entered her room at the Headquarters. Daniel only tapped his knuckles on the wood once before coming in.

"I didn't know Andy Rogers was artistic," he mused.

"I'm not. It's mindless," she said, closing the book and pushing it away. She looked at Daniel, who was tall and broad and had the presence she wished she could exude. Instead, she always came off like that animated angry fairy. If only they knew her kill count. She could never forget it. "What do you need from me?"

"Nothing," Daniel said. "Your time, perhaps. Perhaps your mind."

Andy narrowed her eyes. Daniel was her senior by far. He wasn't a Cleanser, but a drafted Optic who made the decision to stay after his contract. He learned everything about every position he could, making him a well-qualified Head of the Atlanta Squad. He was *willing*. He was also plenty capable, which made this moment an oddity.

"What for?"

"Company," Daniel said. "You're the only one here who thinks like I do. Yet you've stayed so quiet. What are you thinking?"

My kill count, she thought, is more than yours.

"Religion," she said. "I was thinking how the Bible says 'Do not kill' as a Commandment, and yet Christianity has such a history of death. The Crusades in particular, as an example. Consider Leviticus, which states something like 'If a Priest's daughter plays the whore she must be burned alive' although that came before Jesus—which is also mildly hilarious, considering Jesus threw out the Old Testament and yet his followers didn't. If they did, it wouldn't have been printed. Not," Andy said, tapping a colored pencil against her desk, "that any of that is relevant."

"It's an interesting thought," Daniel said. "Why wouldn't it be relevant? This is what you've studied."

"Studying the true statements of religion is different than studying the beliefs of a member of that religion," Andy said. "That's why there are 'radicals,' such as Muslims who participated in terrorist attacks. In fact, Muslims are some of the most pacifistic people on the planet. Example: Paul. Christians have killed more in their history, but the truth is their religion never justified their actions. Simply knowing the religion is never enough." She thinned her lips. "You know this."

"I do," Daniel agreed, "but I like that you do as well. You're smart."

Because she couldn't hold it in, she said, "Not smart enough. I'm supposed to be saving people from demons, not..." Murdering them. But if she exorcised them, who else would be killed instead? Was it her place to make that decision? Wasn't that playing God?

"You're killing demons," Daniel said, who stepped further into the room and leaned against the corner of her desk. "If the Host is already dead, I don't see the problem."

"They're not always," Andy said, finding a pinhole in the wall to stare at. "I can only be so sure, and even then, it's about killing the demon without thinking of the consequences. We don't even know if there's a limit on demons. The possessions have only risen in number. Are we really making an impact? And what about Cillian? He was still speaking to us, Daniel."

"Andy," Daniel said, reaching out his hand to

touch her curls. She recoiled and did not look at him. He sighed. "You're doing what you must for your job."

"I have to do better," she whispered. She put away her colored pencils and stood up, moving towards her bookshelf and hooking a finger on a textbook. "If anyone needs me, I'll be in here reading."

Daniel moved with her and pushed the textbook back into place. "You won't learn what you want to just from books," he said. He was so close. She could smell cinnamon. She wasn't sure she liked it.

"It's a start," she said and pulled the book back out. She sat on her bed and opened it, a clear signal for Daniel to leave. He didn't. He sat at her desk and pulled out the coloring book.

"Do you mind?" he asked.

"As long as you don't bother me," Andy said, but it was soft, a gentle permission to stay hidden by false annoyance. She couldn't show too much pleasure at the idea of him *wanting* to stay. She could sacrifice a page or two in her coloring book for that.

She looked at her textbook, one she borrowed from Paul about sociology, and she started reading from the forward.

Cleansers had to be willing, yes, but she wanted to be more than that. She wanted to be *thrilled*.

# CHAPTER TWENTY-TWO

Davis did not give himself false hope. He did not try to reason that Samuel just reacted that way because the kiss *mattered*. He did not convince himself that Samuel would believe it was just an Italian thing or a friend thing and, quite honestly, Davis didn't believe any excuse himself.

It was simply that Davis had fucked up on instinct, and now, he was paying the consequences.

This is what he convinced himself when he decided to go running instead of going straight back to his dorm. It was on his third pass in front of the dorm, when he was still debating if he was ready to go in, that he was met with a man in a black and silver jacket.

"Davis," the man said, tilting his head ever so slightly in greeting. Daniel Collins. It was strange seeing him here, in uniform, waiting with his hands behind his back. It was hard to ignore how much the position showed his muscles. Davis thought he looked too much like a mercenary going through How to Be Polite camp.

"I didn't hurt anyone," Davis said as his own greeting. "In fact, I've only had *one* attempt and that was my sophomore year."

Daniel didn't look impressed. Davis wanted to run very far away. Still, Daniel didn't move, so he didn't.

"I'm not here to punish you," Daniel said, which Davis thought was funny. No matter what, seeing an Exorcist felt like a punishment.

"Then why are you here?"

"Catch up," Daniel said. The words seemed too informal coming from him and Davis rose an eye-brow.

"From Atlanta?" he asked warily, his eyes flickering around them. There were people walking by who slowed down at the sight of the trademark jacket, then recognized Davis as the child who had been possessed and sped away.

"My team can handle themselves," Daniel said, a slight edge to his voice. "Did you hear about Cillian?"

Davis rubbed his arm. "Yes," he whispered.

"I'm his substitute until a new Optic is drafted." Daniel put his hands in his jacket and observed him. "I wanted to make sure you were okay."

"'Okay' is a relative term," Davis said, "but I can at least assure you the only way I've screwed up has nothing to do with demons."

Daniel's eyes were piercing as they stared at Davis. They were green, the color of life, but Davis could see no life in them.

Davis sighed, feeling rather tired of all this. He wanted nothing more than to mope and listen to the angriest music he could while going on a run. "Daniel, what do you want me to say?"

"I don't know," Daniel said. His voice was rough as his shoulders slouched. "I don't know how to ask about your personal issues."

"That's not your job," Davis said warily. "Why would you?"

He seemed relieved by this response, if just shown by a slight nod. "You can trust the Exorcists here, Davis. They will help you."

"You are *not* good at this," Davis muttered, shoving his hands into his back pockets. "That's not comforting. I don't want to be on their radar. I wanted you to forget about me."

"I can't," Daniel said. "Robbie died for you."

"Oh, so you want to make sure it was worth it?" Davis sneered, but he felt cold and hollow.

Daniel shook his head. "I want you to stay alive."

"Stop that. Stop acting like you care," Davis said, hunching his shoulders. "You get to keep an eye on me so you can kill me if I fuck up. You are here because you want to see—you want the chance— the opportunity to—you want to see me fail." His words were clipped and jumbled but he breathed deeply, evenly. "If you want me to keep it together, to stay focused enough to prevent my own possession, then please leave."

Daniel looked away with a sigh. "I didn't expect you to become hateful."

"I'm not," he said. "I'm bitter."

"Bitter, then," Daniel said. "I'll leave now."

Davis was going to let him. He would have been glad to see him go, to never see another black and silver jacket ever again, but a thought shot into his head so painfully it reached his heart, and he croaked out a solitary word: "Wait."

Daniel looked back at him.

"Samuel Stewart," Davis said. "He wants to be an Exorcist. He applied to the Cleanser Academy. Could you...?" He wasn't sure what he could ask, what would be fair after what he said and how little faith he had in them. Davis let the words hang in the air.

Daniel gave a single nod, the request received and acknowledged, and he left.

It took a moment for Davis to feel like he could move again, and when he turned around, he wished he hadn't. Samuel stood there, looking displaced as he glanced at the students walking past them, hunching away if one got too close, but he looked up at Davis with a painfully neutral expression.

Davis was not prepared for the conversation that needed to happen. He felt like saying "Sorry I kissed you, my b!" didn't quite cover it. He didn't have a reason or explanation for why it happened. He had kissed friends for fun but had only seriously kissed Rachael. Back then, she had guided him through what sin really was, and sex was not a sin. Sex before marriage wasn't a sin. Sex with someone you love wasn't a sin. Even sex with someone you didn't love isn't a sin. Samuel was Davis's best friend, so just kissing him wasn't a sin.

Except Rachael told him sex without consent was

a sin. That was easy for him to understand. Now he wondered if he had truly kissed Samuel without consent, and if he had done something truly horrible to his best friend. He might have been thinking too much about it, but maybe that was better than not thinking about it at all.

He was more worried about how he hurt Samuel than if he were vulnerable to a demon.

"I'm sorry," Davis said, avoiding Samuel's gaze. "I didn't mean to kiss you. Or…I didn't know it would make you so uncomfortable."

"What? Oh," Samuel said, which made Davis glance up. He didn't look wary, which was good. "I was just surprised. I'm not used to that."

"Kisses?" Davis asked.

Samuel shook his head. "No. I'm used to kissing. For a purpose. Not between friends."

Davis's hand went to the back of his neck, squeezing it. "Yeah. My mother's Italian. I guess it was just…instinctual. It doesn't really…mean anything."

"It would be a bit weird if it did," Samuel said, and his lips quirked just enough that Davis let himself relax the slightest amount and smirk back.

"Don't tell me you've never checked me out," Davis said, raising an accusing eyebrow.

Samuel looked about to protest before he huffed and said, "I'm a gay man. I can appreciate the merchandise."

Davis wanted to continue teasing him, to put that memory of Samuel looking so uncomfortable out of his mind, but he couldn't. He tried for a real smile, which could only stretch so far. "Are we good?"

"I was startled, not scarred," Samuel said. "It was just a kiss. We're theatre majors, for goodness' sake."

It didn't quite add up to how Samuel reacted originally, but Davis wasn't going to push. Still, he wasn't sure what to say.

"Did you really just mention me to an Exorcist?" Samuel asked.

"That was Daniel," Davis said in confirmation. "He's an Exorcist from home. Atlanta. I sort of hate him and I think he hates me, so I don't know if I would exactly call it a 'connection,' but...who knows, right?"

"Yes," Samuel said, his expression softening. "Thank you, Davis."

"Consider it any apology for 'startling' you," he said, waving him off.

"Are you really going to make a big deal out of my reaction?"

"Oh yes," Davis said with a mock nod and pout. "You call yourself a theatre major and can't handle a celebratory kiss?"

Samuel flushed. "For the record, I'm a *backstage* theatre major. It doesn't count."

"Oh? What about Ashley? She's backstage," Davis said.

"Ashley is a very confident designer," he said, glancing away.

"You said you were used to kissing."

Samuel inhaled. "I'm not used to kisses without *intent*, okay?" He exhaled and looked at Davis. "I have an exam tomorrow. Do you want to get coffee?"

"Wait, did Samuel Stewart just suggest he was

going to drink *coffee*?"

"Ew, no, *I'm* getting tea," he said, as if offended by even the suggestion.

Davis glanced down at himself, in his rather nasty clothes after running, which really weren't needed anymore anyway, and he looked back up at Samuel. "Let me change first?"

Samuel nodded. "I'll wait, then."

Davis truly hoped this meant they were really okay. He wasn't sure what he would do without Samuel.

# CHAPTER
# TWENTY-THREE

"Here."

Davis stared as Tommy held out a box in front of his face, blocking his view of his textbook.

"What is it?" Davis asked, taking it delicately and glancing at Tommy, who looked rather bored.

"A present," Tommy said. He was wearing another set of pajamas, this time with rainbow colored ponies. "Call it a congratulations for getting the part in the play." There was a smile then. "Don't take it too seriously, okay?"

Davis eyed him suspiciously. "Is this a prank? Because last time you gave me something, it took a week to clean up all the glitter..."

"No," Tommy said, but laughed. Davis found it funny the first day and then every time he found a dot of glitter, he laughed at the memory. Still, he couldn't help being wary. "It's an actual gift. I promise."

"I don't trust you," Davis said.

"Well, I *do* trust you. This is just to make you feel better."

This made Davis take it more seriously, so he carefully opened the small box. Inside of it was a length of leather, knots spaced between different colored beads. It was a necklace, perhaps, or a bracelet you wrapped.

"What?" Davis said, surprised at receiving such a gift.

Tommy pointed at the beads. "Those are raw stones that represent repellent for sins. Sapphire repels envy, things like that, but most are general. Amethyst keeps your mind open, peridot gives you stamina or strength or something, citrine keeps away evil thoughts, things like that. It might sound silly, but I thought it could be comforting or something. And the stones aren't rare or anything. This only cost like twenty bucks. You can wear it however you like, if you want. Maybe stop scaring people with your yoga and just use this."

Davis hugged him. He held on for just a moment and then pulled away only so he could tie the gift around his neck. "I can use all the help I can get," he said, smiling broadly at his roommate. "Thank you."

Tommy shrugged, but his smile gave away how pleased he was. "I'm glad you like it."

"Thank you," Davis said again, fingering the different colored stones around his neck. "I'm never taking it off."

"Please do," Tommy said. "I do not want you getting that leather wet."

"Well I'll take it off when I'm showering or swimming, then," Davis said, his smile not leaving his face.

Tommy patted his shoulder. "Anything for you, bud."

"I'm not stopping yoga."

Tommy laughed. "It was worth a try."

# CHAPTER TWENTY-FOUR

Samuel was not thrilled about going to Davis's performance.

As much as that might sound like a horrible thing, there were many reasons Samuel thought were perfectly logical as to why he did not want to go.

One, it was the last show of the year, meaning there were exams to study for and jobs to hear back from and portfolios to update. Samuel was graduating in less than a month and that fact alone was a tad overwhelming.

Two, it was a performance of *Spring Awakening*. This second point contained multiple points in and of itself. Two-point-one, it meant that Davis would be stage kissing, which Samuel was not sure how he felt about. Two-point-two, it meant that Davis would be having stage sex, which Samuel was well aware how he felt about but would not acknowledge to himself or anyone. Two-point-three, it meant Davis would be helping tell one of the arguably saddest stories within modern musicals. Samuel could not help thinking *I don't do sadness,* mournfully, and ironically because most of his life had been just that. It was just now he no longer *wanted* to be sad.

Three, Tommy was joining him. Normally, Samuel was fine with Tommy, but he couldn't help notice Tommy arranged this after whispering in Samuel's ear, "I know he kissed you." Samuel's first reaction was to snap at him, to tell Tommy it was absolutely none of his business.

Then he noticed Tommy was *waiting* for his response, for any indication of what it meant to Samuel, and all of that meant Samuel couldn't respond at all. He certainly couldn't figure out a way to say *no* when Tommy suggested they see the performance together. Now it was feeling awfully like a date and *that* was something Samuel was uncomfortable with.

"Cheer up," Tommy said, giving a smile that spoke too many languages that Samuel didn't know. "We're here to see a *musical.*"

"That might be more meaningful," Samuel said carefully, "if I hadn't worked on it and if it wasn't a tragedy." He had indeed been a costume technician for the show, and he worked very hard for that to be hardly noticed. Still, he checked the program and his name was there.

Of course, so was Davis's, in multiple places. Actor and carpenter. He accepted a job in the scenic shop and now he would be known as someone multitalented. Samuel was pleased and concerned by this, but he, yet again, couldn't say why.

Tommy talked animatedly while Samuel answered anything vaguely directed at him with nods and halfhearted answers, but soon the show was starting, and Samuel realized this was something he needed to prepare for and didn't: a pop quiz on life.

Davis was not just multitalented with acting and carpentry. Davis was talented at whatever he was asked to do, apparently, and Samuel was left stunned by the sheer onslaught he brought to the stage. Davis was clearly not a natural singer, but he passed off cracks as emotional turmoil and turned the rawness of his vocal cords into a husky yearning. He unleashed suggestive words like a whip, brought tenderness out to contrast arrogance, and used silence as a deadly tool. Most shockingly, perhaps, was his ability to dance. He was able to choose when to be graceful, when to be steady, to be soft or hard, gentle or rough. In that moment, looking from the audience, Samuel could not imagine Davis being anywhere else but on a stage, yet he could not imagine that the character was Davis at all.

This, Samuel thought, made up for any sense of discomfort he felt before. It blew away the aches, the thoughts of the world—of the exorcism, of Cillian—it blew away the thoughts of *his* world and brought him into *that* world so strongly that he was stunned into paralysis by intermission. Ten minutes seemed like ten seconds before it was all back, his whole self was trying to keep up, to stay steady, and it was only when he sucked in an ugly sounding breath that he realized he was crying.

He was a little bit disgusted by it, that it happened now, with Tommy beside him and Davis on stage. He hadn't cried in years and all of it just made him even more upset, which made him feel *angry* at nothing in particular, but maybe every-thing, and he knew that he could never say *why*.

What he could say was Davis belonged on that stage, and Samuel wanted to do anything he could to keep him there.

# CHAPTER TWENTY-FIVE

avis wasn't sure exactly what he expected from the first performance. He expected for everyone to notice he couldn't sing, to notice he maybe got *too* into character, to maybe notice it was him playing the role: the guy who had been possessed and was now playing a boy who lost two people to death too early in life.

He did not expect to be *tackled* once he got off stage.

Once his instinct to crouch and wait until the beating was over passed, he realized it was Steven, pulling him into a hug and shouting, "You brilliant motherfucker! We did it!"

And they *had*. He was pulled back on stage for bows. It was a dream, knowing time was passing and events were happening, but only grasping the edges. Then he was seated, given just a moment to catch his breath before he was reminded he needed to attend the talk back, where people could ask them pretty much anything. Davis had also prepared for this.

He hoped it would be passed over, that no one would comment on who he was, but, perhaps inevitably for a show this size, the question came up:

"Davis, how has being possessed affected your work?"

He had prepared, yet it was worded differently and all he could do was open his mouth and blink before his director cut in.

"As far as I can tell, it hasn't done anything except to make him more dedicated," he said, meeting Davis's eyes just briefly before looking back out at the audience members left. "Davis, can you tell them about your acting process?"

"Ah, sure," Davis said, completely caught off guard. "I do a lot of breathing and stretching exercises. Otherwise, it's a sort of method acting, you could say. I try to convince myself I am whatever character I'm playing. Their clothes are my clothes, their choices are my choices, their emotions are my emotions, and then I walk in their shoes when I'm on stage. It's easier for me if I mess up to already be in their head. When their head *is* my head, you know?" He looked at the audience he couldn't see, and his director with a shrug.

His director gave him a thumbs up. "Next question?"

There was a next question, and a next, a mention of Davis's dancing skills—Why yes, he *was* a double major in theatre and dance. Yes, he *was* an Honors student. Yes, he *did* work in the shop. How did he do it all?

*I don't know what else I'd do* was the answer, but he laughed and said, "It's made possible by the people I'm around. I'm lucky to have the professors I do."

He couldn't see the audience still, the lights were too bright and way too hot, and by the time the talk through was over, he was already past fidgeting and onto feet tapping before he sprung out of his chair and skirted around anyone in his way.

*What about arrogance?* Davis heard the question, and he stopped to turn towards the source. No one. *What about Pride?*

*What about Pride?* Davis asked it back. *There's none here for you.* He played a character, one whose skin he put on for a couple hours, and whose skin he locked away every night. There was no one but him.

"Davis?"

Davis immediately snapped his attention forward, seeing Tommy approach him. He was *still* wearing pajamas, the top being a t-shirt with a false tux and tie printed on it. They greeted with a mutual pat on the back and Tommy grinned. "How do you feel?"

Davis mentally assessed himself to figure out that answer. "Like I never have to be afraid anymore," he said. Then, "Where's Samuel?"

"Around," Tommy said, glancing around himself. "He was rather...upset."

"Upset?" Davis asked.

"Distraught," Tommy clarified. "Murderous, too, maybe. That's why I didn't follow him."

Distraught and murderous weren't things Davis normally associated with Samuel. Well, maybe murderous, but only with people who bothered him too much. Which, given, was sometimes anyone, but it didn't seem to fit *now*.

"So, he didn't leave?" Davis asked.

Tommy shook his head. "He's around."

He was around. Davis only had to avoid other people for a few minutes before he caught Samuel walking back into the building from outside, looking down at his polo shirt like it had betrayed him.

"Hey," Davis said, smiling at Samuel's presence, despite the worry.

Samuel smiled back and everything was okay.

"Hey," he said. He held up a finger for Davis to pause as he rummaged in his side bag and pulled out a bundle of brown paper, pushing it into Davis's hands. "Flowers are…weird, so here's my congratulations present to you." He looked earnest as Davis took the gift. "It's really stupid."

Davis had to bypass many versions of a response before he landed on, "Stupid fits me just fine," as he pulled back the paper.

It was a small metal sculpture of a frog with a guitar. The frog's head was thrown back in euphoria and Davis felt *elated*.

"It's made of recycled *things*. At least that's what was advertised. So, if you want to throw it out, you have to at least recycle it instead," Samuel said.

"*Never*," Davis said, beaming at the frog. "This is from the summer job you had, right?" He knew Samuel hadn't worked there for very long, claiming that he just was not suited to work with customers. It had been months since he would have worked there.

"Yes," Samuel said simply. He cleared his throat, covering the fact he didn't want to make a big deal out of the present, and asked, "Where's Tommy?"

"Getting free wine," he said, waving his hands over to the refreshments, where Tommy was indeed talking to the individual handing out the wine.

"Typical Tommy," Samuel said, then seemed to regret it as his eyes darted to meet Davis's.

"Typical?" Davis asked. "I don't think I've mentioned his drinking *that* much."

Samuel looked strained and he stared at the sculpture in Davis's hands. "Well, I," he started. "I've hung out with him a bit. You know, outside of…you. We came together tonight."

"Together," Davis said. Something settled in his chest and stomach before it even reached his brain. "*Together,*" he said again, in realization, in maybe slight horror at either not understanding earlier or the memory of kissing Samuel before having ever asked if he was *together* with anyone.

"Ah, no," Samuel quickly said, waving his hands, but his face was starting to flush, and Davis felt so overwhelmed by *that* he had to shut down any instinctive responses and instead smirked and raised an eyebrow.

"No?"

"No."

"Oh? Really?"

"Really," Samuel said, his eyes wide. "God no, we've just—it's just that we've—" He glanced around, spotting Tommy's location before looking back at Davis. "It's not romantic."

Oh.

*Oh.*

...Oh.

One of those must have escaped because Samuel said, "Yeah," softly, looking quite like an animal about to flee. "Nothing committed. Nothing serious. We just...know each other."

"Really," Davis breathed, "really well."

"Not that well," Samuel said. "It's not significant."

"Yeah. That...makes sense."

Davis knew the reaction he was supposed to have. He was supposed to pat Samuel on the back, tell him *good job, man.* Or *at least two of us get to get laid* or some other version of socially acceptable bro terms, but he was just trying to get his nose to stop feeling like it was in a permanent scowl.

"Is it that weird?" Samuel asked quietly.

Whatever was holding Davis snapped and he was able to laugh and pat Samuel on the back and say, "*No!* A little, but hey, at least two of us are getting laid," and he immediately felt sick for saying it.

He needed to make it all right. He had to make himself okay with it because those were his best friends and there wasn't anything that would stop him from supporting them. Not even a heart re-broken.

Later that night, he placed the frog statue on his dresser. He stared at it and he ignored everything else in the world except for the feeling that built in his chest when he was on stage. That, he knew, couldn't be taken from him.

# CHAPTER TWENTY-SIX

Samuel pulled at his collar, feeling suffocated in the rented white suit and cursing the college for ever thinking having graduation outdoors in Charleston, South Carolina was a good idea.

He held three graduation tickets in his hand as he walked into the theatre building. There was still some time before he had to check in, yet the streets were blocked off and the sidewalks were beyond capacity. Samuel slipped inside the building and squeezed his way to the elevator.

No one was in the elevator.

As it went up, he stared at his unused tickets, putting a face to each one. His mother, his father, his sister. He closed his eyes and breathed.

The second floor did not hold as many people, but there were still students lingering around the couches. This included one Davis Turner, whose face brightened the moment he saw Samuel. He was dressed only slightly more formally than normal. It was a graphic shirt still, gray with an intricate black design, but it was also a button up and his jeans looked brand new. He grinned widely and practically skipped out of his seat, which Samuel did not think was possible.

"Nervous?" Davis asked in greeting.

"Why should I be? I already have the degree," Samuel murmured, pulling at his collar again. Davis reached out and unbuttoned his collar, then the next button down as well, making Samuel still. Davis quickly took his hand back.

"Sorry," he said, stuffing his hands in the pockets of his jeans. "You looked hot. And nervous. Not because of the degree. But because of the people, your job, living on your own..."

"Thank you for reminding me of all of my current anxiety-inducing problems. Much appreciated. Please, do continue," Samuel said, keeping his face blank as he stared at Davis and he redid the buttons on his shirt. He didn't actually mind touches from Davis in and of themselves. He minded the fact he *liked* them but felt like he shouldn't have them. Davis was his best friend, but there was a type of barrier now—built from his reaction to the kiss, from the fear that had been there already, and maybe simply from the fact Davis was still Someone Who Had Been Possessed and Samuel felt it was unfair to ask Davis for anything more because of that.

But *did* Samuel still think of him that way?

He guessed he was also supposed to think of Tommy, but there was also a reason he wasn't in a *romantic* relationship with him. Samuel didn't feel like he was capable of that type of love.

Davis was still looking at him proudly. Samuel tried to focus on his academic success—and lack of other successes. "I won't be living on my own quite yet anyway."

"But you'll have a degree," Davis said, as if simply continuing his thought. "Your job is confirmed, right?"

"I'll be an Assistant Costume Technician for one summer show as an interview, you could say," Samuel said, considering it both good news and bad. Ten-minute interviews were hard enough, let alone something like this. He wanted security and it seemed the only way to get that with his degree was to go on to get his master's and become a professor. He wasn't so sure he wanted to do that, either. "I feel like I've set myself up for being stressed the rest of my life."

"I think you would be stressed no matter what, but at least this way you like what you're doing, right?" Davis said, giving a reassuring smile.

Samuel matched his smile. "Yes, although..." He wanted to be an Exorcist above anything else. It just simply wasn't possible. Davis knew this and his smile wavered.

"I can try checking in with Daniel, if you want," Davis said, his voice lowering. "It's been a while..."

Samuel shook his head. "Thank you, Davis, but I'm okay. I've found something I'm good at." Then, before Davis could respond, "You're going to be out there, right? For graduation?"

"Ah, no..." Davis said uneasily. "Actually, I don't have a ticket. I was just going to watch from the theatre. They'll be broadcasting it in there."

The tickets were heavy, considering they were just pieces of paper. Samuel counted them, with the names of who they were for, and it took the moment of physically holding them out, of realizing they were still in his hands and not in the hands of who they were for, before he was able to accept none of them were coming.

"Here," Samuel said, his chest tight as he held out one of the tickets to Davis.

Davis did not take it at first, looking at the ticket and then at Samuel's face. He was trying to read it, but Samuel had years of practice in keeping his expression neutral.

"I don't need it," Davis said, softening his voice. "I'll be okay. It's going to be hot out there, anyway."

"No, I need you there," Samuel admitted, feeling his face warm. "Someone has to suffer with me. In fact..." He looked at the couches and the other students there before raising his voice. "I have two more tickets. Anyone need one?"

"What about your parents?" Davis asked, his voice still low, giving Samuel the privacy he needed.

Samuel shook his head. He hoped it was a clear enough answer. It seemed to be, because Davis didn't push. Samuel poked him in the chest. "Why didn't you tell me you needed a ticket earlier?"

"I try to avoid asking for too much," Davis said helplessly. "And I don't know what's too much."

Samuel met Davis's eyes. He thought, perhaps, eye contact was the most important part of their friendship. It wasn't as easy with anyone else. "I want you out there."

"Then I'll be there," Davis said. Then he laughed.

"Tommy will be, too. Happy about that?"

"Will he?" Samuel asked, schooling his features again. Tommy was definitely treating their relationship romantically if Davis saw it as such. Samuel felt rather uncomfortable by that. Davis must have taken his reaction as embarrassment, because he elbowed Samuel's side.

"He wouldn't miss it," Davis said happily.

It was Ashley, with her bleached hair and flowery summer dress, who hopped off the couch and came over to pluck a ticket from Samuel's hands. "If Davis is going to be out there, then I will just have to deal with being out there as well," she said, her smile sly but her eyes soft. The look hinted to Samuel more than he probably wanted to know, so he didn't ask.

"Can't leave my side? Am I too magnetic for you?" Davis teased Ashley, who stuck out her tongue.

"Someone has to protect your pansy ass," Ashley replied, and Samuel did not doubt she could actually do the job. He listened to them banter until he had to make his escape.

"I'll catcall you," Davis said as Samuel was leaving, "Just so you know I'm there!"

"Don't you dare, asshole!" Samuel shouted back, but he smiled. He smiled as he stepped into the heat, he smiled as he handed his last ticket to a man wanting to get in, he smiled as he met up with the other graduates, and (even if he hid it) he smiled when Davis catcalled him as he walked across the stage.

Graduation wasn't an end for them. It was a beginning. Samuel would make sure of that.

# CHAPTER TWENTY-SEVEN

It was as if Davis could feel Samuel's happiness radiating from a dozen yards away. He was grinning and Tommy was laughing and Ashley was cheering and graduation was made *perfect*. It was what Samuel deserved.

They waited back at the theatre department for Samuel to meet up with them, but Davis watched out the window of the second story as Samuel got stopped by two men. They were wearing black and silver jackets.

"One moment," Davis said, sliding away from his friends and taking the stairs down two at a time. He joined the Exorcists just outside the main entrance.

"Recruiting?" Davis asked, his eyes meeting Daniel's before gliding to the other man. He was slender in a way that didn't come with regular gym visits, but from dieting or high metabolism. His ink black hair was cut to a buzz and his eyes looked like they would never focus again. Yet they focused on

Davis and he found himself having to look away. They landed on the man's scarf, blaringly red and outrageous in the heat. "Nice scarf," Davis complemented suspiciously.

The man seemed to startle before collecting himself and petting the scarf in admiration. "Thank you," was all he said.

Davis looked at Samuel to check on him, only to see him looking at the man's scarf as if he just then realized how bizarre it was, too, but he wouldn't dare comment on it. Because no one answered his original question, Davis looked at Daniel. "So?"

It was the look that stopped Davis from wondering. Daniel was looking at him like so many had before—a terror in the edges of his expression, being forced back only by conscious effort. Then it was gone, his features smoothed. He was Daniel again, the awkwardly distant man.

"We're not recruiting today," Daniel said. He tilted his head away. "Davis, can I talk to you? Privately."

Davis looked at the other man and then at Samuel, who looked equally parts confused and giddy at meeting *Exorcists*. Davis was surprised he wasn't bouncing on the balls of his feet. "Okay," he said, smiling towards Samuel before walking off a bit with Daniel.

"I haven't forgotten," Daniel murmured. "We are still holding the draft for Optics. That's why I brought Jenkins, to see if Samuel was one."

"And?" Davis asked hopefully.

Daniel shook his head. "He's not. Jenkins recognized him as someone who hadn't Seen him previously, but we were making sure. However, even if he was…has he ever talked about his sister?"

There was a vague memory of Samuel mentioning a sister, so Davis nodded, even if he berated himself for not remembering until now.

"She died when he was young," Daniel whispered, but his expression seemed non-secretive. They could have been talking about the weather. "When he applied to the Cleanser Academy, his mother called…" He took a moment, watching Davis. Davis wasn't sure what he was looking for. "She said Samuel killed her. That disqualified him from being accepted."

Davis tried to rearrange his image of Samuel, the one who was shy, who liked tea instead of coffee, who wanted to *help* people. He tried to fit this new information into that schema, and he couldn't. There was no place for it to fit. "He didn't," he said confidently, his gaze going to his best friend.

"No, he didn't," Daniel agreed.

"Then why didn't he get in?"

"Too much of a risk," he said. "The case had been under investigation before and reopened once."

"Why?" Davis asked. "What was the case?"

Daniel just shook his head. It was confidential, then. That was probably good, now that Davis took a moment to think. It would probably be better if he let Samuel tell him.

Still, this was his connection for Samuel, and one question wouldn't hurt. "Would he get in if he applied again?"

Daniel looked at Davis sadly. "He would be

behind."

"But he could potentially get in," Davis translated.

"Yes," Daniel said carefully. "There is a chance, albeit a small one."

This was good news. This was a chance for Samuel.

So why did Davis feel so hollow?

# CHAPTER TWENTY-EIGHT

"You didn't tell him," Jenkins said to Daniel. "Why?"

It was a sudden question a few days late, but Jenkins was getting rather bored and Daniel was the only person he could have a conversation with.

Except Daniel was extremely good at acting as if he wasn't an Optic.

"Weren't you going to paint the walls another color?" he replied.

"Daniel," Jenkins urged. "You have to tell Paul what happened."

"It's Davis," Daniel said in a murmur. "He's my responsibility."

"Not anymore," Jenkins said. "You're a temp in our squad. He's our responsibility now, just like the others we've saved."

Daniel seemed disgruntled but did not argue.

Jenkins, however, was about to start the argument *for* him when Paul walked in.

"I might have found something," he said, gesturing for them to follow him into the kitchen, where he placed out a map on the table. It was similar to a normal map, but one you would see on a weather channel, color coding the different temperatures. This one was specifically of downtown Charleston. "Look," he said, pressing his finger over the campus, where the color was a deep blue.

Jenkins looked towards Daniel with a raised eyebrow. "Can we tell him now?"

Daniel ignored him. "There are spikes in temperature because of Davis," he said. "He has always fought off the demons."

"This is different," Paul said. "This is stronger, maybe even multiple entities." He pointed out three different areas on the map. "These areas are focuses. I need you to look into them."

"That's Davis's dorm," Daniel said dismissively towards one of the spots. He moved his attention to one of the other focuses. "Where is that?"

"It's by a port," Jenkins said. "Across from where you pay your parking tickets."

Daniel hummed in recognition. Everyone knew where to pay parking tickets in Charleston, even those who weren't locals. "I'll go there."

"Okay, then Jenkins, can you visit these shops?" Paul asked, tapping the last area.

"Yes," Jenkins said.

"Yes," Daniel translated, if unnecessarily so. Paul was rather good at assuming what Jenkins was going to say.

"Thank you. This is just information gathering. Scooping the area. I would send Andy, but—"

There was a knock on the door. Then another, more frantic this time. Jenkins followed behind Paul as he went to greet their visitor.

It was a girl, barely standing up on wobbly legs. Her hair was long and matted. She wore a long T-shirt that acted as a dress. She was filthy. Most noticeably, however, was the blood dripping from her mouth.

"Help me," she coughed out. She had a trace of a Hispanic accent, an emphasis on her vowels. "I…think I may possibly…be possessed."

# CHAPTER TWENTY-NINE

amuel's interview show turned into an internship for a year, long enough to guarantee an income and proximity to Davis.

It was, he should note, also another year to spend with Tommy. Tommy had certainly taken note, having brought Samuel lunch occasionally, then dinner, then suggestions of late-night ice-cream trips when work took too long. Samuel was very bad at saying no, especially when the nights ended pleasantly warm, tangled in sheets and limbs. He wondered if this was what being in a relationship meant. Except he looked towards the future and he saw Tommy leaving at the end of the year, graduating and going on to possibly pursue a master's degree in computer science. Samuel found himself thankful for that end goal and that was how he knew he was not in love with Tommy Rider.

Still, it was sometimes pleasant to pretend.

"Do you not cuddle for a reason?" Tommy asked

from the bed, watching Samuel sit at the dorm's desk.

"I don't take the time," he said. He also didn't take the time to chit-chat, usually. Sex was a good distraction. If he wasn't worrying about his job or his future, it was about a massacre caused by a demon in Florida or someone claiming they were a Saint and that *Angels* were dying and the very clear reminder he could do nothing to help.

But sex only lasted so long, and he didn't like lingering.

"Davis will be back any moment and I'd rather see him with my pants on," Samuel said.

"Why?" Tommy said, though he closed his eyes and seemed rather content to not move. "He knows what we're doing."

Samuel was still rather uncomfortable with that thought. "Does he know about every time you bring someone home?"

"When I used to bring others, it used to be a joke that they were auditioning for our third roommate," Tommy said with a silent laugh.

"How *did* you get a room for two all to yourself? It makes sense for Davis to have a single in the suite, but this is the Honor's dorm. Wouldn't they try to fill all the rooms?" Samuel asked.

"It's not hard to keep potential roommates out," he said with a shrug. "There are some who are willing, but then a parent gets involved or a friend scares them off. I sometimes scare them off, too, by coming up with a ghost story or just telling them Davis is a loud snorer if I think they're trying to get in for other reasons."

"Other reasons?" Samuel echoed.

"Yeah, like trying to kill him," Tommy said. "It almost happened when he was in high school, he said. It's better to be safe than sorry."

Samuel did not like thinking about that. He wanted to know, to ask Davis about every detail of his experience, but then he was too afraid to ask. He wasn't even sure of his own intentions, even if he knew without a fact he honestly cared to know. "Well, having him know I'm here is still…"

"Still what? You're able to bang in a stranger's house, where everyone knows, but you're…" Tommy trailed off, and Samuel wished it could have been because he fell asleep, but Tommy peeked open an eye at him. "You're special to me."

Samuel felt caught. There was a conversation here, one that Samuel was not wanting to have at all, mainly because he wasn't sure the sentiment was returned. Tommy was a friend, if that qualified for him being special. Samuel didn't get this close to just anyone.

"I need a shower," Samuel said, and he did. He reeked of sex, which wasn't unpleasant unless someone else smelled it. He slipped out of Tommy's room and into the bathroom, glancing only briefly to see Davis's door closed. He took his time in the shower, savoring the water and cleaning every inch of his body while thinking of nothing but the fact Davis hardly ever closed his door. The room was much too small to feel comfortable with it closed. At least, that's what Davis mentioned before, so this was strange. But maybe Samuel was just thinking too much. It was the middle of the night.

Samuel should be thinking of Tommy. He should, maybe, feel guilty. Maybe sad. Maybe he should be planning out the rejection speech. All he could really think was, *You made it significant, didn't you?*

He felt relieved, and for that alone he felt guilty. He had a reason to stop this, to go back to random men in bars or house parties, to…something else he wasn't exactly sure he wanted. He couldn't be certain of what he wanted. Maybe, simply, *out.*

Samuel got out of the shower and this time, Davis's door was open. He was sitting at his desk, glasses perched on his nose, the mentioned nose deep in his notes. He was wearing pajamas, but they were simple compared to Tommy's collection, just a soft shade of green. Samuel leaned against the doorframe and watched him before he cleared his throat.

Davis looked up then and his face lit up, settling part of the internal torment Samuel hadn't let himself acknowledge. "Samuel," he said fondly. "How is it being an adult?"

"If by 'adult' you mean still living with my parents and working an internship that doesn't pay enough for me to live on? I'm doing *grand*," Samuel said. "How's your thesis?"

"Shit fuckery," Davis said, waving at his laptop and piles of books. "The Inferno. Pits of hell. It's as bad as listening to politicians who don't give a shit about human rights try to convince people they care about human rights."

"That bad?"

"That bad."

Samuel let out a breathy laugh and shook his

head. "Need a break?"

Davis seemed to consider this for a moment and said, "Do you?"

Samuel hadn't realized how transparent he was, but he nodded, knowing it was the truth. He watched Davis take off his glasses and push back from the desk. "Come on, then. Charleston is the best in the middle of the night."

"Tommy was the one who signed me in," Samuel said awkwardly.

"Good thing I'm his roommate *and* I know the whole front desk staff. Day and night," Davis said, slipping his feet into his tennis shoes. Samuel did the same. "Plus, they know *you* by now, too."

Samuel flushed and ducked his head. There were some things he just didn't want to think about. Then he realized it probably wasn't due to just his nights with Tommy, but simply the fact the two people he spent the most time with happened to be in the same dorm.

After Davis worked his magic at the front desk, the two of them took a walk. Samuel had lived in Charleston his whole life. He was familiar with every street and at one point or another had sketched most of downtown during his art classes. Yet still, when Davis stopped and pointed *up*, Samuel looked and was forced to reconsider exactly how much of Charleston he really knew. He knew the facts. He knew the shapes. Now it was like he could see the branches overhead, twisting into each other, and he no longer had to see it as a cage. He saw the light of the moon filter through them, casting shadows through the canopy and giving a contrasting feeling of being so close but so far away from the sky.

He closed his eyes.

"I miss you, Davis," Samuel said honestly. It was the first time he admitted it even to himself. He wasn't sure how he meant it. Was it because of the awkwardness? Was it because he felt like he never actually got to see *Davis*? Was it just the fact it was that much more difficult to go to a coffee shop every morning with him? He knew one fact for sure. "You're my best friend."

Davis laughed. For a moment, Samuel thought he would swing an arm around his shoulder or give him a hug, but he didn't touch Samuel at all. He hadn't really touched Samuel in over a year.

"You see me often," he said. "How could you miss me?"

"I see you mostly in passing now, when I'm with Tommy," Samuel said. "But Tommy is not my best friend. Tommy is not my boyfriend, either. It's too much..." *time away from you.* It wasn't fair for him to say that. "He's too much."

"Oh," Davis said, kicking at the ground. "I would visit you, you know. At your house, but I'm not allowed to drive."

"What?" Samuel asked. He hadn't known this. Why hadn't he known this? "Why not?"

"Demon possession attempts can happen at any time. It's like having epilepsy except there's no medication," he explained. "I always just got Tommy to drive for me. Or I took the bus, but those are risky as well..."

"Oh," Samuel said. "I'm sorry."

Davis didn't say anything to that. After a moment

he whispered, "He's going to be heartbroken."

Somehow, Samuel knew who Davis was talking about, but he couldn't regret it. "It got weird between us, didn't it?" he asked. "After you kissed me."

"Yes," Davis whispered. "I messed up."

Samuel rolled his eyes and huffed out a breath. "You've made out with Steven since and you've had stage sex. It's not a big deal." When Davis just grunted in reply, Samuel added, "What do I have to do to get us back to what we were? It's been too long." He wasn't even sure where they had been. Had something else existed at all, or was what he created a false dream of a friendship?

"You would have to go back and not run away from it," Davis said. "Which isn't happening, because time travel isn't an accessible thing."

Samuel nodded. At least it sounded like it used to be different. Better, maybe. "I made it significant by doing that."

"Yes," Davis said.

Samuel huffed again and stood in front of Davis, holding out his arms. "Then hug me."

Davis did hug him. He pushed his arms under Samuel's, wrapped them firmly around Samuel's back and pulled them flush against each other, nearly making Samuel go on his tip toes. It was startling, but Samuel had already been preparing himself, so it only took a moment before he was hugging Davis back, his cheek against Davis's shoulder.

"I missed you, too," Davis whispered. "And I forced myself again and again to not be jealous of your time with Tommy."

Davis wasn't allowed to be jealous. He wasn't allowed to let his emotions be *real*. Davis had to filter everything with *possession* in mind.

"There's no need to be jealous," Samuel said softly, "but this is much too long of a hug."

"Oh, right," Davis said, letting go of him quickly. He seemed embarrassed, but it was dark out so it was hard to tell for sure if he was blushing.

Samuel was careful to not make anything significant this time, but he wasn't ready to go back. Not yet.

"I'm cold-hearted," he admitted, the words coming out in a way he usually restrained them. "I don't love Tommy. Not romantically. I care for him, but I think he's kind of an asshole, and maybe *someone else* would find that endearing, but I don't. I just like sex. Not even necessarily sex with him, just the accessibility of it. Which is horrible, isn't it? I've used him."

"You set the ground rules, didn't you?" Davis asked. Samuel nodded. "Then you've done nothing wrong if he broke them."

"How do you break up with someone you were never actually dating?" Samuel asked.

"I don't even know how to break up with a person you *were* dating. Rachael broke up with *me*."

"Give me advice anyway?"

Davis sighed and shrugged. Maybe this was too difficult of a position to put him in. "Be honest?"

"He'll hate me and it will become awkward to visit your dorm and I'd rather not avoid your dorm," he said.

"I said honest, not blunt," Davis said, wagging a

finger at him. "Be kind."

Samuel was not so sure kindness was a word that would be used to describe him, but he took the advice with a silent nod. "I'll think of something to tell him."

"Honestly," Davis said, "I think he already knows."

# CHAPTER THIRTY

More time passed. Months—too many months, too fast.

There were no more exorcisms made to the public. Still, Samuel was notified of deaths, and it felt like the numbers were rising. He ignored them all at first. Then, he turned off the notifications altogether.

Samuel finished his internship and was then invited as a full-time employee, which he had no room to turn down. It was stability. It was a way to save for his own apartment. It was a path to freedom. It wasn't a marble staircase, but that was okay. He was *fine*. Many people settled in life, and this at least gave him some type of fulfillment.

He successfully avoided Tommy right up until Tommy and Davis's graduation. They were hosting a beach party of mostly theatre graduates and there was no real way for Samuel to get out of it without being rude. It was unfortunate, but he couldn't deny the longing he held for the beach. He smelled it every day, and every day he imagined sinking into the sand until he *was* the sand, the beach, the ocean, and the thought didn't bother him at all sometimes. Sometimes, it was pleasant and peaceful.

That's how he found himself sitting on a towel, sunglasses covering his eyes, bug spray and sun tan lotion at his side, with his back to the ocean. He buried his hands in the sand because he knew if he didn't he would fidget, and fidgeting was a non-verbal form of communication he wished to not show.

"Hiding?" Ashley asked as she plopped down next to him. Her hair was now a shade of green and Samuel didn't have the heart to tell her it wasn't working well. Blue was much more her color.

"Ashley," he said softly, fondly. He didn't realize how much he missed her working beside him in the costume shop or poking fun of him until she was back in his presence. Of course, now she was graduating, too. This could very well be the last time he saw her.

She smiled and rested her cheek on her knees. "You are awful at communication."

"My mother once told me I shouldn't try to communicate," Samuel said, without truly understanding why he was sharing at all. "She said it was pointless. No one wanted to hear what I had to say."

There was a beat where Ashley was very still, and Samuel realized the true extent of what he just admitted. Her eyes were forward but Samuel was still in her line of sight. He dug his hands further into the sand.

"That must have made writing essays difficult," Ashley said, her nose wrinkled, but when she turned to look at Samuel there was humor in her eyes. It was permission to laugh, so Samuel did because, yes, essays were extremely difficult. He was happy with the idea of never having to write one again.

"Hey," she said after a moment, bumping her shoulder against Samuel's. "I want to hear from you. So maybe text someone besides your boyfriend."

"Boyfriend," he repeated, dumbfounded. He thought of Tommy and immediately went to correct her, but how would Ashley know about him at all?

"Davis," Ashley said slowly, as if reminding him of something he should have already known, "Turner? Hot guy with 'trouble' written on his background check and 'kissable' written on his face?"

Samuel had not heard a more accurate description of Davis.

Ashley rose an eyebrow. "Well I was going to say 'hopefully my future husband,' but it seems that might be taken."

"Oh," Samuel said, catching up. He really, really wasn't good at communicating. He felt disconnected and jumbled. "No. I was just—" In a relationship? Thinking how strange being with Davis would be? How impossible—continuing that thought was leading into a danger zone of fate and Samuel did not want to play. He paused, still catching up, and squinted at Ashley. "Your future husband? So you're—have you confessed?"

Ashley snorted. "Like it works that way. I just dream. He's really hot. Kind, but also dangerous, you know?"

"No," Samuel said, "not dangerous. Not at all."

"Well, I mean, *he* isn't, but the whole demon thing..."

"Then everyone's dangerous," he said evenly. "Davis might in fact be the safest because he knows how to fight against possessions."

"Is he really not *your* future husband?"

Samuel shook his head. This he knew for a fact. "He's my best friend."

"Well, all right," Ashley said, spreading her legs out in front of herself. "Then wish me luck."

"Good luck," Samuel said flatly.

Ashley wagged her feet for a moment before springing up and wiping off her swimsuit cover. "Text me," she said, and she walked away.

Samuel was going to call after her, to apologize for his terrible social skills, to maybe apologize for not apologizing well, but all words and thoughts stuck when he saw Tommy Rider's eyes on him.

"Stewart," Tommy said when he approached Samuel. He was wearing only navy swim trunks. Samuel took his hands out of the sand.

"Sorry," Samuel said as his greeting because he could not think of anything else, no matter if he was actually apologetic or not. He started wiping off his hands.

Tommy smiled, which Samuel was very fond of, and then he nodded his head towards the beach house, a suggestion, which Samuel was more than fond of.

This wasn't what needed to happen. Samuel hoped Tommy could simply understand his expression: I want to, but I really can't.

"Can we just talk privately?" Tommy requested, and that Samuel couldn't refuse.

But this was what he was dreading. The silent walk from the beach to the house, the avoidance of eye contact and any exchanging of words, the pit in his stomach that told him it would be so much easier if he could just break Tommy's heart with a lie or falsely fill it with another.

They walked. Samuel saw Davis watch them go in his peripheral, Ashley speaking to him.

He had wished her good luck, and he meant it.

"Finally," Tommy said as they entered a bedroom. He gave a sheepish, apologetic look that made Samuel's guilt and sympathy spike. "I was already embarrassed about my actions. Having other people I don't know see me out there..."

Samuel watched him twist at and pull his fingers and it was clear Tommy was nervous. Maybe this meant Tommy realized the rule he broke. Maybe he realized keeping that rule could mean they could continue. Maybe there was hope for this yet.

Tommy closed the door.

# CHAPTER THIRTY-ONE

Fingers were snapped in front of Davis's face.

"Staring is rude," Ashley said, her hands going to her hips. "And Samuel said you weren't his future husband. I call bullshit," she grumbled.

"In fairness," Davis said, "I was staring at the house. Not a person. Persons. And clearly Samuel was right." He gestured to the place he had been staring.

"Uh-huh, whatever," Ashley said. She seemed much more flippant than normal. "Then what about being mine?"

Davis moved his stare towards her. "Your what?"

"Future husband. Potentially, at least," she said casually. Too casually. So casually Davis was not sure it was serious.

Ashley's eyes met Davis's in equal strength. She was serious.

Davis never even considered her before. She

hadn't even been on his radar, not romantically—but then, no one really was. He wanted to explain that, but it wasn't a reason to say no.

"I'm not," he started, then he felt heat reach his ears. "I," he tried again. "I don't have a job, I don't know what I'm doing, or if I'm staying here or not, or anything—and it's—I."

He knew exactly what was happening. He was moving into an apartment with Tommy using the scraps he saved from working during his schooling, but all the jobs ended and he had nothing truly reliable lined up. It was an excuse. It was the only fair response he had.

Ashley did not look impressed. "Do I look like someone who requires you to have your life together? I'm very independent."

Davis got warmer. "Yes, but—I...want to. Have my life together, I mean. A little more. And—" Rachael had been his last relationship. Ashley was so different. Beautiful, wonderful.

Maybe he should say yes.

Could he?

He shook his head. "I can't. I'm sorry."

She closed her eyes for a moment. She breathed in. Out. She opened her eyes, then they looked *past* Davis. "Is that...an Exorcist?"

Davis turned around to see a girl walking around the house. She was wearing the Exorcist jacket, if the jacket had been specially made to be sleeveless. She was scowling at the sand as she walked, large reflective sunglasses covering her eyes, tight black curls shading her face. It was so obvious she was an Exorcist, but Davis could see the question in it. The girl seemed so casual, her short shorts completing the image.

"Davis Turner," she said, stopping in front of the two of them and looking rather irritated. "I can't believe you're not possessed right now."

"What?" Davis said, his heart telling him this was something to be nervous about. He didn't feel anything. He paused, trying to pay attention, trying to see if any of his emotions seemed like they were someone else's. They didn't. "Why would I be?"

"Paul told us to come here," the Exorcist said, pushing her short curls back with her sunglasses. "Our Finder. Head of the Charleston Squad. Usually when there are signs of a demon possession when you're around, it's you."

"It's not," Davis said, a little wide-eyed.

"Yes, clearly," she mumbled. She looked at Ashley and seemed immediately uninterested. "But someone else is."

Davis's blood ran cold. "Then we need to get out of here." He looked at the house, where he knew Samuel and Tommy were, and then to Ashley. "Now."

# CHAPTER THIRTY-TWO

Samuel was being kissed.

There was no prior explanation, just a shift in mood, a push against the door, and a *want*.

Samuel liked feeling wanted, but he did not want this. He was not kissing back.

"Tommy," he said the moment his mouth was free enough for the name to slip out. He pushed against Tommy's chest. "Stop—"

"We're fine," Tommy said, kissing and *licking* Samuel's jaw, which he was not so fond of.

"*Tommy*," he repeated, shoving a bit harder. He thought that would push him away. It didn't.

Tommy sucked on Samuel's neck, making him flinch. "We've done this before," Tommy said. "I know you want to continue this. It's obvious—you're addicted to it." His hand crept down, grabbing between Samuel's legs and forcing out a gasp. Samuel could feel the smirk against his skin. "See?"

Dread filled Samuel before it all drained out of him, every single emotion going with it. Acceptance for what was going to happen, knowledge that there was no way to change it. Maybe he deserved it. That's what his mother would have told him. He had wronged Tommy—perhaps he had been a tease. There wasn't a reason he could come up with for trying to stop what was happening except the very simple thought of *I don't want this.*

He wondered, absently, if this was why he didn't get into the Cleanser Academy. How could he ever help anyone else?

"You're *mine*," Tommy growled. "Not his. Not anyone else's."

Samuel blinked, his breath labored, his body limp. "Whose?" he asked softly. "Who else's could I be?"

"*Davis's*," Tommy said. There it was again, the assumption made, just because Samuel and Davis were close and Samuel was gay, that they were more than friends. Had that caused this? Tommy's...possessiveness? "I'll prove you're mine. And I'll make sure he can never have you."

Something in his words jump started Samuel, but Tommy's grip on his arm and side was strong—stronger than it should be. Samuel shifted his weight and kicked Tommy's shin.

It hardly did anything. Samuel knew it wouldn't, but he wasn't going to just let this happen. It didn't settle well with him at all. But Tommy's hand was around his throat, lifting him as green eyes pierced him.

"Want me," Tommy said in a nearly desperate

whisper. Samuel wanted to want him. It didn't change anything. Tommy growled, "*Want me!*"

"I *can't!*" Samuel choked out, clawing at Tommy's hand, scratching at it. But even as he drew blood, Tommy didn't even acknowledge it.

There was a bang on the other side of the door. Tommy paused.

"Samuel! Tommy!" Davis called. Tommy growled. "We have to go! Now!"

"Fuck off, Davis!"

Greed. *Greed!* Samuel was so *stupid.*

"Da—ah," Samuel started before Tommy's hand was pressing too tightly into his throat.

"Tommy, I'm not joking! There's a demon possession somewhere!" Davis yelled.

Right here! Samuel wanted to yell. This is not my Tommy!

"We'll be right there!" Tommy called back. "Give us a moment!"

Samuel kicked backwards, hitting the door as forcefully as he could. There was a moment when everything was still and silent. Samuel could not breathe. His vision was blurring, as was his brain.

"...Samuel?" he heard Davis say.

Then the door burst in.

# CHAPTER THIRTY-THREE

When Davis was possessed, the events following went slowly and quickly at the same time. He didn't truly comprehend the years, days, hours, minutes, seconds—and yet each moment was burned into his memory.

That was what time felt like when Andy kicked in the door.

Kicked wasn't exactly the correct phrasing. There was more to it. The whole time Davis talked to Tommy, she messed with the knob. *Then* there was the kick, precisely placed. The door burst open. The two men on the other side were pushed aside. There was scrambling, gasping, coughing…

Factually, Andy entered the room. Factually, a man tried to kill Andy. Factually, Andy did not let that happen. Factually, Andy killed a man.

The details were finer. The two men were, of course, Samuel and Tommy. It was Samuel who was gasping and coughing. Andy ignored him, going straight to Tommy with her bare hands and when Tommy—Tommy, who usually had a lazy smile and a daring mind—attacked her with wild eyes and nails and teeth, Davis knew it was not his roommate. It was not his friend, and it certainly wasn't anyone else's friend.

Andy talked the whole time. She said things such as, "Tommy, you don't want to do this to your friends!" and "You goddamned mother fucking shithead! Stay still!" and maybe this was supposed to be humorous. Maybe it could be retold as such, but the truth was it was a fight and it was nasty and, most of all, it ended up with the blade of a knife in Tommy's throat.

Davis was sure his heart stopped when Tommy's did.

"What—did you—do?"

That was what Davis wanted to ask, what he realized his question should be after Samuel croaked it out.

Davis wanted to believe none of this was real. It was a strange occurrence of time. A nightmare. A fake memory of an alternative universe.

Tommy could totally recover from a knife blade in his neck. Hearts were restarted all the time.

This was how Davis computed the events. It was too much to take seriously but too much to laugh at. He was still standing just outside of the doorway and Samuel was clinging onto Tommy and shouting through a raw throat at Andy.

"The moment you realize you were almost *killed* and—" She grabbed Samuel's chin and pushed it to the side, "—raped, in either order, you can realize *I just saved you.*"

"You killed my friend! You didn't save *him!*" Samuel croaked back, the words having less of an effect when he lapsed into a coughing fit and held his head.

"That wasn't your friend," Andy said sternly. "That was a demon. Tommy Rider has been dead."

Samuel's jaw tensed and he swallowed. "Then who was I friends with?"

"Tommy," Andy said easily. "And then a demon impersonating him and using his body. We've been tracing the demon energy for *months*. We thought it was Davis but there is no way for anyone to have that much demon energy stored within them and still be alive."

"You mean," Samuel said, his voice cracking, his anger switching to pain, "Tommy died *months* ago?"

"Yes," Andy said, rubbing her cheek, which might have been hit at some point. "So I didn't kill him. I killed the demon who did."

That was when Samuel sat back, his hands holding his head, and silence permeated the air along with the smell of blood.

Then Samuel looked towards Davis. Davis's expression was of complete horror and devastation. His cheeks were stained with tears. It was only when he saw Samuel that everything Davis was feeling made sense. His expression mirrored Davis's perfectly.

They both just lost Tommy Rider.

# CHAPTER
# THIRTY-FOUR

The beach house was wrapped with caution tape and blue and red lights. Samuel sat in the sand, facing it. He wasn't sure he was in the exact same place as earlier, but he still dug his hands in the sand and grabbed onto anything, hoping to feel grounded when he was anything but. His mind went through periods of loud nonsense and then to complete and utter silence.

Davis was next to him now, his head on Samuel's shoulder, his body completely still. Neither of them asked if the other was okay. They both knew what the answer would be, or, perhaps, they didn't have an answer. They were required to stay in the immediate area until further notice. Samuel had already given a statement to the police while a paramedic checked him over. He also had a small tirade where he demanded answers and pushed to stay, but he never specified where. Stay with

Tommy? That wasn't an option anymore. Davis, on the other hand, had shut down and refused to say anything. Samuel was fairly sure that was the reason they weren't allowed to leave.

They were both silent, sound surrounding them, moving back and forth as the waves shifted behind them.

Every subject in Samuel's mind involved Tommy. He knew a necklace of bruises was slowly showing, but it caused nothing more than a hoarse voice. He searched for something to say, something to fill the silent bubble around them—something to snap Davis awake.

"What's it like?" he whispered after a moment. He cleared his throat. "I mean, I know it hurts, but what is being possessed really like?"

"It doesn't hurt," Davis said. He was staring at the sand as he took a breath. "It only hurts when you resist it. It's like—the difference between dying slowly in your sleep and taking medication that gives you an unbearable amount of pain so you live a few days or weeks or months more." Samuel was rather fond of the idea of dying in his sleep.

"Ah, but, that's not what you asked. What's it like to be possessed?" Davis's head lolled to the side. "It only successfully happened the first time, when I was nine. There were a lot of articles written about it."

"They said you killed two men, including your father. They didn't talk about *you*," Samuel said.

Davis shifted and rolled his shoulders. "I only killed my dad. Robbie Hodge killed himself."

"Just like Cillian. But your dad was killed by a demon, not you. They got that wrong as well,"

Samuel said. He ignored his churning stomach as he thought of Tommy—of the demon that possessed Tommy—attacking him. "I think it's important to know the difference right now."

"Tommy would never have done that to you," Davis said firmly.

"Exactly," Samuel said. "So what's the real story?"

Davis continued to take long, deep breaths. "My life was perfect. At least, in my nine-year-old, ignorance, I thought it was. What did it matter if my dad lost his job? That just meant there was more time for *me*. What did it matter if my mom was just putting on a smile for me?" He paused and tapped a finger on a broken shell. "What did it matter if I couldn't remember small moments of time? The rumors about me were just rumors—I, little, innocent, sweet Davis Turner, would never bully anyone."

"You don't have to relive it," Samuel said, taking one hand out of the sand and going to put it on Davis's arm. He hesitated when he saw all the sand stuck to it. He wiped his hand on his towel before placing it on Davis's forearm. "Davis?"

Davis looked at him then. It was curious. "You said 'relive' as if you know what it's like."

"You can tell a story or you can experience it again," he murmured. "You don't have to do either."

Still, Davis's gaze stayed on him for a moment before he said, "I don't actually know what it was like to be possessed because all I remember is waking up. There was blood. My mother was crying and cradling me and making sure I couldn't see—" He cut himself off and Samuel watched as his lips thinned. "I saw it anyway. I saw what I had done to my dad. I say that, but the truth is I can't actually remember what it looked like. It was as if the image was burned into my mind so strongly it burnt itself away."

Samuel sighed and looked back at the sand. His eyes felt heavy. "Tommy didn't get to wake up."

"He didn't get to kill you, either," Davis whispered.

"The demon," he corrected.

"Yeah." Davis sighed. "He wasn't able to be used as the weapon to kill you. I keep going back and forth between shock, mourning, and relief. How awful is that?"

"As the one he attacked," Samuel mumbled, "I know exactly what you're talking about."

Davis groaned and rubbed his eyes with his wrists. "He doesn't have to face what happens after. That's the worst part."

Samuel tapped a finger on his foot. "What the church did to you?"

"What my mom did," Davis said. "Taking me there. She...she wouldn't look at me the same. She would tell me she loved me. That she didn't want to lose me, too. But I lost her. I lost what I had with her. It was painful not in a physical way, but in the way we would walk down the pews and I would have to duck my head as we passed others, how they would scorn me and tell me I needed to be exorcised. They would say I was a murderer. That I was the demon that possessed me, and my mom didn't retaliate. She never said a word against them." Davis let out a shuddering breath. "There wasn't a need to retaliate the truth."

"You didn't think that way when I first met you," Samuel said. "You seemed happy."

"Maybe I was ignorant."

"Maybe you've become ignorant."

Davis's gaze shot to Samuel and the question and pain was so clear Samuel had to close his eyes. "I wanted to help you and you didn't need help," Samuel clarified. "You had found your passion and you were going after it, rumors be damned. And now, after this, you're believing those ugly words again? You aren't seeing yourself. That's ignorant."

"You're a jerk," Davis said with no bite.

"Yeah, I've heard that," he said. There was a beat of silence. "I broke it off with him. Tommy. Just by not talking to him, by avoiding him for months. I was a coward. And a jerk. And it might have been the reason..."

"If you're implying this was your fault, then you forget I lived with him the last four years," Davis said, "and that you were not the only thing going on in his life."

"I knew almost nothing about his life. That's the point," Samuel said. His fingers were rubbing the fabric of his shorts.

"You couldn't have known. That's also the point," Davis said. "None of us could have."

"I wish I could have. If I was an Exorcist...if I had noticed sooner..." Samuel pulled his hands from the sand and reached into his back pocket to pull out a small book. He flipped through it silently and went to make sure Davis couldn't read from it. He didn't have to worry, as Davis's gaze was only on his face.

He wrote in the book, just a small addition to his list of wants, before pocketing it again. Samuel turned his whole body to face Davis, forcing him to sit up straight.

"Did he really know you kissed me?" Samuel asked, wanting to know despite the guilt that he felt with it.

"It wasn't an important detail. He knows—knew. Knew...my habits. He called it my Italian blood," Davis said. He fiddled with his necklace—the one Tommy gave him. "Friendly to a fault. I guess I was a bit of a jerk, too."

"It's only significant if you want it to be significant," Samuel whispered. "I think...he made it significant."

Davis shook his head. "I think the demon did," he said. "That's what they *do*."

Samuel put his head between his knees and his hands on the back of his neck. He willed the physical pressure to ease the emotional one. "I thought the hardest part of today would be getting him back, not...losing him completely."

"Did you like him? Love him?" Davis asked gently.

"As a friend," he said honestly, "but I'm going to tell his family I was his boyfriend."

Samuel watched as Davis undid the necklace and instead wrapped it around his wrist. "You were going to continue to live with him still," Samuel said. "In an apartment. What are you going to do?"

Davis shook his head. "I can deal with that later."

"No, I—" Samuel paused. "I need something to do. Productive. I hate not being able to do anything. Let me solve it."

"Okay…I'm down a roommate," Davis said, his words strained. Samuel could see his muscles tighten, how he bent over as his stomach clenched and shoulders hunched. "I don't have money for the place on my own because no one will hire me here."

"It might be a fair reason to get out of the lease, if you had a place to go," Samuel said.

"I don't want to leave Charleston," Davis whispered. He took a pause, a breath. "I don't want to live far away from you. This has been the home I've created."

"Well," Samuel said, looking back down at the sand. Too many emotions battled as a response and he wanted to deal with none of them. "I don't want to go back with my parents."

Davis stared at him, looking for something, his lips nearly forming words as he searched for the right ones. "Are they…you've said a few things to imply they aren't the greatest."

"They know I'm gay and pretend I can still be saved," he said, "even though I already am. And I'm not going to hide who Tommy was to me. Not any longer. So, home might become…unbearable."

"Do they…hurt you?" Davis said, immediately looking down to Samuel's arms and legs. He would only find ghost lines of white hidden by a farmer's tan.

"Not physically," Samuel said, "no. That's beside the point." He steeled himself, fighting against an underlying anxiousness. "Could I…help out with rent in exchange for a room at your place?"

"Yes," Davis said quickly, almost too quickly, and then a pause where his expression was soft or almost...shy. "What I mean is, it could be our place. Equally. Half yours."

Samuel let himself release his nervousness and nodded. "I think I need that. I don't want you to be alone." He met Davis's eyes. He didn't want to be alone, either, but that was much harder to say out loud.

Davis's expression changed, his jaw tightening, his eyes darkening with sadness and fear. He took deep, shaky breaths, one after another. "I don't want to be alone," Davis choked out like it was his own, desperate release. "Thank you."

"Don't—don't start crying," Samuel said, feeling his nose tingle. He had to shut his eyes to try and take control over himself again. "Then I will and I—don't want to."

Davis let out a breath that might have been a laugh, might have been a sigh. "Not masculine enough?"

"No point," Samuel said. "I don't want...if someone sees me cry...Tommy saw me cry, at *Spring Awakening*. It was embarrassing. It's...too raw. I can't be any rawer than I already am right now."

"Emotions were something I always had trouble with," Davis said. "So many are linked to what's considered sin. If something just upsets me, it could be linked to anger—wrath—or jealousy, or pride, or...the list goes on. If I'm happy, even, it could be pride, as proven when I was younger. Emotions are what demons tamper with. So, what was safe for me?" He took gentle, even breaths as he dug a shell fragment out of the sand. "Sadness. Simple sadness. I was pretty much the emo kid in high school after I stopped my medication because at least if I was sad about my situation, it wouldn't hurt anyone else. It wasn't risky."

Samuel felt that sadness, sharp and familiar. His lip trembled ever so slightly, and he pressed them together as he shut his eyes tightly. He put his hands back in the sand, grabbing at it, holding onto chunks tightly.

"I was wrong—sadness can definitely morph into something dangerous, but that's not the point," Davis said. "The point is, emotions happen. No matter how I tried to hold it, it festers, and it can become something else—something that it wasn't. And Samuel?" Samuel looked up at him and with a tilt of his head, Davis made sure he held his full attention. "You can be raw in front of me."

Samuel took one, then two ragged breaths before he wiped his hands off quickly on his shorts and covered his nose and mouth with his palms flat together, like an intimate prayer. His shoulders shook and then, because it could not be helped, tears fell silently from his eyes.

# CHAPTER THIRTY-FIVE

There would never be enough time in the world for people to mourn their friends and family. Jenkins was proof of that in a way no one truly understood. They say after only a few months, the feeling is no longer "grief" but "depression." Becoming a Nondefined was the only undeniable symptom of a mental illness. Not that anyone else saw it that way. People denied it just as they denied demons are real or that people landed on the moon in 1969.

He would never wish it on anyone else.

Maybe it was that thought that pulled him away from the dreary scene inside the beach house. Maybe it was just the need for air. Still, he found himself walking to the two boys sitting in the sand.

"I'm sorry for your loss," he said to their bowed heads. He hoped that was what they expected him to say, that they Heard him. "Please don't end up like me."

It was Davis who lifted his head and acknowledged him, who squinted and said, "Like you?" Jenkins watched as Davis stopped himself. He could tell the moment Davis recognized his jacket, then his face. A year had passed, but it was clear Davis knew exactly who Jenkins was and what that meant.

The other boy—Samuel—turned his head. He looked like he had just smudged away all traces of sadness and replaced them with any other emotion he could grab onto, the current one being confusion. "What?"

"Nothing," Davis said quickly, his eyes wide and staring at Jenkins. "I don't think I heard you right, sir?"

Jenkins shook his head. This was not something Davis needed right now, and it was not his secret to tell.

Except Paul and Daniel walked up beside him and there was absolutely nothing he could do. Daniel couldn't protect him from this, and it was clear in Paul's expression he made the realization as well.

Davis Turner was an Optic.

# CHAPTER THIRTY-SIX

It didn't matter that Samuel said he didn't want to go back home. He had to. Despite having a full emergency bag in his car, there were other things he wanted to get, and parents to talk to. They weren't exactly expecting him to move out.

When he made his way back to his parent's house, he knew he wouldn't be able to say anything. His mother stopped him in the hallway with only her voice.

"It's been hours," she said. She looked so frail, just skin stretched over bone. Her hair was a shade darker than his, thinly falling over her shoulders. There were laugh lines around her eyes, but Samuel had no idea where she got them from. "You are never so late. Were you purposefully trying to make us worry?"

Samuel closed his eyes and took a deep breath as he rubbed his neck. He took too long, apparently, because his mother continued.

"We've given you a roof all this time. Food. Education. You have a degree now. A useless one. When are you going to start paying us back?"

"You took out loans for my schooling," Samuel said, feeling too drained to be anything but factual. "In my name only, so I'll be paying for it. You already have most of that money."

His mother looked affronted, as if that was somehow information Samuel shouldn't know about, even if he was the one who received all the e-mails. "Don't talk to me like that, young man. You know that money went to paying for you."

Samuel wondered how exactly he was talking to her. In what way was it wrong?

In what way did she care?

"If you watch the news," Samuel said carefully, "there was a demon possession at Davis's graduation party."

His mother scoffed and shook her head. "I told you like minded people flock together. And you're one of them. Lucky to be alive."

"I am," Samuel said, and he flinched at the crack in his voice. His throat still hurt. He wondered what color his neck was now and how his mother could ignore it. He realized there was no point in telling her the whole story. Pity was not only something he didn't want, but something that would only be viewed as attention seeking, which he would then receive a lecture about. If he cried, he would be told to clean himself up, to stop bothering them and get his life together.

His life didn't feel put together. It felt shattered, and he felt dirty. However, if there was something

Davis had given him, it was a shred of self-worth. He could get out.

Samuel kept his head low and continued up the stairs. His bag had been left in the car. He checked to make sure he had his keys still when he went into the bathroom. He unloaded his pockets, putting the keys, his wallet, his cell phone, small folded pieces of paper, and a mini notebook on the sink counter. He held onto the counter, rocked as he took two large breaths, and he stripped.

He took a cool shower, not cold enough to shock his skin, but to rinse away the musk and sand. He washed his hair, twice. Conditioned it, twice. Repeated the process. Washed his body in every crevice, and then he slid down until he was sitting in the bottom of the tub. The water was much colder by then, but he didn't care. He wanted to be cold. He closed his eyes and rested his forehead against the shower tile.

He missed Tommy.

Sure, they had just been friends with benefits, fuck buddies, equal opportunists, but all of those held a positive relationship title in the phrase. Tommy was a *friend*. Samuel had ignored him for months and now he was gone.

Samuel clasped his hands together and said a prayer. He wasn't one to believe that any religion was necessarily more "right" than any other, but he desperately wished that this time he was right to believe someone was listening.

# CHAPTER
# THIRTY-SEVEN

When the time for Davis's graduation came, he didn't walk. He didn't want anything Tommy could no longer have. He felt heavy. He thought it was much like how he felt through most of high school, and how he felt in middle school before that. Phases. Moments where it was hard to want to do anything but sleep.

The world wasn't courteous when it came to mourning. Especially Davis's world.

"It was your fault," Tommy's mother spat in his face. She was nearly the complete opposite of her son, with proper clothes, precise make-up, and expensive jewels from head to toe. "Tommy *trusted* you. Look where that got him!"

"Mrs. Rider," Samuel jumped in, his voice as reassuring and gentle as possible. "I assure you, Davis had nothing to do with this."

Mrs. Rider looked at Samuel, who she believed

was Tommy's boyfriend, and she embraced him. "A hidden member of the family, you are, Samuel. I'm sure you don't know all the details of Mr. Turner's life. Tommy had to sign a form saying he accepted the risk."

Samuel looked extremely uncomfortable being held so tightly by a stranger. He politely extracted himself and said, "Davis is my best friend. He cared about Tommy more than anyone. That's why I'll be living with him." Then Samuel complimented Mrs. Rider's shoes and she was distracted effectively.

Davis walked away and dialed a number.

"Was it my fault?" Davis asked, starting to choke up again.

"Davis...you are a bit of a...magnet," Daniel said, who was not good at comforting people. "But no, it was not your fault."

No matter how many times he was told, or in how many different ways, he believed it was his fault.

It wasn't just the hateful words and blame thrown toward him by other people. It was that he had no true reason *not* to believe it.

His true punishment came when he and Samuel were moving into the apartment.

He still hadn't been able to get a job. Whether that was because he wasn't qualified or because people recognized his name now more than ever, he wasn't sure. He felt like a failure for working so hard and now—now he couldn't even pick up a minimum wage position.

There was a knock at the door and Davis went to get it. If it was someone who found out where he lived and had a raw egg ready to throw or anger to release, he was not going to subject Samuel to it.

It was not someone with a raw egg. It was Jenkins Perks, wearing his formal Exorcist attire and a guilty expression.

"I couldn't do anything," Jenkins whispered. "I tried. I promise I tried."

Davis blinked down at the letter before taking it slowly. The Exorcist insignia was silver and stamped in the corner, which was enough for him to know what it was. Still, he opened the letter to confirm it.

Davis R. Turner was to be drafted upon graduation to fill the position of Optic in the Charleston County Exorcist Squad.

This. This was his punishment.

# CHAPTER THIRTY-EIGHT

There was a job description on the second page of the letter. The first page contained things Davis could only scoff at: apologies and explanations for such a draft. Why he was picked. Who Jenkins Perks was and who he would be to Davis. It was a local squad, which meant Davis could choose not to stay in the provided housing if he so chose. More apologies. More promises of accommodations. Condolences. A printed name, a signature.

The second page was the full, detailed descripttion of what an Optic was, and what one could be. To Davis, it was a horror story.

He would have intense training. He would learn how to be Jenkins' translator properly, but most of all he was to learn exactly what he could do with his ability to "see things as they really were." In other words, he was going to be trained how to See when a person was possessed. He would learn the procedures and he would be a full-fledged Exorcist.

He laughed.

"Me? An Exorcist?" He chuckled between words. "One of the most vulnerable people to possessions? You must be shitting me."

"We waited two years," Jenkins explained. "We searched everywhere else."

"It's Samuel who wants this," Davis said, still laughing at the absurdity of it all. "This? Me? It will cause a riot. Haven't you heard? I'm the reason Tommy was possessed in the first place. Kind of counterproductive, don't you think?"

"That has been considered by the Head of our squad," Jenkins said carefully, his eyes flickering behind Davis, where Samuel must have been. At least this way Davis wouldn't have to relay the news. Jenkins looked back at him. "He thinks it works in our favor."

"Favor," Davis repeated sourly. "How so? Able to keep an eye on the trouble? Is the optional housing actually optional or 'highly recommended with no true option to refuse?'" Davis leveled Jenkins with a glare. "We all know what politics this is."

"It's truly optional," Jenkins said, looking even guiltier, which Davis felt smug about. "And while politics has a part in the presentation, you will not be treated any differently, Davis."

Davis clicked his tongue against the roof of his mouth. "I already am." And he shut the door.

He was not going to deal with this right now. It was just one more thing and one more punishment for being *Davis R. Turner* and frankly, he was *tired*.

He wanted to slam doors and punch walls and

throw lamps, but all of that anger expelled when he heard the quietest, "Davis?"

That was when Davis looked at Samuel, when he saw the devastation on Samuel's face and the blues and browns on his neck, and *that* was his true limit.

He leaned back against the door and slid down it. He felt the tears down his cheeks before the sobs started wracking his chest. He couldn't wipe them away fast enough. He couldn't get his body to do anything but squeeze tighter, his knees pushing into his chest, his whole body shaking, rocking, and he felt so *horrible* because not only could he not get himself together, he couldn't ask Samuel to help, and he couldn't *help Samuel.*

"I'm sorry," he croaked out. "I'm sorry. I know you wanted it, but I—I didn't. I never wanted this. I can't do this."

"Davis," Samuel said, not as softly as the last time. "Davis, stop, I didn't want this for you. You're allowed to be upset."

Davis couldn't think of a response right away. He couldn't think much past how horrible everything was, so it took a solid minute before he said, "I just— I look around me and all I see are obstacles I can't get over. All I see are people who don't want me to be happy, or circumstances that are just mocking the fact I've even *tried.* They're just staring me in the face and making me feel so *stupid* for thinking I could ever try to be anything else."

Davis flinched as a hand covered his eyes. He went completely still. "Then stop looking around you," he heard Samuel say, "stop letting them define your future. They only have partial control. A draft has a timeline. Did you read what it said?"

"Yes," Davis whispered. "Two years unless a volunteer takes my place."

"Only two years, then," Samuel said, even if there was a twinge of something in the words. "Then you're going to move to New York, or Chicago, or LA, or stay right here, and you're going to become a famous actor."

"And dancer," Davis said, with a choked sob. "I'm a dancer, too."

"Yes, you are, and you always will be," Samuel said. His voice lowered now that Davis was calming down from his hysterics. "And I'll be here. I'll help where I can. You won't be doing this alone."

Davis blinked against Samuel's fingers, his eyelashes dusting them. "For two years? Will you be in Charleston for two more years? What about training for a different position? What about trying for the Cleanser Academy again?"

"There's nowhere else I want to be but here," Samuel said. "I can't leave it behind. I won't leave you behind."

"Don't let me hold you back," Davis pleaded. "Don't let me cause you pain. Not like Tommy. Not like…I don't want to hurt you. I already did, I know, I know, and I'm *sorry* every day—"

His words were cut off as something touched his nose—Samuel's nose—and he felt Samuel's breath against his lips, a microsecond, maybe, and then he felt Samuel's lips on his. It was a light pressure, a soft kiss to his upper lip. A pause there. A release. Then a kiss to his bottom lip. Then, before Davis could react to it at all, to decide it was okay to let himself kiss back, or to move his hands, or to breathe, the hand was being removed from his eyes at the same time Samuel was pulling back.

Davis looked at Samuel's lips, then at his eyes in disbelief.

"An unexpected kiss for an unexpected kiss," Samuel said. He was not looking at Davis and was blinking more than necessary. He cleared his throat and visibly drew up the energy to make eye contact. "I trust you more than I trust anyone else in the world. I'll sign the waiver, as I'm sure Tommy would again, if he could. It's not you. It's a risk we deal with every day. But having you as my friend makes dealing with it more bearable." After a moment, when there was still silence due to Davis being unable to form thought, let alone words, Samuel tilted his head down and added, "Okay?"

Davis nodded dumbly.

Samuel nodded back, seemingly satisfied. "Okay. Then I suggest washing your face, taking a moment if you need it, and continue unpacking, because there's no way I'm letting you out of this lease." He stood up easily and Davis watched him as he dusted off the knees of his jeans. Then he held out a hand to Davis. "Come on."

They clasped each other's wrists to pull Davis to his feet. Davis closed his eyes and took a breath, but it wasn't enough. It was like he couldn't pull in enough air and he wasn't sure he ever would be able to again. The causes of this feeling were so varied, but there was one he was holding onto. He hoped more than anything that after all of this, he would be forgiven—not by some higher power, but by Tommy Rider.

# CHAPTER THIRTY-NINE

They gave Davis two weeks to let the information sink in. Two weeks to accept he would, essentially, be a soldier. Two weeks to say any goodbyes.

Samuel was given a week off work.

Davis told Samuel he would still live in the apartment, but Samuel had a hard time thinking he wasn't also saying goodbye.

The first few nights were spent silent, but awake. Then Davis pulled his laptop from his room, dragged out the speakers, and set it up on top of a cheap storage bin. Their couch was a find on Craigslist and Samuel felt the need to disinfect it multiple times before he was willing to sit on it. It was pretty lumpy and very yellow, but it was free, so they didn't complain much.

They watched a movie on Davis's laptop. Then another. When he was picking out the third, Samuel kicked at his hand lightly before he pulled out another Hallmark level movie.

"Wait," he said. "I have something." He went into his room and came back with a box set. All three *Lord of the Rings* movies, extended edition. He hadn't been sure Davis was a fan. It was hard to tell if a geek was a general pop culture geek or a Mordor geek, but Davis took the box set gingerly in his hands.

"I've never seen them," Davis admitted.

"Blasphemous," Samuel said. He put the first disc in the player.

Finally, during *The Two Towers*, both of them fell asleep.

# CHAPTER FORTY

The day before Samuel needed to return to work, Davis's parents showed up. They weren't actually his parents, Samuel learned. They were his very young aunt and uncle, on his dad's side. Still, Davis called them mom and dad, so Samuel thought of them as such.

Samuel opened the door to pie.

"I hope you don't have any food allergies," Davis's dad said. "Martha cooked. A lot." He spilled the pie into Samuel's arms, who fumbled to not drop it. "You don't understand. She doesn't cook. Not really, and not for me."

"Oh, shove it," Davis's mother said. Martha? Mrs. Turner? Samuel wasn't even sure that was her last name, so he was even less sure what to call her. She elbowed her way past her husband. She was as tall as Samuel, who was tall until he stood next to Davis, and it was clear she was the one with shared blood.

Her skin was a beautiful dark brown, and her hair long, straight, and pitch black. She was also holding a pan. She winked at Samuel. "He cooked most of this. He's just trying to put the blame on me."

Suddenly, they didn't seem so young. They came in and acted like an old married couple, and Davis hugged them both and kissed their cheeks.

"You met him briefly before," Davis said, gesturing to Samuel, "although he was hiding." If there had not been such specific company, Samuel would have flipped Davis off. Davis grinned because he knew. "Samuel, my parents."

"Martha and Kyle are fine," Martha said, and waved politely. "Anything else makes us feel old."

"Which would have been a compliment back in the day," Kyle said, pointing at Samuel with a wink, and suddenly it was very clear what had created Davis Turner.

There was more food in the car. Enough to fill their fridge and freezer, all brought in via coolers.

"We know what it's like to be fresh out of college," Kyle said as he played Tetris in the fridge. Samuel already calculated which foods needed to be eaten first to make them all last the longest and still there was no way they would be able to eat it all before something went bad, even with freezing some.

After a while, the light chatter settled and the reason for their visit became clear. Samuel labeled the dishes as Davis sat in the living room with his parents. They were whispering, but not in a way that they were keeping it from Samuel. It was just a tender topic.

Once there were tears, Samuel excused himself into his room.

He sat on his bed and wondered if his parents shed a tear for him. He simply packed up and left in the next night.

He checked his phone. There was one missed call from his mother and a voicemail he wasn't ready to hear.

They didn't want him back. They wanted their control back, whether that was through guilting him or by making him believe they cared. The thing was, harshly spat words were the ones remembered for years, and those were the only ones he remembered at all.

# CHAPTER FORTY-ONE

The week before Davis needed to report to the Exorcist Headquarters was spent finishing *Lord of the Rings* and falling asleep on the couch. It became a habit to wait for Samuel to come back from work, heat up a specified meal out of the ones his parents provided, and settle in.

Davis realized one very distinct difference between himself and Samuel that he maybe should have considered before they agreed to live together. When a bout of depression hit, Davis *slacked*. His room had clothes and papers every-where, he was behind on laundry, and he was growing a *beard*. He considered it in the mirror for only a minute before he deemed it unfitting for his young aesthetic and shaved it.

Samuel had the opposite reaction. He *cleaned*. He was immaculate in everything he did. Everything seemed more like a hotel room rather than a place where two boys *lived*, minus the cheap furniture. The order was driving Davis a little nuts, but it was better than having a messy roommate, so he just silently judged.

That was all a good distraction during his countdown, but really there was nothing he would complain about. He still felt like fate had backhanded him, but the only thing he could do was keep moving forward.

Except the day came where he was required to report to the Headquarters downtown, and Davis felt physically ill. He wondered if he could get out of it by becoming sick, having a mental breakdown, or moving to Canada. He could claim he was an illegal immigrant, maybe, to start an investigation. Being deported to Italy didn't sound so bad and at least would be better than becoming the exact thing he worked *not* to become.

"Hey," Samuel said gently. He had been silent most of the drive downtown, but pulling into the parking deck seemed to cue him to speak. "Are you going to be okay?"

"I think we've decided that's a relative question," Davis murmured. "This isn't what I want, and I know you think it's not my fault, but I can't help feeling I should be happy to be doing this, for Tommy."

"Tommy wouldn't have wanted you to be miserable," Samuel said. "Tommy supported your acting—performing." He parked in his same spot, on the top level, but did not get out. Davis appreciated the permission to stay in the car for just a while longer. According to Google Maps, the Headquarters wasn't very far. In fact, Davis probably walked past it before without even realizing it.

"I don't want you to be late," Davis whispered.

"I won't be," Samuel said, his volume matching Davis's as he looked at his lap, where his hands were fiddling with the steering wheel. "That is, I won't be, unless you procrastinate getting out of my car for an hour."

Davis looked at him with a raised eyebrow. "You're an hour early now? You always leave at this time."

"I always get to work an hour early," he said, side glancing at Davis. "There's a lot to get done."

It was then, when Davis saw how much effort Samuel put into his second-choice career, that he realized just how incredible of an Exorcist Samuel could be. The next thought was how skewed it was that Davis was the one drafted and Samuel couldn't volunteer for him. Both of them had been denied their first-choice career. At least for now. Davis could possibly restart his in two years, and he was determined for Samuel to have the same opportunity.

With possibilities and a newfound intention, Davis got out of the car. Samuel followed shortly and Davis stood in front of him.

"Can I hug you?" Davis asked. He usually didn't need to ask, but Samuel had proven that a yes to one thing didn't mean a yes to everything or every time. Still, Samuel nodded and outstretched his arms.

"Just don't get fresh with me, Turner," Samuel teased, before he huffed out a breath as Davis hugged him tightly.

"Tommy was a lucky guy, huh?" Davis teased back as he held Samuel. He could feel hesitant hands rub his back.

"I was a bit of a jerk," Samuel confessed. "Only his boyfriend after he's dead. It's just a pity play. He deserved the real thing."

"Well, maybe I can help prevent this from happening to someone else," Davis said, pulling back but keeping his hands on Samuel's shoulders. "And you can, too. Maybe not as an Exorcist yet, but someday."

"People die every day," Samuel said, "and demons are the cause only a small percentage of the time. When Tommy—the demon—was...was trying to..." He stopped and Davis could nearly see his thoughts rewind. "He didn't seem like the Tommy I knew, but my first thought wasn't possession. It was that there are still horrible people in the world that don't need a demon's assistance." He poked Davis's chest with a finger. "And some who can prove it's something that can be fought against." His hand dropped and he looked to the ground. "I'm not sure I could have done what Andy did."

"I'm sure," Davis started, "that if you had been trained and you saw someone being nearly," he paused, "killed, I think you would have saved them."

"We won't know, will we?"

"Maybe," Davis said. He clasped and then patted Samuel's arm. "I'll come by the theater when I'm done."

Samuel looked at Davis's hand, then his eyes, all before he hugged Davis again, his nose in the crook of Davis's neck. "Be careful. Please be careful. I don't know what they'll put you through, but after what happened to Cillian, and now Tommy...I can't lose you. I refuse to. I'll argue with the Angels if you die."

It took Davis's breath away. He let his hands go into Samuel's hair, to hold him there and take up just a minute more of his time. He pulled away only when Samuel did.

"I won't die," he told Samuel as he flicked the lip of his hat. "I look too pretty to die." He winked.

"Asshole," Samuel murmured as he readjusted his hat, but he was smiling, and Davis had to rub his tingling nose.

They parted ways at the entrance of the garage.

Davis still felt like he was walking to his doom.

# CHAPTER
# FORTY-TWO

It took maybe ten minutes for Davis to arrive, standing in front of the Headquarters at Too Early O'clock and wondering if he went to the wrong place. It was a historical house, as many businesses in the area were, but it didn't look like a typical renovated government building. Certainly not for Exorcists. Still, there was a metal plaque that named it as such. Metal plaques didn't lie.

Davis gave himself the remaining ten minutes he had before his check-in time and considered what would happen if he was late. It wasn't like they could fire him. He was *drafted*.

He went up to the door on time only because of his principles.

It was Andy Rogers who opened the door. Davis's instinct was to scowl and push all the emotion he felt about Tommy's death toward her via anger. He was not very good at fighting this particular instinct.

"Oh, get over it," Andy said, putting her hands on her hips and looking very unimpressed. She wasn't wearing her uniform. Instead, she had on a light blue tank top, shorts, and a slew of belts with a wide arrangement of pockets and zippers on them. Her fingerless gloves matched her leather boots.

Davis did not drop his scowl, but he didn't try to shove past her. It was just difficult to control his face at the moment. "You hadn't confirmed Tommy was dead."

"Ninety-nine percent certain," Andy said bluntly. "Enough to not worry too much when protecting your friend."

Davis did not like that it made sense. It didn't feel right that the person who literally put a knife in Tommy's neck was not to blame.

But he knew—he *knew* it wasn't her fault. And he knew what it was like to be possessed. For a long time, he wished he had been killed by Robbie Hodge instead of the opposite. Now he just felt lucky he hadn't been. So, he understood every action and yet he was still upset.

"I don't want to be here," he said plainly.

Andy shrugged. "Well, I do. Is there anything else you want to say, so we can get it out of the way and move on?"

There were many things Davis wanted to say. He said none of them. He shook his head.

"Good." Andy stepped out of the way and Davis entered the house.

It was a large house, but while the outside was obviously historic, the inside had a more modern layout. The entrance was an open concept: part of the kitchen seen to the left, a dining room to the right with a few doors for closets or a bathroom, and a stairway that connected to a bypass, connecting two separate areas upstairs, but leaving the downstairs with tall ceilings. Despite there being a wall under the bypass, Davis could see the ceiling continue to the other side. It was a large area, probably used as a family room or another dining room, or both. It had clearly been renovated, and probably multiple times from the look of it. There were still some areas of the bypass that needed another layer or two of paint, and out of three columns holding it up, two were simple exposed beams that looked very out of place.

It was still very much a house, not a Headquarters.

"You know, I didn't know what to expect but...what...is this?" Davis asked.

"Exorcists aren't that well-funded since half of America is still in denial and don't believe we're needed. There are only teams in major cities—which means, yes, we will travel some, but the Columbia squad also has a range, so we never go far unless there's a crisis," Andy explained. "Because of the lack of funds, we deal with what we get, and we got a house. Which we only have because of Jenkins."

"But it's...it's been renovated. It looks new," Davis said, letting his eyes wonder over the details. There were fake plants in the corners and paintings on the walls, antique furniture fitting into the space very purposefully. It felt like a warm welcoming, despite the contrasting Andy Rogers.

"Yeah, well, Paul likes to make people feel like the world is a fuzzy place," Andy said, flicking her wrist dismissively as she walked towards the kitchen. "Come on. We have paperwork to do."

# CHAPTER FORTY-THREE

During his lunch, Samuel received a Snapchat from Davis. It was weird, one, because he could not ever remember installing the app, and two, the picture was a stack of papers and a black and silver jacket with the caption "fuck me."

There was also another missed call and voicemail from his mother.

Samuel was a nervous wreck.

He didn't understand why the snapchat disappeared.

He hated lunch breaks because his boss forced him to stop working and he didn't have anything to distract his mind while he ate his packed lunch.

He felt incredibly guilty.

That was what his mind went back to, as chaotic as it was. He had not been there for Tommy. He was sure somehow Davis being drafted was his fault—for not being qualified himself? For not hiding the fact

Davis was?—and he was positive the voicemail on his phone was his mother telling him what an awful state he left them all in.

*I did it for you.*

He was suddenly glad his lunch break was an hour, because his hands were shaking and all he could do was find a place to sit against the wall and hold his knees to his chest.

When he knew he could at least speak, he took out his phone and dialed.

"Hello? Samuel? Don't tell me this is a butt dial."

"Hey," Samuel said, letting out a slow breath. "How, um. How is everything?"

There was some shuffling and Samuel heard a harsh wind blow into the phone before a *clank* and his heart stopped. "Ashley? Ashley?!"

"Sorry, I dropped you," Ashley said, carefree and easy. "Actually, you caught me in the middle of packing."

Samuel begged his heart to act normal. "Packing?"

"Yes, Samuel. Packing. Moving?" She sighed. "You'd know that if you kept in contact."

"Right. I'm sorry," he mumbled. "I'll be better. I called, didn't I?"

There was silence for a moment before Ashley asked, "Are you okay?"

"Why wouldn't I be?" Samuel asked quickly, and realized the question was very stupid. He had many reasons to not be okay and no, he was not. Ashley already knew that.

"Tommy," she said simply. "Everyone there was told what happened. That he attacked you."

"Tommy didn't," Samuel defended quickly and fiercely before taking a deep breath. "Tommy didn't. The demon did. Tommy would never have hurt me." A pause. "He was my boyfriend."

"No, he wasn't," Ashley said, "But I understand his significance to you for you to say that."

"You don't know he wasn't," Samuel muttered, resting his head back against the wall and closing his eyes.

"You're a stubborn one, aren't you?"

"Yes," he admitted. Ashley was silent, as if she knew there was more that Samuel wanted to say, and there was. "I haven't ever had a boyfriend. Just...friends with benefits. And when everyone spread those rumors about me being a whore, they weren't a lie. I have never loved anyone romantically. I wouldn't know what it felt like if I did. I just know I..." His words caught and he banged his head against the wall in sheer frustration for not being able to explain himself. "Sex with Tommy didn't exactly involve talking to him much, so it was fine."

"I'm pretty sure that's a good indicator that you weren't romantically attracted to him," Ashley mused.

"And I don't appreciate people calling Davis my boyfriend," Samuel said. "He isn't. I don't even know if he's into guys or if that would upset him."

"He kissed you," Ashley said. Samuel heard a chair slide against wood floor.

"He also kissed Steven and—others. He's an actor. Maybe he grew up in a different culture. He's from Atlanta. He is part Italian, you know. The kiss is not really an indicator," Samuel grumbled. He now leaned forward to put his head between his knees.

Ashley clicked her tongue. "And the fact he's had a girlfriend?"

"Well that doesn't rule it out because bisexuality exists. Or—what is it called? Pansexuality."

"So why does it bother you that people call him your boyfriend?"

"Because he's not," Samuel said honestly.

There was a small laugh on the other side of the phone. "Samuel, are you saying you're bothered that Davis isn't your boyfriend?"

Samuel paused. He certainly hadn't meant it that way. He felt a bit weird that his words had been twisted, or perhaps it was a Freudian slip?

"I don't know," he whispered. Then, "He's been drafted as an Exorcist. Today is his first day."

"Did you really just call me for romantic advice, Stewart?" Ashley accused with humor, but there was also an edge to her voice. This was not news to her. It was a reminder. She didn't want to think about it either. Possibly, she wanted the same thing he did.

"I wanted to make sure you were okay," he said softly.

"I'm okay," she said softly back.

Samuel clenched his phone. "I'm going to miss you when you move."

"Then keep in contact," Ashley said, as if it was the simplest thing. Maybe it was, to her.

"I'll do my best," he promised, and he meant it.

# CHAPTER FORTY-FOUR

The paperwork for becoming an Exorcist was extensive. There were liabilities and acknowledgements and oaths: blanks in which he had to fill in the same information a dozen times for a dozen different purposes. They had his medical records, which were not extensive, and they had his criminal records, which were extensive, if only because it included every time someone called the cops regarding a situation he was involved in.

"None of these are my fault," Davis pointed out. Then, "But, oh, hey, you can't have an Exorcist with this kind of criminal record."

Andy peered over the paperwork. She seemed like all life had been drained from her simply because she was forced to babysit instead of stick knives in throats.

"They're all just records of people feeling 'threatened,'" she said, using air quotes. "Exorcists should be threatening. People should try to not get them-selves possessed."

Davis still couldn't control his face. He scowled.

"Be *happy*, teammate!" she said with an unusual amount of excitement before her face fell and she matched his scowl. "I'm not in charge."

In all his life, no one got under Davis's skin like Andy did. He ignored her and the jacket laying on the table. He was going to put off wearing it as long as he could.

The next sheet contained his salary.

The paperwork was suddenly interesting.

"Holy shit," Davis said, rubbing his eyes under his glasses, not because he thought his vision was wrong, but because he thought he must be sleep-ing, daydreaming, wishing too much for some good to come out of all of this.

There was definitely some good.

"I thought you said Exorcists weren't funded well," he said in astonishment and looked accusingly at Andy.

"Where do you think all the money goes, if not the Headquarters?" Andy drawled. "It's not like we're in need of ammunition—at least not in the same capacity as, say, the army. We have our jackets, our vests and formal wear, and funding for research." She rolled her eyes. "And *some* weapons, but those don't all need replenishing as much as just upkeep, which I do."

"I don't know if I completely understand what I'll be doing," Davis admitted as he glanced at the next page, then went back to make sure the money figure had not changed. It hadn't.

Andy turned to the next page for him. "There you go. Job description. Optic: Translator for the Non-defined. Demon spotter. Back up to the Cleanser. That's me. Yay." She rested her cheek on her fist, her elbow on the kitchen table. "This job is very similar to, say, a firefighter's. There's not always a fire going on, but you always have to be ready for it. In the meantime, there are other things that need to be done to prepare. We're only one squad—a small one, compared to larger cities—and that means we can't rotate shifts like firefighters can. We are constantly on call, whether we're living here or elsewhere." She gave him a meaningful look.

Davis was able to control his face now, but he was unable to control his middle finger. Andy smirked in approval.

"So, you'll be working mostly with Jenkins, your Nondefined," Andy said. "I'm sure you've heard enough about them, but the short of it is I can't see what he's actually doing or saying because I don't care who he really is. His identity was *spiritually* taken, you could say. I see him as a scrawny white kid tagging along because that's what he feels like to me."

"You're prejudiced," Davis said, unsurprised.

"Something like that. But we all assume things about people. Optics just do it the least amount," Andy explained. "So, you'll go to meals with him and make sure he actually gets what he wants instead of the server assuming he's actually your girlfriend ordering a salad and water." Davis scrunched his nose. "Hey, it's a disability. It just also happens to be useful for us."

"Got it…" Davis mumbled.

"There will be further lessons. Your training will be as much physical as it will be textbook. That will be mostly with me, but the others will assist. As the Cleanser, I'm the stereotypical Exorcist from the old movies. The ones who actually perform whichever ceremony is needed. Plus combat, minus the title of Priest. We bring in an actual Priest if needed." She tapped her fingernails on the table, much like a witch would. "Let's see…Vanessa is our Specialist. That position is different in every squad. They have a, you guessed it, *specialty* that's useful for that particular squad. You'll learn Vanessa's soon enough."

*Ominous*, Davis couldn't help but think.

Andy gave a long sigh. "Noah is our Medic, which is pretty self-explanatory. Still, respect his experience in trauma. Oh, and if you have a mental breakdown, he's trained as a counselor until you can see someone else. We don't have a psychologist in the squad. So good luck."

"Uh, thanks," Davis said, although he was thinking the squad would definitely benefit from a psychologist.

"Lastly, Paul. He's the Head of the squad, served as a spook in the Navy, but is now our Finder as well. He can locate whatever we need, whether it's an artifact for a ritual or a person. He also helps Jenkins do the paperwork." She paused. "Right, Jenkins deals with paperwork because it's not like just anyone can torture information out of a Nondefined. Like I said, useful. Any other questions?"

"Uh," Davis started, trying to mentally catch up

after the rather morbid information. "Sure. Let's go back to…demon spotter?" He pointed at where it was printed. "Clarify."

"You're an Optic," Andy said snidely, as if she also had said, "How are you so stupid?"

Davis gave her his best impression of her meaningful look.

"You can—ugh." She twirled a finger at her eye. "See them. Demons. People who are possessed. You might not be able to yet, or you can't tell you're seeing them, but you'll learn."

"I do not want to see demons," Davis said. He said it plainly, but then the panic set in a moment later. "No, really. I don't want to see them. I—don't want to do this."

"If you were able to," Andy said, "you would have been able to tell Tommy was possessed and we might have been able to save him."

"If you knew he was possessed long enough to know he was dead," Davis growled, "then why didn't *you* save him?"

For the first time since meeting Andy, he saw her expression falter.

"Because I thought it was *you*. I wasn't positive it was him," she said, "until I saw him trying to kill your friend." She blinked. "But mostly because we thought it was you. You've been able to take care of yourself, so we weren't worried until the…signs spiked. That's why I was sent to check in on you. Then I made a calculation based off all the previous signs." She huffed through her nose and dropped her hand to the table. "I *am* sorry about your friend."

"Now, now," Davis said, narrowing his eyes at

her. "Don't go changing up on me. I was just forming a schema for you."

"Finish the paperwork," she said, and Davis did.

It was in the afternoon when the rest of the team arrived. They were all in uniform and Davis only recognized two of them. Daniel bowed his head. Jenkins looked guilty but also happy to see him. It took a moment longer, but then Davis did recognize one of the other men who approached him.

"Paul," Davis said warily. "Er. Do you have a title?"

"Officially, I'm a Petty Officer. CTI1. But just 'Paul' is fine," he said, holding out a hand, which Davis shook. "My apologies for not being here earlier. We had a few locations that needed our attention."

Andy nudged Davis. "What the firefighters do when there's not a fire," she said. "Phase one: Check suspicious activity. Which is, by the way, everywhere. We live in Charleston, one of the most haunted cities in the world. Or, at least in America. It keeps us busy."

Paul smiled through his salt-and-pepper beard. "Caution, yes. We have to investigate every possible demon activity so we prevent what we can. We also have to be suspicious, not of the possibility of someone being possessed, but of it having nothing to do with a demon at all."

"I thought that's what an Optic is there for," Davis said, wondering if Andy was just trying to scare him. He looked at Daniel instead of her for answers.

"Yes," Daniel said, crossing his arms. "Although no one has truly perfect vision. Even Optics can miss something. Not to mention more powerful, older demons can hide very well." He seemed to think about this for a moment, "However, newer ones can be just as sneaky simply because they're the most... human."

Davis rubbed his sweaty palms on his jeans.

"Okay," he said carefully. "Sure."

"We'll go over more later. Slowly, or as slowly as we can, so you can best understand," Paul said. He turned to the two remaining Exorcists. "This is Vanessa Vu, our Specialist," he introduced. The girl looked young in her face, but she almost matched Davis in height, which was rare, and her face was soft edges, monolid eyes, and sassy lips. Her hair was the type of brown that was a shade away from black, and purposefully curled just at the ends. She wore a cross around her neck and a dozen bangles on her wrists.

"Pleasure," she said, dipping her head and smiling politely. Davis gave a shy smile back.

"And Noah Debuu, or Doc," Paul said.

"Hey, Newbie," Noah said, grabbing Davis's hand into a handshake Davis had no control over. Noah had a huge hand, but the rest of him seemed scrawny, all long spine and limbs. For someone so slim, his arms were strong. He grinned so wide that the contrast between how white his teeth were and the darkness of his skin was startling. "I'm the Medic. Physical injury? I got you. Psychotic break? Also got you. My job is to keep you stable until you get to some kind of hospital. I do have field experience and a doctorate."

Davis did not doubt it for a minute. "Then you know the psychological effects a draft could have?" he asked, simply because he was bitter.

"It's why I have double duty," Noah answered.

"I'm here to help."

Davis licked his dry lips. "Right."

A hand landed on his shoulder and Davis flinched. He turned back to Paul.

"*Astaghfirullah*. I'm sorry about your friend," Paul said genuinely. "We failed you and yet now we're asking for your help."

"It's a draft," Davis whispered, ignoring the foreign word he didn't know. "Nothing about this is asking."

"We're asking for participation," Paul said. "We need you. Daniel has been here for two years with only rare trips back to his own squad."

"I'll stay to train you," Daniel said, "and I will check in on you, but I have to go back. It was always temporary."

Davis took a deep breath and shrugged. "You're paying me enough. Plus...if I can help prevent another incident like the one with Tommy, I'll try."

"Then let's start your training," Daniel said, walking out of the kitchen for a moment before coming back in and tossing him a thick vest. "Get used to wearing that and your jacket. Put it on and follow me to the...gym," he said. "Let's find out what we're dealing with."

# CHAPTER FORTY-FIVE

At five o'clock, Samuel was done with work. Usually he stayed a little after, but he received a text telling him Davis was waiting outside. Once he exited the building, he found Davis sitting on the sidewalk, head against the wall and eyes closed. One peeked open.

"I'm tired," Davis admitted.

Tired meant Davis was alive, so Samuel was okay with this. He took the spot next to him.

"What movie do you want to watch tonight, then?" he asked.

Davis closed his eye and leaned his head against Samuel's shoulder. "You pick. My brain is too occupied."

"That bad?"

"It's bad," Davis whispered. "Except...it pays really well."

"It better," Samuel grumbled. "Come on, tell me

about it on our way home. I have outlasted my tolerance for the sidewalk's level of cleanliness." He nudged Davis's head up before helping him stand. "What did they do to you, make you do physical training all day?"

"Physical tests, mostly. They need to know where I'm at before they know how to train me. Which would be worse if I wasn't used to choreography training. I just didn't sleep much," he confessed. They had, again, fallen asleep on the couch, but Samuel was the first to do so for once. He wondered how long Davis stayed awake after the movie ended, because Samuel knew he didn't start another one.

"Then we'll watch *Mirrormask*," Samuel said as they walked towards the parking garage. "And… maybe you should sleep in a bed."

"I'll sleep on anything," Davis said, stifling a yawn.

It took a bit longer than normal, but Samuel got Davis home and forced him to eat some soup while he put on the movie.

"I'm going to save it," Davis said suddenly, putting his half empty bowl aside. "The money I make," he clarified. "I'm going to pay for you to go to med school or…something. To be some sort of Exorcist. To bribe them back into letting you become a Cleanser."

Samuel opened his mouth, to decline, to say he wanted to earn it, but then he closed it. Then he opened it again. He thought about how there wasn't a single other person who had ever supported him the same way Davis did with just those words—not to mention the idea of putting away money for him. The closed his mouth again. The thought itself was overwhelming. He felt like until now he had never been given a true gift, and now he was given Davis.

He was speechless.

Davis seemed very confused by this. "What did I say?"

Samuel was unsure how to proceed. He went back to his basics.

"I don't want your money," he said, but it was soft and his mouth was dry. No, he did not want Davis's money. He wanted everything else about Davis.

Maybe it was because he admired who Davis was. Maybe it was the fact Davis was now able to do what Samuel so badly wanted to do: to be available to help others, to be able to breathe easily enough himself that he could see others.

Davis looked at him as if Samuel was something he didn't understand, like a math problem with flying trains and the gravity of Jupiter. He didn't say anything. Samuel was glad for it.

They watched the movie. Neither fell asleep to it. Samuel felt like he was having a panic attack for absolutely no reason at all.

It was too early for bed but Samuel gathered his blanket and stood. "I have some—I'm going to go..." He pointed to his room. "Are you okay?"

"Yeah," Davis said, his eyes following Samuel as he walked towards his room. "Will you be bothered if I watch another movie?"

"No," Samuel said. "Only if you don't clean up your dishes."

"Got it," Davis said, holding up his bowl as he

stood up to go to the connected kitchen. He glanced up, catching Samuel standing in the hallway, watching him. Samuel thinned his lips, meaning to say something more. He didn't. Davis smiled. "Goodnight, Samuel."

Samuel almost took a step towards Davis, to explain how worried he had been all day, to apologize for not being able to spend the night on the couch with him.

He turned away.

"Goodnight, Davis," he said, and he went into his room.

# CHAPTER FORTY-SIX

The days as an Exorcist were unpredictable. Just as Andy had said, it was most similar to an average day as a firefighter. Day two, there was an alarm.

"Come on," Daniel said, throwing Davis his vest and jacket as they scrambled from the gym-not-gym. They piled into an SUV with Noah behind the wheel. Davis quickly learned why he was the designated driver and he clung to the handle on the roof as they sped down the opposite direction on a one-way street.

"He's had practice driving an ambulance," Vanessa explained, who was holding onto the back of the seat with one hand and trying to put her hair in a ponytail with the other. She somehow was able to make it work.

They slowed down as they exited the peninsula. Davis watched worriedly as they neared his apartment, only to pass it and instead enter a small neighborhood.

"This is for you to observe," Paul told Davis as they stopped in front of a small house. It was one story with a screened porch attached to the side. Children's toys were spread across the front lawn. Davis couldn't do much but observe and hope this was not a child who was possessed. He wasn't sure what his stance was on what to do. Could he let another child go through what he had? The years of bullying? The look his birth mother gave him as she left?

Davis stumbled as his arm was caught in a tight grip.

"Observe," Daniel said with a tone that left no room for argument. "It isn't the child."

Davis nodded, although he couldn't help think how horrible of a decision it was to draft *him* in such a vital position. He stayed behind Daniel as they approached the front door.

"Sir," Paul called as he tapped his knuckles on the door. "We received your call. Is everything okay?"

Nonspecific. If there was someone else inside, they had no clue who was at their door. Neighbors? Cops? Davis didn't think a demon would much care. Then, maybe demons were aware of Exorcists. They had once been human, after all.

There was no answer.

Paul made a hand gesture to the screened porch and Andy pulled away from the group with Noah following behind her. He tried calling out again. "Mr. Greene?"

There was a dull *thump* before soft sobs could be

heard. Paul closed his eyes, mouthed a word, or maybe a phrase, before he looked at his team.

The door was locked. Paul whispered, "Jenkins," and Jenkins immediately knelt in front of the doorknob and pulled out tools before he started working on the knob. Davis stared at him, wondering why he had such a skill. Although, Andy had been able to do the same thing. Jenkins didn't say a word. The lock clicked open.

"We're coming in," Paul announced, and they all pushed inside. They were quiet, but swift, crouching as they passed through the living room before heading where Paul pointed them. Davis continued to stay with Daniel, thinking of un-important things like *this is not good lighting* and *for having a child, the house is pretty clean*.

They followed the muffled sobs until they entered the small kitchen. This, unlike the rest of the house, was a mess, littered with food congealing in the sink and small fruit flies getting caught in a stick trap. Davis covered his nose at the smell. How long had it been like this? Why was it like this at all?

The cries were louder, but only barely. Daniel gestured to the pantry before staring down Davis. He had to be ready, even if he was there only to observe. Daniel opened the pantry.

There was a little girl standing just between the door and the shelves behind her. Her hands were over her mouth. Her eyes were red and puffy, her cheeks were filled with freckles, flushed, and tear-stained. Ginger curls were pulled into pigtails with unnecessary star clips around the ties. She was so tiny.

Daniel kneeled in front of her. "Where are your parents?"

She shook her head, her whole body shaking as she tried to back up further, but there was nowhere to go. Daniel glanced back at Davis. Davis leaned back enough, seeing Paul let Andy and Noah in through the side door. He waved when Noah spotted him.

Once Noah joined them, Daniel moved out of the way.

"You might be needed," Daniel told him. "Just stay with her."

Noah nodded, his expression hard and serious before he turned to the girl. He had the widest smile. "We'll go on a small trip. I heard there are cookies."

The girl cowered but her eyes were steady on Noah. Cookies weren't convincing enough.

"And a bath. Do you like baths?" Noah asked.

Daniel elbowed Davis. "Come on. He has it."

They joined the others, who gathered back in the dining room. Andy gestured to the bathroom door. The bedroom doors were already wide open.

Paul stepped forward. He knocked on the bathroom door.

"We know you're in there," he said. There was no reply. Then, sobbing. The door was unlocked. When they opened it, a woman stood there, her summer dress drenched in blood.

"He tried to hurt her," Mrs. Greene said, eyes wild. "Please, you have to get an ambulance. If he's alive—please!"

None of them moved for a moment, then they all did. Daniel moved forward and Vanessa ran back, presumably to get Noah.

Davis stepped back, out of the way. He watched as a large man was brought out, his red beard and pale face splattered with blood. So was the entire front of his flannel shirt, holes revealing wounds. The blood on the woman was clearly not hers. Davis only stared. He wondered if that was how his father had looked. He couldn't remember at all.

Except, Mr. Greene was still breathing. He knew that was a difference.

"Get out of the way and call 911!" Noah spat as he moved over to the man and pulled his pack off.

Davis looked away. He tried his best not to gag.

Paul was the one to make the call.

"Neither were possessed," he heard Daniel tell Andy. "This was just a domestic event."

"Then we should leave," Andy said. "This was a waste of time."

"No," Paul said as he closed his phone. He looked directly at Davis. "This was good. This is exactly what you needed to see, Davis." Davis highly disagreed, and it must have shown. "I mean it. You needed to witness the facts: it's not always a demon when someone thinks it is."

"And it was the father who called in," Andy recalled. "Said the mother was possessed. People jump to that conclusion all the time." She was staring at Mrs. Greene, who sat on the floor of the bathroom now, Jenkins watching her nearby. Except he wasn't exactly watching her. He was looking past them, towards the kitchen. Davis followed his gaze, where he could barely see Vanessa's back in front of the pantry.

What a mess this was.

Davis vomited.

He hadn't meant to, but it was uncontrollable. He ignored Andy's sounds of disgust and just coughed until his stomach had nothing left and his throat was raw.

"I don't want to do this," he rasped. He was shaking, but there was no stopping it.

"Too bad," Andy said. "We have to smell your puke now, so consider it even. We can't clean it up because of evidence."

Davis didn't have the energy to argue with her, but he thought it was very far from even. He wished he had something left to throw up on her boots.

It wasn't long before they heard the sirens. Police officers and medics barged into the house. They took over the scene while the squad was forced out of the house.

"Do you understand?" Paul asked.

"I understood before," Davis said. "I don't exactly understand what happened in there, but I don't think I need to. There wasn't a demon involved, but there could have been. That's why we showed up. The guy thought his wife was possessed."

"If my wife was about to stab me, I'd think so too," Andy said, her head lulling to the side in thought. "Especially if she used to be docile. There was clearly an abuse situation here."

"And the kid?" Davis asked quickly. "What'll happen to the kid?"

"I'll stay here and see that through," Daniel said. "She'll go to child services unless the investigation deems one of the parents innocent."

Jenkins jerked forward but then stilled. Davis and Daniel looked at him. "I want to know she'll be okay."

"She will be," Daniel assured him.

It wasn't long before they were allowed to go back. Paul answered any questions the cops had for them and Noah stayed with the paramedics. As promised, Daniel stayed with the child. Her name was Cassie.

Davis went straight to the gym-not-gym and closed the door. He paced as he put his fingers in his hair and pulled. He shut his eyes. It was the image of the father, of the little girl peeking and seeing her father like that. Of her mother, covered in her father's blood.

He had looked like that. There had been blood on him. His father's blood. He had seen—something he never wanted to remember. He couldn't remember. He just knew bits and knew enough now to form his own gruesome images in his head.

He saw Tommy, with dead eyes and a blood-soaked shirt.

Davis dry-heaved. He only let himself do this for another ten minutes before he pushed off the floor and stumbled towards the punching bag. He had to get his emotions under control. He couldn't let them get out of hand. He had to focus.

He punched the bag until his knuckles bled. No one bothered him. They let him have a tantrum and they gave him privacy to do what he needed to. He was thankful for it, but it didn't help his latest memories. He just hoped this was something he wouldn't have to see again.

Day three, there were no sirens. No calls. It was silent. They taught Davis how to use a gun.

# CHAPTER FORTY-SEVEN

Samuel picked up Davis from work. On the third day, he watched as Davis slowly walked to the car and slid in the passenger seat. He leaned his head back and closed his eyes. His hands were bandaged just as they were the day before.

"Bad day?" Samuel asked, because he wasn't quite sure what else to say.

Davis breathed in a large breath through his nose, his eyes stayed closed. "Yes," he answered. "It was another bad day."

Samuel closed his own eyes and swallowed. There was nothing he could do. Nothing at all. Nothing.

He turned on the car and drove them home.

The next day wasn't much different. He wasn't sure it ever would be.

# CHAPTER FORTY-EIGHT

It was day four. Daniel Collins leaned over Davis as he was lying on the bench press.

"Did you put the sign on the door?" Daniel asked. He was wearing a grey button-down un-tucked over blue jeans. It was the most casual Davis had seen him.

"If you mean the one that says 'pretend gym' then yes, that was me," he said. He had found some colored pencils and borrowed the pink one. "I was thinking of adding little drawings, but they probably wouldn't look like what I would mean for them to."

It was a moment before Daniel said anything more. Instead, he spotted Davis as he raised the weights.

"It's impressive you can do this much," he said. "I wouldn't have expected it."

"I'm a dancer. I have to keep in shape," Davis said between labored breaths. He wondered if he could demonstrate exactly how much strength he had in his legs alone.

"A dancer? Do you know Capoeira?" Daniel asked.

Davis knew of Capoeira. He hadn't had much practice with it, seeing how there hadn't been a class and most people did not want him included in their extracurricular activities, especially when it required a partner, but he nodded anyway.

"Just because it's like fighting doesn't mean I'll be able to fight," Davis said. "It's a dance for a reason."

"No, but your main goal isn't to fight," Daniel said, "It's to handle a situation where a person might have paranormal levels of strength. You won't be able to win. You have to be able to be fast. To dodge." He leaned in closer over Davis. "You've been fighting demons your whole life. Now, we'll teach you how to do it right."

"You think I haven't been?" Davis asked, giving up on the bar once Daniel put his weight on it and sliding out from under it, away from his teammate.

"No," he said, straightening. "You've just had good luck."

Davis took a slow breath. "Then tell me something," he said. "Answer honestly with your opinion. Was Tommy my fault?" He knew he asked the question before, but it had been over the phone and unspecific. It still bothered him. He wasn't sure that would ever stop.

"We all failed him, Davis," Daniel said. "No one can be blamed for a demon's actions."

"And Angels?" Davis asked.

"Angels," Daniel said, his voice lowering, "are simply to blame for never interfering at all."

"So you do believe in them? That they exist?"

"I do," Daniel said, his words carefully measured. "I just also believe they're too busy with idealistic plots to actually help. That's why Exorcists exist. Angels aren't doing shit." He stopped himself and looked at Davis. "You need to talk to Vanessa."

Feeling that this was more of a dismissal than anything, Davis wiped his face with his shirt and slid off the bench.

"I'll leave you alone then," he said, ducking his head and leaving the room, feeling...disappointed. He hadn't really believed in Angels before, but now? Now, he wasn't sure.

He walked out of the Pretend Gym and was stopped by Jenkins.

"Are you doing anything?" Jenkins asked. He was wearing clothes that were so covered in paint Davis wasn't sure of their original color. One glance around told him the beige primarily on him was the same color as the walls, which had been blue the day before.

"I was heading to Vanessa," Davis said. "Daniel told me to."

"Oh," Jenkins said, looking slightly disappointed.

Davis sighed. "However, the first point on my job description is being your translator. What do you need?"

The shift in Jenkins' expression was so sudden it startled Davis. "*Really?*"

"Really," Davis said, not being able to resist smiling at the energy. "What do you need?"

"I need to find my son," Jenkins said.

"Isn't that a job for, I dunno, the *Finder*...?" Davis asked warily. "Oh. Do you want me to ask Paul? I can do that."

Jenkins shook his head. "No. Paul knows. He understands me well enough, if by assumption. No, he can only find living things."

"Living," Davis repeated, "as in...your son...?"

"Is a ghost," Jenkins said. "He has to be. And I want to find him."

# CHAPTER FORTY-NINE

Samuel's phone vibrated on his work table. It was ignored in favor of wondering if a work table was a better use of his money than an actual bed. He decided yes, it was, if only for his sanity's sake.

Davis was called in on Samuel's day off, as was going to be a normal occurrence, apparently, and so Samuel worked at home. He had a pile of deep red fabric, thick and durable, but flexible. He was starting a project, although this was the first time he didn't have a solid plan.

His phone stopped vibrating. Then it started again. He checked the number, then placed it back down.

The fabric was perfect for his project. The bronze trim he picked out complemented it perfectly.

Samuel could not ignore the third time his phone went off. He pulled it out. The word "HOME" had never been so intimidating as it was in large font across the screen. He closed his eyes during the second and third vibrate. He picked up on the fourth.

"Hello?" he said, as if he did not know the number and he wasn't terrified of who was on the other line.

"Sammy," his mother cooed. "My baby, I thought you died! Where are you? Are you okay?"

"I'm okay," Samuel whispered, feeling small and guilty. He wondered why it took so many weeks for his mother to be so frantic.

"Oh. Well, if you're okay, then I need an explanation right now. You just left me with your abusive father—" There it was. This was his mother, the one only covered by the illusion of caring. She didn't give him a moment to speak. He waited and listened to her tell him how awful of a son he was, how he didn't contribute to the family, how this was why he could never expect to be worth anything to anyone else. He just sat and listened.

She had to breathe at some point, so when she did, Samuel said, "If I'm worth so little, then you won't miss me," and he hung up.

Then he proceeded to curl into his blanket and shake, ignoring his phone as it started vibrating again until it fell off the table. He did not pick it up.

# CHAPTER
# FIFTY

I t was impossible for Davis to come up with a sympathetic response to Jenkins when he was so clearly focused on the theory that his son was a ghost. So, when Jenkins started talking about how he asked to be assigned to jobs that sounded more ghostly than demonic, Davis just accepted he would be going along wordlessly. This was at least better than seeing blood.

It was a day after rain, so the weather was muggy as they walked from the Headquarters toward downtown Charleston. At first, Davis thought they were heading toward the campus and he got a very intense fear of being spotted at all, let alone in his jacket. Then they turned down another road, just a block away from the campus. King Street, known for its expensive but fun shops, was filled with tourists. Davis didn't really want to be recognized by any of them, either. He really wanted to burn his jacket.

"Jenkins, I—" Davis started, but then Jenkins

turned into one of the shops and Davis was able to breathe. It was a small antique store that was packed with too many items: chandeliers, tables, and desks. Books, scrolls, pieces of things Davis couldn't put a name to. Neither of them could walk down an aisle without their shoulders or the toes of their shoes brushing something. Jenkins was the one who found the way to the counter, which was un-occupied.

"One moment!" shouted a woman from the back.

Jenkins looked at Davis. "You'll have to talk to her, but I'll tell you what to say. Explain I'm a Non-defined. Or, better yet, say I'm a silent type. Maybe then, if I speak, she'll assume I'm actually not talking, and she won't hear anything else."

"That would be lying," Davis said. "You are not a silent type."

Jenkins looked prepared to argue this, one finger raised, but then stopped. "Daniel is an asshole and didn't really listen to me, okay? I don't usually get to talk when someone understands me."

"It's not a problem," Davis said easily. "Do you mind if I summarize?" He smirked. "Like the Ghost Whisperer. Fitting, right?"

Jenkins shrugged, but there was the slightest recognition in his lips. "I don't mind. I just hate when I'm misunderstood. And yes, it is like the Ghost Whisperer." He seemed pleased.

"Sorry about that," the worker said as she came out from the back room, looking tired but cheerful. She noticed their jackets and she suddenly looked incredibly less tired. "Oh! You're here! And so quickly!"

Jenkins did not say anything. He was staring at her.

Davis held in a sigh and just looked at Jenkins.

"Oh," Jenkins said. "Right. Ask her to explain what experiences she's been having. But, you know. Be nice. Human."

Davis hadn't expected his previous retail experience to be applicable to being an *Exorcist*, but he supposed wearing the blue vest had done him some good. He put on his greeter smile, charming and approachable.

"We treat each call to the Exorcist Headquarters with the utmost importance. Let me introduce myself. My name is Davis Turner, and this here is Jenkins Perks." He gestured towards Jenkins. "I am his Optic, so please excuse what he says. I will translate. But tell me, what is your name?"

The woman flushed, her cheeks matching her burgundy hair, which curled to frame her round face. She wore a small hairpiece with a dark green feather surrounded by black ones, all coming from a small gear. She was cute, for someone who was quite possibly twice Davis's age.

"May. Ringer," she said. She looked at Jenkins. "So, you're a Nondefined? I've never met one before. I'm sorry I can't, um. 'See' you." Her apology seemed so sincere it was almost as if she was chastising herself.

Jenkins looked like he had never heard an apology in his life. He looked at Davis, then back at May, then back at Davis with an expression that clearly said he didn't have any clue what to say. Davis wondered if translating Jenkins' thoughts was also part of his job description.

"Don't worry, Ms. Ringer," Davis said kindly, having checked her hand for a ring. "I assure you, being an Optic is not a dream job." He puffed out a breath as Jenkins elbowed him in the stomach. "Case in point."

May just smiled shyly. "Well, at least you don't make assumptions about people. That's all I see." She sighed softly. "I appreciate the work you do. I'm sure you're used to strange things happening in antique shops."

Davis did not know if it was common or not, so he shrugged. "Do you mind telling us what's been going on?"

"Ah," May started. "Some of the smaller pieces have been found on the floor in the morning, across the store. I've found skid marks where furniture has been moved..." She stepped around the counter and led them to where the marks were. "I have cameras, but they're not very high quality. I'm sorry."

"You don't have to apologize," Jenkins said to her. Then stopped, as if realizing she wasn't an Optic, as her expression changed to one of worry.

"He says you don't have to apologize," Davis said quickly. "Which I agree with. We've had to work with much less."

Jenkins raised an eyebrow but shrugged. "It's definitely a ghost. Demons are people focused. This is a classic haunting. My guess is it came in with a new object. However..." He glanced around the store. "It sounds almost...playful." He looked at Davis. "Childlike."

Davis hadn't even been sure ghosts were real

before, but he always admitted there was more proof than, say, *Angels*. He wondered where ghosts fit in with the belief of Offers. Pushing that curiosity aside, Davis relayed the information.

"Oh, good," May said, a hand over her breast in relief. "I don't mind a ghost, as long as it won't hurt anyone."

"Jenkins believes it might be a child," Davis said, even though he was of the opinion Jenkins thought that because he so dearly wanted it to be one. "Can you recall if it started after receiving a specific item?"

"You know…let me check my log," she said, going back to the counter and pulling out a binder from underneath it. She rifled through it before tapping on a line. "If you think it's a child, then…" She trailed off as she walked through her store familiarly, stopping and presenting them with a small figure. It was a boy carved from dark wood, his limbs disproportionately thin. He was crouched to the ground, looking curiously at something unseen.

Jenkins picked it up very gingerly, holding it in his hands as if it were glass.

"This is Negrinho Do Pastoreio," he said, pronouncing the name with an accent and peering at it almost…sadly. He looked at Davis and shook his head. This ghost could not be his son. He placed the figure down. "Although the name might be updated by now. Still, this could be a very historic ghost, if it is Negrinho. He was the inspiration for the first Finder."

May looked lost. Davis wondered what she heard. "Jenkins explained how this is a figure of—" He looked at Jenkins as he said, "Negrinho Do Pastoreio," to make sure he pronounced it right. He wasn't sure how he felt about saying that name. "That might be your ghost."

"Oh, I knew who the figure was, but—that is a historic and—and *tragic* myth!" she said, putting a closed fist to her mouth as she held herself with her other arm. "Do you really think he's here?"

Davis looked at the figure. "Possibly," he said, because Jenkins didn't say anything. "I have a friend from Brazil, if you would like some direct information. I know him from high school."

"Oh, that would be *wonderful*, thank you," May said, her eyes soft as she smiled.

"We can give her contact information for people who deal with ghosts," Jenkins told Davis, digging in his pocket and pulling out a business card. There was an icon of a ghost looking suspiciously like Casper in the corner. Davis handed it to May.

"For you, just in case you want a cleansing or something," Davis said. "We mainly deal with, you know...demons."

May was absently nodding as she looked at the business card, but she looked up at Davis at the mention of demons. "You're *the* Davis Turner, aren't you?"

Davis ignored his pounding heart and instinct to flee. "Yes, ma'am," he said.

She looked at him sadly. "It shows how horrible people are when they assume you're evil, yet you are an Optic—you see things for what they are. Even I can't..." she trailed off and frowned at Jenkins, "be...free from assumption. But it victimizes people. So please, let me apologize to the two of you, and thank you again for your hard work."

Davis was shocked still by the response. This was not what he expected as a reaction to being recognized. This was not anything close.

He rather liked it.

A look at Jenkins told him he was not alone in that.

# CHAPTER
# FIFTY-ONE

It was starting to get late and Samuel had already eaten dinner by the time he heard a key in the door. Davis told him he would get a ride back but as the hours went by, Samuel had been ready to kidnap Davis from the Exorcists just so he could be home.

The door opened and Samuel greeted Davis as he closed the door behind him.

"Hey," Davis said tiredly as he dropped his bag. Samuel took a step closer to him. Davis blinked and said, "Uh, hey?"

Samuel's mind was noise, only static as he stared into Davis's eyes. Then he took a step closer, making Davis step back until he was leaning against the door, eyes wide.

"Is everything okay...?" Davis asked, his eyes never leaving Samuel's. Their eyes were locked until Samuel took one step closer, tilted his head, and his eyes dropped to Davis's lips.

Get the hint, Samuel thought at him. I'm horrible at words and I'm horrible at communicating, but I need you right now.

He could see Davis swallow. He wondered if he was making a mistake.

He couldn't back down. He needed this.

"Can I kiss you?" Samuel asked, so close he could feel his breath hit Davis's face.

Then Davis's hands were on his face, pulling him closer, closer, *closer*, and then they were kissing and Samuel could *breathe* again. It wasn't tentative. It wasn't hesitant. It was bold questions and equally bold answers, hands clenching in fabric, muscles tensing and relaxing under touches that had become foreign. It was Samuel yearning, Samuel testing, Samuel asking where they could go.

It was Davis putting a hand to Samuel's chest and giving him a gentle nudge. It was Davis looking at him sadly. It was Davis shaking his head, saying *no*.

No.

Samuel wanted to throw a tantrum, to stomp on the ground and yell *can I not even have this?!* He didn't know what he was doing. He now couldn't even explore what he didn't understand. He might have just royally messed up the healthiest part of his life. He closed his eyes and he willed himself to stay collected.

Then there was something cool against his forehead. He opened his eyes and was met with Davis's.

"I can't be Tommy," Davis whispered. "I can't do anything without being careful. I can't...have casual sex. I can't be friends with benefits."

Samuel flinched back. "Right. Because it's sinning, right? It's probably why Tommy got poss—"

"No," Davis said, holding Samuel's face, giving very little room for Samuel to look anywhere else. "No, Samuel. Sex is not sinning. That—none of that is relevant here."

"It's me," Samuel said. He didn't want to react, but he could feel himself trembling. He had already been shredded until he was raw. He wasn't sure how much of this he could take.

"If by you, you mean how I could never separate my feelings for you from our actions."

Samuel couldn't breathe.

Davis looked *guilty*. "I'm sorry, Samuel. I just...I tried. And I have to keep trying, to respect...I can't do it. Anything physical, with you just...It makes it difficult for me to get past it, okay? I don't want you to disappear, though. I don't want to scare you off because I can't control my emotions." He looked frantic at this point, wild in the eyes.

What had Samuel been doing all this time?

He took a step back, away from Davis, staring at him, unable to look away from his messy hair and bruised lips. He had done that. He wasn't sure how he felt about it except he was glad someone else hadn't.

He shook his head and rubbed his face. "I wasn't—asking for you to be a replacement fuck buddy," Samuel muttered through his fingers.

It took a moment for Davis to respond. "Then what were you asking?"

"I don't know," Samuel said, and then *he* felt

guilty, because the truth was simple: he knew. He didn't know if he loved Davis romantically, but he knew this moment wasn't about trying to find out. It was one simple thing: "A distraction."

He could see Davis's breath, how it was deep, slow, and controlled. It was the opposite of Samuel's.

"I can't distract you that way," Davis whispered, and there was a crack in his voice that controlled all of Samuel's attention. "I'm sorry."

"No, no, I—" Samuel said, taking another step back. "I'm sorry. I just—kisses are so…" Insignificant. That's what he thought, but if he said it, it would be a lie. If they were insignificant, Samuel wouldn't have been bothered by their first one years ago. He calmed his breathing enough to carefully say, "I don't know what it feels like to be romantically attracted to someone."

Davis's breathing became a little less controlled.

"You knew you didn't like Tommy that way," Davis said.

"Yes," he confirmed.

"And with me…?"

"I don't know," Samuel said truthfully. Then he took another step back, and then another until he was leaning against the back of the couch. "I don't know," he whispered.

"You don't have to," Davis said, taking a step away from the door and then going to sit next to Samuel. "But hey." He nudged his shoulder against Samuel's with a shy smile. "I'm willing to explore. But I'm also all for waiting and focusing on the other things life throws at us. Such as whatever you need a distraction from."

"My mother," Samuel said. "My family, really. I'm not living there anymore but I hear echoes of her words, of my dad's silence, and of my...sister."

Davis nodded slowly. He was looking at the ground and Samuel could see the gears turning. "Well, if you need a distraction, let me tell you about this *ghost* in an antique shop downtown," he said, and just like that, he captured Samuel's full attention with his words and with his hand gestures, and things were normal.

Samuel wondered if he wanted things to be different, or if they would always be the same. What they had was good. It never had to change. So, if Samuel could be content with it staying the way it was, there would be no point in exploring further.

Perhaps that was simply a thought for another day.

# CHAPTER FIFTY-TWO

Davis was *buzzing*.

Excitement, nerves, simple fear maybe, or pure thrill.

His lips felt very soft, half a day later.

He had not let himself think about Samuel as anything but a best friend ever since Samuel pushed him away. When Davis first kissed him. When Davis did not allow it to mean anything.

Now, he could not stop thinking about it.

"Davis," Daniel chastised. "You're supposed to be training to fight *demons*."

"Yes, sure," he said, nodding. "Demons." He fully admitted he wasn't listening.

This was the seventh day of work and honestly, they could not expect him to fully pay attention when he was worn out every day and he had been kissed and touched in a purely *intimate* way. Not that they would know the details, but still. It was so much different than the roles or games he played.

It hadn't meant what he wanted it to mean, but there were now *possibilities*.

He was not given time to process it. He wasn't able to sleep. He had laid in bed and thought of truly inappropriate things he could do with Samuel and he couldn't find himself regretting them.

He slouched over a file he wasn't reading, a report of something doing something. Maybe he was supposed to be updating it. He wasn't doing much.

"Vanessa," he heard Daniel say.

A hand touched his, smooth and small, and then Davis wasn't inside of the Headquarters' kitchen at all. He was looking at Vanessa and he was standing now, as if he had never been sitting. He could see past Vanessa, where there was a hallway not unlike the one his high school had. There were cork boards and glass cases lining the walls, spaced precisely every dozen feet or so.

He reached out his hand and felt glass.

"What?" Davis asked, putting his palms flat on the glass and *pushing*. It flipped open, swinging like a door, and Davis stumbled out and turned to see where he had been.

It was a display case, his name on a gold plate at the bottom.

He swirled to glare at Vanessa. "What the fuck is going on?"

"Let me reintroduce myself," Vanessa said, polite and clear through her accent. "I'm the Specialist of this squad. I have a very specific purpose."

"And that is?" Davis said, just to get her to talk.

He was a bit freaked out and impatient for an answer. She had seemed so innocent and sweet before.

"Possession," Vanessa said. Her smile was sharp but not cruel. "I'm here to teach you what to do if a demon possesses you."

"I already know," Davis said, crossing his arms. Still, he was nervous and glancing around, noticing each of the cases held a person standing inside them.

No, not just any person. They were all versions of *him*.

"You don't understand the mechanics," Vanessa explained. "And you push demons out. You need to know how to trap them."

Davis scrunched his eyebrows. "I think that would kind of defeat the purpose of preventing yourself from being possessed."

"You're not trying to prevent it," Vanessa said. "You're trying to *control* it long enough for you to…" She wavered. "Well, to do what Robbie and Cillian were brave enough to do."

"Robbie and Cillian…?" Davis asked hesitantly. He knew they both died. More specifically, he knew both died in the line of duty, if you could call killing yourself as such.

"Davis," Vanessa said gently. "How do you kill a demon?"

"I don't know, with a mental sword?" Davis said sarcastically.

Vanessa shook her head and sighed. "I can't believe—why do they leave this to *me*?" When she looked at Davis, he saw a childish annoyance turn into devastation. "There's only one way to kill a demon that we know of—not just exorcising it. Exorcising doesn't kill the demon; it just separates it from the Host. Killing a demon requires it to be trapped in an incompatible Host." She paused to make sure Davis understood what she had said so far, then continued when he nodded. "Exorcising makes the host incompatible, yes, but then the demon can escape. Therefore, Exorcists are taught to prevent them from escaping, and then becoming incompatible themselves." She glanced to the side. "Unfortunately, exorcisms aren't perfect, so Exorcists are taught to...make themselves incompatible."

"Please, just spit it out," Davis said. "What are you saying?"

"I'm saying dead bodies are incompatible Hosts, Davis," Vanessa snapped. Her eyes shone and she closed them for a moment. "If they can't be exorcised."

It took Davis a moment to fully understand what she meant.

Dead bodies were incompatible with demons. Andy had explained why she killed Tommy (or at least his physical body) to kill the demon. Robbie and Cillian died in the line of duty. Cillian was said to have committed suicide.

He was being told what to do if he was possessed.

When he had been possessed those years ago, he woke up to find two people dead.

Robbie was said to have saved him.

"Robbie Hodge committed suicide," Davis said slowly, his eyes wide as he stared at Vanessa, hoping she would deny it.

"He was originally the Nondefined of the Atlanta squad," Vanessa said. "He wasn't taught how to do exorcisms involving children. In fact, I don't think he was officially an Exorcist and he couldn't have still been a Nondefined anymore at that time. We don't know how he did it, but he was able to take the demon from you and into himself." She closed her eyes, perhaps out of respect. "He killed himself to kill the demon—to save you."

Davis shook his head. His breathing was shallow.

"I can't," he said breathily. "I can't do that. I can't kill myself. Not for this—I'm *drafted*. I don't want to die for this. I don't want to hurt..." Samuel. Calmly, he said, "Please get out of my head."

"But we haven't—"

"I don't care," Davis interrupted. "You've been without me until now. You can give me time to accept all of this."

Vanessa seemed to hesitate, looking down the hallway. Davis followed her gaze, where there was a door. Not a regular door, but one used for loading decks. It was covered in colorful graffiti.

"Is that the way out?" Davis asked.

"No. That's where we're supposed to go," Vanessa said. "But that can be another day."

"Another day," Davis agreed. He was going to leave it at that, to not push back at all, but...if Vanessa got to see into his mind, couldn't he see into hers? Shouldn't he be allowed that?

And so he tried. He felt the pull of his conscious and he tried to *push*.

Question marks. That's all there was. So many,

too many, creating and overtaking this space. It couldn't really be understood as a real place, just abstract concepts. The search for answers, pastel colors, loneliness, anger, fear.

"Nice try," Vanessa's voice rang out from all around. "But you're not like me."

Then, as if nothing happened, Davis was sitting at the kitchen table, the file still in front of him. He met Vanessa's wary gaze before looking around. Everyone else had left. The clock indicated hours had passed.

Davis's scar on his back was stinging.

"I want to go home," Davis whispered.

"Okay," Vanessa agreed, making it pretty clear with her expression she wanted to as well. It was then, when Davis was so close to her, that she did not simply look young. She *was* young. He wasn't even sure she eighteen.

He got up and couldn't even say goodbye before he left.

# CHAPTER FIFTY-THREE

Samuel received a text message from Davis requesting a ride. Samuel didn't hesitate to grab his keys.

He had not been asked to go to the Exorcist Headquarters, however. He had been asked to go to the Battery instead.

The Battery was a park that was surrounded by water on two perpendicular sides and historic buildings on the opposite ones. Samuel found Davis leaning over the railing at the corner, where he could see miles and miles of water. Samuel parked as closely as he could.

This, he knew, was close to where Cillian O'Dougherty had died. He avoided looking over the railing as he approached Davis.

"Is everything okay?" Samuel asked softly, taking a place next to his friend.

Davis's shoe scuffed the ground.

"It's supposed to be," he whispered. "They act like I should want to be an Exorcist. I feel like it's propaganda: 'You should be proud to serve your country!'" He held up a fist and jutted out his jaw. "You should fight and be willing to give your life for the cause!" His fist dropped and he looked at Samuel. "Is it so wrong I don't want to die for it?"

It sounded like a dream to Samuel. How he wished he could feel like he was doing something *important*. He understood that it was not Davis's dream.

"It's not wrong," Samuel said, because as he thought about it when adding Davis in as a factor, none of it seemed so shiny. "You shouldn't be forced to do that."

"And yet," Davis gestured to his jacket, "here I am, being told to—to do more than just risk my life." He stared at Samuel. "I was told—we're supposed to—we have to kill demons."

It took a while, with many pauses and breaths, for Davis to explain what he had been told. During the whole conversation, there was one word that stuck to Samuel's brain.

Suicide. Suicide. Suicide.

He gripped the railing until his knuckles were white. He felt queasy.

*I did it for you.*

It was only more proof towards his theory. His sister must have been possessed. Surely there would be records of some kind where he could look it up. Maybe that was the reason for her letter, instead of—

One thought cut off all others.

"You can't," Samuel blurted out. Then he wasn't holding the railing anymore, but holding onto Davis's arms just as tightly. "You can't do it. Promise me. Promise me you will never kill yourself."

Davis looked startled before his lips thinned. "I don't want to," he said, and Samuel thought he could relax until Davis added, "but I don't want to hurt others more."

Samuel dropped his hands. He rubbed his fingers and retreated inward. He didn't want to lose Davis. He couldn't. He couldn't be the cause.

"I don't," he started, then stopped. How could he convince Davis not to do it? How could he possibly get someone to listen to him?

He took a deep breath. Then he reached into his back pocket and took out a small book. Davis seemed to recognize it, even if Samuel never explained it.

"It's a wish list, mainly. Things that would make life easier." Samuel opened the front cover, showing a folded piece of paper. The edges were worn from nearly daily abuse. He handed it to Davis wordlessly.

He watched Davis unfold it, read it, and then understand it.

His eyes were blazing when they met Samuel's.

"This is your sister's suicide note," Davis said. It wasn't a question. Samuel didn't answer. "Why the hell are you carrying this with you all the time?"

"It's for me," Samuel said, "to remind me to keep living because she didn't. She..." He blinked. "I have to live for her now, too."

"No," Davis said. "You live for *yourself*." Samuel tried to speak, but Davis held up a finger. "No, listen to me. If you are struggling and need to find a reason to keep living, don't rely on a suicide letter that is *implying the blame is on you*. It is not. This is a *horrible* thing to do. This—" He waved his hand towards the letter. "This is like Robbie Hodge leaving me this note, like every person—like Rachael, whose father was Robbie's teammate, telling me I had to live my life based purely on honoring his death."

"Davis—"

"Yes, I dated the daughter of an Exorcist. Yes, it was awkward. Don't look at me like that, it's not the focus here. You," Davis pointed at Samuel, then gestured at all of him with both hands. "You are worth living for. For yourself. We shouldn't live our lives based on other people. That's why, even though I loved Rachael, I couldn't stay with her. She wanted me to live for her and for Robbie, but you *can't* rely on that. You have your own life that sucks, but your decisions should be based solely on what you want, not on others.

"So, in the same breath, you shouldn't die for someone else, either. That shouldn't be a thing. I get it, it is. More lives can be saved potentially, blah, blah, blah, but these decisions can't just be made for other's sakes. Call it selfishness, I don't care, but here is my thought: If I'm going to commit suicide, I'm going to do it *for myself*. That means that if I am in a situation where it's either I kill someone or myself, you *bet* I'm going to kill myself, because otherwise I will have an added guilt that *I know intimately*, that I never, ever, want to go through again. It took years of recovery and I would still wish for my father's life, or Robbie's life, to replace my own."

There was a pause where Davis caught his breath. "But that can't happen. They're dead and I wasn't given a choice. Now I have one. And I'm doing it because *I want you around.* I don't ever want to be the monster they think I am. *And,*" Davis continued, taking a deep but quick breath, "your sister didn't kill herself for you. She did it for herself. Suicide is a selfish thing, but *that alone doesn't mean it's bad.* The word 'selfish' has been given a negative connotation, but the truth is your life is in your hands and it's your final call what to do with it."

Davis had to take in more deep breaths. He seemed done. Maybe he was done. Samuel wasn't sure. He was just staring at Davis's flushed face in complete disbelief.

His heart hurt.

He didn't know what to believe.

"Suicide is not always selfish," Samuel croaked. "You said it yourself: You would do it for someone else. But some people genuinely think the world would be better without them." His voice was eerily calm, but he didn't care. He felt so cold. "Some think they would be relieving a burden. So, don't you dare—don't you dare lump them together and call them selfish, even if it's not bad. You can't know their reasons and you sure as hell can't know my sister's."

"I," Davis started, his breath still labored. He looked startled by Samuel's retort, then horrified. "I'm sorry. You're right. I don't know why others would do it. And I'm...sorry for the outburst. I was...thinking about it a lot. When I was younger. When Cillian...all of this—we're being surrounded by talk of someone taking their own life and it *bothers me.* I was just instructed to do it without being able to make that decision on my own, even if I would do it."

He quickly handed the letter back to Samuel, who pinched it between his fingers. Davis rubbed his face.

"Your sister. Gosh. I'm—so sorry for rambling and…not thinking…I don't get to have very many of those. Outbursts, whatever. I should have thought it through more. I…" He trailed off slowly.

Samuel couldn't look away from the letter.

"I don't want you to die," Samuel whispered, and his voice cracked. His heart was pounding, but he didn't feel like he had to be as defensive, so his shoulders slowly slumped. "I don't want to die, either."

Davis stood silently, putting his hands in his pockets and rocking slightly before saying, "Then let's turn it into something else. Let's make some house rules. Roommates usually have those, don't they?"

Samuel looked up at him.

"Rule number one: No dying," Davis said. His gaze was steady.

"Rule number two," Samuel said. "No putting yourself in situations where the other feels like they need to die."

Davis gave him the smallest of smiles. "Rule number three, no keeping suicide letters in small notebooks in your back pocket."

"Hey," Samuel said, shaking his head. "Not that one."

"Throw it away," he said, gesturing to the ocean.

"I am not polluting the ocean," Samuel said.

"Well, stop polluting your pocket," Davis countered.

Samuel paused and he flickered his eyes, thinking about the comment, wondering what he was supposed to do. This had not turned out how he thought it would.

"It's biodegradable," Samuel said instead, "but I'm not throwing it into the ocean."

"Then we'll burn it or perform some ritual of your choosing on it," Davis said. He brought up a hand and his thumb touched Samuel's cheek. "Don't carry around that baggage with you anymore."

"I don't want to let her go," Samuel said. *I don't want to let you go,* he thought.

"Then keep her somewhere else," Davis said. "Like something with a positive memory. Do you have something else?"

Samuel shook his head, then paused.

"Maybe at my parent's house," he said carefully, dreadfully.

"Then we'll get something else," Davis said. He didn't know what that entailed, but Samuel did, and it was terrifying. Still, he nodded, because quite honestly, Samuel was tired of being sad and scared. He wanted to smile when he thought of his sister. He wanted to live despite her death—or, perhaps, because of it.

"I was supposed to be comforting you," Samuel said, "not going through therapy."

Davis shrugged. "You helped me realize what I actually believe."

"I don't…necessarily agree with all of it," Samuel said, his words hesitant.

"Of course not," Davis said, giving a helpless laugh. "You wouldn't be your own person if you agreed with everything I thought." Then he winced. "But we can keep the two rules, right?"

"Yes," Samuel said. "I believe we can."

When they got home, Samuel took a dry erase board and put it on the refrigerator. In handwriting that mimicked Times New Roman, he wrote the two rules.

"Rule number three," he added once Davis retired to bed. It was two simple words:

"Be selfish."

Despite the conversation the day before, it was still difficult for Samuel to see Davis put on his jacket.

He knew what was underneath. The stretch of two purposeful scars. The memories of what someone else had wrongfully done to him. It felt too much like history was repeating itself.

"You should get a tattoo," Samuel said as they walked out of the apartment.

Davis laughed. "Of what? Where? I'm pretty sure they have enough to try to cover when I start acting again."

"They wouldn't," he said, "if you got it over your scars."

Davis paused and looked at Samuel.

"Take it back," Samuel said. "Make it yours. If I get rid of Abby's letter, you have to get rid of your baggage, too."

Davis blinked in the doorway of their apartment and Samuel ushered them out so no more bugs got in. It was as Samuel locked the door that Davis started laughing. When he looked at him, Davis's grin showed all of his white teeth.

"Deal."

# CHAPTER
# FIFTY-FOUR

Davis was avoiding Vanessa.

As much as this was true, and maybe he should have felt a little bad for it, at least he was doing it by fulfilling his first assignment: being Jenkins' translator.

Because demon possessions didn't happen as often as fires (and their main cause for concern in the city was currently contained within their team), the squad allowed for guests to come into the Headquarters on scheduled visits for 'pro tips' and counseling sessions. At least, that was how Davis viewed it. He was pretty sure it was a press conference in disguise because of the number of reporters. Paul simply called it a public meeting.

Jenkins would also be available to answer questions, which was why Davis was required to attend. Otherwise, he was sure he would be hiding in the closet to avoid them all. He was dreading it with every fiber of his body.

He helped set up the living room with folding chairs while Jenkins pulled a dark wood table along the back wall, which would serve as Paul's pedestal. The others simply got their own folding chairs. That, at least, was perfectly okay with Davis. He wanted to be on everyone else's level so he could become as invisible as possible.

Davis and stage fright had a very strange relationship of coming and going. When he first started acting, it nearly ended his career before it started. By college, it was completely gone. Now, his hands were sweating just from the thought of people looking at him. He blamed the jacket, as he always did, because it forced people to associate his name with 'demon' in some context.

He needed something else to occupy his mind.

Jenkins brought in a large portfolio bag, which he placed on the table as he pulled out a single canvas. All Davis saw at first was flashes of color—black, red, orange, more red, more black, sparks of yellow and dots of white.

"What is that?" Davis asked as he continued to unfold chairs.

"A painting," Jenkins said. He looked over his shoulder and grinned at Davis's unimpressed expression. Then he just shrugged. "They won't understand me, but they can understand art." He turned it so Davis could fully see the image. There was only one word came to Davis's mind at the sight of it: Hell.

In truth, it was a mix of realism and impressionism, with bold strokes of color here and precise lines there. Still, it was fiery, with something that might have been a volcano in the background. Reds and oranges leaked towards the foreground, where Davis realized there were actually splotches of green, and small, unspecific figures.

"It's the Creation, at least as passed on by demons," Jenkins said. He turned the painting to look at it himself. "A bit dreary and messy. My usual work is much more…precise."

"Yours," Davis said. "Usual?" he questioned. "Creation? Not to offend, but this doesn't look like the Garden of Eden. It's Hell."

Jenkins hummed. "Well, that is what Earth is like, isn't it? No, this is before the garden. This is part of the story of how demons and Angels were created." He looked at Davis. "You're going to have to retell this, so listen closely:

"When God was creating humans, He was interrupted," Jenkins explained. "There was too much chaos trying to ruin his work, so He sent off these unfinished creatures on their own mission, to do what he couldn't. They were to go to the Garden of Eden, where they would be completed. Only, it wasn't a garden then. It was corrupted. The only way for these creatures to finish God's work was to sacrifice themselves." He pointed to one of the volcanoes. "By going in there. The only problem was some of them didn't want to sacrifice themselves for God. They disputed it and caused more chaos. Still, when the time came, every one of those creatures split into three parts. Together, they combined to form man and beast. Separately, those who were willing to sacrifice themselves became Angels and those who weren't willing became demons."

"I haven't heard of this," Davis said. "Did you…is it just a theory?"

"It's mythology, as all religions are," Jenkins said, looking at the painting as if analyzing every part and judging any mistakes he found. "It could be true, it could be just a story, but we hear all sorts of things from demons. They carry knowledge that are from places we can't go. It's through demons we found out about the Offers."

"Was it really demons?" Davis asked, surprised. "I would think Angels would be the ones to tell that. You know, as messengers to try and make us work to be good or something?"

"No," Jenkins said. "No one's heard of an Angel's message except a few in the church with small claims. Nothing as solid as what demons have said, though. Nothing that the public was exposed to hearing." He looked away. There was a pause and a breath where Davis understood he was seeing something else, a memory or a nightmare. "It was broadcasted through a possessed man in the Exorcist channels."

Davis chilled. The thought of that being a possibility was terrifying. The man had to have been an Exorcist himself, and not low ranked at that, which meant…he didn't want to think about how strong that demon must have been.

"Why would demons reveal that?" Davis said. "How can anyone trust demons?"

"We don't, really. We just relay what we've been told," Jenkins said. He put the painting face down. "However, the demon went on to explain how demons are superior to Angels, how Angels will die out because they are too pretentious and too few, and how they—the demons—will rule the world." He said this with a completely straight face. "Seeing how Angels haven't really helped us, and I have a job for a reason, I can at least believe parts. Still..." Again, he had a faraway look. "I believe my wife is an Angel."

Davis believed people said things like that, the idea of them being ghosts or Angels, purely as a way to avoid accepting what death really was: the cessation of existence. He wasn't cruel enough to voice that in this moment, though.

"I'm sorry for your loss," Davis said instead. "For your family."

Jenkins shrugged it off. "It's illogical. My wife was possessed when she was..." His fingers tapped on the table. "When she died. Then my son? What happens to two-year-olds who can't even conceptualize sins and virtues? He was just...pure."

Davis already said what he could. He never even thought about children dying. He had been nine when he was possessed—clearly old enough to have sin. But one who was two years old? Could they receive offers? Was the only option true death?

"What are ghosts, then?" he asked.

"They're the in between," Jenkins said. "People who have died but haven't accepted an offer. They're only as strong as those who believe in them."

"That's why you believe your son is a ghost," Davis said gently.

Jenkins did not respond. He just looked at the folding chairs. "People are going to start arriving soon."

It was only when guests started spilling in that the other Exorcists started to arrive. Noah immediately took up the other seat next to Davis.

"I have to write speeches for these things," he whispered. He scanned the room. It would have seemed casual if his eyes didn't look so sharp. "You know, since I'm trained in grief counseling. Most of these people have lost someone to a possession."

"Could you, instead, by chance, give them a speech about how they shouldn't hate me?" Davis asked in a harsh whisper.

"They don't hate you."

"They're *glaring*."

"Have you considered their faces might just be stuck that way?" Noah laughed as Davis glared at him. "Don't worry, bud. We're here as a team. That includes you."

"Yeah, well, I sort of want to just puke. Or take a really long bathroom break. And quit."

Noah seemed only amused. "Social anxiety? Exposure issues? Stage fright? Sounds like I'm needed."

"That's the first psychological sounding thing you've said," Davis said, not sure whether to be offended by it or confused.

"I know," Noah said, grimacing. "It comes out sometimes. You have a completely different way of thinking when you know how thinking works. I try to avoid shrink talk."

"The last time I talked to a counselor they only told me 'good luck,'" Davis said.

"Then they needed to be fired," Noah said. "You need more than luck."

"Thanks," Davis drawled. Noah gave him a thumbs-up before walking a few steps away to greet a few uniformed officers. Watching their exchange made Watching their exchange made Davis realize two things: one, that the National guard was attending this gathering, and two, Noah had served. There was no other explanation for the shift in Noah's posture, going from relaxed to straight and formal.

Davis also recognized a few of the other guests. Rather, he saw the cheap I Can Graphic Design demon eye pins on their shirts and he immediately tensed.

"I'll keep an eye on them," Andy whispered to him in passing.

Davis glanced at her worriedly. "You know who they are?"

"The so-called 'Demon Offerings?' Annoyances," she said. "I won't let them approach you." Davis believed her.

At first, it was perfectly fine. There were wary glances, frightening glares, and complete avoidances of eye contact, but for the most part the audience that gathered was not there to chastise Davis. Even when he had to stand and translate questions for Jenkins—What is it like to be a Non-defined? How can we trust you? What made you this way? (Davis might have added his own response to some of them that were not so polite)—and then when he had to tell the story of the Creation (as told by demons) they did not ask about *him*.

"This is my town and I will not allow for it to be overrun by demons," Paul said in his speech regarding the state of Charleston.

Then Andy, when asked about basic tips for what to do if a loved one is possessed, said, "First, assume they're not. Second, don't be an idiot and deal with them yourself. Call us."

"I trust that Davis Turner will be able to fulfill the duty as Optic sufficiently," Daniel said in his own speech about leaving Charleston.

It was only after the other speeches were done that questions were directed towards Davis.

"Was the death of Tommy Rider caused by his proximity to Davis?" It was a reporter who asked, a microphone in hand, a camerawoman as his side.

None of them answered at first. Davis begged for Daniel not to answer because he was not good at reassuring anyone. Davis thought Paul would say something, as the Head of their squad, hoping it would be something positive, but he stayed quiet.

It was Andy who spoke up.

"Tommy Rider was a tragedy," she said, folding her arms and leaning back in her folding chair. "There has been a steady rise in possessions that can be traced over the last two decades. As you all are probably well aware, Davis has only been in Charles -ton for four years. While he himself is more suscep- tible to possessions, it is not his fault. Let's not forget who the real enemy is here." She leveled a glare with the reporter. "We, as humans, do not want to be- come worse than demons, do we?"

There was a slew of questions all asked at once, and Davis felt like throwing up, but then Paul must have addressed a single citizen because everyone quieted except for her.

"Demons took my child," she said, pleading. She

looked worse for wear, her hair matted under clipped extensions, her clothes dirtied and stained, her arms wrapped around her midsection. "I know they took my boy. Doesn't that make it your problem? Won't you find my child?"

When the others hesitated to speak, Jenkins was the one who said, "We don't normally investigate kidnappings..." and Davis looked at Daniel, who met his gaze. They knew why Jenkins spoke up. He was the only one of them who had been a parent.

"We'll look into it," Davis said before anyone else could say anything. He felt Daniel's glare on him but ignored it. "If you could, uh—if you could stay afterwards to give us information...anything to help us locate him."

She looked at Davis with wide eyes, as if unsure whether to trust him or not, but she seemed to be drained of any energy she had to protest, or not in any position to be picky on who she had to help her, so she closed her eyes and bowed her head.

"Thank you," she said. "His name is Darren. Darren Weiss. *Thank you.*"

After the talk, people shook Davis's hand, some grips tighter than others, some with harsh words, but Davis just looked each of them in the eye. He couldn't back down here. They had to be able to trust him and that meant he couldn't show them how terrified he was. This all was a responsibility he never wanted.

He wondered if they could impeach him.

Davis was not the one to talk to the woman. It was Vanessa. Kind, soft, young Vanessa, or at least that was persona she showed, who took down all the information she could and gave the woman every ounce of reassurance. That was how Davis had seen her and how she appeared now. She was the calm in the storm, the soft biscuit in a squad of knives. He realized that she needed to appear that way so the world didn't just see them all as weapons. Davis looked at his hands and wondered if he counted himself as one of those knives.

It was not until Paul told Davis to go home, to rest his body and mind, that anything truly bad happened. Davis was walking to a bus stop when a hand came from behind him, covering his mouth and pulling him back into the shadows between buildings.

His resolve hadn't changed in years. That was one thing he could rely on: he would never fight back.

# CHAPTER FIFTY-FIVE

With Davis constantly busy with Exorcist training and tired when he got home, Samuel was left to himself. Usually this was fine. That's what he should have been used to. Yet his life had merged seamlessly with Davis's, so it felt...unusual.

He was rather terrified of the idea of going to his parent's house. He texted Ashley, explaining in very simple terms what was going on: His parents weren't the greatest in the support department, he had to retrieve an item from their house, and he wanted someone to know where he was that wasn't Davis. He didn't explain further. He didn't know the words to.

Ashley sent back words of encouragement and the offer for him to visit her afterwards. She needed help packing. Having plans for after the visit made it seem less...morbid. It wouldn't be the death of him.

So, he took some time off in the afternoon and headed away from downtown Charleston to Mt. Pleasant. His parent's house didn't look intimidating from the outside. He had been the one to keep up with it, so he noticed the smallest of changes others probably wouldn't. The paint was slightly peeling on the stairs of the porch, the bushes were beginning to overgrow, and the windows were dusty from the Charleston wind. Samuel parked at the street. He could feel his nerves battling against his determination for change, to make something right out of this household.

He wanted Davis there.

After a few deep breaths, Samuel got out of his car.

Then an onslaught of every single negative possibility entered his thoughts and he stumbled back against his car, his hand on his chest as he tried to catch his breath, or calm his heart, or steady his quivering bones. His parents had never touched him—neither hit nor hugged him—and his thoughts regarding the house were so illogical he could only berate himself.

When he was in high school, his teacher had sent him to the counselor's office. It was because Samuel had a bruise on his cheek, but he had caused that through his own clumsiness. The counselor heard Samuel explain that no, his parents weren't hitting him, all while Samuel was pacing the room and rearranging the books into alphabetical order before apologizing for doing so. The counselor had listened and told Samuel he didn't do anything wrong. Then, Samuel was given tools. If he felt like there was an impending doom, he could create logic that would prevent it. Rituals. It was like good luck charms and bad omens. It was a fallacy, Samuel knew: a way to trick himself into believing he had control, but it worked for him. For now.

He locked and unlocked his car three times, and that meant it was safe. He walked up the stairs and back down the same amount. Three was his number. It was how many times he touched each corner of the door, and all of this was to ensure safety in passage. He didn't always need it this badly, hadn't really needed it in years, but he did now. Three was a holy number, and the God he believed in wouldn't let harm come to him unless it had a purpose in His plan. It was to make him stronger, not to destroy him.

He wondered why Angels didn't show themselves like demons did.

He knocked on the door, mentally counting: one, two, three.

He took in a breath. One, two, three. He held it. One, two, three. He let it out. One, two, three.

The door opened and his father stood there, looking at him. He was more beer belly than man. The worst thing he had done to Samuel was be absent—physically there, but mentally anywhere else.

He frowned at Samuel. Samuel ducked his head and avoided eye contact. His father stepped to the side.

"Who is it?" he heard his mother yell from the living room.

"Trickster," his dad said. Samuel slipped passed him, determined to just go upstairs and get what he needed and go. But he stopped. This wasn't how he wanted to do this. This wasn't making the change he needed.

Samuel straightened himself and walked into the living room, past a wall of crosses and paintings of Saints he was sure were judging him.

"It's me," he said. His father followed him before going to his chair and opening another beer. Samuel always suspected that was how his father dealt with his mother.

His mother was sitting in her own chair, looking thin and frail. She stood up as quickly as she could, which was not quickly at all, when she saw Samuel.

"Sammy," she said and held out her arms. Samuel looked at them and squinted. He did not understand the gesture at all. "Come here, don't deny your mother a hug. Not when you've finally come home."

He could hug her. He could allow himself to believe it was meant as a show of affection, of comfort, but he would be lying to himself. Just like on the phone, he heard endearments before criticism. All of it was false hope. It was the perfect exterior hiding the crumbling interior. He shook his head.

Samuel could make up an excuse. He could say *I don't like being touched* but, again, it would be a lie and it would not be a change.

His mother's expression shifted, her mouth frowning, her eyebrows scrunching, her eyes squinting. He could see part of himself in her then, but only a part.

"Still ungrateful, I see," she said. Her arms dropped. "I've already lost your sister. Look at what you've done to our family."

One, two, three. One, two, three. One, two, three.

He was never showing his mother Abby's letter.

"I've just come to get something, then I will leave you be," he said. He turned and walked away.

"Samuel Stewart, get back here! You need to apologize to us!"

He did not stop. He felt a different sort of power come from disobeying her. He realized there was really nothing more she could do to him. He was legal, he was financially independent, and he had been taught what support and love felt like.

He wished Davis was here, if only to see if his *mother* was possessed. Maybe it would make the underlying ache disappear. It had with Tommy.

He went up creaky stairs and turned not into his room, but into Abby's.

It was perfectly arranged. Everything in its place. Books were in order; the desk was organized so notebooks lined up with the corners. Organizers meant for drawers were on top for supplies. The bed was made. Clothes were either hung or in the dirty laundry basket. It was perfect. Abby had been perfect.

That was what both of them were taught, and what Samuel failed to live up to as far as his parents were concerned.

As Samuel stepped in and looked past the order, he realized that this was the room of a thirteen-year-old girl not yet in high school. She was ahead of her time, worrying about her grades, having a boyfriend, being popular. She had excelled in it all.

Samuel never understood her letter, but he always accepted it anyway. Now he questioned the motive and found it flawed. If she had thought her death benefited him in any way, she had been wrong. Things became only worse after she left.

Samuel wasn't sure if he was on a time limit or not, considering his mother's outcry, but he thought she would hesitate entering Abby's room, so he gave himself time. He sat on her bed. He laid down on it and looked at the ceiling, where glow-in-the-dark stars were stuck, all equal distance from each other. He got up and moved around, touching what he could, observing what he couldn't. He sat at her desk.

He clasped his hands and bowed his head. He believed, even with everything that happened, even if she had been possessed, that Abby was given the offer of an Angel. She must have. So, he thought of her and prayed to her, a simple thought: I love you. I miss you.

And he thought of what he missed. Of the times he had been in here, shushed when he giggled too loudly. When she read to him after their bedtime. When he showed her his first drawings. He remembered being nine years old and saying, "I want a boyfriend like yours," and she had smiled and said, "Well, mine's taken. We'll find you another one." She had never critiqued him. She had never discouraged him except if she wanted to protect him.

Samuel stood up from her desk. Davis had suggested finding something to remember the good, but there was nothing that he could hold onto that felt sufficient. He had the first ten years of his life with her. He would remember all that he could. That, he thought, would be enough.

He ignored his mother completely as he left the house, even though her words were full of hatred and accusation. He took out his phone and called Ashley.

"I'm heading over," he told her. "You have a lighter, right?"

"For my kitchen. Why?"

Samuel held Abby's letter tight in his fist. "I need to ceremoniously burn a letter."

His phone started vibrating to indicate another call was coming in, and he looked at the caller ID.

"Never mind," he said quickly to Ashley. "Change of plans."

# CHAPTER
# FIFTY-SIX

Someone was cursing.

It was so eerily similar to when he had been nine that for a moment, Davis didn't want to wake up. He didn't want to see his father's dead body. He didn't want to see his mother crying.

*Please tell me I didn't hurt anyone,* he pleaded to the world. *I'd rather never wake up.*

Then he felt the pain. It was *everywhere* and hurt even more if he moved, but it was nothing like what it felt like after a possession. It wasn't every single nerve being lit on fire. Nothing was as bad as that. So, he let out a sigh of relief and opened his eyes.

Silver and black.

Davis thought of Robbie Hodge, a man he never knew. He thought of Rachael, who loved him up until he showed his priorities and they didn't match up with her image. He wondered what she would think of him now that he was drafted.

The Exorcist jacket did not belong to Robbie, but Noah.

"Man," Noah said, his expression contained as

he looked over Davis, a flashlight shining over each eye. "Why'd you have to get yourself beat up? I'm supposed to help you when *demons* are involved, not people. I gotta sleep when I can, you know."

"They ignored my warning," Andy said, who was standing over them, arms crossed. "People are sometimes worse than demons."

With Noah's help, Davis sat up, if painfully. He didn't remember much, and he wouldn't even try to remember faces, but he now knew what happened.

"They were scared," Davis whispered, putting a hand to his chest. It was a little difficult to breathe, but not painfully so. He felt Noah's fingers pressing in his side and he stilled, closing his eyes at the pain and trying his best not to wince.

"Scared or not, we'll find them," Andy said, scowling. She looked *dangerous*, even more so than when he saw her in action. She was the Cleanser for a reason. In the same thought, he *couldn't* see Samuel looking anything like that. He wasn't sure Samuel was capable of being dangerous.

"Nothing seems to be broken or ruptured," Noah said. "Just bruised. You're lucky." Davis gave him a look. "Well, sort of. At least they avoided your pretty face." Noah took Davis's chin and moved it so he could back up his words. "Yup."

Davis let out a small breath hearing that. He didn't want anything permanent to come from the next two years, no matter how likely it was. He was going to be a performer, dammit, and he didn't want there to be any extra reasons for him to be denied a part.

"We called your emergency contact," Andy

said. "He should be at the house."

"You weren't out long, but I want you to stay with us tonight," Noah said. "I'd rather you be in the hospital, but I don't trust the doctor on staff right now. Downright dirtball. Thinks some people deserve to die. 'Course he can't say that, but he prioritizes…"

Davis clapped Noah's shoulder.

"Thank you," he said, knowing all too well his name would be recognized. Hospitals were, perhaps ironically, one of the most dangerous places for him.

Noah gave a laugh and together they stood. "Can you walk?"

Davis took a hesitant step and nodded. His midsection hurt like a bitch, and his left upper arm hurt as well, but that had taken most of the damage—kicks. No punches, just kicks.

"You could have fought back," Andy said as they slowly walked out from between the houses and towards the Headquarters. "I know you could have. Even without the training you could have by brute alone."

"No, I couldn't have," Davis muttered. He wasn't *that* fit, not enough to take on multiple people, and he had stomped down his 'fight or flight' instinct long ago. "I can never be what they think I am."

"You can have some *sense*," Andy retorted.

"Yeah? If I fought back, what do you think would have happened?" Davis snapped back. "This is *nothing*. Imagine what would have happened if I retaliated. Either they would have tried *harder* or they could claim *I* attacked *them*. My bet is on the latter—in fact, my bet is that was their whole plan. They want a reason to prove Tommy's death was my fault so they can sleep better at night with me locked up."

"We won't let that happen," Noah said. "We know how demons work."

Davis glared at Noah. "If I ever get possessed and hurt someone, you *better* lock me up."

Noah looked ready to protest, but Andy cut him off. "If *you* hurt someone, I'll swallow the bloody key."

"Good," Davis said, then sighed. Wanting to ignore how terrifying Andy was, he focused on where they were going. Then he stopped.

"Wait. Who did I put down as my emergency contact?"

His suspicion was confirmed once they reached the Headquarters and he saw Samuel's Civic in the front, along with a jeep he didn't recognize.

"Shit," Davis muttered as he rubbed his face. It wasn't that he didn't want to see Samuel (quite the opposite, really) but that he didn't want to stress him further than he already was.

When they walked inside, there Samuel was, sitting at the kitchen table with a mug held tightly in his hands. He was wearing his more comfortable clothes, a large sweater that fell off one shoulder and his favorite white skinny jeans, his hair mostly covered by a white beanie. Surprisingly, Ashley was sitting with him, wearing a crop top with the word "Sugar" written on it in pink and a skirt that matched the color. Both turned away from Paul to watch as Davis entered.

He watched as Samuel's eyes traced over him and was glad nothing was really visible. Instead of commenting on Davis's condition, Samuel asked,

"I'm your emergency contact?"

"Who else?" Davis responded with a shrug. Looking at Samuel, Davis noticed something that made him smile. He was tapping his fingers together. It wasn't rhythmic, but almost like a tune. He was *excited*. Of course he would be. He was in the Exorcist Headquarters, the place where he wanted to work since he was a kid. "You can be excited, you know. Giggle, even, if you must."

Samuel covered his mouth, and a grin, with his hand.

"Shut up," he said, but his eyes held no malice.

"You're okay?" Ashley asked. "They said you were injured."

"Yeah," Davis mumbled, looking away. "Just some people trying to goad me."

"You still got knocked out," Noah said helpfully. "Very briefly, but you can never be too careful." Davis could not remember gaining a head injury, which might have been something to be concerned about, but he wasn't. He was mostly tired.

"Goad?" Samuel asked, dropping his hand. He wasn't grinning anymore. "Who were they?"

"I don't know," Davis said, which was a partial truth. He had seen them at the gathering, but he didn't know their names. "Don't worry about it, okay? They probably did it for some sense of justice. Let them take from it what they will."

He saw Noah and Andy look at Paul. He had been silent thus far and looked awfully tired himself.

"It will be dealt with respectfully," Paul said calmly. "Noah, what's your diagnosis?"

Noah looked at Davis, then at his friends before

responding. "Enough to be watched overnight and given a few days of rest, but it's nothing serious—yet. We should watch for internal bleeding. We can't know the full extent without taking him to the hospital."

Paul's gray eyes caught Davis's. "And you won't go to the hospital?"

"Not if it can be avoided," Davis said. "Sir," he added.

"Why do you have to be so goddamn stubborn?" Andy growled towards Davis. "Is this a guy thing? Avoiding hospitals? Suffering in silence? Trying to be the tough guy? It's stupid. What use are you to us if it gets worse?"

"Well, considering I don't want to be here anyway and you can't legally force me to go to the hospital..." Davis said, crossing his arms, and then regretting it as he was reminded of his bruising.

"I could force you, legally," Andy said. "As long as everyone closed their eyes."

"He's staying here," Noah said. "I'll watch him. I'm an expert, remember? This was by my recommendation. Trust your teammates, Andy."

Paul was looking at Noah. "Is Dr. Fieldsmen working at the hospital?"

"Yes," Noah said simply with a clear expression of distaste.

"Then I trust your judgement," Paul said.

Andy did not look pleased by this result, but she backed down.

"Could I," Samuel started, then stopped. He looked hesitant. "I'd like to keep an eye on him, too. He's my roommate. I'd like to help."

"Roommate," Andy said. "Right." She raised an eyebrow.

"That is true," Ashley said, who looked rather uncomfortable as the only one there not in, or wanting to be in, a black and silver jacket. Still, she was a fiery spirit and didn't back down. "If the only thing you can do is insult and mock, I don't see how you're qualified for your position."

Andy looked *furious*, her eyes ablaze and her gloves creaking as her fists tightened. "Go suck a—"

"Andy," Paul said calmly.

"—fuck," Andy finished, and her face contorted as if she were either conflicted by Paul calling her out or by how strange her insult came out. She breathed out through her nose, and with it seemed to go most of her anger. She said nothing more, just leaned against the wall and flexed her hands as if checking her gloves.

Samuel looked at her with a mixed expression. She was, after all, the one who ended Tommy's life, whether he was actually still alive or not, but she also saved *him*. Davis still could feel the exact conflict inside himself.

"You can stay here," Paul said in answer to Samuel. "I'm sure Noah would appreciate your help."

"Anything," Samuel blurted out, then flushed and Davis smiled. His eagerness made this all seem a little more bearable.

Noah nudged Davis with an elbow. "Good friend you have there." He winked at Samuel in a way that said *I got you*. "Try to keep up with me, alright?"

Wide eyed, Samuel nodded. "Anything you

need."

"Oh, I'm gonna be spoiled with this one," Noah said, giving a laugh before jerking his head away. "Come on, I'll teach you some basics of things to look out for."

Samuel practically leapt out of his seat to follow Noah, giving Davis a look that was somewhere between "Oh my god, is this happening?" and "I don't look too eager, right?" Davis waggled his eyebrows in return.

"I don't think I've ever seen Samuel like that," Ashley said, "and I worked directly with him for a year."

"He really wanted to be an Exorcist," Davis explained. "He should have been the one drafted."

"He's not an Optic," Andy butted in. Davis's conflict over her was leaning towards murderous.

"Well, he was worried sick. You should have seen him," Ashley said, brushing her hand through her purple locks. "He thought of *everything*. We took separate cars just in case. Did you know he has a full medical kit in his car? He wiped down this whole table with disinfectant, too. We weren't sure how bad it would be."

None of this was very surprising, but it was also nice to know Samuel was worried before he was otherwise distracted by the Headquarters. Davis smiled. "That's all he did?"

"No," Ashley said, wide-eyed. "He ran through a yellow light."

Davis let out the beginnings of a laugh before he stopped, his muscles clenching painfully but he grinned through it.

"Samuel being extreme," he said. "I'm very touched." And he was.

It wasn't long after that when Ashley left, saying she had a lot of packing to do. She made it seem like she was packing a mansion by this point, but her move was just two weeks away. Davis was escorted into the guest room, which was tidy and held too much furniture. There was a twin bed tucked in a corner and an air mattress on the ground.

"I'll be the one keeping a close eye on you all night," Samuel said in the doorway. "Apparently, that's the job they give assistants."

"Is that what you are?" Davis said, gently sitting on the bed. "Noah's new assistant?"

"Just for tonight," Samuel said. He smiled shyly. "Even if it's just for one night, it's...pretty cool. I like the idea of helping you in some way. That is, helping anyone."

Davis laid down with some difficulty and let out a slow sigh when he was horizontal. He cursed the fact he still had on all his clothes but there was no way he was going to move now. So, he turned his head and looked at Samuel.

"You always help me," he said. "You don't have to be an Exorcist to help people."

"I know." Samuel was smart enough to take off his socks and jeans before getting on the air mattress. Davis looked at the popcorn ceiling. "People pick what fundraisers they give to, right? Their cancers to fight? They have their battles. Demons are what I picked. I just have to find a way to do that as...me."

"You'll figure it out," Davis said confidently.

"But...why did you pick demons and not...well..."

"I'm not fragile, Davis," Samuel said. "You can say it."

"I know, I just..." He paused. "Why not suicide prevention?"

Samuel took his hat off, placing it on top of his folded clothes and sighed.

"I almost burned her letter," he whispered. "I went back to my parent's house. You know, to find something else. I'm not convinced she—my own sister—would have left a note like that. And my mother—well, let's just say I've never been truly convinced demons haven't played a part in my life." He laid down with practiced ease. Davis usually forgot Samuel still had an air mattress for a bed back at their apartment. He was so courteous about when he inflated it.

"Hey," Davis said. He waited until Samuel turned to look at him. "I'm really proud of you for going back there."

Samuel ducked his head so his arm was hiding most of his face. "Yeah, well, when I actually burn the letter, it just means you have to get your tattoo. You better get ready."

"More pain. Yay," Davis said, not hiding his sarcasm. But really, he was looking forward to it.

"Maybe in a few days," Samuel said. "It will probably take multiple trips anyway. I can burn the letter before we go."

That was something Davis definitely did not look forward to doing. "It'll be worth it," he said, if also trying to convince himself.

"It will," Samuel agreed. "Now, sleep while you

can. It's going to be a long night."
It hardly felt like a night at all.

# CHAPTER FIFTY-SEVEN

When Noah cleared Davis in the morning, Samuel was equally relieved and disappointed. As the hours passed, the shine wore off enough for his chest to tighten. Oh, how badly he yearned for his own black and silver jacket. This was like getting a taste of something he could never have. Being around the other Exorcists and working with Noah made it abundantly clear exactly how unqualified he was, and how far away from *being* qualified he was.

Of course, after Noah checked him, Davis immediately fell back asleep. Samuel woke him up at seven.

"Fuck my life," Davis said, batting Samuel away. "Let me sleep."

"I have to go to work, which means I have to go back to the apartment first," Samuel said. He felt odd watching Davis like this. It wasn't fondness, necessarily. It was like an unreachable itch. "Do you want me to bring you anything? A change of clothes?"

Davis must have not been fully awake yet. He was slow to respond, even as he sat up with his eyes still closed. When he blinked them open, he finally said, "No. I have an extra—pair? Set?—there are clothes in my bag. You're leaving now?"

"Yes," Samuel said, wishing he could take his time, but he needed a shower and he couldn't take one here comfortably. He felt so hot and disjointed, as if he had slept with a fever.

"Good. Then I can sleep," Davis said, falling back down on the bed. Samuel threw a pillow roughly, making Davis startle enough to glare. "I hate you right now."

"Sure you do," Samuel said, patting his pockets twice to check he had everything, then dug his hands in them to triple check. "Make sure you get up. I don't want to hear you slept the day away because you're lazy." He headed for the door.

"What? No goodbye kiss?" Davis said, mocking a kiss with pursed lips. Samuel paused and looked back at him. Davis rolled his eyes but was smiling fondly. "I'm kidding. I'll see you later."

Samuel left with his messenger bag. It was early enough he wasn't sure if others would be awake, so he descended the stairs quietly.

"Samuel."

He flinched at his name. He closed his eyes as he reminded himself he wasn't doing anything wrong. There wasn't anything to be anxious about. It took another moment to mentally berate and then re-assure himself before he opened his eyes and looked up.

"I was just finishing up a prayer," Paul said. He was already in his uniform, the jacket buttoned up to his neck. He had a mug of coffee in one hand and a book in the other. "You look nervous."

Samuel wondered if he looked *suspicious* and Paul was just being nice. He could think of many things someone could do if they were inside the Exorcist Headquarters, but he didn't understand why. He wasn't even sure the front door was locked. Surely it had to be, if only to keep possessed people out. Were demons even aware enough to know their enemy? Samuel caught himself derailing and rubbed his hands together.

"Sorry. I just need to get to my apartment before work," he explained, his thumb kneading the inside of his palm.

Paul seemed to accept this easily enough. His posture was of complete calm with his shoulders back and weight shifted onto one leg. He hadn't even seemed tense when Davis was brought in. Samuel wondered what his secret was.

"Do you have a moment or are you running late?" he asked.

Weighing his options (and checking his watch), Samuel said, "I have a moment."

Paul inclined his head and they both moved into the kitchen, where Paul pulled out a chair for Samuel before sitting across from him. Samuel took his seat stiffly with his hands tucked under his thighs. It was silent for a moment and Samuel wondered if he was actually in trouble for something. Had he accidentally heard something he shouldn't have? Seen something? Interrupted something without knowing?

"Samuel," Paul cut off his thoughts. Samuel forced himself to make eye contact. "You haven't done anything wrong. Quite the opposite, actually."

Knitting his eyebrows together, Samuel stayed quiet, listening, but still tense.

"Your name has been given to me by more than one person," Paul explained. He leaned back in his chair and was just *watching*. "I recognized your name when Daniel first mentioned it a few years ago."

This held Samuel's attention. He knew Davis talked to Daniel about him but wasn't sure it actually reached Paul or that it would result in anything. Samuel shifted anxiously.

"And?"

"And you applied to the Cleanser Academy," Paul said, leaning forward and resting his arms on the table. "You've wanted to be an Exorcist for a very long time."

"Yes," Samuel said, because it was truer than anything he knew. "Ever since I was little. I still do."

"The odd thing is," Paul said, "they didn't deny your application because you weren't qualified."

"What? Then why?" Samuel asked. He could feel his heart in his chest when before it had been unnoticeable. Years of feeling like he wasn't enough, and that wasn't it?

"It didn't get past initial submission," Paul said. He rubbed his mouth, the only sign he wasn't completely without concern. "It was pulled right away because of what happened to your sister."

"But," Samuel said, but found the words stuck. His

sister, the reason he *wanted* to be an Exorcist, was also the reason he *couldn't* be one? He rubbed the back of his neck. In a small voice, he simply said, "She died."

"Suicide," Paul said. He said it easily, like it was just another fact. Samuel wasn't sure how to feel about it. "You found her."

Having *just* been planning to burn her suicide letter, Samuel did not feel he was as ready to talk about this as he should have been. He hadn't done it yet. His stomach still twisted, and he still heard her voice: *I did it for you.*

"I think she might have been possessed," he said, trying to force himself to think instead of feel. "I was young, but it seems so strange she would...that she..." He tried to gather himself. He needed to pass this. He had to conquer it. There was a still a block. It still hurt in his heart. He wondered if that ever went away. It hadn't even gone numb in more than a decade.

"You don't have to talk about that," Paul said softly. "I didn't ask for your time to bring up bad memories." Samuel looked up from the table. "I think you could be an excellent Exorcist someday, Samuel."

Samuel was caught off guard. He gaped. He was always so carefully guarded it seemed impossible, but here he was, his eyes wide, his mouth open, and he knew words were trying to come out and were instead just sounds that made no sense. He cleared his throat and ducked his head in embarrassment. He dared not try to speak.

"You have the passion," Paul said, as if continuing his previous words with no pause. "The skills can be learned. Your friend is a valuable asset, but I'm sure you know how much he doesn't want to be here. Having someone that does is invaluable."

"He was drafted," Samuel whispered, glancing behind him, up to where the bypass was. He couldn't see if the door was still closed or not. He settled back to face Paul. "Even if he wanted to—which he didn't—it's not as much fun being forced to do something."

"Exactly," Paul said. "That's why I'm against the draft."

Surprise. Confusion. Anger.

"Then *why did you draft him*?" Samuel asked in a harsh whisper.

"Because having him may save dozens of lives," Paul said calmly. "If we had him earlier, we might have been able to save Tommy."

"Don't," Samuel said. "Don't bring Tommy into this. Andy was there and she couldn't do anything. Davis—Davis *was* there."

"He wasn't trained," Paul said, which didn't help calm Samuel's mood. "He still isn't. I understand my superior's reason for the draft, even if I don't agree with it. This is why people like you, who want to be an Exorcist, are so important."

"Well there's nothing I can do now. I don't qualify, and I'm too old for the Academy."

"Don't give up hope, Samuel," Paul said. "When you are qualified, we'll make a place for you here."

"I," Samuel started, "have to go." He stood. His heart wanted to stay. He wasn't sure what he was doing. He felt much too warm.

Paul bowed his head. "Good luck, Samuel."

"Thanks," Samuel murmured as he rose from his seat and quickly left.

When he reached his car, he got inside, turned the keys in the ignition, put the car into drive, and couldn't move his foot from the brake. He sat there, just outside the Exorcist Headquarters, and wondered if he was destroying his own dream.

# CHAPTER
# FIFTY-EIGHT

Thirty-six hours was considered more than enough time for Davis to recover from his injuries, and thus, was forced back into his position. He was pulled from bed and into the backyard of Jenkins' house with an abdomen that was screaming at him.

"You don't get forever to recover," Andy said, standing a few feet from him with Daniel at her side. "You shouldn't need any. Like I told you before, you could have protected yourself and we have to reteach you that instinct."

"I don't want to hurt anyone," Davis said, gritting his teeth with his arm holding his midsection for protection. Under his shirt revealed a rainbow of color, but he knew bruises tended to look worse than they were. Still, he thought that should be enough to keep him in bed. That, or the wait for one decent night of sleep.

"If you don't hurt them, they might kill you," Andy

said as she pulled on her gloves.

"Let them," Davis snapped. "I'd rather be dead than prove to them they're right about me."

"Okay, so you die," Daniel cut in before Andy could. "Then what? You've left your team one man down. They're the next dead. That's on you."

"Why should I care? I'll be dead," Davis grumbled.

"You care because of who you are," Daniel said. "If you won't hurt them, you have to at least learn to defend yourself well enough. Killing is easy compared to keeping them alive, but you won't be able to get there if you keep letting yourself get nearly killed."

Davis was too tired to ignore his annoyance.

"Then come on," he said, dropping his arm and clenching his hand into a fist. "Teach me."

He was surprised when Andy didn't try to just start punching him. Instead, she walked up to him and grabbed his arm. When Davis tried to pull it back, she held it steady.

"Chill," she said. "You have no experience in sparring. We're here to teach you how to *not* get hurt. Meaning…" She patted Davis's fist with an open palm. "We have to teach you how to punch. Open your hand—not all the way, keep your fingers curled. Right." She pressed her thumb into the ball of his palm. "If you can, always punch with an open fist, otherwise you might break your hand, or at least hurt it. Remember your knuckles? Let's avoid that. This is the way to deliver the most damage to your opponent instead of yourself."

Davis stared at his hand and tried to image

punching like that. It was a strange image. He clenched his jaw and nodded.

"Block with your arms," Andy said, grabbing his elbow and giving it a shake. "Hold it. Don't let it be loose. Let your legs be loose. They get you away. Your arms and hands are your only guaranteed weapons."

However much Davis hated being in his position, and however much he was hurting, after a while he couldn't deny his interest in what Andy was teaching him. Attacks were defenses, weak spots were strengths. Her training technique involved manipulating Davis's body in a way that wasn't always comfortable, but allowed him to feel the meaning of the words she used.

"We want you to survive this," Andy said after a while. "We'll find someone to take your place, so survive until then. We'll protect you. Trust us to protect you—from demons and from people."

Davis held her gaze.

"Okay," he said. "You can't trust I'll be able to kill someone, though, possessed or not."

"That's why I have a job," Andy said. "I do the dirty work, remember?"

She reached her hand up and Davis flinched away as it neared his ear, but he forced himself to stop. They paused, their eyes locked, and then Andy put her fingers through his hair.

"One more thing." She grabbed the hair on the back of his head and *pulled*, forcing him to bend back awkwardly and flail as he tried to get out of her hold. "Don't think I'll coddle you."

"Ow. *Ow*, fine!" Davis said, grabbing her arm

and digging his nails into her skin. He twisted himself and her arm enough to pull away, and stumbled a few steps away from her. He held his abdomen and the back of his head. "Shit," he huffed.

"Oh? Not ready to spar yet?" Andy mocked. "Still ready to get beaten?"

"No," Davis said, taking another step back. "I'm injured. I don't want to make it worse. Like you said: I want to survive this. I won't if I get pummeled in a *spar* and am too weak to do anything when we have field work."

"Ah, so he learns," Andy said, dropping her hands to her hips. Davis scowled at her. "Hey, you might be doing this to survive a job you don't like, but we're doing it so *others* survive. Get over it. Work the two years. Survive the two years. Then you can get out."

Davis watched Andy take off her gloves and, without another word, enter the house. Davis collapsed onto the ground, his breathing shallow as he resisted the urge to curl into the fetal position. It *was* slightly embarrassing how little he could do now.

"She's not a bad teacher," Daniel said as he approached Davis.

"No," Davis admitted. He rubbed his face and then looked at Daniel. "You were drafted, weren't you? Why did you stay? Why didn't you get out after your two years?"

"I had nothing else," Daniel said, "and then there was a boy named Davis Turner who was possessed."

"Ha. Ha," Davis said with narrowed eyes.

"I lost a teammate then," Daniel continued, and Davis realized he was being serious. He felt the familiar pang of guilt. "Gained another."

"He was a Nondefined, right?" Davis asked.

"Yes," Daniel said. "Although not in the end. I was his Optic during his time as a Nondefined. Then, he Found himself." He frowned, his eyes downcast. "When a Nondefined is…cured, for lack of a better word, they are no longer allowed to be an Exorcist and the position is filled by another. However, Robbie was…passionate. Being an Exorcist ended up being what saved him—only for it to be taken away." He looked up at Davis. "He was determined to show he could still be an Exorcist. That's why he went to your house."

"Where he died," Davis whispered.

"Yes. He did exactly what he wanted to do. He saved your life." Daniel put a hand on Davis's hair and ruffled it, much to Davis's dismay. "I became the Head soon after and I followed the model he had pitched: prevention, protection, defense. We might not know how he had been able to save you on his own, but he did it, and there has only been one casualty in the team since."

Davis batted Daniel's hand away. "Well, I wouldn't want to take over Paul's position. I want to be a performer."

"And imagine the skills you'll learn here," Daniel said, holding out his hand and helping Davis up. "Stage combat, right? You'll be very practiced in Capoeira."

"Sure," Davis said, even though that was not at all how it worked.

"Let's get you inside and check on your bruises," Daniel said, leading them inside.

"Hey, Daniel?" Davis asked as Daniel opened the sliding glass door. "That one casualty. Who was it?"

Daniel looked at him and all playfulness disappeared from his features. "Benjamin Taylor."

The name struck hard. Rachael never told Davis her father had died. But then, it wasn't her place to anymore.

"How?" Davis asked.

"As an Exorcist," Daniel said simply. "That's all you need to know."

# CHAPTER FIFTY-NINE

Samuel was getting frustrated. Extremely so. He thought of numerous things it could be: work was at a stressful peak, he had no time for his personal projects, and he was frustrated with his worry over Davis.

It had been more than a week since Davis was attacked and he seemed nearly back to normal, so that couldn't be it. Maybe it was the idea that he couldn't be an Exorcist. Maybe it was Paul's words that were meant to be hopeful. But he didn't like the idea of any of this being the reason. He was always stressed, but he never felt like *this*. What was it? What was different?

He was both embarrassed by and accepting of the answer: sex. He had never gone so long without it. It didn't help he was confusingly attracted to his roommate, but that could be explained away by the teasing and his physical needs not being met as well. So, making the decision that Davis wasn't going home until late that night, Samuel went to a bar.

He hesitated before going inside, wondering if he should tell Davis where he was, or even going so far as to ask if this was okay. But of course it was okay. They were independent adults. He went inside.

There was a band playing live music, setting a different atmosphere than if the regular pop playlist was playing. People paid attention to live bands. Well, if they were good, and this one was. Samuel sat on a stool at the bar, one of many that were free, and he listened as he sipped on a beer.

What was he doing here?

A guy walked by, topless, and Samuel's eyes followed. That. That was why he was here. He was out of practice. Tommy had been so easy and consistent. He felt a pang in his chest, feeling as if he had never treated Tommy fairly. He knew there wasn't a complete lack of feelings involved, and he let it go on.

He swallowed and closed his eyes as he remembered Tommy—no, the demon—telling him what he wanted. Maybe that was a sexy situation for some, but not for him. Not for them.

He didn't normally let himself remember what happened, or what almost happened, the day of Tommy's death and he wasn't going to now. Still, he felt a bit ill remembering why exactly he hadn't come back to a bar or club since.

A guy sat heavily in the stool next to him and pointed at Samuel's beer before holding up two fingers to the bartender. He had a wicked smile that promised talent in the bedroom and Samuel was having trouble focusing on anything else. Good. That was good.

"Usually people take their hats off indoors," the guy said, glancing toward Samuel's newsboy cap. "But you look cute with it. Your hair..." His hand brushed down Samuel's face to behind his ear, where his hair was just barely curled around his hat. The touch was warm, the guy's fingers were large and calloused. Samuel was very aware he was being treated as if he were feminine. Usually that was something he could play along with. A lay was a lay. Samuel's heart was never really into sex, just like it wasn't with food, until...

Samuel could talk about his hair. How it was really just wavy but cut so it looked like it would curl. He could put a few more gestures into his speech, bring in his knowledge of fashion, play up the twink in him. That would surely earn him a trip into this guy's pants.

"Military?" he asked instead, looking at the guy's shaved head, then his sun-kissed skin, tattoos, and large build. "Navy."

The guy seemed impressed. Samuel did not think it was that impressive of an observation, but he had higher standards for himself than others.

"You familiar with it?" the guy asked.

"I considered joining once," Samuel said honestly. He was not too fond of being in large bodies of water. He did not consider it twice.

Samuel's comment was enough to get the guy interested. He started talking about his daily schedule, strange experiences, and Samuel actually found he liked his sense of humor.

Samuel could easily sleep with him. Just one

comment about it, one suggestion, and that would be enough. Samuel's body would be very pleased by that.

It felt very wrong everywhere else.

Being very bad at social interaction that didn't involve getting someone to sleep with him, Samuel awkwardly fumbled in his pocket as if his cell phone was going off, and subtly turned the vibrate on and off so that it buzzed.

"Ah, sorry," he said to the guy. "I have to go."

It was much easier to seem like he had a reason to go besides simply wanting to. He didn't feel like trying to spare feelings with words at the moment. He closed his tab, making sure to pay for the drink the guy had given him. The guy seemed disappointed but accepting (and still intrigued) as Samuel left.

He thought maybe it was strange the only thing he missed from the bar was the music. The rest felt so different now. He knew he would have been able to stay and have a very successful night, but...he didn't want to.

He took a walk along the more crowded streets to work off the beers before he made his way to his car with a newly emptied water bottle. Because he didn't trust others driving him, he first conducted every single test he could think of to assess his sobriety. Then Samuel sat in his car for another hour, all before making the decision he would drive cautiously and slowly as he went back to the apartment.

# CHAPTER SIXTY

It was a breath of relief when Samuel walked into the apartment. Davis wasn't exactly glancing at the clock every minute, as much as he was doing exactly that and convincing himself it was for an entirely different reason that did not exist. He tried to look casual about waiting up, with a book in his lap and his feet crossed over the couch's armrest. He must have looked eager, still, because Samuel stopped and loomed over the back of the couch.

"I went out," Samuel said, his eyes focused and observational. "To a bar."

Davis thought he was maybe supposed to react a certain way, but he wasn't sure. His stomach kind of flipped, but not from anxiety. He sat up and gave Samuel a half smile.

"Trying to get laid? How'd it go?"

Samuel walked around the couch and sat next to Davis. He looked at his own hands, where he was fiddling with his fingers. "I wouldn't talk about it knowing how you feel about me. That's a bit cruel."

"But you are talking about it," Davis said because Samuel wasn't wrong. He turned to better see Samuel and tucked his long legs under himself. "Is it weird? I don't want you to avoid talking ab—"

Samuel kissed him. It was a kiss made purposefully to shut him up. Davis blinked when Samuel pulled back. He had been so focused on everything else, so determined to not even let himself feel the things he was, this seemed almost crueler than hearing about Samuel's sex life that didn't involve him. He was about to voice this when Samuel kissed him *again*. The kiss staggered Davis's train of thought, as if all his brain power needed to be used to remember to breathe. He felt the kiss travel through his body and he knew he was leaning forward, as if just to catch the tail end of a dream.

He pulled back when he realized it was real.

"Samuel," he whispered. "We talked about this."

"We talked about friends with benefits," Samuel said. "We didn't talk about being...dating." His face was starting to flush and his eyes were averted, but he had clearly leaned forward quite a bit and he wasn't pulling back. "Feelings," he added, as if unsure he had been clear. "Potential boyfriends?" He seemed less sure about that.

"So," Davis said, just to say something as his brain caught up. Samuel was still too close for him to want to do much thinking. Kissing—*really* kissing—sounded better. "Feelings?" he was able to get out.

"Enough to be completely cockblocked," Samuel confirmed, and that was about as romantic as

Samuel got. There was a hand on the back of Davis's neck, slowly pulling him closer, but leaving enough room for Davis to answer either way. "So?"

"So," Davis breathed out, letting himself be moved, "I didn't expect this tonight."

"Is this okay?" Samuel whispered, his lips touching Davis, ghosting a kiss, teasing him mercilessly. How could he say no? He couldn't, because it wouldn't be true.

"Kiss me, please," Davis said, his hands clutching his jeans. His stomach felt like it was sending bouncy balls all over his insides. He sort of wanted to laugh but, even more, he wanted to be kissed in a way that was all-consuming. To be touched in a way that made it so clear he was wanted. To feel the heat of someone else so close. Samuel provided that, pushing the kiss past exploration and into memorization. Davis had denied himself this need for so long—not kissing, but intention, where it was so clear they weren't doing this for fun, but for the purpose of sharing an experience.

Maybe a little bit for fun, as well.

It could have been minutes, or hours, that they kissed with Samuel cradling Davis's neck and working his jaw. At some point, Samuel had shifted them horizontally on the couch, and that was entirely different and consuming and it was becoming too obvious to Davis what their position was and *who Samuel was*. His best friend. A man. Tommy's past Friends with Benefits.

Davis closed his mouth.

Samuel opened his eyes, the question held there, but also quiet patience.

"This is going to sound extremely silly," Davis fore-warned, looking between them, where Samuel's elbows were braced on either side of him, where his own hands were hooked on Samuel's belt. He removed his hands and cleared his throat. "I'm not… ready…"

His face felt warm. He hadn't felt like this when he had fumbled around with Rachael and hadn't exactly lasted long. He blamed that on being four-teen. This, however, was all him.

But Samuel didn't seem bothered. He kissed Davis's nose, maybe because he felt the same want to just *kiss* that Davis still felt.

"That's okay," he whispered. "I can wait. I know what it would mean for you and I need to learn how to make it mean the same thing."

"Love?" Davis asked. Samuel shifted his weight to one elbow so he could pinch Davis's nose. "Hey!"

"You are much sappier about this than me," Samuel said, but he was smiling, and Davis couldn't think back to when he last saw that smile. "I'm not so sure how much I like titles around everything. The meanings behind them seem so complicated to me. Even if…I knew why I told Tommy's parents I was his boyfriend. It seemed like a tool."

"So I can't call you my boyfriend?"

Samuel scrunched his nose. "It seems so foreign."

"I'm foreign."

"You're pretend foreign," Samuel said, tugging on Davis's nose again. He moved his hand down and tapped on Davis's lips with a single finger. "I do like this."

"*Mi piace tu*," Davis said against the finger, the

simplest Italian he knew, but it seemed to focus Samuel's attention further. "Are foreign languages a kink, Samuel?"

"No comment," Samuel murmured as he took his hand back. "You're distracting. We were talking about something."

"About how I can't call you my boyfriend because I'm foreign—oh, sorry, *it's* foreign," Davis said, smirking.

Samuel shook his head softly, but the smile was still there along with a light in his eyes. "You can try it out. I'll try not to cringe too much."

"We'll see," Davis said, because his number one priority was making Samuel comfortable with this. "But I do have a request?"

Samuel eyed him skeptically. "Yes?"

Davis shrugged and tapped Samuel's lips with a single finger. "Kiss me until the sun comes up."

Samuel smiled.

"God, you're sappy," he said, and then complied.

# CHAPTER
# SIXTY-ONE

There was so much to be done.

Daniel was well aware Davis was in no way ready to be on his own. They couldn't risk it yet. There were also times they couldn't risk him on a mission at all.

"Temperature's low," Vanessa whispered, looking down at a small portable room thermometer. "And dropping."

"Yes, I can tell," Andy muttered, her breath visible.

They were downtown, where the history of Charleston produced vast quantities of manifested sin. The houses were built on graves.

It was dark, but that never meant there weren't people out. The College of Charleston was rated second on the list of party schools in South Carolina, and that ranking was not an exaggeration. It was not quiet, even though the Exorcists were trying to be.

"Davis *is* off campus, right?" Vanessa asked.

"He would avoid it," Jenkins said. "He did when we went to Ringer's Antique Shop."

Daniel translated that and added, "I know he's home. This isn't him."

Paul was in front, leading them into the campus. "Do you hear that?"

It was the quietest of sounds, something muffled, but that was only more reason to investigate. Paul gestured for Andy to go first, which she did, pulling out a knife from her belt.

"Prevention, Andy," Paul whispered. "Remember that."

"I know," Andy hissed. Daniel stepped forward to back her up. The muffling grew louder, and they rounded a corner between two houses.

Daniel could see the aura, much like many psychics could, but this was very specific. There was a dark, almost cracking aura surrounding a young man. It swam around him, through him, inside of him. His pants were down. There was a girl. Her dress was hiked up. She didn't want this. That was all that mattered.

"He's possessed," Daniel said quickly, even though Andy was already springing forward. She ripped the guy away, making him sprawl on the ground, but that hardly seemed to matter to him. He jumped back up, stumbling only because he was trying to get his pants back up, but Andy gave him no time. She crouched and spun a kick at his ankle, which resulted in an unpleasant noise as the guy stumbled. But demons didn't care about broken ankles. The sides of the buildings were starting to shake, a street light buzzing louder and louder until it burst out.

Vanessa and Noah were helping the girl by leading her away. Jenkins had his own knife out as he prepared himself to be their backup should the demon break away. Once Daniel knew the area was clear, he stepped in to help Andy, even though by the time he could, Andy had the guy's face pressed into the concrete with his hands behind his back. He was still straining against her, pushing beyond the limits of a human, ignoring any pain threshold. Daniel wasn't sure what would be enough to hold this one, but he still slapped on handcuffs and took the hold from Andy.

"I would have done this, demon or not," Andy spat as she pushed away from him, pacing only once before crouching in front of him. She glared directly into the face of the young man. "I should just kill you, you disgusting fuck."

"Andy," Paul said calmly. "It was the demon, not the boy."

She growled in frustration and pulled at his hair. "It's him. Toby McCain. Nineteen. No religion, except if you include anime." She pulled his head back by his hair as she observed him. "No signs of rotting. Toby's still alive. Toby?"

There was thrashing and inhuman screeches coming from Toby. Then, the words began. They were in English, although with a British accent, but the words were put together in a way that made no sense. Then, one phrase that could be heard clearly: "*Benevolentia* is dead! *Castitas* next! Kindness is dead! Chastity will be dead dead dead dead DEAD

DEAD DEAD..." It grew louder and louder. Andy adjusted her grip on her knife.

"Andy," Paul warned.

"I *know*," Andy growled, but she raised her hand and, with the knife pointed down, went to plunge.

Daniel watched as the aura spilled out around them, forcing them all to hold their ground as a gust passed over them. They looked, and the tip of Andy's knife was just barely touching Toby's hair.

Andy pushed herself up and looked at Paul. "You didn't want to kill it. Well, it didn't want to be killed. It fled."

"That's all we can do for now," Paul said solemnly. "Continue performing exorcisms."

"Well, here we are," Andy said, lighting kicking the unconscious Toby McCain. "Another to add to the collection of vulnerables."

"Get Doc to tend to his ankle and check his arms," Paul said. "Then we will have a long talk with him."

There was so much to do and more just kept coming. The time was ticking by much too quickly.

Daniel tried to excuse himself.

"Where are you going?" Jenkins asked. Daniel ignored him and kept walking, but Jenkins caught up. "Daniel, where are you going? Why are you acting like...like you can't See me?"

Daniel whirled on him, eyes glaring, but he made sure it wasn't enough of an action to attract the others' attention. "Because you're not *my* Non-defined," he said, voice low but no less harsh.

Jenkins was shocked and maybe a bit angry, but it was no longer Daniel's business. He had been a placeholder here, and there were other things he was focused on.

He turned away from Jenkins, from Andy and Paul—the whole Charleston team—and he decided it was time to leave them for good. After all, they had Davis now. His job with them was finished.

# CHAPTER
# SIXTY-TWO

It was entirely impossible to kiss as long as Davis requested, but Samuel sure did try. It was a strange experience, kissing without using it as a means to something more. Although, eventually, both of them had to take separate showers. When this was done, they moved to Davis's room. Then his bed. When they did, Davis fell asleep, much to Samuel's disappointment and amusement.

They faced each other, neither used to sleeping—actually *sleeping*—in a bed with another person. Samuel didn't understand how Davis could just fall asleep with the events of the night, but the stress lines and creases in his brow were indicators. It would all be so much easier if they could switch places in life. It was immeasurable how much Samuel wished for that.

He might have fallen asleep, or into that sort of in-between state that never quite fell into REM. Davis was warm next to him and he was someone Samuel was unable to ignore. He didn't want to. He felt as if his life was tied to Davis's by chance. To think he had ever thought otherwise was ridiculous. To have ever thought he did not want to be with Davis like this was even more so.

He woke (if one woke from not really sleeping) before the sun rose, so he opened his eyes and he saw Davis and he smiled. He kissed Davis because he *could*.

He felt Davis smile and he felt Davis's hands in his hair, and he smiled and laughed into the kiss and Davis did, too.

"Good morning," Davis said, stretching his long body.

"You should brush your teeth," Samuel said.

Davis hit him with a pillow. "So *romantic*, you are. You kissed me awake. Give me a moment, would you?"

Samuel held onto the pillow, hiding his smile and laugh. He couldn't care less about anything else right now. He had never felt like this before. Maybe everyone else was onto something when they raved about relationships. Then again, Samuel wasn't too thrilled about the "I told you so" that was bound to come from Ashley or any of their other mutual friends. He thought about what came with typical relationships: meeting the family, having obligations to each other, *compromises*, titles and expectations...would they have joint accounts now? What the hell was involved in a relationship and how could Davis still seem so relaxed? They had to get up for work in an hour. Samuel was no longer smiling.

Davis tapped on Samuel's forehead. "You're overthinking, aren't you?"

"I'm thinking enough to be prepared," Samuel mumbled, giving Davis back the pillow. "What does this mean to *you*? What all will change?"

"Change? Well," Davis said, "I get to kiss you, right?" Samuel nodded. "And we can go on dates. We can switch who pays, and whoever is paying picks the place?" Samuel's smile was coming back, and he nodded again. "And we can wear each other's clothes?"

"Your clothes are too big for me," Samuel said, plucking at the shirt covering Davis's broad shoulders, "and not nearly my style."

"Style, huh?"

"Davis, you wear graphic t-shirts. I need to look somewhat professional and knowledgeable of clothes when my job is *making them*."

"Speaking of jobs," Davis said, pulling out his phone, which was apparently the first time he had thought about their obligations. "Can you call in sick to a work that you've been drafted for?"

Deciding that was a rhetorical question, Samuel sat up and stretched himself. His muscles felt very tense, but he felt at peace.

"Life goes on," he said, letting his head drop forward as he tried to actually feel awake. He peeked a look at Davis, who was just watching him. "What?"

"You're beautiful," Davis said, not bothering to hide his grin, "and I'm able to tell you that now without worry."

"Sappy," Samuel said, because he could not

think of anything else to say.

"Distracted," Davis replied. His grin was like a golden retriever's, honest and full of kinetic energy. It was also followed by sloppy kisses, which wasn't the worst thing at all.

They dozed lazily, becoming rather counter-productive to Samuel's want to get up and *do* something, but when their alarm clocks buzzed—first Samuel's, then Davis's fifteen minutes later—they knew they had to get up.

"You know, if we shared a shower—"

"No, Davis."

It was silly—ridiculous, even—how much Samuel enjoyed Davis like this. He was always *flirty*, but now it was directed at *him* with *meaning*. Davis practically skipped around the apartment, humming with a few occasional lyrics slipping out.

"I could just not go," Davis said as he slid across the kitchen in his socks to grab toast. "What could they do? Fire me?"

"No, Davis, you have to go."

Samuel could only hide his smile so much. So, when Davis wrapped his arms around Samuel's waist while he was cleaning dishes, he definitely couldn't hold in the laugh.

"We need more rules," Davis said and hummed as he rested his chin on Samuel's shoulder.

"Oh?"

"Yes. You can't ever stop laughing. It's a new rule—ah, see, you're already breaking it! Stop that."

Samuel rolled his eyes. He was sure if he laughed any more his stomach muscles would pull. He turned around and Davis took a step back, but his expression was open and giddy. Samuel pointed at him. "No making me late."

"No leaving the apartment without a kiss."

Samuel paused before he nodded in agreement to this one.

"No sharing of food." When Davis looked confused, Samuel added, "Can't do it, sorry."

Davis shrugged.

"No lying." Davis said it much more seriously, so Samuel paused. "I mean it. I want communication. If I do something you don't like, tell me. I'll do the same. I don't want this to be in any way unpleasant if I can help it. And," he continued, frowning. "I want to have a serious talk about my…condition."

"Your possessions," Samuel clarified, "attempts."

"Yes. What it means for you. What you'll do if I can't stop it. Can you promise me we'll have that talk soon?" His eyes were steady, but Samuel realized Davis had checked the time on the oven behind him, making sure Samuel wouldn't be late.

"Yes," Samuel said. "As long as we can have a talk about mine as well."

Davis's brows furrowed and he leaned back. "Yours?"

"Nothing like yours," Samuel said. "I just meant— I need to tell you about my parents."

He could tell that instantly made Davis more curious. Davis pursed his lip and nodded once.

They finished getting ready, the pattern of moving around each other already set, but now it had charged. Neither could ignore the other. Really, neither wanted to.

"It's real?" Davis asked Samuel as they left their

apartment.

"I think so," Samuel said, giving Davis a simple glance, then a simple smile. "I hope so."

Davis grinned. "Now who's the sappy one?" he asked as they shared a final kiss in the car before they departed.

# CHAPTER
# SIXTY-THREE

"I," Davis said once he entered the Head-quarters, pointing at Andy, "do not want to hear a word from you. I am blissfully happy. You like ruining those things. Let me be happy today."

Andy raised an eyebrow that spoke more accusation than any words could. She seemed exhausted.

"Life continues on and demons still exist, so," Jenkins said, tossing Davis wraps meant for his hands, "training continues."

"I understand now," Davis said. "I should have told you not to say a word either."

"Well someone has to say it, since Daniel went off to who knows where," Jenkins said bitterly as he went and leaned against the door to the kitchen.

Davis glanced at Andy, thankful she couldn't understand Jenkins. However, she must have been thinking about Daniel, because her eyes looked between them.

"Let's just stick with talking about demons," she said. "And training. It's time for a spar."

"And there are the words," Davis said with a sigh.

Training had been slow but educational in the past week. They were mindful of his injuries and instead of training his muscles, Andy had fed his mind enough information to truly test how good his memory was.

Today ended the easy treatment. With his hands wrapped and Andy's gloves on, it was clear it was time to use that information.

He wasn't sure who started it, but he knew he was the one constantly dodging. Andy did not just use her arms as weapons. She used every part of her body, from her head to her toes, and every part of *Davis's* body, catching him off guard enough times he was sure he would gain back every bruise he just healed from. It was expected, but it was still aggravating. She never seemed to slow down, keeping him on his toes, taunting him with words against his masculinity, and then he just started *laughing*.

Andy took a step back then, one eyebrow raised and looking at him as if she thought he had lost it. He might have.

"I'm not sorry," he said, covering his laugh with a hand. "I know, demons aren't a laughing matter, but you know what? I'm happy. Can't let demons take that away, huh?"

"Is this about you getting laid? Because I really don't want to talk about that," Andy said, visibly cringing.

"Oh, no, that didn't happen," Davis said flippantly. "However, something did."

"Don't say a word more. Please," Andy said. "Now, can you take this seriously?"

"Andy, wait," Jenkins said from the entrance to the house. Then he frowned and looked at Davis. "Tell her I said to wait." Davis passed on the message. "I want to hear about this. You actually have a love life?"

"Believe it or not," Davis said, grinning widely. "You met him. Samuel."

Both of Jenkins' eyebrows raised. Davis heard Andy groan but ignored her. "Samuel," Jenkins repeated. "Wasn't he your roommate?"

"Is," Davis said.

"Well I'm glad one of us is about to have something normal," Jenkins said.

"And what about May?" Davis asked, waggling his eyebrows. "Have you asked her out yet?"

"May? That's not...possible," Jenkins said. He looked more hurt than shy about the topic. "She can't exactly understand me. Not even body language."

"You could send her flowers. Look, see, I'm in *such* a good mood, I could even translate for you. I can vouch that you're not a creepy stalker."

"What the hell," Andy said, who was only getting half the conversation correctly. Davis wondered what she heard. "Stop goofing off. Time is valuable."

"There's not enough of it to just waste it all," Davis said.

"Then there are Nondefineds, who are basically a waste of—oh, Paul," Jenkins said as he moved out of the way so Paul could walk out. Vanessa and Noah followed him.

"I have some news," Paul said. "Do you remember the woman who asked us to find her child?"

Davis remembered very clearly. He stood straight and looked at Paul. "Did you get a lead?"

"Possibly," Paul said. He handed a single piece of paper to each of them. There was a picture of a young boy taking up most of it with notes of information at the bottom. "That's him. Darren Weiss. Someone said they saw him near the Market, but he looks like some of the boys who sell the grass flowers there."

"What does this have to do with us?" Andy asked. "I don't get why we're doing the cops' job."

"There have been strange readings near the Market," Paul said. "Temperature drops. Some store owners have complained about customers leaving because of a sense of dread. That, combined with the mother's claim he was taken by demons, makes it ours."

"Any place specific?" Andy asked.

"A candy store on the corner of Market and East Bay Street."

"Then let's get going. Get your jacket on," Andy said, the latter part direct at Davis. "Daniel's busy, so this will be your first mission without him."

"Aye aye," Davis said, even though his earlier bliss was rapidly turning into nervousness. He'd told the woman he would find her son, and now, he would go through with it.

# CHAPTER SIXTY-FOUR

Despite the unbearably happy past fourteen hours or so, work was a reminder of the rest of the world. It wasn't that Samuel hated his job. In fact, he quite liked it, but he didn't *love* it. It was a job that gave him stress to the point of acne but satisfaction enough to sleep at night. It was just that when he slept, he dreamt of grander things. That hadn't changed. He felt like he was in a long battle in the pursuit of happiness and had snagged a sample, enough to make him feel alive and enough to make him yearn for more.

However, work *was* distracting. If it wasn't the work itself, it was the music filling his brain and, if not the music, the gossip. He acted as if he hadn't been gifted a piece of happiness and then when his lunch break came around, he truly learned what the word *jittery* meant. He never stayed in the building for his break, preferring to avoid being teased for eating chips with a spoon, and it was when he could let his brain catch up to what he had been avoiding thinking about.

He missed Davis's lips.

He was not looking forward to talking about his parents. It meant acknowledging something was wrong. He wasn't sure anyone *else* would believe something was wrong. After all, a past counselor pointed out it was hard to prove abuse when it wasn't physical.

If anyone were to believe him, Samuel thought Davis would. Then again, Davis had a visible wound and *he* chose to hide it. Samuel just wasn't positive enough he could predict Davis's reaction, and he knew it would determine where they went in their relationship.

Samuel thought everything through as he walked away from his work. He wandered until he was close to the Market, where he used to work (and vowed never to again), but heading there would be...awkward. He hadn't left on bad terms, just with an unpleasant feeling on both ends.

As he walked in the opposite direction, inwardly cursing his boss and wondering how rude it would be to contact Davis during work, a boy stopped in front of him, holding out a flower made of grass and presenting his innocence with wide eyes and round cheeks.

"Would you like to buy one of these?" the boy asked. He was young, maybe five, and all alone. Samuel glanced around, knowing this must be one of the flower boys typically around this area, but he looked a bit messy, the braids in his hair starting to fuzz.

Samuel sighed and dug out his wallet, pulling out two ones and handing them to the kid. He was handed the flower, but when the boy's hand touched his it was cold. Much too cold for being outside during the summer.

"You want what he has, don't you?" the boy said.

"What?" Samuel asked, holding the flower close to him as he rubbed his hands together.

The kid looked sad as he scuffed his shoe against the ground. It was just like what Davis did when he was nervous.

"Like that guy who's a new Exorcist," the boy said. "You like helping people."

Was Davis already that well known, that a kid on the streets would know him?

Was it that obvious Samuel wanted to be an Exorcist?

"How do you know that?" Samuel asked.

The boy shrugged. "I dunno. I just know." He took a step back. He never once made eye contact. "I gotta go."

As the boy left, Samuel whispered, "Bye," and wondered what just happened.

The one thing he was sure of was that the boy was absolutely right, and that was gnawing at Samuel more than anything else.

# CHAPTER
# SIXTY-FIVE

They checked out the candy store, recorded readings, and asked locals for any specific information, but there was hardly anything to follow. Just heat and tourists.

"Don't go near there," Davis heard Andy tell Vanessa as they passed one of the information centers. "They don't need demons around to be complete creeps."

"Isn't that an official tourist place?" Vanessa asked, glancing back at the store front.

"No. They say they are, but they aren't. Stay away."

"Okay, *mom.*"

Andy scoffed. "Apparently you need one if you don't take the warning seriously."

That seemed to shut Vanessa up. They silently went back to their search.

Davis kept his eyes and mind open, knowing his

sight was more valuable than the recordings. Still, he wasn't used to looking for possessed people and it was difficult to know what he was even looking for.

"There's nothing," Andy said, her voice filled with disappointment. She was the smart one in the group, having put on her sleeveless version of the jacket and wearing her black shorts. "Not a peep. There are too many boys selling the grass flowers. No one looks close enough at them."

Davis stayed quiet beside her. He had to admit, the oddest part about this trip was feeling the knife at his thigh and gun at his hip. Andy had trained him the basics of both, but he wasn't about to start on a *boy*.

They were walking down East Bay Street when something caught his eye.

"Samuel?" He looked towards Paul and then, after a nod of consent, lightly jogged to catch up with him. "Samuel!"

Samuel turned around, clearly surprised. He also looked tired and…blurry? Davis didn't know how to describe it. He looked Davis up and down and then past him, to his squad. "What's going on? Why are all of you out here? Why are you in jackets in this heat?"

"It's the uniform or something—I don't—we're just gathering information," Davis said. He pulled out the folded sheet of paper with Darren's picture on it. He put on his best cop voice. "You haven't happened to see this boy, have you?"

Samuel studied it, squinting. "No…I don't think so. It's hard to tell."

"You're good with distinguishing faces," Davis

said. "You've seen the flower boys here often."

"I have, but I don't know if I could point them out specifically," Samuel said, frowning. Davis wondered what he saw when he looked at the boy. Did he notice the boy's eyes? His cheeks? His hair? "I don't pay that close of attention. And I'm really not that good with faces. At all."

"Right, well, keep this," Davis said, handing him the poster. "If you see him, let me know right away. He's lost. His mother wants him back."

Samuel took the paper gingerly, staring at it, his eyebrows furrowing. "It's strange, because he seems familiar, but I—I don't know." He folded the paper and looked at Davis. "I'll let you know."

"Right away."

"Yes, Davis, right away."

"Good." There was a pause. Davis slipped out of his work mode and now he was just looking at *Samuel*. "Hey, are you okay?"

"Yeah, I just have a bit of a headache," Samuel said, rubbing his temple. "Work. You know. I needed a break."

"You never take breaks. Work *is* your break," Davis said, teasing lightly.

Samuel laughed. "It seems you do know a thing or two about me. But don't worry, I'm fine. Don't you need to go back?"

"Yes," Davis said, but he didn't even look away. "I'm still wishing we both had the day off."

Samuel's eyes softened and his lips quirked. "The weekend is soon enough."

"Not soon enough," Davis said. He leaned in, giving Samuel the option whether to make "them" known or not.

Samuel lightly put his fingertips on Davis's chest to keep him at bay. "I'm not the biggest fan of PDA."

"Gosh darn. Here I thought I could express my exhibitionist side openly."

This seemed to amuse Samuel, which made Davis feel happy enough to not feel sad over a denied kiss.

"A few more hours," he said. "I'll take you on a date this weekend."

"Davis!" Andy called. "Stop flirting on the clock!"

Davis rolled his eyes. He grabbed one of Samuel's hands and squeezed it. "I'll see you later tonight."

"Tonight," Samuel said, squeezing back. It was enough. Davis smiled, nodded, and headed back towards his teammates. He was counting down the minutes.

# CHAPTER SIXTY-SIX

There was a lighter in his hands and Samuel couldn't use it.

"It'll be okay," Davis whispered against his ear. He was behind Samuel, chin on shoulder, hands lightly on hips. "It's just a piece of paper."

"It's not," Samuel said. "If it was, I wouldn't be needing to burn it ceremoniously. Actually, I would just put it in the recycling." He flicked the lighter. It didn't catch. He flicked it again. Nothing.

Davis reached around him. "Let me try—"

"No," Samuel said, moving the lighter away from Davis's hand. "This is for me to do."

Davis was silent just a moment before saying, "Okay."

"Thank you," Samuel said. He tried to flick the lighter again. Nothing. He threw it against the wall.

"Whoa there," Davis said, moving away from Samuel to pick up the lighter. "We want to try and get our deposit back on the apartment, you know."

There was very little worry about that. Samuel was obnoxious, even to himself, with how paranoid he was about the apartment's condition. That's why they didn't have any pets. Well, one of the reasons. Still, this didn't feel right. There was the smallest of marks on the wall, nothing to be concerned about, but it was evidence of an outburst. He stared at it, then at his hand when Davis placed the lighter in it.

"You don't have to do it right now," Davis said gently, putting his hand over Samuel's, covering the lighter. "It can wait."

Samuel didn't want to wait. He had already procrastinated. He had taken any excuse to put it off for another day. He tried to focus on his breathing.

"My parents," he said. "They're not horrible people."

"I believe you," Davis said.

Samuel nodded. "They weren't violent. They never..." He looked at the mark on the wall. "They never touched me." Davis didn't say anything, so he continued. "I moved here without saying a word to them. I couldn't. I felt trapped but there weren't any bars. When...when Tommy died, it felt like there was a death to something else. When he died, I realized I could, too. Maybe not physically, but he didn't die physically for months."

He was trembling.

Davis took the lighter back from him.

"Another day," he whispered.

Samuel closed his eyes in saddened defeat. "Another day."

# CHAPTER
# SIXTY-SEVEN

It was surprisingly difficult to break the habit of avoiding kissing Samuel. The fact was, it was still connected to so many other thoughts Davis still had. He had to ask, had to hesitate, had to wonder if his feelings were truly reciprocated. But he had very little room for self-doubt: it wasn't just anyone who was willing to be with a guy who fought off demons (internally and externally) fairly consistently.

Davis also had to remind himself that Samuel dealt with things alone. While Davis appreciated people's company when struggling, Samuel preferred privacy. This was why he was in his own room now and not Davis's. That was where he slept, and that was where he was when Davis woke up the next morning.

When Samuel did emerge, he gave the smallest of apologetic smiles and Davis wrapped him in soft hug. They didn't say anything. It was Samuel who, with careful movements, initiated their rule of sharing a kiss before work.

They shared another in the parking garage.

When Davis arrived at work, he immediately approached Vanessa.

Her hair was tied up in two loose buns, which just made her look even younger, especially when she looked at him with such surprise.

"I have to make sure I can protect Samuel," Davis said. "And myself."

"Okay," she said, standing and smoothing her yellow dress. "Come with me."

They walked into the kitchen where Vanessa sat and laid out her hands, palm up. "You can choose when it starts."

Davis blew out a slow breath before sitting. He put his hands on hers.

Being possessed by Vanessa was not like being possessed by a demon. With a demon, he felt torn from his body. With Vanessa, it was like a request to share space.

Davis stepped out of his case, looking at the rows of versions of himself. He walked, Vanessa following, and observed. He recognized every one of them. He stopped in front of one not too far down the hallway. He looked years younger, a tad rounder in the face, maybe an inch shorter, and he was wearing a German school uniform from the late 19th century. He would normally not be able to recognize clothes with such detail, but he knew this one well. He knew all of them well.

"These are characters I've created," he said, to acknowledge it out loud and to inform Vanessa.

"I was wondering," she mused, her hands clasped behind her back. "Every mind is unique. This is the representation of yours. It's a visual and interactive way for you to make sense of being pushed back while still conscious."

Davis put his hand flat on the case. He gave himself a moment, then continued walking. The farther they went, the younger the characters were.

"These aren't just the ones I've performed. There are practice ones, too," he observed, each case giving him a hint of nostalgia. He stopped as he reached the very last case before the spray-painted doors.

The case was very similar in make to the others. Glass on three sides and the top, solid dark wood framing the back and sitting on a small pedestal. This one, however, had a metal frame where the glass met, and a padlock on the front. The version of Davis was young. He was crouched. His hands were plunged into the blood that filled the case up to his ankles. There were small hand marks on the inside of the glass, telling the story of just how much he wanted to get out. But now, his eyes were closed, and the blood had long since been dry and crusted.

Vanessa joined Davis in looking at the case. "Not the prettiest of scenes, is it?"

"It was how I coped," Davis said emotionlessly, factually. "When I was younger. I made *myself* into a character I was playing so it wasn't me."

The hall echoed their silence until Vanessa put a gentle hand on Davis's back.

"Come on," she said. "This is just the entryway. Let's go inside. That's where the training will take place."

Davis just turned away from the case and they approached the large door. The graffiti was clear now, but there was no sense to it. Davis guessed that was because of his lack of visual art skills and he ignored it as he pulled open the door.

It was pitch black on the other side.

"Is this…normal?" Davis asked.

"No," Vanessa said warily. "Do you feel like you shouldn't walk in there?"

Davis looked into the blackness. "No," he said. "I think I should go inside." He should have maybe been worried about why he felt this pull drawing him in. He had fought against demons tempting him long enough to know warning signals, but that was just it: there weren't any warnings going off. It felt familiar. Nothing about it felt tainted. As he stepped inside, his eyes started to adjust, and he realized why.

There were rows and rows of seats, split by an aisle down the middle. They were raked, rising up until he could see a small window emitting the softest blue light.

"What is that?" Vanessa asked. Her hand was gripping onto the seam of his shirt, but he didn't mind much. He thought maybe she should feel uncomfortable, seeing how she was in *his* mind.

"It's the booth," Davis explained. "It's where the cues for a show are called out."

"Cues?"

"By the stage manager. You know, for lights, sound, and other special effects," Davis said. He continued walking and stopped. A light suddenly burst on, highlighting him in a spotlight. He could feel the heat of it starting to warm his face. It felt so familiar, so wonderful, that for a moment he wanted to just believe he was back in school, when he was still living out his dream.

It was now clear that they stood on a blank stage. There were curtains hanging on the sides—legs, Davis reminded himself. The ones above them, hanging horizontally, were borders. There were batons swaying ever so slightly between them, as if they had been bumped.

"Oh my god," Vanessa said as she turned around. Her eyes were wide as she took in the surroundings. "It's a stage. It's—there's nothing here, though. It's just an...empty stage."

"Of course it is," Davis said, and he felt the smile stretch his face. This, more than anything else, was proof of who he really was. It was like having a reminder. He only had to survive two years as an Exorcist. Then? Well, then, he would have this back.

He watched Vanessa curiously before asking her, "Why did we have to come in here?"

"Well, this is where you'll trap a demon," Vanessa said. "It's usually...there's usually something to work with. Like scenery. Something that you could build a trap with. Usually it's affected by your thoughts, but this is...a fresh slate."

"Well, I wasn't thinking of anything," Davis said, which wasn't completely true. He had been thinking about Samuel, but Samuel was rather tied into theatre now and he doubted Samuel would just show up physically in his head. He thought that might be a tad awkward.

He thought for a moment about how he began his acting ritual. He needed to build the character, as shown by the cases in the hall. He had to walk in their shoes, and he needed to *become* them. Once he became them, he had to immerse himself into their world. This was always best done when there was scenery, but sometimes it was so abstract he was forced to visualize a different place. After all, sometimes a sock was supposed to be a puppy, thin air was a person, or the audience was a wall.

"I think I know exactly what to do," Davis said, and he was grinning with glee.

"What?" Vanessa asked.

"Don't worry, I'll show you." And Davis led her back outside the stage and closed the door.

# CHAPTER SIXTY-EIGHT

Davis was not able to show Vanessa his idea before what felt like an earthquake was set off inside his brain, and suddenly both of them were sitting back at the kitchen table, their hands still clasped together. They were having difficulty catching their breaths, but it soon became obvious what happened.

"We have a mission. We have to go," Andy said, removing her hand from Davis's shoulder. He hadn't even felt it there.

Davis checked his watch and was surprised to realize only forty-five minutes had passed. They were in his mind much longer than last time, yet it had actually taken hours before.

"Time is weird," was all Vanessa said as an explanation. "It's just a mental concept."

Davis looked around. "Where's Daniel? Is he still not back?"

"He's not fucking here, that's all that matters," Andy hissed. "Now get ready. You're our only Optic."

It took them five minutes to get into their uniforms and basic equipment before they were piled back into the SUV with Noah at the wheel.

"Historic house on a farm," Paul briefed as they surpassed the speed limit. "Very old. There *is* a history to it. Many deaths, which means a higher chance of an older demon. The older a demon, the more likely it is to be stronger. I don't expect this to go very well. The family has already called and mentioned bruising appearing on their bodies throughout the day and night. There is a man, a woman, and three children, all of which have acted strangely at different times."

"All of them?" Andy asked from the front passenger's seat. "Usually it's just one. Maybe another if they're clairvoyant."

Davis turned around to look at Jenkins, who was sitting in the back as he always did. "What's the difference between someone being an Optic and someone who is clairvoyant?"

"Clairvoyants can see ghosts and very strong deities, maybe even demons. Optics can see all of that no matter their strength, and," he pointed at himself. "Nondefineds."

"So, am I considered clairvoyant?" Davis asked.

"To a degree. There are different ways in which you can be considered clairvoyant, ranging from just seeing auras to seeing full apparitions. They typically can see more about ordinary people. You'll be able to see when they're possessed," Jenkins said. "Think of it like this: most clairvoyants are Optics, but not all

Optics are clairvoyant. They have opened their minds and are able to take in information others might not be able to. That includes demons and, most of the time, Nondefineds. Some are just more open-minded than others. The fact you can see a Nondefined is what classified you as an Optic, however."

"So why didn't you go to clairvoyants in search of Optics?" Davis asked.

"We did," Jenkins said, and nothing more.

Davis turned forward and rubbed his hands. Daniel wasn't with them, which meant this was another mission where he felt completely unqualified—even if he unwillingly was. He just didn't know what to look for. He really hoped he didn't have to punch anyone.

The thing about living in Charleston was that every house could be considered a classic haunted house that would be seen in paranormal movies. Charleston was a battlefield turned graveyard turned tourist and college town, and most of the houses creaked and smelled of rotted wood. They passed over a bridge and Davis looked out over the water, solemnly remembering no one could keep count of how many people had jumped, and there were still bodies left unfound in the blue depths. He would have questioned why he wanted to stay in a city filled with horror, if he had not also experienced the liveliness of it. He never wanted that part of Charleston to die in his heart.

It was still a while after they exited the bridge before they turned onto a long, dirt driveway.

"The family is rich," Paul said from beside Davis.

"They lived off an oil plantation in Kansas before moving here."

"Mistake number one," Andy muttered, her cheek against the window. She seemed bored until Davis noticed how sharply her eyes were focused as they approached the farmhouse.

As they emptied the SUV, Paul handed out orders for different situations. Familiarly, Andy and Noah circled around the house as the rest approached the front. Paul addressed Davis.

"Don't feel the need to risk yourself this time," Paul said. "If you are going to try and be a hero at any point, you should be educated first. For now, I want you to keep your eyes open. Observe. Focus. Notice what doesn't seem right."

Davis's hands were getting sweaty. He wiped them on his jeans. "Okay," he said, and thinned his lips. Where was Daniel to tell him this? How long had it been since he saw his real trainer?

Paul knocked.

The door opened.

"Oh, good," a man said as he opened the door. He was starting to gray around the edges of his hairline but seemed younger than Paul. He looked extremely healthy and was able to pull off a wife beater and plaid combo without looking like beer was his every meal. His skin was a shade of brown that seemed to glow. Davis worked very hard not to envy him.

"Maureen!" he shouted into the house, moving to the side to let them in. Davis was surprised when Andy and Noah came up behind him, but made sure to try and hide it. The man looked back at them.

"My wife's upstairs with the kids. They should be down shortly. Thank you for coming."

There was a period of meet and greet where they learned the man's name was Hugh Shay and his three girls were Latisha, Laura, and Louise. They all had extremely different heights, different volumes and color of hair, different weights—in fact, they were so different from each other, Davis was sure they were adopted. They had two things in common: they were all adorable and looked under twelve.

"We'll be here a while," Jenkins whispered to Davis. "But you should probably be looking more closely at the family. Just because they seem nice doesn't mean one of them isn't possessed."

Davis looked at Jenkins. He could see the convenience in being a Nondefined: he was able to have secret conversations. Then he kicked himself for thinking such a thing. Jenkins was miserable and separated from the rest of the world with Davis as his only connection. He was forced to have this job because he had nothing else he could do, but also because he couldn't be trusted. You couldn't trust someone you couldn't understand. Still, maybe Nondefineds were searching for any positives they could.

Davis looked at the family and saw nothing unusual. He looked closer and he noticed bags under their eyes. Even the children. None of them had been sleeping well. They were also wearing jackets and Davis realized why Exorcists wore them: they always went where it was cold. Even Andy was wearing her long sleeve version.

No recordings were set out. No cameras, no microphones. Nothing but their portable thermosmeter in Vanessa's hand, which she was showing to the girls. There was a benefit to having someone so young on the team, even if Davis still wasn't too sure about her real age.

"We're not trying to gather proof," Andy explained. "We're here to fight. We can't do that unless it's here. Demons can't take physical forms so there will be a possession—there *is* a possession, we just have to wait for it to stop being dormant." She looked pointedly at Davis. "It's your job to spot it if it's not obvious."

"Great," Davis said.

An hour later, he realized exactly how long that might take.

# CHAPTER
# SIXTY-NINE

Samuel received multiple texts from Davis within the past hour. This was not including the dozens of texts in the hour before. He had casually responded to Davis's obvious boredom without showing his anxiety over the fact his significant other was in a potentially dangerous situation and he was supposed to sit at home and sew clothing. The situation did not sit well with him.

So instead of moping around all night, he contacted some of his co-workers to see if anyone was available. When they were, Samuel also texted Ashley to invite her for a final night out before she moved. Once she confirmed, he also asked Davis to join them when he was done.

Davis sent him a thank you text.

Samuel went downtown.

When they all met at a bar, Ashley almost immediately threw an arm around Samuel. "So, what's the occasion for this bout of social activity?"

"You're moving away," Samuel said, as if that was the only answer. Ashley eyed him in disbelief.

"You wouldn't want to say good-bye," she said, and she was right.

"Davis is working," Samuel mumbled.

Their group was silent for a moment, all well aware what Davis's occupation was, and what it meant for him to be working at this time.

"He'll be okay," one of his peers, Joan, said. "He always has been."

Samuel looked at her. He had mentioned Davis and they had seen him a few times, but sometimes he forgot what knowledge came along with the name Davis Turner. "He hasn't always been," he said. "But he's survived." He shook his head and waved his hand. "I didn't want us to come out just to get serious."

"But we're also here for you," Ashley said seriously. "He's my friend, but sometimes I worry more about you than him."

"I'm okay," Samuel said quickly. There was no one to say *okay is a relative term*, but he thought it. His chest ached. "We're, ah. We're dating, actually. Trying it out. It's been going well, I think. We haven't exactly—it's new. He makes me…happy."

"It's like that's how relationships are supposed to work or something," Ashley said, elbowing him and waggling her eyebrows. Samuel wondered how anyone could move their eyebrows like that. He had stared at the mirror once trying to do it with no success, but there was no way he was going to ask now. "You know you have to tell us how he is in bed, right? We have to know what we're missing out on!"

"Ah, no," Samuel said, leaning a bit away. "That's weird, for one. Our private life is private. Two, I don't always jump into bed with guys." He pointed at Ashley. "And you know what happened with Tommy. You know what...what..." He took a shaky breath and removed his hat, combing his hair with his other hand. He wasn't as okay as he thought he was.

Ashley looked horrified. "Oh, no, Samuel—I'm so sorry. I didn't realize..."

"Didn't realize what?" he snapped. "That 'dating' doesn't always mean 'fucking?' That maybe a gay man doesn't want his sex life questioned at all? That maybe even teasing about it when—when—" He let out a shuddering breath. He felt something in him building, growing, morphing into something bigger than it needed to be. He closed his eyes tightly and tried to push it all into a small box to put under a metaphorical bed and forget about.

"Sorry," Samuel said. "Sorry, I shouldn't have said that...well, not like that. Not—I'm just worried. I want to be there, with Davis. More than anything, I just want to be there instead of him," he whispered. He hadn't meant to say so much and when he looked around, he was embarrassed by all the concerned faces.

It was Debbie, another one of his coworkers, who spoke up. "Well, that's why we're here, right? Let's get a few drinks in you. Then Davis can join us later, okay?"

Samuel nodded slowly. The others headed towards the bartender to order the first round of drinks.

Samuel stayed with Ashley near the entrance. It took a considerable amount of energy and mental cheering for him to look at her. Her lips were parted, her eyes shining. She blinked and no tears were shed. She cleared her throat.

"I didn't realize what I was really saying," she whispered. "I'm sorry."

Samuel faced her completely and took both of her hands in his. "Hey. I don't want you to move away feeling like this. I was just—I'm stressed. I never do that, and it wasn't like…" He lost his words and thinned his lips. He tried again. "I directed my anger toward you and I shouldn't have."

There was a stillness between them before Ashley gave a small lift with her lips that spoke volumes. "It's like you're just bad at communicating or something."

"Something like that," Samuel said, matching her expression with a guilty smile. "Your first drink is on me."

"First two and we have a deal."

# CHAPTER SEVENTY

It was almost ten o'clock before there was any-thing to catch their attention. That was when the floodgates opened.

Like always, Davis processed things in factual ways, split into different sections and taken in bit by bit.

Lights flickered, doors slammed open and clo-sed, Andy drew her knife, the light bulbs burst, and one of the children (indecipherable in the dark) tried to attack Hugh. Hugh received small fingernail scratches down his face and arms. Andy went to approach Hugh, and the girl attacking him dropped to the floor before she got there. Facts. It was facts, like he was delivering a report. He had to stay separated from it. It continued. There was a flicker, a *something* Davis was supposed to notice. His eyes adjusted as everything went still.

"Latisha!" Maureen called out beside her child,

holding her as she looked at her husband, who had fallen back and held his face as it bled. Noah stepped in immediately to tend to it.

It stilled. It happened so quickly, without any true warning.

That, Davis realized, was just the first round.

The stillness was broken. Maureen coughed and gasped. There was a strange something to her movements—a blur? Then her hands lashed out to grip Latisha's throat, though the girl was still unconscious. Hugh pulled her away, only to have Maureen switch from Latisha to him, choking *him* violently as her fingers dug deeply into his throat. Andy and Jenkins jumped in to pull her away, and it did take both of them, then Paul joining in a minute later before they could pry her fingers off his neck. Hugh was now unconscious. Multiple people were screaming. Maureen—Davis could *see* Maureen, then not Maureen, like a different face was lagging behind her—no, *she* was lagging behind it. Then, she collapsed.

Another pause.

"What the *fuck* is going on?!" Andy yelled, her legs spread to be able to move at any minute, her eyes wild. "Two possessions in such a short time? That's not possible."

"It is when they're old enough," Paul said as he assisted Noah with checking on Hugh and Latisha to make sure they were still breathing. The other two girls were crying and huddled by a grandfather clock. Vanessa went over to them, taking on the façade of tender caregiver as always.

Davis sort of wanted to cry and huddle in a

corner, too, but he knew he couldn't. He was working and he needed to not be completely useless, even just to save this family and stay alive.

He caught Jenkins' attention. "How could Daniel see when someone was possessed?"

"Uh," Jenkins said. "He didn't much talk about it, but that shouldn't matter. Each Optic sees them differently. It's how your brain makes sense of it."

"I see a...before image?" Davis said unsurely. "It's like an after image, but before and...not them."

"That's it," Jenkins said, and there was a mix of surprise and approval. "You got it. Do you see anything now?"

Davis turned away from Jenkins and looked around awkwardly. He didn't exactly like looking at strangers for something that might not be there. Still, he did it, and it was when his eyes landed on Laura and Louise that round three began.

"Louise—" was all he got out before Andy took action, pushing Vanessa out of the way and grabbing at Louise just as she tried to attack her sister, but right when Andy had her restrained, she collapsed into her arms and Andy let out a frustrated growl.

"Won't you just *stay in one person?* I swear, this must be the real reason we're taught to trap them in our heads," Andy ranted as she stomped around rather childishly.

"He's not breathing," Noah said suddenly, and all conscious attention went to Hugh as Noah started to perform CPR. Latisha was just starting to wake up and Paul immediately pulled her away from Hugh.

There was that flicker again, the image of a

figure that guided the next actions. Davis knew Hugh's eyes would open before it happened. "Noah!" he yelled. "Get away from him!"

That was when the final round began.

Noah pulled away.

Andy strode towards Hugh as he was getting up.

Andy yelled something about the kids and tried to stick her knife into the side of Hugh's head.

Hugh—no, the demon, caught her wrist.

There was no moment of surprise. There was a button on the handle of Andy's knife. One she pushed that sent the blade directly into Hugh's skull.

Everything fell silent.

It was so difficult to process the events, so hard to believe that Andy would *kill again*, that Davis almost emptied his stomach just because of that knowledge: he had to work every day with someone who could kill so easily in front of a family.

Maureen and Louise started to wake. Laura collapsed in complete shock. Noah was staring at Hugh as if trying to figure out if there was a way to fix a stab wound to the head while knowing there wasn't one.

"You..." Latisha started, her hands trembling as she stared at her father. "How...how *could* you?! You killed my dad!"

"I killed the demon," Andy said, her expression detached. "Your dad had already stopped breathing because of it. This way, his death saved all of you."

"But that guy was performing CPR!" Latisha protested. "There must have been another way."

"Not that would have gotten rid of the demon

for good," Andy said sharply. "This is what it takes to protect others in the world now. You might as well get used to it."

"Andy," Davis snapped. "Outside. Now." He escaped the dreadful scene.

He heard a protest behind him before Paul ordered Andy to follow him.

"What?" Andy said. "Haven't you questioned me enough? Did it give you flashbacks or something?" she mocked.

Davis shoved at her shoulders, which barely moved her. "Don't you *dare* talk about flashbacks like that. Don't you dare lighten what you did to Tommy, especially when you just *murdered a man in front of his family* when *he* asked for our *help*!" He had never felt so angry and he had never let out so much emotion without a hint of a demon possessing him, but he knew this was all him. This was all real and it was no sin.

"How could you do that? How can you not even hesitate? What, does it take not having a soul to become a Cleanser? Or did you just take the easy route?"

"He was *already dead*, Davis. Alive only enough for the demon to enter him, but the demon would have switched easily with a death so slow. I wouldn't have done it otherwise," Andy snapped back. "Don't question how I do my job and I won't question how much you jeopardize the team, because if anyone's a killer, it's going to be you once you get all of us killed."

There were too many things Davis wanted to say, all fighting to come out. "You would have done it," was the first he was able to get out. "Even if he hadn't stopped breathing. You picked Hugh. Is that what they tell you to do? Just pick someone?"

"We never learned about a situation like this," Andy said. "I wouldn't have killed him, just like I didn't kill a guy who was about to rape a girl downtown."

"Prove it," Davis spat.

"*Fine.*" Andy went to the entrance of the house and yelled for Jenkins. "The three of us are going back. Y'all do damage control. I know they won't want me here."

"What?" Davis asked as Jenkins stepped out of the house, looking rather terrified.

Andy looked at him sharply. "I'm going to prove my intentions. Now get in the car."

# CHAPTER SEVENTY-ONE

The car ride back to the Headquarters was completely silent. Andy drove as aggressively, if not more so, than Noah. Davis and Jenkins sat in the back. Davis was reviewing the argument in his head, coming up with better comeback lines and cursing himself for not being witty enough to use them on the spot.

Once they arrived and got out of the car, Andy grabbed Davis's arm and yanked him inside, with him protesting the whole way. She pulled open a door that Davis thought was a closet before manhandling him through it.

Davis stumbled as he reached a step. "What the hell?" he said, looking down a stone staircase with unlit torches along the walls. "There's a *basement*? In *Charleston*?"

"We had it specially built to prevent flooding, so get over yourself and get going," Andy said. She flicked a switch and a string of lightbulbs lit overhead. Davis hesitated, but then he started the descent.

It wasn't a very long way down, but it still started to feel claustrophobic, even if there was no difference to the size of the stairwell. It was that everything was dim, and it had clearly been difficult to bring down electricity safely. Then, when he nearly reached the bottom, he saw a cage. There was a girl sitting in the middle of it, her legs spread out, her hair long enough to fold on the floor. There was a flicker, but that was all. She wasn't really moving. Then, Davis saw a head tilt up before hers did and he felt a full body chill.

"Ah," she—no—a demon said, tilting its head, guiding its Host. "Someone new?" Then the demon perked up. "You feel familiar. Inviting. Maybe not so new, then."

Davis stared at it in horror, fighting the urge to just run away from it. He could not say anything.

"She's been here a while," Andy explained. "We've taken care of her, keeping her body alive as the demon tries to starve her. This whole time, we've been trying to exorcise her."

Davis could not look away. "This...doesn't excuse you killing others."

"Maybe not," Andy admitted. "But it shows I try." She made a scoffing sound and Davis could hear her start back up the stairs. "I'll be sleeping when you come up. Jenkins can give you a ride."

Jenkins stepped in Davis's periphery before putting a hand on his shoulder, and it still made him flinch. "Sorry," he said. He looked at the cage. "Her name is Jazmin Sosa. She came to us. She asked for us to protect others from her." He paused, then looked at Davis. "The demon killed everyone she was close to. Demons find the purest people they can to manipulate."

Davis scowled at the demon as his heart clenched at the thought.

"Oh," the demon said again, twisting the girl's head. "I *do* know you."

If he paid attention close enough, Davis thought the voice sounded like an echo. He ignored the demon.

"Yes," the demon said, laughing. "I've been *inside* you. When you were worried about that little play."

It was then Davis understood why demons needed to be killed.

# CHAPTER
# SEVENTY-TWO

There had been a few too many drinks, Samuel realized, before switching completely to water. Davis could arrive at any moment, and he didn't want to be entirely sloshed. He wasn't sure exactly how much he would say, considering he already babbled about how hot Davis was. That is, he simply said, "Davis is *really* hot," with no expansion of details, but he did say it repeatedly.

Slowly, everyone started to get sober, then tired, and that was when Samuel received a text message that Davis was outside.

"Just hold out a bit longer," he told his friends. "I know Davis will want the company. He's the extrovert." They all seemed to want to try their best, so Samuel went just outside the bar.

Davis had unzipped his Exorcist jacket, but had not taken it off, which was the first sign that something was wrong. The second was when he wrapped his arms around Samuel's neck and buried his face into the crook and *sobbed*.

There was a moment Samuel wasn't completely sure what to do. They were outside on the sidewalk, with dozens of people around and his friends inside, and Davis was crying. He was not good with dealing with tears.

However, he knew how to deal with Davis. He knew what Davis was asking for, which was words. It was touch. So, Samuel rested his hands on Davis's sides, then ran them up his back to hold him close.

"You're okay," Samuel said, his voice soft and calm. "You're here. Today is over."

That was all he could do and that, it seemed, was all Davis wanted. He held onto Samuel until Samuel whispered, "Let me tell the others we're going home, okay?" and Davis simply nodded.

"I'm sorry to end your night early," Davis apologized quietly as he pulled away, if reluctantly. His face was a mess and Samuel didn't resist the urge to wipe under Davis's eyes. "I'm sorry for putting you in a weird situation in public."

"For you?" Samuel said. "It's worth it."

# CHAPTER SEVENTY-THREE

It had been so long. So much happened since the last time Samuel heard from his parents, besides the surprise visit home. It made the text message from his father seem more surreal than normal, and any contact from his dad was already abnormal.

It wasn't a series of texts shifting from sweet promises to scornful insults, like he would have received from his mother. It was a simple invite to dinner.

There was the possibility his mother had figured out the only way to get Samuel's attention was through his father, but he doubted his father would have played along. He never involved himself in the affairs between Samuel and his mother. It was his biggest crime and most honest decision. Samuel would never blame him. He only wished they would get divorced so there was less alcohol involved.

Maybe then he could learn who his father actually was.

But maybe this was an opportunity. If his father was taking the initiative, there was hope. As much as Samuel tried to convince himself otherwise, the truth was he wished for his family to be normal. He wished for the chance to sit down for dinner and not have to be on edge. This could be that chance, or at least the path to it.

"Davis," Samuel called as he stood up from his work station in his room. It had been a few days since the farmhouse incident and Davis had been acting solemn, but there was also something else, a determination that wasn't there before.

"Yeah?" Davis called back.

Samuel hesitated. He meant to just tell Davis his plans. The dinner was the next day, which was too short of notice for Samuel's anxiety, but something he was trying to come to terms with. Davis was fairly fond of spontaneity and they were…something now. A potential unit, or some sort of unit anyway.

It had apparently been too long since Samuel said anything because he heard the floor creak and Davis walked to the doorway. "Samuel?" he asked.

"I'm fine," Samuel said. He looked at Davis. This man was so terrifyingly important to him the idea of sharing his family life produced only nightmares. Still, he had to try. He wanted to. More than that, he wanted Davis's support.

He took a slow breath. "My parents invited me to dinner tomorrow night," he said, "and I was wondering if you wanted to go with me."

"Yes," Davis said, taking a step into Samuel's

room. He waited for permission before entering farther and he cupped Samuel's face with both hands. "Are you okay?"

Davis's hands were warm, but Samuel still had to fight the instinct to flinch away. It was foreign to be able to accept a loving touch.

"It depends on your definition of 'okay,'" Samuel said. That, and a weary smile, was the only way Samuel felt he could answer most honestly.

Davis matched his smile. "What are you worried about?"

"I'm worried you'll think I'm crazy," Samuel said honestly. "My mother is…convincing."

"Well, so am I," Davis said. "I'm an actor, after all."

Samuel shook his head and took Davis's hand in his, looking at their fingers. His own had tanned because of the summer, meaning Davis's were now nearly a dark brown. They were working hands. Samuel's were simply chapped from over-washing.

"It's not that I need you to be convincing. I need you to…" How could he phrase it? How could he say that he so desperately wanted Davis to solely believe him? He couldn't ask that so simply. It wouldn't feel right if it was requested. He sighed. "I just want you there."

"I'll be there," Davis whispered, leaning forward until his forehead touched Samuel's.

Samuel scrunched his nose and leaned away. "Sappy," he said, as a fact and a reminder. It was meant to lighten the mood, but Davis still seemed concerned.

"What aren't you telling me?" Davis asked. It

wasn't a demand, but his own request, his thumb now running over Samuel's knuckles. Samuel stopped it with his own thumb.

"I don't know," Samuel said honestly. "But I'll show you what I can."

"Okay," Davis said, his eyes speaking volumes for how serious he was. Samuel would never tire of that undivided attention. "I'll be there."

"Thank you."

# CHAPTER
# SEVENTY-FOUR

Davis wasn't sure how to best prepare himself to meet Samuel's parents. He tried on so many outfits, some that were the absolute *worst*, before going to Samuel's doorway.

"Help," he simply said.

Samuel looked at him, where he was clearly deciding his own attire, and let out what Davis could only call a *giggle* before it abruptly ended, replaced with an expressionless face before it cracked into a barely contained smile. "A suit, Davis? Really?"

"It's just a suit jacket," Davis said, frowning down at himself. Sure, it was over a white, buttoned down shirt, and his pants were black, but it was hardly an appropriate suit.

"Change out the shirt, then," Samuel said, pointing at Davis's current shirt as if it offended him. "Just wear one of your normal t-shirts—not black. At least not *mostly* black, but not too bold, and not with a design that's too recognizable. Wait—the splatter print one should be fine. And change your pants. Just wear jeans—but no holes."

"I knew I asked you for a reason," Davis said before he quickly went to change.

It was as he was changing his pants that his phone went off. It was a horrid sound, set for one purpose only.

He closed his eyes in dread as he picked it up. "Hello?"

"Davis," Paul said. "We need you. Doc will be there soon to pick you up."

Davis mouthed curses but knew he couldn't say no. It was in his contract and Paul wouldn't be the one contacting him if it wasn't a life or death situation for someone.

"I'll be ready," he said, and he hung up.

When he turned around, Samuel was at his door, his expression unhidden. He was terrified. He knew what the ringtone meant.

"I'm sorry," Davis croaked. He felt so guilty, breaking a promise he probably shouldn't have made in the first place. He felt torn, especially when the farmhouse incident happened so recently.

"No, don't—you're fine. It's your job. I want you to help, if you're able," Samuel said, although the words were strained. "That's not—don't worry about the dinner. Worry about yourself. It could be a dangerous situation."

"I'll be okay," Davis said, approaching Samuel and raising his hands to...he wasn't sure what he wanted to do but just *touch* Samuel. Maybe to rub the creases between his eyebrows, or to lift his lips in a smile. Samuel noticed his hands hovering there and took the initiative, grabbing them, putting his own hands over them as he placed them on his cheeks. He leaned in and kissed Davis. It was meant to be chaste, if Samuel pulling away was an indication, but Davis moved his hands into Samuel's hair, knocking his flat cap off as he pulled Samuel back into the kiss.

He was scared, too. Even more, he was sorry to be one more thing for Samuel to worry about tonight.

Davis barely pulled away, still keeping Samuel in place, not wanting him a single inch farther. "I'll text constant updates," he whispered.

"Don't expect constant replies," Samuel said lowly, pulling back just to pick up his hat. "But still send them. I'll text you when I can."

"Please do."

They said their good-byes silently, and Davis couldn't help feel like Samuel was facing just as many demons as himself.

# CHAPTER SEVENTY-FIVE

Samuel was not thrilled to be at his parent's house without Davis. He made sure to leave a full hour earlier than he needed to, which was when Davis left, just so he could sit in his car a block away and allow himself to freak out. His hand itched to call Davis, to ask him to come and just be with him, screw whoever was having a crisis.

A half hour before he was supposed to arrive, he pulled into the driveway. He got out of his car and walked up the stairs and onto the porch. Then he walked off the porch and back on. He did this one more time before he was able to gather himself enough to stay there. He remained rooted to the spot until he had exactly fifteen minutes before he said he'd be there and then he knocked, knowing fifteen minutes early was considered on time to his mother.

He was supposed to be civil here, he reminded

himself. He was doing this for his father.

It was his mother who opened the door. When she did, her arms immediately crossed. "Are you here to apologize?"

"No," Samuel said, finding the word much easier to say than he thought it would be. "Dad invited me to dinner."

She clicked her tongue and stepped out of the way. "I'm going to have to talk to him about making plans without me. I knew about no such thing." Samuel was already starting to regret this.

There was, yet again, no true warm welcome. He remembered a sermon then. The pastor proclaimed people who were homosexual became that way because they were not hugged enough as a child. Samuel didn't think that was true, especially when he knew he liked men before he hit double digits, but also because he knew Davis was one of the touchiest people he had ever met, and it wasn't to make up for a lack of it while growing up. Not with his family.

How different would his life have been if he had been hugged?

The house was a complete disaster with empty cups on every surface above two feet and laundry or trash everywhere else. It was curious how messy things could get when both Samuel and Abby had been so careful about keeping everything neat.

"Your father has been acting strange," his mother said as he entered the house. It was like walking into a blast of air conditioning and Samuel actually shivered.

"I'm sure he's having trouble adjusting to

unemployment," Samuel said, knowing but not being surprised by his father's recent job loss. It was just another text among dinner plans. "I know it can be difficult without that income."

"It would be better if you helped out your family," she quipped.

"He has unemployment," was all Samuel said. He also knew this wasn't a preferred option for them, seeing how both of his parents tended to lean conservative when the topic of the government handouts came up.

"It's not nearly enough," she said as they entered the living room. Samuel's dad sat there in his old chair as usual, a beer in his hands, his eyes looking distant.

"Dad?" Samuel asked, taking the beer from him. It was mostly full, but the bag of chips next to him wasn't. "Are you okay?"

"Samuel?" his dad asked, blinking, focusing on him. "Oh, no. Not Samuel."

"What are you talking about? Of course it's me," Samuel said, feeling his heart tighten. He knew his dad was slowly losing himself, but whether to the sanity of the household or Alzheimer's, he wasn't sure. He just hoped his dad wouldn't forget him.

"No, no," his dad said, his chapped lips stretching into a grin. "You're *Envy*."

"What are you saying?" Samuel asked, his eyes wide as dread chilled him. His heart was now beating faster. This could not be happening. Not here. Not his dad. Not...him.

"I will do anything to complete my job," *something* said through his dad.

"Please, Dad, don't let it—" He wasn't able to finish as his dad leapt from the chair, faster than what should have been possible for him, and then his hands were on Samuel's neck, tightening, shaking him harshly.

"Da—!" Samuel tried to scream, to claw at the hands around his throat to stop the strangling, but he could barely breathe. He saw his dad. *He saw Tommy.* He felt *fear* and *hurt* and, more than anything, *determination.* He didn't want anything to happen to his dad like it had to Tommy. He kicked out, catching his dad in the shin and they both fell to the ground. This was worse, with his dad on top of him, pressing down against him as he struggled against the much stronger man—the man who had been so weak he was unable to work.

"Come on out, Envy! Come out! Defend your Host!" his dad mocked. "It's time for you to *come out!*"

Samuel's heart was pumping as he choked and struggled, feeling his fear swell, thinking back to how this was so similar to what Tommy had been doing and—

And he could have had such a different situation. Why couldn't he have? Why did everyone else get to live so happily and here he might die, from his father's hands. *Why did he not get happiness?*

But he pushed back the thoughts as he was able to finally catch a break, hitting his dad's stomach with his knee, catching him off guard just enough that Samuel was able to scramble away, coughing, gasping, and rubbing his sore neck.

"Dad?" he croaked out, watching as his dad straighten. He could see his mother at the edge of his vision, standing stock still in the doorway. "Mom, you need to leave! Call Davis!"

"I don't want—"

"*Call Davis!*" Samuel snapped, tossing his phone to her. His dad went after it, but missed. His mom missed as well, but she was able to scramble enough to snatch it from the ground and stumble into the kitchen.

"Hey! Dad! Or...or demon, whatever!" Samuel called. His dad turned sharply from his mom to look at him. His heart was pounding, his palms sweating, but he had to keep it together now. He had to control this situation as much as he could. "What do you mean by Envy?"

"I mean the demon lingering inside of you," the man said, a sick grin tainting his face. "Don't you remember the boy?"

"The...boy?" Samuel asked, not remembering anything specific about a boy.

Except...except he remembered something. A young boy, misplaced. The missing child with round cheeks from the poster Davis had given him. That's why it was so familiar. It was the same boy whose braids had started to frizz. Why hadn't he recognized him?

"Ah, you remember now, don't you?" the demon said. "Envy has been there, waiting until the moment you could believe the influenced emotions are your own. All it has to do is heighten your emotion, any emotion, and then *switch.* But something keeps stopping you. Something keeps preventing it."

Samuel thought back to the night of the farm-house incident, when he had blown up at Ashley, then when he threw the lighter. Had that been him, or *something else*? If he hadn't shoved that emotion away…if he hadn't been surrounded by caring people…he didn't want to think of what could have happened.

"Samuel?" the demon said, making Samuel focus back on him. "Do you want to talk to your father?"

Samuel choked, his hands shaking, and he quickly covered his mouth. This was his dad. The man who was absent, but not contributing to his mother's antics. This was the man who held the only hope Samuel had for decent parents. He stayed with his mom because she needed someone. He hadn't necessarily been there for Samuel, but that didn't mean he wasn't a good man for trying. So, Samuel nodded, desperately.

"Too bad." The demon used his dad's hand, pulling out his pocket knife and with one, swift slash, it cut his dad's throat.

At first, Samuel couldn't do anything. He couldn't see anything but the cut, the smirk, the moment when all life left the body and it fell to the floor with a sickening noise. He heard his mom scream.

Then Samuel screamed.

He crouched, squeezing his head and shutting his eyes. He felt like the world crumbled away until it was pulled out from under him, making him fall and fall and fall with no hope of an end.

He couldn't take it. He didn't *want* to take it. He

didn't want any of this. He wanted his sister. He wanted his mother to love him and his dad to be happy. He wanted Davis to be able to sit with him during a holiday dinner. He wanted to be able to laugh and smile and be proud of himself in a black and silver jacket.

He wanted what everyone else seemed to have.

He wanted to stop suffering.

He didn't want this.

Not this.

Not this.

*Not this.*

# CHAPTER
# SEVENTY-SIX

Davis was taken back to the Headquarters, where Paul laid out a plan. No one called in, he learned. It was just that Paul had been doing work as the Finder he was, and he located a spot with a sharp spike of activity. Everyone listened closely to his explanation and Davis completely ignored Andy.

Husband and wife, fluctuating between middle and lower class, known especially for going to a Catholic church consistently. Andy had to point out that going to church didn't necessarily mean anything and Davis decided continuing to ignore her was the best option.

They buttoned their jackets closed, checked weapons, and arranged themselves in the SUV. They were headed towards Mt. Pleasant and Davis fiddled with his phone.

"Let me see your gun," Jenkins said from behind

Davis.

"Hm? Okay," Davis said, pulling it out and handing it over. He wasn't supposed to use it, really. They had only given him the bare minimum in target practice and quite honestly, he hated it. He was fine with handing it over.

It was several clicks later before Jenkins handed it back. "Just checking it."

"Daniel should be here," Andy muttered, her arms crossed. "We aren't prepared yet. I can't be the only one with combat training."

"Sometimes it's brains and not brawn we need," Jenkins calmly said back, making Davis smirk. Andy looked back at them with a glare.

"What did he say?" she demanded from Davis.

Davis just waved her off. He was sure Andy probably would have retorted with something if his phone didn't go off.

"Oh, look at that. Sorry, Andy, can't talk right now. On the phone," he said just before answering his phone as it flashed Samuel's name. "Samuel?"

"Is this Davis?"

Davis frowned. It was a woman's voice and sounded nothing at all like Samuel. Samuel had a mix of sounds to his words and a reader's accent. This woman sounded very Southern.

"Yes, this is Davis. Why are you using Samuel's phone?" There was only one person Samuel let mess with his phone, and that was Davis himself.

"This is his mother, Julia Stewart," she said. "Please, I don't know what to do. My husband just— Samuel just threw me his phone and said to call you and I—I think my husband is dead. No, he is. He's dead. There's so much blood. And Sammy—"

"What about Samuel?" Davis snapped into the phone.

"Davis," Paul said calmly. They were pulling in front of a house. He did not move, just grabbed onto his phone with both hands.

"Hold on," Davis told him as he listened to Julia Stewart talk.

"He kept saying *Envy* and my Sammy—he's been trouble all his life, you see, but—"

"Get to the point. Is he okay?" he asked hurriedly.

"Well, I can see why you're his friend—"

"He's my *boyfriend*. Now tell me: *Is. Samuel. Okay?*" Davis would say anything and drop everything to be there.

"Davis," Jenkins said, and he was only able to get Davis's attention because Jenkins couldn't talk to anyone else. "Look at the mailbox."

"Well," Julia Stewart said as Davis looked at the mailbox. "I think he's been possessed."

Along the bottom of the mailbox, in carved cursive letters, was a name Davis knew well: *Stewarts*.

# CHAPTER SEVENTY-SEVEN

It was cold. It was not supposed to be this cold during July in Charleston.

Samuel curled into himself, trying to find warmth where there was none. There was no blanket to grab onto, no comfortable bed even beneath him. Maybe it wasn't really cold. Maybe he just had a fever. He blinked open his eyes.

He saw a glow in the dark stars, all evenly spaced apart. He could see his own breath.

I did it for you.

It was Abby's room. It was so obvious now. As he tilted his head against the soreness up his neck, he saw ice spreading in corners and along edges.

Samuel couldn't understand what that meant. He was so tired and so cold. All he wanted to do was go back to sleep. At least then he didn't have to deal with any problems.

So, he closed his eyes again and let the darkness surround him.

# CHAPTER SEVENTY-EIGHT

"Davis! Get back here!" Andy yelled, but Davis already jumped from the SUV and was running towards the house. He ran onto the white porch and immediately started pounding on the door, checking the handle only to confirm it was locked before continuing.

He had to get there first. He didn't care what else happened. He had to get there first, and he had to stop Andy from killing Samuel.

"Mrs. Stewart!" Davis yelled. "It's Davis! Samuel's—I'm Samuel's boyfriend! We were already on our way!"

It was only then the door opened, and a frail woman stood there, shaking and pale with blood on her hands. "I didn't know what to do," she cried. "I didn't know. I can't be alone. I can't live alone."

*What a selfish way to think*, Davis thought as he pushed his way inside the house.

He was almost shocked by the sheer contrast from the outside and inside. The exterior had made the Stewarts seem rich, while the interior expressed how poor they were. If not in money, in something else. It was in shambles created by cheap fixes and neglect. There were patches on wall holes that had been filled but not sanded or painted, footprints of dirt filling gaps on the bowing wooden floor, and there were dead bugs filling the lights overhead. That was just a start to the disarray. Davis nervously licked his lips and he continued inside, checking each room, bypassing the sight of what must have been Mr. Stewart.

Samuel wasn't there.

Davis dug his fingers in his hair and pulled at it as he shut his eyes tightly. This couldn't be happening. It couldn't be. He wanted to convince himself this was a nightmare, but he knew reality.

Suddenly, he was shoved against the doorframe with Andy's forearm against his collarbone and her face in his. "Don't you *dare* go running in like that again! I'm trying to protect your ass so we don't have to go drafting yet another piss poor Optic who doesn't give a fuck about anyone but himself. I am *not* letting you die, and I am definitely not letting you take any of us with you."

"Samuel could have been in here!" Davis argued. "He could have been here, and I don't want to see you put another blade in someone! Not anyone and not *him*!"

"Then let us *do our job* so we can help him! You getting killed by the demon won't help matters!" Andy snarled. She lowered her arm. "Now calm down so we can get enough information to find him."

It was not a very quick process for Davis to calm down. Right when he thought he was finally calm enough to move forward, he would imagine the demon using strength beyond Samuel's body limitations to hurt him, or the demon destroying his mind, or Andy killing him in different scenarios.

He wasn't made for these situations. He wasn't built for it. He wasn't some kind of hero. He was only a twenty-two-year-old who wanted a roof over his head, Samuel happily at his side, and to perform on a stage. He wanted to pass this on to the experts to handle, only to realize he was supposed to *be* one of those experts. He wasn't. He was far from it. How did they ever think he could do this?

Jenkins stayed with him, blocking his view of all the other activities as they crouched near the back entrance. Jenkins was silent, but his expression indicated he was available if Davis wanted to talk. He didn't.

Vanessa was the one to approach them. "Paul is tracking Samuel now. Andy went with him. They'll call us if they find him, so we need to be ready."

Davis stood up and Jenkins went with him. As much as Davis wanted to take action and keep an eye on Andy, there was nothing he could do now.

They waited at the house for news.

# CHAPTER SEVENTY-NINE

"This is a very sensitive job," Paul said as they walked the woods behind the Stewart household. "I advise you, as someone I trust to do their job, to treat it as such."

Andy kept her head lowered, watching Paul's steps. "Every job is sensitive," she said, "to someone." That was why the rules were the rules. She had lost sight of the point in saving people after years of doing this job. There were no limits to demons, as far as they could tell. There was just trying to control them before too much damage was done. A couple deaths by her prevented dozens more. Being cautious and careful seemed so much less effective than being quick and to the point.

"This one is sensitive to the team," Paul said. "Davis is one of us."

Andy was pretty sure Paul was biased towards Davis. She was also pretty sure Paul didn't trust her as much as he said he did. That was one thing that did bother her. "You were in the army," she said. "You had a job to do and you did it."

"I was in the army," Paul agreed as he fingered a twig that had been broken. "I did my job. I helped kill many people. Despite it being my job, I hated myself for it every day. Then I learned about the people we were killing."

"Let me guess," Andy said. "That's when you took on their religion."

"I was wrong to kill innocent people. I was reborn and now I can live my life using my skills to help," he said as they continued on. "I am the Head of this squad, which means every decision you make, whether correct or not, I take on as my own."

Andy was silent for a moment. She respected Paul as much as she respected Daniel, even if they were different, just like they were both capable in different ways. Even though Paul was useless in combat now due to the same reason he was no longer in the Mideast, he still had the mind of an Army General and the tracking expertise of a hunter. He held the team together and cared for it deeply. He was their leader. She never questioned if she was included in that. She just knew. He had not once chastised her for her methods.

"At the farmhouse," she started. "Did you agree with my actions?"

"You saved four lives, possibly more," Paul said. "And we know they were good people. Demons don't bother with those already tainted. They deserved much more."

"That doesn't answer the question."

"Yes," Paul said. "I did. You are a terrifying force, but you are also intelligent. You have only ever gone through with killing if you think they are already dead or on their way towards death."

"You believe that?" Andy asked. "How do you know I don't use that as an excuse?"

"Because you're asking that question," Paul said.

Andy blinked at the ground. She felt more settled than she had in weeks. "Thank you for trusting me."

"You wouldn't be on my team if I couldn't."

Soon, the trail led to another neighborhood. From that point, there was only so much farther they could follow the signs of passage before it was mixed with the traffic of other pedestrians.

"Let's keep going," Andy said. "We can split up and try to pick it back up again. Maybe go door to door—"

Paul put a hand on her shoulder. "Thank you, but it's getting dark. We should go back. We'll get a search team out for the night. Tomorrow, we'll have to try again with the whole team."

Andy would not go against the orders of her superior, so she nodded. She shoved her hands inside the pockets of her jacket and shrugged her shoulders. She was going to need advice on how to deal with Davis Turner.

# CHAPTER EIGHTY

"So you're Sammy's...boyfriend," Julia Stewart said after a while. Her eyes were red.

Police were on their way to make their own reports, so everyone moved to the front porch. The paint was starting to peel. It was obvious there were many layers. Davis had been hoping to talk about the house or the weather or anything but where this was going.

At least she was actually able to use the word 'boyfriend.'

Davis had not heard a single good thing about this woman, but he also hadn't heard much in general, so he decided to be careful and keep in mind she just lost her husband and possibly her son. "We're dating," he said.

"We lost his sister, you know," she said. "Years ago. She was thirteen."

Davis stared at her, remembering Abby's suicide

letter and how much that ruled Samuel's mind. "I'm sorry for your loss. Losses," he said genuinely, but he could only muster up so much strength. He looked at Vanessa.

"How about we make you a warm beverage," Vanessa said, clapping her hands together. Cheery. Fake, but apparently not many caught it. She would make a great actress. "Just something to keep ourselves busy." The house had enough walls that the living room couldn't been seen easily from the kitchen, so Vanessa led Mrs. Stewart inside. Davis could hear just catches of conversation.

"You know, I tried to raise Samuel right. I thought he had grown out of...boys."

"Oh, yes, I'm sure he did," Vanessa said. "He seems to like men now, which is a vast improvement over boys."

Davis blinked as he tried to smile, and he tried not to cry. He rubbed his face. They continued to wait.

When they finally did receive news, it was not good news. They lost Samuel's trail and would be starting again in the morning while a search team took over the night shift.

"Shit," Davis cursed. "Fuck." He kicked at the porch stairs. A minute later, he called Ashley and then Samuel's workplace to ask if they'd seen him, and if they had, to call Davis back immediately. Most importantly, he noted, they could not trust that Samuel was himself.

He had not been seen. Ashley was hysterical, but she let Davis call her back just to he could talk to *someone*.

"They'll find him. We'll help him," Ashley said,

who was the only one Davis mentioned *possession* to. She wasn't even in town anymore, though. She was too far away. "You're in a fucking Exorcist squad. It's going to be okay."

"He's my best friend," Davis said, finally sitting on the stairs and hunching over. "I lost Tommy. Steven moved away. You moved away. Most of Charleston knows who I am, and not in the good way, and... and I don't know what I'll do without him if anything happens."

"You'll continue living," Ashley said. "You'll serve the rest of the two years and then you're going to become a performer. It would just be harder. Much harder. But you don't have to worry about that because nothing is going to happen to him. He has you, after all. He has all of us."

Paul and Andy arrived around the time the police did, and everything was handed off to them—minus confidential details, such as Samuel's name. A while later, they headed back to the Headquarters, where it was suggested Davis stay the night. He did not argue.

He was ushered into the spare room he previously stayed in. He sat on the bed, feeling lost and scared, but most importantly, he missed Samuel. He wanted the air mattress to be on the floor, just waiting for Samuel to come back from the restroom. He wanted a different reality.

He just stayed mostly still, fiddling with his fingers, picking at his nails, and finding no want to even lie down until sometime later, when Jenkins stood at the doorway. It made him wish he had pretended to be asleep.

"We'll get him back," Jenkins said. "I promise. We'll get him back for you."

"Don't make false promises," Davis said, sneering. "Don't lie to try and make me feel better. It doesn't work."

"Then trust that I'll try," Jenkins retorted. "You have to try and trust me on this. But I'm also going to trust Paul and Andy. They're my teammates, and yours, too. And believe it or not, they care about people's lives. Why do you think Jazmin is downstairs? We could have just killed her. But we didn't. We want to save her, and I'm sure the others will want to save Samuel for you."

Davis looked at him through the dark room, seeing Jenkins silhouetted by the hall light. "Why are you with me? Why promise me this?"

"Because dealing with it alone...having to do the last option alone is the worst feeling in the world," Jenkins said. His hands were fisted at his sides, his shoulders hunched. "I don't want anyone else to have to go through that. Not if I can prevent it."

"The last option?" Davis asked him.

"Mercy killing," Jenkins said. "I do not want you to be put in a situation where the only options are killing him or him killing others—or killing him because he could not live with what he's done."

Davis stared at him, his hands bunching in his jeans. "I couldn't kill him," he said. "I just couldn't."

"I thought the same thing about my wife," Jenkins said. "And then she killed my son."

# CHAPTER EIGHTY-ONE

Davis was right to assume he wouldn't be able to sleep that night. It wasn't just thoughts of the evening, of knowing Samuel was out there, possessed. It was images of Jenkins having to kill his wife, then of him, in his black and silver jacket, having to kill Samuel.

He knew what it was like to have been possessed and know that he had killed. It was the worst feeling and it caused the world around you to change. If they were able to get Samuel back, what would have happened by that time? What casualties? Would Samuel be able to handle it, after already struggling to handle so much else?

But Davis was willing to be there. Davis would not mercy kill him for that reason. Even if Samuel begged him to, he wouldn't—it would be the cruelest punishment of all. He could be there for Samuel and feed him back the words he was told by the people he had found. He could remind Samuel of the exact words he told Davis. He made a plan in his head, deciding that no matter what they were going to save him. They had to perform an exorcism. There had to be another way to kill the demon. They knew Samuel's religion. Davis *knew* him. They had to get him back.

He would have Samuel back.

After a while, he gave up sleep altogether and went downstairs. The living room was oddly lit, with moonlight coming through the floor-to-ceiling windows. The night air cooled the room the same way it stilled it. This house still felt like an imitation of a home, where the furniture was brought in by professional stagers. He decided he did prefer it over what he thought a normal Headquarters would look like, and he sat on one of the most comfortable couches in the world, his knees drawn to his chest, and he stared at the painting of The Creation.

It wasn't long before Jenkins joined him.

They didn't talk about the fact they were still up. They didn't try to have small talk. They both stared at the painting and thought about the knowledge that came with it.

"I don't know if I believe in any of that," Davis said, staring at the red of the painting, remembering the blood of his childhood and the blood of his present. "Angels—God? I think we're on our own still. We wouldn't need Exorcists if we weren't."

"Do you think this mainly because of what happened when you were a kid?" Jenkins asked.

Davis looked at Jenkins, wondering if he knew exactly what the church had done, then just shook his head. "I've come to realize the truth of what happened that night. It was one church, one group of people who thought they were doing the right thing—but Samuel is..." He clenched his fists. "He's Christian—Catholic, even, and he's...he's always been wonderful and accepting. He would never want to hurt me. And I have a friend from high school, Jacob D'Cruz—he's from Brazil, whose citizens are mostly Catholic, too. But they're both incredible people. And Samuel...how in the world did he get possessed? How could he, of all people?"

He understood still that demons didn't just go after sin. He knew what they did, how they got into your head and made you believe in false feelings, but he never imagined *Samuel* having to deal with it. He had always been so attentive in analyzing every emotion he had.

"He was innocent," Jenkins said, shrugging. "Demons like to pull out any sin. They're attracted to it. Andy will be asking you a lot of questions about what the demon could be latching onto. We need to figure out the root cause to be able to try and talk directly to Samuel."

Davis looked at him. "Were you able to talk to your wife?"

Jenkins took a slow breath. "Follow me," he said, standing and heading back upstairs. Davis followed him wordlessly until they reached the two doors he had yet to see into. Jenkins opened the first door.

"This was my son's room," he said, standing at the threshold, clearly showing he did not want to enter. The room looked like a stereotypical baby boy's room: light blue walls, white furniture, a crib, rocking chair, toys scattered on the ground.

"Carson," Davis read from a small sign hanging on the wall.

Jenkins nodded, looking pained. He closed the door, moving to the other one. This was where he usually went, when everyone else was busy and there was no work to be done. He opened the door and walked in, holding it open for Davis.

"This is our...well it's a library or sorts, but...a resting room."

It was much more dimly lit than the baby's room, with a total of five bookcases lining two perpendicular walls, three to the left of the door, two on either side of the window. It was a small room, no bigger than the baby's room, but it also had a small raised section with two steps leading up it, a La-Z-Boy chair perched on it, and a basket to the side with more books. Davis was careful when he walked inside, observing the books one case at a time before he made a realization. It started with larger, flatter books that came in different shapes and bright colors. As it went, the colors became more bold or dull and the sizes were more uniformed with visible titles along the spine. It was in order by age group: baby's first, then children's, young teen, young adult, and then adult.

"Eve, my wife, collected books with the idea of letting our son grow up with them. We had hoped he would love them," Jenkins said, taking the few steps to the chair and sitting down in it. He looked like he belonged there, but also as if something were missing. He didn't quite fill the chair enough. Davis could imagine him holding a child there, reading to him, laughing and enjoying a simple story. He saw Jenkins' hands tighten on the arms of the chair.

"What happened?" Davis asked, this time filling the question with his sadness, wanting to know for his own sake, for Samuel's sake, but also for Jenkins'.

"Eve got possessed," Jenkins said, his voice shallow, staring at nothing. "It was when I got home from a gallery showing. The kitchen and living room were a complete disaster and there she was, standing amongst the mess with a grin on her face." He closed his eyes tightly, as if in pain.

"You don't have to tell me," Davis said quickly. "I'll understand."

"No, you need to hear this," Jenkins said, taking a shaky breath. "For Samuel, you need to hear this."

Davis gave a single nod.

"I realized pretty early what was going on, even if I didn't want to believe it. I asked her where Carson was, panicked because I knew I was already losing my wife, but what about my *son*, my baby boy…and she told me she killed him." A cold chill went up Davis's back at the way he said it, like it was just a fact. There was no emotion behind it until the next few words, which were filled with nothing but anguish. "She described in detail what she did to him. There was *blood*. She dropped him over the rail at the Battery, into the water and rocks. That's why when Cillian…" He paused, took a breath. "I—I *couldn't* believe it." He looked at Davis. "She attacked me with a kitchen knife and I—there was nothing I could do. She almost killed me. There was a struggle much worse than what you've seen, much…more painful, she…I had to kill her in self-defense."

"Jenkins..." Davis said sympathetically. "I'm so sorry..."

"You have to understand that I regretted it at first—I *killed* my *wife*... but she killed my two-year-old son. She would have killed me. If she were exorcised...would she want to live with that?" Jenkins shook his head. "We were everything to her, just like they were to me. I'm...like *this*," he said, gesturing to himself, "a Nondefined, because of that. Because I lost them both and I lost my purpose and I can't let that happen to you, too."

"I can't kill him," Davis said. "I already said that. It's not that I won't. I can't. If you try to put me in the situation where I'll have to, I'll just freeze."

"I know," Jenkins said. "You're different than I was. You don't have that instinct to fight back. But you have to let us do our job. You don't want someone else's life in danger because of him, do you?"

Davis didn't answer. He couldn't. He could barely accept the image of Samuel hurting anyone, possessed or not.

"Just please, keep it in mind," Jenkins said gently. "We don't need another Nondefined. Samuel needs you to do what's right."

"Everyone has a different opinion on what 'right' is," Davis said. "Samuel and I made a promise to each other that we would find another way."

Jenkins stayed quiet for a moment, just sitting in the chair, feeling the fabric of the arms. "Well, then I hope you can keep that promise. I will help you where I can."

"There's no hoping to it," Davis said, hardening his resolve. "I'm going to find a way to save him. I have to."

375

# CHAPTER EIGHTY-TWO

When it first started to lighten outside, every member of the Exorcist squad was gathered in the kitchen except for Paul. They waited patiently as he prayed, using his whole body. It was a calming thing to watch in the midst of such chaotic thoughts. Arms outstretched, body open, accepting to an invisible connection. When he was done, he pulled out a map and spread it over the table. He had a tablet showing a time lapse of temperature readings.

"This is where we started," he said, pointing towards Mt. Pleasant and the Stewart household. "This," he said, drawing an invisible circle around a dark blue mass, "is probably Samuel. You can see how it wasn't there for most of the night, but reappears just a half hour ago and disappears again."

"Wait," Andy said, pointing to where the blue

mass appeared. "That's the park across from the police station. We've seen temperature changes there before. Are you sure it's Samuel?"

"No," Paul admitted. "But this is different. Colder. Stronger. I believe this is our main lead."

"It should be investigated either way if there aren't any other clues," Davis said. He was already in his uniform, his knife left in the spare room and his gun in its holster, ignored but not forgotten.

The others, he noticed, were already geared as well. He felt touched by the gesture. He had not been very kind to them as a group and here they were, up as soon as was logical and ready to find Samuel.

"Thank you," he said, even if he wasn't sure how this day would end.

The SUV took them to the park, where Vanessa took the initiative to warn a family that was lounging at the playground.

"I don't see him," Davis said, looking around. There were woods just beyond the playground to one side, and bushes and branches of small trees along the entrance to the pier. They went to the small group of trees first, calling out Samuel's name, but there was nothing but crabs and spiders. Of course, there wouldn't be anything else. Of course, Samuel wouldn't be there.

But then Davis saw the pier. There was a figure at one end, sitting on the ledge. "There. We should look there," and he began to walk along the bridge, towards it. He felt eager, but he didn't rush. He had to do this correctly.

Paul called out a formation and Davis was pleased to hear it was surrounded by his movements. He ignored the frazzled fishermen that were on the left pier and turned right, slowly stepping down the stairs. One of the others, probably Vanessa or Noah, could deal with any bystanders.

It was easy to see it was Samuel sitting there now, casually, as if he had been waiting. A step closer and he could see a flicker.

"This keeps him locked," Samuel's voice said. It was so quiet, so casually said that it made Davis doubt himself. Then, an image of a warped head moved just before Samuel's followed it. Davis had to take very purposeful breaths. "It was difficult, staying alive inside of him. He was very strong. But I found his weakness."

"Shut up," Davis said, but was rather stricken by the idea he was having such a conversation with a *demon*. "Why aren't you doing anything?"

"Oh, but I am," it said. Now Davis could hear two voices. One of Samuel's, his words specifically pronounced. Then there was an echo, an added accent. Samuel's eyes looked at the water, watching as something dropped from his outstretched arm, into the water below.

Blood. Samuel's blood. Davis's mind was loud with screams and he had to clench his teeth to not let any of it out.

"What are you doing, then?" Davis asked. This, of course, was being asked so Davis himself could think of what to do. He couldn't just be physical, but he didn't want to just start babbling to Samuel when he knew how impossible it was for Samuel to be conscious at all. Was this where Andy should step in?

She knew the most about religions, about what might shock Samuel conscious and maybe even make him incompatible. Somehow, Davis didn't think it would work. Samuel was Christian, yes, but it hadn't ruled his every action.

"Did you know," the demon said, "that Samuel found his sister in a bathtub? He found her because the water had started to leak underneath the bathroom door. Pink stained, of course. She had cut her inner thigh."

Davis's lungs felt like they had gone up to rest in his throat, but the demon continued.

"There were many things I could have manipulated inside of him," it said. "Many things he could envy. Your position, your family, the other Exorcists, or even the venders along the Market that don't struggle with social interaction. However, each of those was more difficult to be truly convincing. It didn't seem real to him. Do you want to know what did feel real, Mr. Turner? What he could accept being jealous of?" Davis stayed silent, watching as Samuel's body was used, turmoil tearing him apart inside. The demon's head turned to look at Davis through the corner of his eye, and then Samuel's followed. "His sister's death."

# CHAPTER EIGHTY-THREE

Samuel couldn't sleep, but he didn't want to open his eyes.

He had read somewhere that when someone had insomnia, it was still best to lay down and rest anyway, so he did. He didn't want to face the waking world. There was a part of him that knew the room was colder, that the ice would overcome him. He would let it.

There was a familiarity he felt in his chest. A sense of something that was never supposed to belong to this room. This dreadful room.

There was something else in it.

He opened his eyes.

The stars were glowing on the ceiling, neon green against the dark surrounding.

He was supposed to do something today. Obligations, maybe. A personal project? He had been making something for Davis, he remembered. He hadn't known it was going to be for Davis. He had thought it was going to be for himself, but it wasn't. It was for Davis.

Davis. That's what it felt like, the feeling foreign to his room. He could hear Davis, even if he could not hear words. He knew Davis, knew the feel of his presence just as well as he knew his absence.

Samuel looked around the room. Davis was not there, but the feeling didn't go away. It was enough for him to sit up, then look on either side of the bed, then under it. He slid from the bed and even checked the closet before going to the door.

It was locked.

Why was he here?

It wasn't that he felt like he shouldn't have been in Abby's room as much as it felt like maybe it was only supposed to be a visited place. He wanted to go home. He started knocking on the door.

"Hello? Is anyone out there? Mom? Da—" He stopped. He had seen his dad. He had—no. He pushed the memory away, far away, where he couldn't truly acknowledge its existence.

"Do you want to see what living means?" a voice said. It was proper with a hint of an accent, but it also sounded like a recording of himself.

"I don't understand," Samuel said, staring at the door. He thought the owner of the voice must be on the other side.

"Then look. Realize why you don't want to rejoin them," it said, and the door opened.

Water. So much water, spilling from under the bathroom door. *Pink* water.

Samuel screamed and stumbled back, and the

door slammed shut on its own. He pushed the heel of his palms into his eyes and pushed back against the side of the bed and wished and hoped and yearned to go to sleep.

This, he felt, had already happened many times. He did not go back to sleep.

# CHAPTER EIGHTY-FOUR

Davis had stood at the railing of the Battery, facing the ocean, contemplating the sadness that was his life. Samuel had come to him without question. He had not looked at the water. He had not looked away from Davis. Davis had ranted about his views on suicide. He had told Samuel he never wanted to be forced to end his own life. He had talked about it being a choice. He had meant every word of it. He found he still meant every word of it, but he was finding a logic to the decisions Exorcists had to make. Although he would gladly die for Samuel to live, that was only partially his decision. If Samuel truly wanted to die, it wasn't in Davis's power to prevent it.

However, it wasn't two people making a decision about who would die. Davis thought about Jazmin and the demon within her, how it had traveled from him to her and how it had killed everyone she was close to.

He started to make a final decision. It wasn't one he liked, but there weren't many options and he was tired of waiting and watching.

He took a step forward and the demon's head turned sharply towards him, Samuel's eyes were glaring at him.

"I wouldn't try coming closer," it said. "This is the only way your boy will stay alive."

Davis heard a sound from behind him. He glanced back, towards Jenkins, who looked ready to leap, and Andy, who was looking at him, waiting for Davis. He looked back towards Samuel. "He'll stay alive," he said. "He'd be breaking our first rule if he didn't."

The demon scowled at him and it was so *wrong* that Davis had to close his eyes for a minute before blinking. "You were the one that said dying was his decision," it said.

"Then it should be an informed decision," Davis said, "and it's something he could talk to me about. Samuel, try to hear—" The wood plank beneath his foot cracked and he almost lost his footing, but caught it until the crack expanded, forcing him to quickly step back until his foot landed on—and then through—one of the planks. He stumbled and was caught by two arms under his, pulling him away. He saw Andy start to move forward and he quickly held out his hand. She stopped. His heart was pounding.

"Why wait for us at a pier?" Davis asked as he got his footing back under him. "You're cornered."

"You think that," the demon said, and then it stood with a grace Samuel didn't have, but Samuel's body performed, and faced Davis directly. "But drowning is one of the slowest ways to die. Samuel can't swim, you don't want him to die, and I'm sure we're all aware I would be able to escape just fine to start this process all over again. I'm stronger every time."

Davis gritted his teeth as he tried to figure out something he could do. What could *he* do?

A memory stuck in his head. It was of when he was younger, when he would sit in his bedroom and create characters. They were all very different and he would design them to have potential for great emotions, all the ones he couldn't have. He thought of one particular character, a man who wished to be a rock star. Davis had given this character all of his dreams of becoming famous, but most importantly he had given the character his anger towards others, the anger that said *this is not fair*. He had given it away so that he was never upset when others had it easier than him. He had worked harder and felt better.

Now, he started to take those feelings back.

"Where would you go?" Davis asked. "Would you go possess someone else right away? Let them experience what it's like?" Maybe he wouldn't be so feared if they understood. He only let himself toy with the idea, let it have a passing thought—let it have *potential*.

The demon was staring at him curiously. Samuel took a step back, which was a step closer to the water. Davis glanced back at Andy. He hoped she understood what was about to happen.

"I just want Samuel back," he said, looking back

at the demon. "There are too many people who would miss him. Ashley, his mother, me," he said, "and he still needs to get his black and silver jacket. There are reasons for him to live." Davis shrugged and looked towards the cracked planked below his boots. He took a tentative step forward. "I think he deserves that chance."

"Ah, but," the demon said, but there weren't any other words. It stood completely still in Samuel's body.

"It's retreated internally," Vanessa said softly. Davis didn't know when she'd joined, but he looked back at her, then at Andy.

"What should we do?" he asked her.

"Wait," Andy said. "This is Samuel's battle now."

# CHAPTER EIGHTY-FIVE

"...Samuel..."

Samuel blinked, taking in a deep, heavy breath as he started to become more aware, shivering as he opened his eyes and faced the door to the hallway.

Why was he awake again? What was the purpose? At least here he was safe. Here, no one could hurt him. He wouldn't have to deal with the cruelties of the world. He wouldn't have to remember. He could just sleep...

"...first rule..."

The words echoed in the room, making some of the furniture shake as if an earthquake was rocking the foundation.

But that would suggest he wasn't safe, wouldn't it?

He hunched against the bed, looking around fearfully, putting his hands over his head and shutting his eyes. He willed for it to go away, for everything to just go away. His limbs felt so stiff, so incredibly cold, and he knew he wouldn't be able to fight back.

Why couldn't he just fall asleep again? Why did he wake up?

What rule...?

That voice was awfully familiar. He had *felt* it before, had just put a name to it. It didn't seem to be threatening. In fact, it seemed...comforting.

Samuel blinked as a name fit into the space. "Davis...?" he asked into the room.

"I just want Samuel back."

It was Davis, but it sounded like it was coming out of a speaker. It was coming through the door. Davis was there, past the...past his memory.

Davis was safe.

"...Ashley..."

Samuel bit the inside of his cheek and forced his freezing limbs to work, breaking from the ice that had started to bind him and standing on his numb legs.

"...and he still needs to get his black and silver jacket."

He had a reason to move, a reason to wake up and keep going. In fact, he had more than one. It was hard, but the last thirteen *years* had been hard. He struggled to make his way to the door, feeling much heavier than he had before. When he tried the handle, he found it locked.

"No! I want to leave!" Samuel shouted, his voice hoarse as he banged his fist against the door, trying the handle again and again before it burst open, making him stumble out, slipping on the wet surface and catching himself with his hands. His nose was almost touching the pink tinted water. He shook and he fisted his hands and he couldn't make himself stand. Still, on his hands and knees, he forced himself to look up.

He was looking at a face with wide, bloodshot eyes and rotted teeth, the skin flaking, wiry hair falling out of a nearly bare scalp, limbs hardly even bones dressed in ragged clothes.

Samuel screamed and stumbled back, taking in deep breaths as the full realization of what was happening dawned on him.

He was a prisoner. He was trapped, against his will, inside of his own head. Which meant…

He remembered his dad. He remembered his death. He remembered the word—no, the name—*Envy*.

"Hi there," the demon said, cackling, the voice now sounding dusty and old. "Don't you think," it said, "that it would be better for you to go to sleep?"

"Don't you think," Samuel sneered back, "that it would be better to go to hell?"

"Oh, but that's much too boring, Dear. The chaos is already there—but *here*, though. Here, I can create it." There was the laugh again, awful in tone and pitch, making Samuel cringe. He scrambled to stand and tried to get past the demon, to head towards the front door of the house, looking for *some way* to get out. His ankle was grabbed and *yanked*, forcing him to fall, but he screamed and kicked and pulled his leg away.

Then he heard Davis again. "Come on, Samuel! Come back to me!" It was coming from Samuel's room.

"I'm *trying!*" Samuel cried out, running into his door in his haste and having difficulty turning the knob to open it because his hands were wet and shaking, but he managed it and stumbled inside, shutting the door behind him.

He turned around, and the demon was standing in front of him.

"Do you really want to be trying?" the demon asked. "Don't you remember what's out there? Remember your sister? What happened to your father? Do you want to see what you did to your mother?"

"Mother?" Samuel asked, thinking back, trying to figure out what he had done. He didn't remember doing anything to his mother.

"Do you remember what *she* did to *you*? What she made that man do?"

Samuel stood, staring unbelievingly. "What man?" he asked after a moment. "What are you talking about?"

"See the file cabinet beside you?" the demon said, much too happily. Samuel turned his head and saw it. "That contains your memories."

"It's small," Samuel commented, his curiosity growing, turning into more of a *need*. He needed to see the truth of his world. That, whatever it was, needed to be factored in his decision to keep fighting. He observed the demon, realized it wasn't moving, and he knelt down in front of the file cabinet and tried to pull the top drawer open, but it was locked. He growled and hit the top of it. "Come on!"

"You can't open it because they are the memories *you* locked away," the demon said.

"Then why tell me about it?" Samuel asked, starting to be rather pissed off now since it was obvious the demon was no longer in attack mode. "You can't use it against me if I can't remember it."

"You'll know if you leave, though. Don't you want to see if it's worth living before you face it?"

Samuel looked at the drawer. "It's always worth knowing everything before you make an important decision," he said, examining it as if it were something more than just an old filing cabinet. "How do I open it?"

"You're the one who locked it," the demon said. "How should I know?"

"Me?" Samuel said, staring at it. "Then…I should be able to open it. I should have the key, right?" He patted himself, his t-shirt and then his blue jeans, front and then back pockets, where he stopped. He dug in his back pocket and pulled out a small key, one that was so simple it must have been universal, yet somehow…wasn't. This was all in his head, wasn't it? This was how his head was making sense of everything going on.

He put the key in the lock and the drawer popped open, a puff of debris and mold spores coming out with it, forcing Samuel to cough and wave his hand to try and clear the air. When it cleared enough for him to look, he saw it wasn't just dust and mold. It was ashes of papers that were crumbling at the edges, some completely destroyed and settled in the bottom of the drawer.

"What is this?" Samuel said as he looked in with horror.

"They're your blocked memories—you make

sense of the rest," the demon said, clearly seeming less amused now.

Samuel gathered some of the ashes in his hands, realizing as he held them exactly what they were.

"They're gone," he said, letting the ashes slip through his fingers. "They're the memories I've destroyed."

The demon didn't say anything, so Samuel gave a moment to look through the files that were left, dated back since he was nine years old. He went to pick it up, to look at the first one, but he stopped. When he was nine...that was before his sister's death. He wanted to look at it, to try and remember what he had forgotten, but he didn't. He put the file away and went to the most recent, pulling out a single piece of paper.

Just looking at the paper flooded his mind with the memory. He could see it again, his dad, possessed, holding the knife. The knife cutting his throat. The body dropping to the ground. It was blank again, something he hadn't registered, but then he could see his mom, fearful, backing away from *him*, calling him a monster, praying to God, quoting Bible verses—and he had just left. He had not killed his mother. He hadn't touched her.

He took a breath and went back to his earlier years, when he had been nearly innocent. He pulled out a paper. He stared at it, feeling separated from what it showed him. Then, the rest of the papers burst out from the drawer.

The papers floated down around Samuel's hands as he gasped and shook as all the memories washed over him.

It was too much. Too much he remembered, too much he had to push through, it was *too much bad*. What his mother had done—what his sister had said, as a result.

"I'm so sorry, Samuel," she had cried to him. "I'm so sorry. Maybe…maybe if I was gone, she'd treat you better. She would be able to see how wonderful you are."

"Don't leave," he had said. "I'm okay when you're here."

Then she had left her letter. *I did it for you*. She had been wrong, though. When she left, nothing was okay. It was *worse*. His mother never had to physically abuse him when she could get someone else to do it.

The demon was right. Maybe it was better to stay here then deal with what happened. He could hear it laughing with victory.

"Samuel!" his name was called out. Again, it was Davis. He couldn't face Davis. He *couldn't*.

But he had to. He would, because there were other memories now. Ones he had made and kept, others to be made. He steadied his breath, walked over the papers littering the floor, and he faced the demon, staring into the demon's haunted eyes. "It's time you let me out."

"No," the demon said, seeming less sure. "I will just take you back."

"You can try," Samuel said, still feeling fragile and raw, but determined. "But this is my mind."

"If that's how you feel," the demon said, tilting its head before its mouth split into a strange grin. "Then I'll just have to move to Davis."

"No!" Samuel screamed and lunged at the demon, but it disappeared. Samuel gasped as pain shot through his body, hitting his nerves, feeling as if *something* was skinning him alive from the inside. The room warped and changed.

Then, he no longer saw a room, but Davis standing in front of him on the dock.

The demon was going to possess him.

He knew what Davis had been told to do if he was possessed.

He had to kill himself, and there was nothing Samuel could do.

# CHAPTER EIGHTY-SIX

Davis watched Samuel. He saw him starting to sweat, to shake, to whimper. Davis called out any encouragement he could, knowing there was little else he could do. Andy had been right. This was Samuel's battle.

Then Samuel's breathing changed.

There was a flicker, an image of the demon turning towards the water, but it was shot back into Samuel's body, which did not move.

Samuel's expression wavered, then it stilled into one of utter horror and pain.

"Davis," he breathed out. "*No.*" Then, with a shock of fear, he tipped back into the water.

That was when the demon of Envy switched Hosts, moving from Samuel Stewart to Davis Turner.

Davis felt it happen as he always did: the cold, the pain, the invasion of it, the influence over his emotions. He felt the manipulations of those feelings he had taken back, twisting them and turning them into truly awful things, and Davis let it happen. He let himself feel as if everyone else deserved what had happened to him. Everyone deserved the unwarranted blame placed on them, the misplaced hatred, the knife cut into their back—or *worse*.

He was the person wanting that. He was no longer Davis Turner, standing on the pier, trying to save his best friend. He was on stage, with multicolored lights shining on him, a crowd cheering in the audience, watching *him* as he glided across the stage in a custom costume piece, entertaining them, feeding from their energy, feeling safe in the knowledge that *he finally had this*.

It was hard to pull himself away from it. It was hard to stop enjoying himself long enough to look around the crowd he had created.

"Where are you?" he asked into the microphone. The words echoed through the theatre.

"Right here," the demon said behind him. It was grotesque, looking more as if it was from a zombie movie than anything Davis had seen. It was falling apart. Yet its back was still straight, and its face was still smug. "Isn't it a lovely view? A grand stage, made just for you."

"Oh, yeah," Davis said, nodding along. "I mean, I helped make it."

"Oh?" the demon said.

"Yeah. I used to do some carpentry for the college," he said, tapping his foot on the platform. "The thing is, you're not in control here," he added casually.

"You really think that?" the demon said, looking

unimpressed.

"Yes. There are certain…things I built into this stage, you see," Davis explained. He was grinning as he looked at his foot. It was hovering over a carefully camouflaged button. He pushed it.

Cage walls shot up from the floor around the demon, boxing it, and a top dropped from above. The demon hissed and ran to the bars, grabbing onto them before jerking back with smoking hands. "What did you *do*?"

Davis shrugged. "I built a demon cage. This is *my* head, right? I've been aware of it for years, making myself believe and become something else, somewhere else." He put his hands on his hips. "I'm not an Exorcist. I'm a performer. An actor. It's in the job description."

"I can still manipulate your emotions!" the demon screamed. "I might be trapped in here, but that doesn't mean I'm not in control!"

"But that's where you're wrong," Davis said calmly. "You don't have control if you have nothing to hold onto. My emotions might be high, but my jealousy isn't real." He slid off his studded jacket and rubbed a hand through his hair, letting his created character go back into its case. Those feelings had no place within him anymore.

He knew what he had to do now that the demon was trapped within him. He had to make it incompatible. He had to push himself back out. He had to kill himself. He was procrastinating, if just for a moment longer.

He was scared.

"You'll never get to be one! Not as long as you're

stuck being an Exorcist!" the demon screamed. "What about your friends who were able to leave Charleston while you're stuck here? Steven? Ashley? What about those who are able to audition for Broadway, your dream?"

"I'm not jealous of them," Davis said, rubbing the sleeves of his t-shirt as he searched his true feelings on the matter. "I'm happy for them, just like I'm happy being here. My time will come. In the meantime, I have another job to do." He slipped on a black and silver jacket and he closed his eyes, preparing to wake up and use his gun for the first and final time.

He jerked his eyes back open as he heard the demon's painful cries, watching as its skin started to boil and then *melt*. Davis grimaced as he watched in confusion.

Then he realized what was happening. He needed to make the demon incompatible with himself and he *had*, just by getting rid of his jealousy.

The demon was still alive, though, sizzling on the floor of the cage. Davis felt a *rush* at the idea of not having to die, of finding another way, just as Samuel had said he would. He ran off the stage, grabbing a bat from a props closet, and he ran through the graffiti covered door and into the hallway.

There he was. A version of himself, maybe thirteen, maybe fourteen, with black eyeliner, spiked hair, and a studded jacket. He took the bat and he smashed the case, shattering the character and everything false it had contained.

He heard the demon's screams and he heard the demon die.

When he woke up, he thought he would be able to feel the relief. He had trusted his team to take care of Samuel. It was over.

He woke to blood.

# CHAPTER EIGHTY-SEVEN

Andy was *pissed*.

Here she was, trying to be a supportive goddamn teammate for once, taking the lead from someone *other* than the Head of *her* squad, and Davis went and purposefully got himself possessed so the rest of them had to save his fucking boyfriend.

Jenkins jumped in after Samuel, pulling him out unconscious, but alive. Noah got him breathing again, which he did in coughs and spits before he freaked out and almost fell *back* into the water before they stopped him. He was distraught, which she guessed was understandable, but really, there were other things to focus on.

Such as Davis, who got himself fucking possessed on fucking purpose.

Sure, she wasn't an Optic. Their current Optic was possessed. Fucker. Their last Optic went and left them out of nowhere. Fucker. Not Fucker. That one was her fault. She was still pissed. However, the change in expression and attitude was enough of an indicator. His face was being strange, though. The demon didn't seem to be in complete control, which meant Davis was definitely trying to do what Vanessa taught him. The thing was, he hadn't stayed conscious enough to stop the demon's actions, which meant the demon pulled out Davis's gun, took the safety off, pointed it at Andy and pulled the trigger without a moment of pause.

Andy wouldn't have been able to dodge it if it had actually been loaded—but it wasn't. There were no bullets, thanks to Jenkins, and therefore she was not shot.

That didn't stop the demon completely, though. It, using Davis's body, attacked her with hands like claws, scratching at her and grabbing at her waist. She was pushed over, but that had never slowed her before. She just wasn't used to fighting someone she wasn't actually ready to kill. It was much more difficult. She elbowed him in the face (if she broke his nose it's *his fault* for getting himself *fucking possessed*) and kneed his stomach (the previous statement also applied to ribs and organs) and was able to get him off her just as he swiped her knife, slashing it against her shoulder and down in a curve around her arm, all the way to her elbow.

There was nothing for a moment—no pain, no comprehension, and then a *burst*. It *hurt*. The blood was easy enough to ignore. Scratches were *nothing*, but she thought she could see *white* which meant *bone* and she couldn't feel her fingers. She twisted away, cradling her arm in whatever awkward way she could, but he had her knife and she was down one arm.

It was Vanessa, of all people, the youngest and least trained in combat, who whistled before throwing a rock at Davis's face to get his attention.

Then it was Jenkins who tackled him from the opposite side (at least she thought it was Jenkins. He looked hairy, but her vision was starting to blur) and then there was some brown blob (Noah, probably) and she had lost too much blood. She was extremely pissed.

Yet she felt that, *finally*, she did her job right. Maybe it was okay if she was the one that died this time. She wasn't playing God; she was letting the Universe work, and this is what It wanted. It was *right*.

"Andy!" she heard Paul call. "Don't let her die! Do whatever you have to! Don't let her—"

# CHAPTER EIGHTY-EIGHT

When Davis woke up, he had no choice but to pay strict attention to Andy. It was the blood that drew in his eyes, and it was the knowledge that brought on the devastation. He had done that. He hadn't prevented the demon from hurting her. He might have *killed* her.

For the first time, Paul was hysterical. It took Vanessa's soft tone and Noah's harsh words to keep him back.

"Call 911," Jenkins snapped at Davis.

Davis scrambled for his phone and did just that.

As they waited for the ambulance to arrive, Noah tended to Andy's arm as best he could. Davis watched because he couldn't move. He wasn't sure what he would feel if he actually was the cause of Andy's death when she had so purposefully been careful for him, for Samuel.

He felt Samuel's hand on his shoulder, the touch

familiar, and he looked to see a mirrored expression. It was Samuel the demon had possessed originally. This was the *real* Samuel. In a moment, they understood the guilt the other felt. They were both at fault for this—in the exact same way they weren't.

"It was a demon," Samuel whispered, eyes downcast. His hair still dripped water occasionally. He must have lost his hat at some point.

"Yeah," Davis choked. "I killed it."

Samuel quickly looked up to him, shocked. "Killed it?"

"Yes," Davis said, his eyes intent on Samuel's. "I found another way."

Samuel's smile uneasy. "I knew you would."

Davis took a breath. "Here, take off your shirt at least," he said, slipping off his jacket and handing it to Samuel. "You don't need to add anything else to the list of things for us to check just by staying in wet clothes."

Samuel stared at the jacket. *The* jacket. Black and silver and very obviously made for an Exorcist. "Yeah," he breathed, taking off his shirt before slipping the jacket on. He couldn't take his eyes off it.

"It suits you better," Davis whispered with a smile, kissing Samuel's cheek. Samuel did not say anything.

When the ambulance arrived, Paul and Noah went with Andy, and Vanessa drove the rest of them in the SUV, insisting Samuel have his arm checked along with a full physical just in case the demon did any other damage. Davis noticed Paul was very careful in his wording. Samuel was a victim of a demon attack, but he never once said he was the one possessed.

Davis did not mention the pain in his own face or stomach. He could piece together what happened and Noah could look at him later.

When they arrived, Andy was already in surgery.

"That boy from the missing poster," Samuel told Paul. "I saw him. He…" He paused, searching for the explanation. "I can't explain what happened, but I was told he passed the demon on to me."

Paul was still not completely composed, but he had prayed once Andy had gone through the swinging doors and had been calmer since. Andy's life was in the hands of someone, or something, else now. "That would explain the mother's theory of him being kidnapped by demons," he said, but it was clear that was something they would be investigating at another time.

Then Samuel tilted his head towards Davis, looking down at their linked hands. "The demon. It… made me remember some things—a lot of things. From my past. I had known about them, I just…chose to forget them."

Davis watched their hands as well, staying silent for Samuel's sake.

"I know what happened," Samuel whispered. "But I don't think I can talk about it yet. I need to believe they're real memories first."

"Take all the time you need," Davis whispered back.

They had to wait an hour before Samuel could be seen, and Andy was still in surgery. Davis became increasingly worried, especially now that Samuel wasn't by his side.

"He'll be okay," Jenkins said. "It was a small cut caused by his belt. They'll probably give him a tetanus shot and put a Band-Aid on it. Plus, you have no worries paying the bill."

"Andy," was all Davis said in response.

Jenkins had no response to that.

They waited.

Samuel came out after a while, looking sheepish and rubbing his shoulder, where he had indeed gotten a tetanus shot. "Any news?" he asked as he took a seat next to Davis.

"No," he said, laying his head on Samuel's shoulder—the one he didn't get the shot in. "She's still in surgery. Are you okay?"

"Nothing unexpected," Samuel said as he rested his head against Davis's, which was only a surprise because others were starting to look at them.

They stayed silent, not knowing what to say or what to do, just listening as the nurse kept calling people back, and then...

"Samuel?" At first, they ignored it, because he had already been seen and there could have been another Samuel waiting. Then, "Samuel Stewart?"

Davis lifted his head to look at Samuel, and Samuel glanced at him before standing up. "Yes?"

"Could you come back here for a moment?"

Davis stood. "I'm coming with you."

Samuel did not argue.

They were led back to one of the examination rooms. It was when Davis saw blonde hair and a familiar grin that he grabbed Samuel's arm.

"Tommy?" he asked, staring unbelievingly at his deceased friend.

Samuel had looked at Davis's hand when his arm had been grabbed, but his head shot up as he stared presumably at the same image before him.

The door was closed quietly behind them.

Tommy swung his legs from where he sat on the small counter. "Hiya," he said. His grin was wide and his cheeks were flushed with positive energy. There was a white mask pulled off to the side.

Samuel's hands flew to cover to nose and mouth. "Tommy," he said despite the words being muffled. He dropped his hands to his heart. "Tommy, how?"

Tommy's smile dimmed as he tilted his head. "I accepted the offer to become an Angel," he said. Then he frowned and looked at Samuel. "I'm sorry for what happened. I would have never…"

"I—no—what?" Samuel said, his hands reaching out. "Can I touch you?"

Tommy smiled and nodded. "I wouldn't mind hugging the both of you, if that's okay."

"Definitely," Davis said breathlessly. Tommy hopped off the counter and they hugged in a group, hands twisted in fabric.

"Where are your pajamas?" Davis asked as he pulled back, now taking in all of Tommy after the initial shock.

"Really? That's what you ask a *real, in your face* Angel?" Tommy teased as he looked down at his white t-shirt and loose pants.

"Yes," Davis said, then laughed. He had more *answers* than questions. Angels were real. More importantly, someone who had been possessed could still receive the offer to be an Angel and *that* gave him a hope he had never felt before.

"Burned like the sin it was," Tommy said, winking. "Replaced by this mask, although mine's blank for now," he said, tapping the smooth mask. Then his face was serious again. "I'm here for a reason. The other Angels thought it would be best I was the one here because you know me."

"For what?" Samuel asked.

"You," Tommy said.

Davis's heart tightened. He wondered if Tommy's feelings had carried over. He wondered how Samuel felt about all of this, but when he looked, he saw only hesitancy on Samuel's face.

"What about me?" Samuel asked.

Tommy leaned against the counter and looked fairly disturbed. "There have been...many Angels being killed lately," he said. "There has been more recruiting, such as myself, but it's far from out-numbering the killings. We're dying out."

Davis was suddenly dismissive of any anger he had ever held towards Angels. They had been trying this whole time.

They had given Tommy an afterlife.

"Recruiting has become more difficult, though," Tommy explained. "The requirements were never made known, but they are specific."

"It's not just living a decently human life?" Davis asked.

Tommy shook his head. "No. It's facing the very worst version of a sin and then making the decision to repent for it." He looked at Samuel. "You have to know the enemy intimately to defeat it."

Samuel looked pained as he stared at Tommy,

still looking as if trying to understand such a phenomenon. "And this," he said, "has something to do with me?"

"Yes," Tommy said. He was looking at Samuel, only at Samuel, but it also seemed as if he wanted to look away. "The Angels have become desperate over the years, to the point of...influencing events."

"Influencing how?" Davis asked sharply. "What are you talking about?"

"I'm not supposed to be telling you this, but consider it a gift." Tommy glanced at Davis. He seemed almost nervous. "They—Angels—plan things. They try to work it so that more people will be qualified." He looked at Samuel. "They needed someone who was sure to accept, someone who had a want to help. They put together events so that you, Samuel, would be qualified to receive the offer to become an Angel."

Davis froze. It took him a solid minute before he could turn his head enough to see Samuel's shocked expression turn into horror as he started shaking his head.

"No, that's not possible," Samuel said. "I'm not dead. I haven't died. Right?" He looked at Davis, who quickly nodded, then he looked back at Tommy in a pleading exasperation.

"They can't always wait until death," Tommy said. "Not anymore."

"You're telling me," Samuel said, "that Angels have purposefully manipulated me to make sure I qualified and accepted? They—they made *sure* I was possessed?"

"They did more than that," Tommy said, although

he was seeming more hesitant at revealing this information. Still, it was clear he felt he had to answer Samuel completely. He looked around as if he could see through the walls, ground, and ceiling. "They made sure you had reason to want to become someone who opposed demons. They had to make sure you felt a sin." He glanced at Davis. "Although they expected that to come from Davis's draft."

"What?" Samuel asked, his eyes wide and he put a hand in his hair stressfully. "That was..."

"Influenced," Tommy said. He wasn't looking at either of them anymore. This was not part of his job. This was him revealing the truth. "They made sure the two of you met. They made sure Davis would be drafted. They...did not expect for the two of you to become...so close, or for Samuel to be possessed for a different type of envy, but the child..."

"Was used for me." The understanding was visibly clicking, and Samuel's hands dropped to his side.

"Your father," Tommy said. "What your mother did, what your sister did, your theories were all influenced."

Davis couldn't breathe. He couldn't say anything, not just because *he* was still trying to understand it all, but because of the parts he did understand. Because, despite any anger towards Angels now being *justified* for all the horrible things they had 'influenced,' he still could not express this anger even in this moment. In the end, this was Samuel's conversation. This was his journey. Davis had simply been a pawn.

"And Davis?" Samuel asked. "Why not him? He's been possessed—he's defeated it many times!"

"Davis," Tommy said calmly, "will receive a different offer."

Davis felt sick. The only other offer was for…for… He blinked. He had assumed it would be the case for so long, but to be told the only choice he would have is dying or becoming a demon? He felt sick.

"Then no," Samuel said. "I refuse the offer."

Both Davis and Tommy stared at him now, both equally shocked.

"But you've always wanted to help—" Davis started.

"I've wanted to be an Exorcist," Samuel said. He was staring at nothing on the wall. "I never wanted others to be harmed for that to happen. I want to make my own decisions and—" His sharp gaze looked at Tommy. "I will never forgive the Angels for Davis's draft."

"You don't need to deny it for me," Davis said quickly, even though it hurt to say. He was guilty of loving that Samuel said no because he just could not imagine what saying yes would have meant.

"It's not for you," Samuel said, his voice only slightly softer. "At least not only for you. It's for me, too."

Tommy didn't question Samuel's decision. He simply bowed his head. "I'll let them know."

"Tommy?" Samuel asked. Tommy looked up at him guiltily. "Thank you for telling the truth. Thank you for not manipulating me into accepting."

"It's the least I could do," Tommy whispered, "after what I almost did."

Then, Tommy Rider was simply not there anymore.

Davis and Samuel sat down. The necklace-turned-bracelet felt too tight around Davis's wrist. It was going to be a long day.

# CHAPTER EIGHTY-NINE

There was a guilt that started to settle in the pit of Jenkins' stomach. He had essentially advised Davis to prepare himself for killing Samuel—and he had nearly died himself. They had both survived and Jenkins had barely considered that outcome.

He wondered if he would have been able to prevent his wife's death. Had he been someone else, with other instincts, other priorities, other morals...if he had been able to be more selfless, would she still be alive? Would she have been possessed at all?

Would his son still be alive?

He had been searching so long for the ghost of his son, who maybe deserved better all along. Maybe even now, he was better off. Jenkins couldn't be a father. He couldn't even be a *person*.

He had to give up the search. He had to let

Carson go. That was the only way he was going to move forward, if he even could.

Who was he? What could he be? He couldn't pretend to help others if he couldn't help himself. He could only be nothing disguised as something human.

He wanted to be more. He wanted to be someone else, to *do* something else than just stare at his failures.

That was how he found himself walking away from the hospital. He walked down King Street, through the crowds of tourists, and he stopped in front of a small antique shop.

Maybe it was time he took a different approach to life.

# CHAPTER NINETY

If there was a specific reason why Davis became an Exorcist, one that didn't involve the manipulation of Samuel Stewart, he thought maybe this was it. It wasn't orchestrated by Angels or influenced by demons. It was something he hadn't asked for, but something he discovered—something he would use on his own terms. It was Jazmin Sosa, caged in front of him, fighting for her life against a demon, and him, with the ability and want to help her.

He wasn't an Exorcist. Not at heart, no matter what his jacket meant. He was, however, someone who knew what it was like to be possessed, who knew the consequences of life, and who now held a secret about Angels.

Jazmin was clearly possessed and clearly dying. She might even already be dead. They hadn't known with Tommy. They hadn't been able to ask.

There were so many things they still had to ask. But this, Davis could do something about. If Davis could help Jazmin—if he could save her life, it would be a symbol of exactly what he could do. If this worked, he could save others. He could put in his time and feel good about what he'd done. Two years of his life didn't have to be forfeited. It could be given, willingly, by his own choice. When he closed his eyes and saw Samuel's warped expression during the possession, he had accepted all he would give up to help him. Except Davis had found another way. Nothing had to be given up. It simply had to be postponed.

A postponed life was much better than being dead. He could handle that if it meant preventing deaths. He would have his chance. Two years didn't have to be so long.

His teammates were giving him the space and time he needed. Andy was there, her arm bandaged to her chest along with the knowledge of many more surgeries for just the hope of repairing all the nerve damage, but she was alive and trying to jump right back into work.

She had insisted on helping Jazmin the minute she had been released from the hospital. It was their job. Now, they could finally do it properly.

It was still an eerie sight. Jazmin was still in a cage in the impossible basement of the Headquarters. It was still terrifying to think of being possessed by a demon—to allow it to happen instead of resist it—but Samuel had promised him a surprise after helping Jazmin and there was no way Davis was missing that.

The problem was, no matter how patient his

teammates were, no matter how long Samuel was willing to wait, there wasn't an exact science to Davis willing the demon to transfer. It was method acting—an art. He had been so scared and so desperate, driven by his emotion more than an obligation. He had been willing to consider killing himself if he had found no other option. He had been so against death he had been able to make it work. Could he get to that place again? Could he reach that peak for someone he didn't know?

He had to try to be able to know. He took a deep breath, and he imagined a tangible world that held his feelings. He imagined it, and he placed a character of greed.

No, not a character. *Himself*.

The way to make it the most real was to bring it out from something he knew intimately. He knew what it was to *want*. He wanted his life back. He wanted to act, to dance, to perform in front of a crowd that was excited to see *him*. He wanted to be able to drive and to dream about cars. He wanted to be able to have sex without any fear. He wanted to just sit on the couch with Samuel and *breathe*.

But he couldn't have that. He couldn't have it for this very reason: the cold sliding through his body, the spikes that made his hands into fists, the disconnect he felt from his own body, the tearing at every nerve—then the struggle. He had to visualize—why was it so hard to visualize?—a hall. No, a case. He was in a case. No, past that, he was in the theatre. The demon was above him, crouching on the baton holding stage lights, eyes gleaming down at him. It was hard to see it past the blaring light, and still Davis could tell it was only an impression of a human; something left behind when the actual humanity burned away. The baton swung, Davis covered his eyes as the light shone into them, and—

No. The demon couldn't lunge at him. There was a glass pane in the way. No—not a pane, a box that was rigged to close when something fell in it. He heard the demon's growls and cries and scratches and Davis lowered his arm from his eyes to see it.

He couldn't look at it.

It calmed.

Then the whispers began. They weren't aloud. They were in his head, directly affecting his emotions.

"No," Davis said. "These aren't mine. They're not who I want to be." And he released the emotion— the *character* holding it, smashing the case, killing it, and the demon *screamed*.

Davis gasped and flailed, another pair of arms binding his to his side and he realized he was out. He looked around, noticing everyone relaxing from where they had been tense. No one had been hurt. Not this time. He slumped.

"Thank you," he said, drooping his head. He was so tired.

"Yeah," Jenkins said, helping ease Davis onto a stool.

"Davis?" Andy said, her attention away from him, then to him.

"Hm?"

"You did it," she said, and there was a *smile*. "*Look*."

Davis blinked open his eyes, just as he saw the girl doing the same.

There were murmured words, ones Davis could vaguely make out. Not English, but Spanish. He was hardly fluent in Spanish, but he could grasp the similarities he did know, so he translated, "*Am I me? Is it safe?*"

Then, with a breath of relief, he answered, in Spanish, "*It's safe.*"

Her eyes were black. Large and focused and *hers*. Davis gave her a tired smile. "Welcome back."

"Thank you," she said in an accented English. She looked around and covered her mouth when her binds were released and she *sobbed*. Davis looked at her pityingly. He knew exactly what it felt like to regret living.

"Oh, *wonderful*. Happy days," someone said, and Davis turned around quickly to see someone standing in the stairwell, arms crossed and looking just as sarcastic as they sounded.

"Bailey," Paul said as an introduction. "It's nice of you to join us. Davis, this is Bailey. He," Paul said, looking to Bailey as if for approval, and receiving it with an annoyed nod, "is the Finder of the Atlanta squad."

"I'm not joining you," Bailey said. His feet were fitted with combat boots, and he wore the trademark black and silver jacket. His hair was jet black, shaved on the sides, and his ears, fingers, and skin were widely decorated with silver and ink. "I'm here for one reason only, and that's to find Daniel. Where. Is. He?" He was glaring at Davis, who was tired and had more important things to attend to right now then to be accused of...something.

Except this Bailey just confirmed Daniel was missing and that kept Davis's attention.

"Daniel's missing?" Andy asked in genuine surprise. "We thought he just left. He did that sometimes."

"He didn't come home this time," Bailey snapped. "He's the Head of my squad. I would know. And it's when *this guy* shows up in the team that Daniel disappears."

"I don't think you understand how okay I would be with not being here," Davis retorted. "But I'm here, having just *killed* a *demon*, by the way, and accusing people isn't exactly the best way to effectively get things done." He crossed his own arms, mimicking Bailey's stance.

"Davis," Paul said calmly, and Davis looked at him in disbelief.

"I don't give a fuck who did what," Bailey said. "I'm here to find Daniel. If you plan to actually help your teammate, who could be *dead* for all you know, then find me. I'll be searching for him." Then Bailey turned on his heels and went up the stairs, making one of the most dramatic exits Davis had ever seen.

Add missing teammate to the list of problems going on and Davis was glad he and Samuel had decided to keep their meeting with Tommy to themselves.

"Go," Noah said to Davis. "Take a break. You're meeting up with Samuel, right?" Davis nodded. "We're going to have to discuss what happens now that he's been possessed, so take this time while you can."

Davis glanced at Paul, who nodded. "Our

Lieutenant will be visiting in a few days. We'll cover everything until then."

Lastly, Davis looked at Jenkins. "I'll be okay," he said with a single nod. "I have things to do."

His nerves were building again, the need to just keep working was fighting his want to leave. But Samuel was waiting for him, and Davis was eager to go.

"Thank you," he said, and he left.

# CHAPTER
# NINETY-ONE

"**O**kay, so I know I probably said being blindfolded was hot at some point, but I know I never said you could do it just so you could prove me wrong." Davis flailed slightly as he took another step on the death traps known as Charleston's brick sidewalks, even more deadly when he *couldn't see*.

"That's not the reason!" Samuel said quickly, though he had to admit it was a tad chilly, as all evenings were when it wasn't crowded with tourists or college students. "Just bear with me a bit longer. We're almost there."

"Is 'there' warm, or are we going to make it warm?" Davis asked casually, and Samuel couldn't tell if he was just making a sexual suggestion or if it was a legitimate question. He felt it was probably neither and that this was how Davis coped when his mind was scrambled and his eyes were covered.

"Just be patient," Samuel mumbled, guiding Davis by his hand.

They were both aware of everything going on that needed their attention. Demons, Angels, people who were vulnerable post-possession, missing children, recovered memories, a disabled teammate, a *missing* teammate. They ignored all that so they could become more aware of each other. This mini adventure was brought on as a way to show they couldn't just ignore how everything affected them. Samuel hoped he would be able to show that to Davis.

Samuel had been to their destination before, though mostly as a kid. It was during a lunch break, when Andy was still in the hospital and Davis had mostly stayed with her, that he had remembered it. He hadn't been able to stay, which led to his whole purpose in dragging his boyfriend there now.

Eventually they stopped walking.

"You can take off your blindfold now," Samuel said hesitantly, still holding Davis's hand even though it wasn't needed anymore. He watched as the makeshift blindfold—one of Samuel's ties—was slipped off to reveal Davis's eyes, bright hazel in the street lighting and highlighted more with confusion.

"Is this…?" Davis began, chancing a look at Samuel.

"The jailhouse?" Samuel supplied. "Yes, it is."

"The most haunted place in all of Charleston," Davis said, the question implied.

"Yes," Samuel answered.

Davis blinked. "You brought us to the most haunted place in all of Charleston."

"I think we have agreed this is true," Samuel said with a raised eyebrow. "Is there a problem?"

Davis's eyes went wider at this. "You brought *us*, two of the most vulnerable people in Charleston for possession, to a place where demons probably *thrive*."

It was Samuel's turn to blink, though he did so emotionlessly. "I don't see the problem here."

Davis seemed perplexed, which didn't happen often, and only made Samuel feel smugger in his decision for their late-night date. "It's risky. You don't want to be possessed again, do you?" he asked, his body visibly tense as he shifted uncomfortably.

"No," Samuel said simply. "Of course I don't want to, but I don't have to worry about it. In fact, nor do you."

Davis looked back at him like he grew another head. In a moment's time, Davis shifted again and humored Samuel. "Why is that?"

Samuel moved so he was standing just an inch from Davis's nose, his head tilted slightly. "Because you're here." After the confused look he earned, he continued. "So many times, you've taken a bad situation—no, not a bad situation. Just—when I start thinking about my own issues, you have always been able to charm your way into getting me to relax and not *worry* so much over everything. You helped me bring myself back." He brought his hands up to cup Davis's face, tracing his thumbs over his cheekbones as steady eyes watched him. "You've done so much for me. Just your presence. My best friend." He paused again, closing his eyes briefly to try to will away the embarrassment that was sure to come with his next words.

"Samuel, you—"

"No, I have to say this," Samuel said sternly. "The one thing I can do is trust you and show you it's not all bad. So here we are, at the most dangerous place we can be, vulnerable from our possessions, and yet here we are, perfectly fine." Samuel took a breath. "I trust you to bring me back every time. I trust you to be able to fight your own, but I'm also here, fighting along with you." He placed a hesitant kiss on Davis's lips, which Davis accepted and returned, if with bewilderment. "It's all I can do right now. I wish I could do more, that I could talk more about what happened, but all I can do is show you how much I believe that you are strong."

"Samuel..." Davis's voice cracked, though he didn't seem bothered by it. He was looking at him with the most baffled look. "I...I still hurt Andy. I don't know if I could do what I did again. I mean, I was able to with Jazmin, but what if both were just a fluke?"

"I'm not expecting you to be perfect," Samuel said, his gaze locked with Davis's. "You're new at this, but I know you'll always succeed with me and with yourself. I just wanted to remind you of that and of my trust in you—in *you*, Davis. Who you are, as a person."

"You just brought me out here for that?" Davis asked.

Samuel flushed slightly and gave a crooked grin. "Would it make you feel any better if I said I wanted to come here but was too chicken without you?"

"You are too cute," Davis said with a small, slightly pained laugh before he gave Samuel a short, sloppy kiss and turned towards the inside of the building. "Let's go, then! I'm sure there's just more ghosts than demons here anyway."

"Ghosts," Samuel said flatly. "Yes, of course."

Davis glanced back as they reached one of the cells. "You don't believe in them?"

"I grew up in Charleston," Samuel said, as if that answered everything. Which it did. "I believed you about Negrinho Do Pastoreio, didn't I?"

"Ah, right," Davis said with a nod. "Good, because I've been on the ghost tour before and I have a story or two for you."

Samuel vaguely listened to Davis's tale, and the numerous other ghost stories he decided to share while in the creepiest place in Charleston, but Samuel didn't mind. He shivered and had the feeling of being watched more often than not, but then he felt Davis's warm grip tighten and his beating heart was able to slow enough for him to realize this was a date. An easy, comfortable date. He only hoped his idea had helped Davis's uneasiness, because this was his limit. It was all he could do.

Well, this or accept being Angel, which wasn't an option.

...Right?

# THE END

# ACKNOWLEDGEMENTS

The number of people involved in this book is outstanding and a bit overwhelming looking back. I think back to the very beginning, so many years ago, and how this started as a possible theatre trope story with my dear friend Kat. Thank you. The next seven years was filled with people who read horrid drafts, listened to me ramble more ideas, did one of many sensitivity readings and called me out and allowed me grow. Thank you all, and thank you to my friend Angel, who always supported me. Carrie, for editing and formatting while tolerating my many questions about this whole process. A. E. Hayes, for being so understanding, hardworking, and truly understanding what I was trying to do with this story. Molly, who made me feel like I could really do this and more. Drei and Shayne, who created inspiring works of art. My friend and my love, Morgan, who dealt with me through every edit of the final draft, every low, every high, and all the time in between.

# ABOUT THE AUTHOR

Annie O'Quinn grew up in Greenville, South Carolina. After graduating with a theatre design degree from College of Charleston, she went on to study illustration at The Academy of Art University, all while writing as a hobby.

Being in the queer community herself, Annie hopes to accurately portray characters within the community while tackling hard issues such as mental illness and other disabilities within all of her books. Her goal is to be able to teach from her experience, but also continue to learn from others for the rest of her life.

You can find Annie O'Quinn at her website, www.annieoquinn.com, or on other social media at annieoquinn or oquinn53, with updates occurring most frequently on her tumblr.

www.ingramcontent.com/pod-product-compliance
Lightning Source LLC
Chambersburg PA
CBHW021952120726

47898CB00001BA/83